YTO

PH

A Family's Affairs

WINNER OF THE HOUGHTON MIFFLIN–
ESQUIRE FELLOWSHIP AWARD, 1961

SOME PREVIOUS HOUGHTON MIFFLIN
LITERARY FELLOWSHIP AWARDS:

To E. P. O'Donnell for *Green Margins*

To Dorothy Baker for *Young Man with a Horn*

To Robert Penn Warren for *Night Rider*

To Joseph Wechsberg for *Looking for a Bluebird*

To Ann Petry for *The Street*

To Elizabeth Bishop for *North & South*

To Anthony West for *The Vintage*

To Arthur Mizener for *The Far Side of Paradise*

To Madison A. Cooper, Jr., for *Sironia, Texas*

To Charles Bracelen Flood for *Love Is a Bridge*

To Milton Lott for *The Last Hunt*

To Edward Hoagland for *Cat Man*

To Eugene Burdick for *The Ninth Wave*

To Herbert Simmons for *Corner Boy*

To Philip Roth for *Goodbye, Columbus*

To William Brammer for *The Gay Place*

by Ellen Douglas

A Family's Affairs

HOUGHTON MIFFLIN COMPANY BOSTON

THE RIVERSIDE PRESS CAMBRIDGE, 1962

FIRST PRINTING

CONTENTS

A Courtship

◄§ CHARLOTTE ANDERSON, by her own and her family's standards, made a good marriage. She married late, at twenty-five, for it took her a long time to find a man who met her standards and who wanted *her*. She intended to marry a man who was more intelligent than she and, indeed, considering the rest of her requirements, that one was a logical necessity. She meant to follow the letter of the marriage service, and she wanted a man she could trust to be respectable in the literal sense of the word; in fact, if only she had been interested in glamour, she might have been accused of waiting for the impossible. As it was, she told herself that she did not care about good looks or money, but about strength and honor, and intelligence; and if the strength and honor were real, it would take considerable intelligence to support them. It did not occur to her then that a good disposition might some day be more important to her than any of these.

Like her two sisters and her brother, Charlotte was small, fine-boned, and white-skinned. The four children all looked like their half-Creole, half-Scotch father. The lightness of their bodies gave a first impression of fragility that was almost immediately erased by everything else about them: the strength of hand and wrist, the characteristic, bouncy, slew-footed walk, the overarticulation of chin and jaw, and the weight and solidity of their individual personalities. Charlotte had a clear unsentimental eye and a figure any man would turn for a second glance at. She thought her bosom too large for good proportions and her legs a trifle thin, but her hair was long and almost black, and her skin smooth; everything taken together, she felt she could hold her own. She had flirted with half the young men in Homochitto, and at least half a dozen of them had claimed to be in love with her. She had bucked her mother when it was necessary and was aware, from the beginning, that she might have to look a long time to find a man both stronger and more intelligent than she. Not that there weren't enough strong men in the world — it wasn't conceit — but that they usually didn't stay long in Homochitto.

When Ralph McGovern began to call, Charlotte knew her search was over. He was a quiet man, a young engineer who had struggled a long time in his soul before he was sure God had not called him to the ministry. Charlotte had known him all her life with the intimate, impersonal, small-town knowledge that begins at children's parties and grows with the marriages and deaths of mutual cousins. Summers when he was home from college they had gone to the same parties, and he had danced his duty dance with her. He was a poor dancer, but she had followed him as well as she could and asked leading questions about his school and later about his work. The winter of 1916–1917 he contracted for a job grading the road from Homochitto to Natchez, and for the first time in eight years spent a year at home. She was not surprised when he asked her after church one Sunday if he might come to call. She had seen him at church every Sunday for weeks, and had amused herself by admiring his shining blond hair, his stern cleft chin, and his erect, slightly sway-back carriage, and by listening for his strong baritone to ring out with solemn enthusiasm above so many quavering sopranos: *Blest be the tie that binds.* Charlotte was between beaus, so to speak, but she never meant Ralph to be just another beau. One Sunday when the McGoverns came out of church after the service, Ralph following his mother and guiding his grandmother with a steadying hand, Charlotte stopped to speak. She looked at Ralph, held out her hand, and smiled, and before they separated that morning he had asked if he might come to see her.

For six months he came regularly, twice a week, to call. At first Charlotte found him hard to talk to. He was so quiet she thought he was bored, and she chattered on about whatever nonsense came into her head, anything to fill the void of silence as they sat alone together evening after evening on the sofa in the Anderson parlor. Every now and then the boom of his *Ha, ha, ha* rang out as she paused for him to appreciate her stories. Slowly she began to understand that his silence was neither shy nor sullen. When she touched on a subject he knew and cared about, he talked easily. He had the facts in his head and his conclusions carefully and methodically worked out. When she asked his advice, as she did, more often than not, only to put their relationship on an intimate personal level, he examined her problem as thoroughly as if all the world depended upon his answer. Once he stated his position, once he discarded every imaginable alternative, he never changed his mind. This was possible because he did not have to consider the subject again: he already understood it.

Such a point of view and method were new to Charlotte and she was ready to accept them without examination or criticism. At the time even the obvious flaws were virtues to her. Fatherless since she was sixteen, used to a household of women, she took to his self-assured masculinity and imperturbability, feeling as if she had never before had room to breathe.

When six months had passed, she knew she *had* to marry him and was in a passion of impatience for his proposal. It was February and still he came, as regularly as the milkman, on Tuesday and Friday nights, at seven-thirty, and stayed until ten-thirty. She sat beside him one Friday night, alert, excited, half miserable, and waited for him to decide what would happen next.

The rest of her family, or at any rate Kate, her mother, and her sisters, Sarah D. and Anna, were in the dining room, busy at their own affairs. But their presence was as palpable as if they had been sitting in a row on the straight-backed Victorian parlor chairs watching her, particularly watching Ralph; Kate with an ironic inquiry in her eyes, as if she said with exaggerated concern, "Young man, are your intentions honorable?" To Charlotte the irony which she knew to be her mother's support made the inquiry tolerable. Kate had prepared her daughters for nothing but marriage, which she considered the only serious business in life; but she lightened the gravity of her view by her implicit attitude that except in the eyes of God we are all, even at our most serious, somewhat absurd.

The huge dining room in the old house had always served the family as a sitting room. Bounded on each side by the bedroom wings, on the front by the parlor, and on the back by a long porch with crisscrossed green lattice to keep out the summer sun, it was shadowy, scarcely lighter during the day than at night when electric wall sconces on either side of the mantelpiece dimly lighted its far corners. Above the wainscoting the walls were covered with shredding brownish paper, its pattern dimmed to a gray tracery by layers of dust and time. The wide oak floor boards were so splintery it was dangerous to go barefoot, and the rug showed far more warp and woof than it did pile. A battered oak dining table put together with wooden pegs stood in the middle of the room. Charlotte's father had fished it out of the river after a passing stern-wheeler had blown up near Bois Sauvage, the family's Louisiana plantation. A narrow, scroll-backed day bed stood against one wall below a gilt-framed mirror so large and heavy and leaning at so precarious an angle that it seemed to threaten the lounger with its crushing weight; and the shabbiest and most comfortable chairs in the house were drawn about the fireplace. Every detail of the room and its furnishings said *genteel poverty*. But Charlotte did not see it in that way. Where Kate might long for new upholstery and wallpaper, Charlotte only knew that it was just the same as it had always been and that she was comfortable there. She did not notice the worn spots on the rug, and automatically put on her slippers in the morning before walking on the splintery floor; but she was drawn by the fire in the coal grate and the exciting conviction that no matter what the time of day or year something was always going on in the dining room.

The parlor might have belonged to another family. The two rooms shared a chimney, but, unless there was company in the house, the parlor grate was cold. It was a cold room, cold and uncomfortable, its furniture too small and fragile — Victorian love seats and straight-backed chairs with legs that had been broken again and again by big men who tilted back and stretched out their legs in an effort to make themselves comfortable. Starched white doilies protected the table tops and were scattered like big snowflakes on the arms and backs of the chairs, and cold, gray velvet hung at the windows. In spite of its gloom and shabbiness, the dining room vibrated with the life of the family, and in spite of its effort at elegance, the parlor had no life at all.

Now, as Ralph and Charlotte sat by the fire, she listened to him and with one part of her mind mechanically replied, while with another she jumped from thought to thought in a sequence by no means incoherent to her. She was tired of courting in the parlor, and she listened to the murmur of voices on the other side of the wall and wished that just one evening she and Ralph could change sides with the family. If they could get comfortable . . . She knew herself to be helpless within the limits of courtship against his ingrained formality, and she could think of nothing to do about it. *Nobody can help me, and there's no use blaming it on the parlor*, she thought to herself. *The truth of the matter, one reason I think he's so smart is I can't get him to propose.* She shifted uneasily on the plush-covered love seat and felt a broken spring give way unevenly. The clock struck ten, and her face grew hot with a flood of uninvited anger. *Another evening gone, and we're just where we were three months ago.* Her heart began to pound, and she knew she could not sit beside him until ten-thirty, waiting for the clock to strike again. Abruptly she got up.

"I'm awfully tired tonight, Ralph. Would you mind if I said good night early?"

Calmly and pleasantly she saw him to the front gate, but her thoughts had driven her to a furious resolution. If he wanted to be slow, she would be slower. If he wanted to be formal, she would be more formal. *What's so smart about his not proposing?* she said to herself. *I must take the prize for stupidity if I think that's clever.* But she recognized almost at once that she had caught herself in her own trap. She was angry with the very things in him she cared for most. *All right,* she told herself. *I may be willing to wait for him. But I'll be damned if I'll help him out.*

In her rage she had forgotten that ten minutes earlier her mind had been on Kate and the girls, and now she was half surprised, when she came into the dining room, to find them still sitting there, Anna reading, Kate playing solitaire on the dining room table, and Sarah D. sitting cross-legged on the day bed, staring at herself in the big mirror, and rearranging her long brown hair. Kate, still slender and handsome at fifty-four, bent over the table and examined her cards. Her straight, gray-streaked brown hair was carefully and softly piled on her head to conceal the spots where she was beginning to be bald, and caught in an invisible net. Her greenish eyes, light, alert, and half concealed by characteristically ironic, humorous, and once seductive drooping lids, jumped quickly from card to card. She played an ace to the board, picked up an unexposed stack, and looked through it.

"I can't win without cheating," she said, slipping a card out of place and playing it to the board.

Charlotte drew a chair to the table and, without speaking,

sat down beside her mother and watched her play out the game. When she finished the Canfield, Kate began to lay out a game of Wandering Jew.

She glanced at Charlotte inquiringly. "You sent him home early," she said. "Is something the matter?"

Charlotte shook her head.

"He must find you amusing," Kate said. "I never heard such a laugh."

"Is he really serious?" Sarah D. asked, still gazing into the mirror.

"Sarah D.!" Anna, the second daughter, looked up from her book. "You ought not to ask questions like that. It's none of your business."

Charlotte looked gratefully at Anna.

"Why not?" Sarah D. said. "It's all in the family. What does Charlotte care if I know whether he's proposed or not?"

"I like him," Charlotte said. "But I certainly haven't given him an opportunity to propose at this point."

"Opportunity!" Sarah D. said. "At this point! He's been coming to see you for *centuries.*"

"Six months," Anna said.

"Well, he'd better hurry up, if he's going to," Sarah D. said. "Winston Wilkinson told me he's almost through with that road, and he'll be leaving soon."

"Sarah D., have you been talking about my affairs to your friends?" Charlotte said.

"Oh, don't be silly, Charlotte," Sarah D. said. She was trying to pin her fine, unmanageable straight hair over a rat and into a high puff, but the rat slipped out and dangled limply on her temple. She looked at it meditatively in the mirror and then looked over her shoulder at Charlotte. "Winston's been working for him on Saturdays," she said, "and he told me that the job is almost over." She raised one eyebrow in an effort at quizzical sophistication. "The conclusions are mine," she said.

Charlotte put her elbows on the dining room table, leaned her head on her hands, and laughed helplessly.

"I don't see anything funny about it," Sarah D. said. "If you want him, you better do something quick."

"It's that rat," Charlotte said. "Is that where you're going to wear it?"

"Sarah D.," Kate said, "Charlotte may not be so bent on worming a proposal out of every boy in Clayton County as you are."

"He never says a word," Sarah D. said. "He must be *very* serious. Does he like to dance?" She was seventeen and had just discovered that she wanted to spend the rest of her life dancing. "Let's have an unbiased opinion. Sis, is he a good dancer?"

"He can hold his own," Anna said.

"Dancing is not the most important thing in the world," Kate said.

"It is to me," Sarah D. said.

"All the McGovern men are quiet," Kate said, "but Charlotte talks enough for both of them."

"Ralph's a nice fellow," Anna said. "I've always thought he was attractive. He's a fine, *steady* fellow."

Steadiness was one of the qualities in him that had appealed most to Charlotte from the beginning — steadiness and unimpeachable reserve. If she had formulated her judgment of him more specifically, she might have thought that it was necessary not to break his reserve or to destroy his privacy, but to establish herself within them, so that she would be supported and bounded by the strength of his barriers. But she could not say any of this to her family, and she felt faintly uneasy when they began to talk about him. She was afraid they might say something she wouldn't like, something to make him seem ridiculous in her eyes, to spoil the tender, fragile beginning of romance, so necessary to her in any relationship with a man, and so difficult to bring to flower between herself and Ralph.

It was, after all, ideally, not enough that he should be steady, and it would have suited her ideal vision of him better if Anna had been able to say, in some polite and commonplace way they could all have accepted, that she knew how much passion must be held in control by his strong sense of propriety. But, there was the question. Was the passion there?

"There are lots of things we could do to perk him up," Kate said thoughtfully as she shuffled the cards and began another game of Wandering Jew. "Lots of things. I've been thinking about it."

Anna and Charlotte looked at each other, as if to say, *Here she goes again.*

"For one thing, you need a new dress, Charlotte. I have yards of yellow dotted swiss left from that bolt I got on sale last summer. We can go down to Hamlin's tomorrow and find a pretty pattern and start it. For another thing, we haven't had a party in years. That would give you an excuse to wear the dress, and would liven things up a bit. Don't you think that's a good idea, Sis? We could borrow Fanny Lee's Japanese lanterns and have a party outdoors. Here it is the end of February. In a few weeks it'll be warm enough for an outdoor party. The third week in March would be just right, and that would give me plenty of time to make your dress, Charlotte." She sighed, and, dropping her cards, gazed into the fire. "All those lanterns hung along the grape arbor," she said. "Think how lovely!"

"Mama . . ."

"When is the moon full? A night when the moon is full would be perfect. You know, Charlotte, Ralph McGovern will never get you out in the moonlight without a little help from somebody."

"Mama, I'm not going to maneuver Ralph into the moonlight. He'll have to get there under his own steam."

"You *are* serious, aren't you?" Kate said.

☙❧

Kate went ahead with her plans for the party, gathering force and enthusiasm as she proceeded. She bought patterns for Charlotte and Anna, got out the yellow dotted swiss, and found an old dress of her own that could be ripped up and re-made for Anna. ("You don't mind, Sis," she said. "The party is really important to Charlotte, you know." And, in truth, Anna did not care what she wore.) Kate loved to sew, and the following weeks she spent in cutting, fitting, and stitching, talking to her children through a mouthful of pins. The floor of her room was covered with pieces of patterns, pins, needles, empty spools, scraps of cloth, and papers with measurements jotted down on them. "Don't move anything," she would cry when someone came into the room. "I know just where every-thing is." The bed was draped with cloth and patterns which at night she folded over onto one side, while she crawled un-der the covers on the side she had cleared, being careful not to disturb anything. A small coal fire burned in the grate and one rocking chair sat beside it. There was a clear space in the middle of the floor for the girls to stand and be fitted. Here Charlotte stood patiently one morning while her mother made the last adjustments on her dress.

" 'S'not jus' f'you 'n' Waff," Kate mumbled to Charlotte as she worked.

"Mama, take the pins out of your mouth. I can't under-stand a word you're saying," Charlotte said. "Besides, you might swallow one."

Kate spat the pins into her hand and stuck them into her dress. "I've been sewing with a mouthful of pins for fifty years," she said, "and I haven't swallowed one yet."

"What were you saying?" Charlotte said.

Kate bent her head and began to adjust the placket under Charlotte's arm. "Lift your arm, dearie," she said.

Charlotte held out her arm.

"I said, this party is not just for you and Ralph. I'm using you as an excuse. Didn't you guess as much when I first mentioned it?"

"Who's it for, then?" Charlotte said.

"Sis," Kate said. "Sis is the one I'm concerned about. She's hardly been out of the house all winter, except to go to work, and she needs a party more than you do. But you know I couldn't say that to her. I'm going to invite Douglas Wills for her. I've always thought he'd be attentive to her if she would give him the least encouragement. And James and George Peabody, and that nice young doctor from New Orleans who's visiting the Reids. And, Charlotte, you can help me out. All you have to do is kind of stir things up, if you see she's getting stiff and desperate, like she does sometimes."

"All right," Charlotte said. "I'll keep an eye on her. But, Mama, you know she'll see through you. You're as transparent as a sheet of glass."

"I can't understand why she *never* has an engagement. When I was her age . . ."

"She goes out sometimes," Charlotte said. "But she'll probably stop if she gets the notion you're worrying about her. You know how she is about that. Mama, may I put my arm down?"

Kate nodded. "If some of these young men could just get to *know* her," she said. "If she would forget herself for a little while."

"I don't think the trouble is that she's thinking of herself all the time," Charlotte said thoughtfully. She shifted her weight from one foot to the other.

"Keep still, or I'll get the hem crooked," Kate said.

"Of course she's shy. But the main thing is, she expects too much. She wants a man to be perfect."

Kate pushed a pile of scraps out of her way and crawled around to the other side of Charlotte. "My dear," she said, "put your weight on both feet if you want this to hang straight."

And then, "My, all these fine scraps. I have almost enough to begin a new quilt. Where's my scrapbag?"

"I don't see how you can find *anything* in here, Mama," Charlotte said. "I never saw such a mess. It's a disgrace."

"Oh, I can find things," Kate said. "Wherever anything is, it's exactly where I put it, if you all don't meddle."

"Don't you know your idiosyncrasies get exaggerated as you grow older?" Charlotte said. "By the time you're seventy, you'll be completely buried in scraps."

"About Sis, what were you saying?"

"I said she wants a man to be perfect." She stared dreamily into the fire. "That's not so unreasonable," she said.

"Well!" Kate said. "I think it's even worse than having her mind on herself, if it's not the same thing. Who does she think she is, to decide who's perfect?"

"I mean perfect for *her*."

"I wish her luck, then," Kate said. "She'll need it." She savagely thrust a pin into her bosom. "Ouch," she said. "You see, that's why I keep them in my mouth. Then, when I get excited, I don't stick myself."

"You could use the pincushion," Charlotte said.

"But will you, darling?" Kate said. "Will you help?"

"I'll try, Mama," Charlotte said. "But you know Sis is going her own way. The best I can promise is that I won't let her get trapped with somebody she can't talk to."

Anna was not as patient or else not as interested a model as Charlotte, and at her fitting she stood in the middle of the cluttered room with a look of boredom and frustration while her mother hitched up one side, pulled down the other, rearranged gathers, and fitted in the waist. Patterns were always too large for Anna, who was smaller than the smallest size that Hamlin's stocked. But cutting down a pattern and fitting it onto pieces of an old, ripped-up dress was a challenge that stimulated Kate.

After enduring her mother's absorbed attention for a few

minutes, Anna said, "Wait a minute, Mama," found a book, and began to read standing up.

"I can't fit you like that," Kate said. "You'll have to put your arms down."

Anna sighed, put down her book on the sewing machine, shifted from one foot to the other, and gazed out the window at the brick wall of the house across the alley. Kate, kneeling at her side, worked quickly and skillfully. She glanced up at Anna's profile.

"Sis," she said, as she continued to pin and baste.

"Hmmm?"

"I have a favor to ask of you."

"All right," Anna said. "What is it?"

"I want you to help Charlotte out at the party," Kate said. "If she won't encourage Ralph, somebody has to."

Anna woke up. "What do you mean?" she said.

"Oh, you know what I mean. You know. Just — just let him know, without really saying anything, of course, how much Charlotte likes him. You can find a way to do it. Those things just *happen*, if you want them to."

Sarah D. was sitting on a cleared spot on her mother's bed, watching the fitting, and now Anna looked doubtfully at her. "Sarah D.," she said, "don't you repeat any of this to Charlotte."

Sarah D. leaned back against the headboard and half closed her eyes. "I'm not even listening," she said in a bored voice. "I'm simply sitting here waiting for Stanley. I *am* occasionally absorbed in my own private life, you know."

"Sarah D. has better sense than to tell Charlotte something that might offend her," Kate said. "She's no child."

"Mama," Anna said in her quiet, gentle voice, "why don't you let Charlotte alone? What are you trying to do—a John Alden and Priscilla in reverse?"

"She's entirely too reserved," Kate said. "Reserve is all well and good with a forward man, but two people as reserved as

Ralph and Charlotte will never get to the altar. I feel like I'm trying to drive a six-foot wagon through a five-foot gate. Something's got to give."

"You aren't supposed to be driving this wagon at all," Anna said, looking down sternly at the top of her mother's head.

"You know they're ideal for each other," Kate said. "Why shouldn't we help?"

Anna smiled. "They do suit each other, don't they? I saw it right away. But, Mama, I can't encourage Ralph for Charlotte. In the first place I don't know how, and in the second place, if I did, it's a terrible idea. Stop and think about it a minute. You're so busy trying to make everything turn out right, you're getting carried away. If you aren't careful, this party is going to be like one of those birthday parties where all the children are too self-conscious and dressed-up to play."

"When I was your age, I kept things lively," Kate said. "I wasn't above a little scheming."

"I'll bet."

"It wasn't a matter of getting too dressed-up to play. I could dress things up to a fare-thee-well, and have the time of my life."

Anna laughed.

"Why, at twenty-two I was engaged to your father, and Dr. Shields, *and* David McCay."

"All at once?" asked Anna, who knew by heart the story of her mother's multiple engagement.

"Yes, all at once. Of course, David lived in Natchez, and your father knew about Dr. Shields. But you've heard that tale. Anyhow, we *all* had a grand time."

"Everyone can't manage that well, darling," Anna said.

Kate groaned and Anna helped her up from her knees.

"Stiff," she said. "Stiff. I get stiffer every day. Now." She turned Anna around and looked critically at her. "It's going to be lovely. Just a pinch more off the shoulders . . ."

"May I take it off now?"

"Wait a minute. Just one minute more." She adjusted the shoulders in silence and then watched Anna wiggle out of the pinned-together dress. "Don't scratch yourself."

"Mama," Anna said when she had laid the dress on the bed, "Charlotte's a grown woman. I'm not going to interfere between her and Ralph."

"You always put things wrong," Kate said. "I don't want you to *interfere.*"

"Then I'll be as sweet to him as if I wanted him to marry *me.* I do like him."

"All right, all right, I give up," Kate said. "You girls are impossible."

After Anna had gone upstairs with her book Sarah D. lay on the bed looking at Kate, who had sat down in the rocker with her work. First Kate stuck herself on a pin and said, "Plague take it," and squeezed her finger until a drop of blood appeared. Then she caught a hangnail on a basting thread and, exasperated, dropped her work into her lap.

"Why are you staring at me?" she said.

"I didn't know I was," Sarah D. said. "I was thinking about Charlie Dupré."

"Oh," Kate said.

"Do you think he's handsome?"

Kate considered the matter. "Well, he's a bit skinny yet," she said, "but he has nice features; he'll fill out."

"He dances like a dream," Sarah D. said. "I don't care what he looks like." Her foot tapped gently as if to the faint sound of music.

Kate picked up her sewing again. "Yes," she said, "just like his father. And he carries himself so straight on the dance floor. I hate to see a tall man stoop."

"He doesn't stoop even to a short girl," Sarah D. said. "I don't see how he does it."

"Looks like he's hanging from a string hooked to the top of

his head. He floats. He just floats. It's a joy to watch you two dancing together."

"I may have to fall in love with him," Sarah D. said.

"I wouldn't do that," Kate said. "The Dupré men are all queer — either too bright or too dumb — except Father."

"Why do you work so hard over us, Mama?" Sarah D. said.

"Work!" Kate cried. "Why I love to sew. If I weren't making these, I'd be making something else. I can't understand why none of you girls like to sew."

"Maybe because you never would let us finish anything," Sarah D. said, "but I wasn't talking about that. You know what I mean — about Charlotte and Sis. You're going to get yourself in trouble one of these days."

"I've been in trouble before," Kate said, biting off a basting thread.

"And even me," Sarah D. said, "although not so much."

"I'd hardly be thinking of marrying you off yet," Kate said. "Besides, you're like me. You can take care of yourself; if anything you need holding back. While Charlotte and Sis . . . Oh, you know Charlotte and Sis. 'Specially Sis."

Sarah D., clutching her knees, thoughtfully rocked herself back and forth on the bed. "Mama, why didn't you get married again after Father died?" she said.

"That comes under the heading of my business, Miss Pry," Kate said, grinning at her. And then, "I'd like to know what man would be fool enough to take on you four."

"Dr. Howerton would," Sarah D. said with a giggle.

"Wuff," Kate said, as disgustedly as a dog that has missed a squirrel.

"I like him," Sarah D. said, "and so do you, you know you do."

"He's a darling man," Kate said. "Yes, he's a lovely man when he's not drinking. He's bought you many a pair of shoes, dearie, although I wouldn't want that generally known. But if I were married to him, I couldn't send him home when he was drinking. He'd *be* at home. Besides I have enough on my hands getting you children grown and organized. I can't take on a husband."

"Maybe you shouldn't organize us so hard," Sarah D. said.

"Now, that's enough advice from you," Kate said. "The organizing I do, I have to do, and I'm very careful to keep it under cover."

"Ha," Sarah D. said.

"Nobody knows the difference and everybody is happier for it," Kate said.

"It's better to tell people straight out what you think and what you're doing," Sarah D. said. "They don't get as mad as they do when you begin to maneuver."

"What do you know about it, my dear? At your age."

The doorbell rang. Sarah D. sprang up and kissed the top of her mother's head. "There's Stanley," she said. "Don't worry about us, Mama. Miss Fanny is chaperoning."

"Go along with you," Kate said. "I'm not worried about you. It's Miss Fanny who's in danger."

◆§◊◆

All four of the Andersons expected, each on her own terms, a response from Ralph: Kate felt sure he would succumb to the alchemy of moonlight and yellow dotted swiss; Anna decided that he would stay blissfully unaware of her mother's motives, and resolved to do everything she could to keep him so; Charlotte was both hopeful and fearful for him. She wanted him to see what Kate was doing, because she could not bear for him to be either stupid or a victim; but she also wanted him to see that she, Charlotte, would neither prevent nor apologize for her mother, and that she could allow her the pleasure of the chase without being a party to it. Sarah D. decided to take matters into her own hands, and the next time Ralph came to call, she did so.

Charlotte was in her room dressing, and Sarah D. came out to entertain him.

"What are you doing at home tonight?" he said. "Where are your faithful swains?" He always asked her that question, if she was at home when he came to call, and she always answered as if it were the first time.

"Mama doesn't allow me to have more than two evening engagements a week during school." She settled herself beside him on the love seat and spread out her full skirt so that she would look as graceful and glamorous as possible.

"Shouldn't you be studying?" he said. "You don't have to bother with me, you know."

Sarah D. shook her head. "I suppose Charlotte told you Mama is giving a party," she said.

"She told me about it," he said. "Are you coming?"

"Of course I am. It's for all ages — from your crowd on down."

Ralph laughed.

"Oh, I don't mean you're so *old*," Sarah D. said. "Charlotte doesn't think you're old a bit. But after all, when you stop to think about it, you're nearly twice my age."

"But I think of you as quite grown up," he said gravely. "And after you're grown, a few years' difference in age doesn't seem to matter so much."

"The party is really for you, you know," she said, "even though no one says so."

"For me!"

"Well, for you, and then partly for Sis. I won't go into that."

Ralph began to look uncomfortable. He twisted on the love seat and cleared his throat nervously.

"The trouble is," Sarah D. said, "you don't know Mama as well as you should. If you knew her better, you'd see it without my telling you."

"I'm mighty fond of your mama," he said, "and I think she

likes me, but I reckon if she were having a party for me, she would say so."

"No, indeed," Sarah D. said. "Not like that. I didn't mean she meant you to know it's for you."

"Aren't you getting into deep water?" Ralph said. "Maybe we'd better not talk about it any more." He got up and, walking over to the mantelpiece, began to examine the gold and red Empire urns with which he had spent the evening twice a week for six months. "These are lovely vases, aren't they?" he said hopefully.

"I can't stop now," Sarah D. said. "You'll just have to listen to me, or else you'll get the wrong idea. Now come sit down."

He stayed by the mantelpiece, leaning his elbow on it and looking down into the fire.

"Mama always wants people to be at their best," Sarah D. said, "and she always wants things to hurry up and happen. And a party is the way to make things happen when people are at their best."

Ralph looked up at her and smiled indulgently. "You're being awfully cryptic tonight," he said.

"I don't mean to be," she said. "It seems to me *you're* being dumb on purpose. It's just that no one else around here will tell you what to think, so I've decided it's up to me. Now don't run off, and don't stop me. I'm not going to hurt you."

Ralph sighed and sat down. "Do you think Charlotte would like it if she knew you were telling me what to think?" he said.

"*No!* But Charlotte doesn't have to know anything about it."

"Well, since you've got to tell me, what *should* I think? Because I haven't thought anything, except that I would like to come to the party."

"I'll tell you how I would feel, if I were Charlotte," Sarah D. said, "and if I were Charlotte you would know how I feel, because I would tell you."

"You're not Charlotte, but go ahead."

"I believe people should be frank with each other," Sarah D. said.

"I see you do," Ralph drily replied.

"Well, you know what I just said about Mama? How she tries to make things happen? She's so funny and so much herself with it that an outsider never knows what hit him. But if a person *sees* what's happening he might be alarmed. So if I were Charlotte, I'd tell you not to be alarmed, because Mama's really harmless. I wouldn't want you to think we had designs on you."

"Maybe it never occurred to her that anybody has designs on me," he said. "It hasn't occurred to me. In fact, as far as Charlotte is concerned, designs aren't necessary."

Sarah D. looked scornfully at him. "Really!" she said. "I don't believe you've been listening to a word I've said. I'm not talking about Charlotte. I'm talking about Mama. But, as far as that goes, Charlotte knows perfectly well how Mama is."

"Yes, I have been listening," he said. "I understand you. But I don't believe Charlotte's worried about her mother. And since we're being so frank, I'll tell you that I don't think you ought to interfere in Charlotte's business. I was giving you an easy way out."

Sarah D. frowned and began to twist a loose strand of hair that had dropped down on her forehead. "I didn't expect you to be so difficult," she said. "You ought to know I'm not doing it to be bad. Besides, you needn't act so high and mighty. You've been listening."

Ralph was silent.

"Well, haven't you?"

"I just about had to," he said, "but I'm going to forget it."

"All right. Forget it, if you want to. But I can tell you one thing about Charlotte you needn't forget. She's not like me or Mama. We blunder around stirring folks up, and then, if we can, we talk our way out of it. But she makes up her mind, and she likes other people to make up theirs. She doesn't smother anybody with good advice, like I do, and she doesn't ever *use* them." She hesitated a moment and then added, "But, my, she certainly has some fixed ideas. When she gets on a tear, look out!"

Ralph smiled at her. "I see you're trying to protect her interests," he said. "But you needn't worry about me. I wouldn't be here, if I didn't see that she's as straight as an arrow."

"Oh, *straight*," Sarah D. said. "She's no saint, if that's what you mean. She just likes to get her money's worth."

"Now hush," Ralph said. "She'll be coming out in a minute, so don't say any more."

The party served one of its purposes in ways that Kate had not foreseen and did not recognize. It turned out to be one of those evenings when everything goes well. The weather was fine — a late March night, warm as May. The moon, whose help Kate had so trustingly invited, rose early, huge and red in the clear eastern sky, like a cool fairy sunset in reverse, and by eight o'clock stood, all dazzling white, high above the Anderson garden — the daytime side yard. The three old laurel trees that grew in a row and screened the side porch from the morning sun cast black shadows against the house and, where the moonlight struck their dark trunks, oozing drops of sap glimmered like clear water. Moss-filled wire baskets, thick with pale green curling ferns, hung from iron hooks in the ceiling, and the washed and shining leaves still dripped occasionally into puddles of moonlit water on the floor. All the ragged edges of the untended shrubs melted and merged in the shadows of the trees, and the Spanish daggers thrust out green spikes from their impenetrable hearts. Even the bare, grassless ground under the arbor was transformed; darker shadows against the bare darkness moved in the light breeze like ghosts of lace and made leafy patterns, first on its hard surface and then, springing up as if alive, on the pale dresses of the wandering ladies. The tender new leaves of the grapevines that dragged heavily at the sagging arbor shone, veined and translucent, in the light of Fanny Lee's Japanese lanterns, and the heavy, round cut-glass punch bowl on the table under the arbor seemed weightless and made of moonlight, as if it might take flight through the foliage with its brood of cups, like a fat fairy mother and her soap-bubble children.

To Kate's obvious delight, Charlotte and Sarah D. were surrounded all evening by beaus, and Anna responded quietly to the attentions of the young doctor from New Orleans, a man who obviously knew what was expected of eligible bachelors by hopeful mothers, and who was more than willing to fulfill their expectations in return for an evening's hospitality. Even Will, Kate's son, who at fifteen tried to see as little of his family as possible, put in a token appearance and was reasonably polite. Kate beamed on everyone and was never too busy checking the punch bowl or entertaining the chaperons to keep a sharp and interested eye first on one daughter and then on another.

But all the favorable external circumstances did not mitigate Charlotte's anxiety. Three weeks had gone by since the evening when she had sent Ralph home early, and her mother had said, "There are lots of things we could do to perk him up." Still he had not spoken. She had stuck to her resolution to be even slower than he, but as far as she could tell, he had not even noticed that she no longer made an effort toward him. He was absorbed in the events of that exciting spring of 1917 and, like a great many other young men, held himself still, almost held his breath, waiting for an explosion, afraid as much that it would not come as that it would. The world spun faster and faster; but their courtship, like a dying top, canted and wobbled and jerked to a halt. Charlotte did not worry about the war. She had heard people say again and again, "We're going to get in it. There's no way to avoid it," and she thought she was excited and concerned. But in truth she did not believe them and she paid no attention. She was thinking of Ralph and of herself, her plans were made, and she worried only about how to implement them. Caught in her obsession with Ralph's deliberation, her mother's intractability, and her own desire, she did not wonder if Ralph had his own reasons for caution, if he was thinking methodically and conscientiously how wrong it would be to marry her and then go off to war. If she had, she might have proposed to *him* out of relief and joy and willingness to enter a general sacrifice. Instead, she reviewed the lines of her private battle. For weeks she had protected Ralph from Kate, and tonight she resolved to be gracious and impersonal with him. She had told herself that she was bound by Kate's maneuvers to remove all pressure on her own part, forgetting that she had sworn the same thing to herself in anger, even before Kate mentioned the party; that she had said, "I'll be damned if I'll help him out," simply because he would not show his passion. She smiled and chatted and moved from one group to another, sometimes with Ralph at her side, sometimes without him. As the evening advanced, she paid him less and less attention. She had begun to feel trapped by her own foolishness, and she turned her frustration against him. Everything he said seemed to her a retreat, all his reserve and gentle courtesy meant, *Look out. I see I'm under attack. You may as well know I'll have this my way, or I won't have it.* And a moment later his most habitual gesture would seem so unbearably stupid and blundering that she would turn away in embarrassment. She thought of him more and more in relation only to her private unsayable demand.

For a long time, in the middle of the evening, Charlotte stayed in the parlor where the rug had been rolled back and the young folks were dancing. Music came through the doors and windows from the front porch where the four pieces of a local Negro band were playing. Charlotte had left the garden when Ralph went over to pay his respects to Kate, for she felt unable to watch her mother's boundless optimism and subtlety at work. It did not cross her mind that Kate might be obvious, or that she might embarrass Ralph. She knew that she would simply make a picture in his mind, a picture of the Andersons, lively, unselfconscious, and amusing; and plant in him a firm conviction that he, too, was lively, unselfconscious and amusing. *This is how we are,* she would say, in effect. *How can you help loving us when, as I can clearly see, you are already one of us?*

But what's wrong with it? Charlotte asked herself as she automatically went through the *hop, slide, hop, slide* of a polka with one of Sarah D.'s more vigorous friends. *What's wrong with it?* Immediately she saw what was wrong with it for her. She wanted him her way. She wanted her family, no matter how well-meaning, to have nothing to do with charming him and winning his love. They refused to let her alone at a time when it seemed most essential to act independently.

She whirled, smiling, round and round the parlor.

She was sick of them, sick of the loving chatterers who had daily, all her life, advised her about her clothes, her beaus, and her future, against whom she had steadily to exert the pressure of her will in order simply to stand still. *I'm going to leave,* she thought. *I'm not going to stay in Homochitto another week.*

As she danced past the parlor door she saw that Ralph was standing just inside the room, watching her and waiting for the polka to end so that he could claim her.

Thank the Lord for that, anyway, she said to herself. *Sarah D.'s beaus are too strenuous for me.*

The music swelled out in a violent whirl and her partner spun her around and stopped on the last abrupt chord directly in front of Ralph, who nodded and smiled and took the boy's respectful "Good evening, sir" as if he were indeed as old as the greeting implied.

"I wish I could dance with you like that," he said to Charlotte. "I always seem to have ten feet in a polka."

"It's not me," the boy gallantly said. "All the Anderson girls can dance. Miss Charlotte's just like the rest of them."

All! All! Even the children are doing it, Charlotte thought. *Anybody knows I can't pretend to dance like Sarah D.*

The boy excused himself, and Charlotte and Ralph climbed over a rolled-back rug and sat down on the love seat in the corner as the band began to play "Three O'Clock in the Morning." A few couples waltzed slowly around the room.

"It's a lovely party," Ralph said.

Charlotte smiled stiffly, feeling as if her face were cracking. "Don't you think so?"

"Oh, yes. Yes, I do. Mama's parties always are." She gave him a cold hard look. *You'll never figure it out,* she said to herself, only half knowing what she meant. *And I can't help you.*

He was looking straight at her and she saw him wince.

"I've been talking to your mother," he awkwardly began.

"Yes, I saw you."

"You know how hard it is for me to get to know people, Charlotte. How slow I am," he said, coming as close to self-analysis as perhaps he would ever come, and speaking with the stiff uncertainty of one to whom personal conversation is almost impossible. He was still looking earnestly at her, his knees spread apart, his big hands clasped tightly together, as he leaned toward her. The light shone on his crisp blond curls, and his mouth was as stern as an angry father's. "Your mother is the easiest person in the world for me to talk to," he said. "She never thinks about herself, does she?"

As Charlotte looked at his stern mouth and shining hair, a wave of tenderness swept over her, and the painful knot in her chest began to loosen. *I'm impossible,* she said to herself. *First I want him to see how Mama is and to like her for herself, to say nothing of understanding what I think without my telling him. And then I turn around and decide that when Mama gets the bit in her teeth, even I don't like her. And to mix matters up even worse, the reason . . .* She hesitated, even in her thoughts. *There,* she said. *It's true. Yes. The whole reason I'm so mad is I want him to make love to me.* She turned on him a blank, faraway look of concentration. *His hair is shiny,* she thought. And then, *I've got to do better.*

"What's the matter?" he asked. "Aren't you having a good time? What are you thinking about? You look at me as if you're angry."

She laughed nervously. "Sometimes I think I must be crazy, Ralph," she said. "I get the queerest notions. I'm not angry, and, yes, I'm going to have a good time. What were you talking about?"

"I was telling you how much I like your mother and how easy she makes me feel — I guess because she never thinks about herself."

"Oh, she thinks about herself, all right," Charlotte said. "But in a different way from you or me. She was born for the stage, and she's got one tonight. With an appreciative audience, she outdoes herself."

Out of irresolution she had said first less and then more than she intended to say; but now Ralph looked steadily at her, and she saw that he was concerned only with her, saw a faint spark of understanding in his eyes that lifted from her the dragging weight of her own self-absorption.

"You know what I mean," she said.

"I think I understand her a little bit," he said, "even though she's so different from my own family. And I see how much she cares for you and the others. Maybe she likes an audience, but after all, the effort is for you, isn't it? For all of you, I mean. That's enough for me."

She drew back, as if he'd touched her with a needle. "For *you!*"

"Well, I'd like you to know how much I like your family,"

he said, still slowly and methodically. "You're important to me, and I know they're important to you." He caught her hand. "Come on," he said. "It's a beautiful night. Let's go out in the garden."

She was satisfied. That was all he said, but she was sure he had seen and understood and accepted everything. She spent the rest of the evening flirting extravagantly with him, and he responded with affectionate amusement. She knew that neither she nor Kate had budged him one inch in the rock-bed of his life. Out of himself, he was ready.

When? she said to herself. And then, *I'll never have to make up my mind again. He can find all the answers for me.*

When he said good night at the creaking iron gate, everyone had gone, and Charlotte had decided what she would do next. They stood with the gate between them, and she told him that she was leaving.

"Why are you going?" he said.

"I want to take a trip," she said. "I've been saving the money."

"Stay here," he said.

She looked at him, and in her heart she said insolently, *Do you think I'm going to sit around Homochitto and wait for you to propose?*

"I want you to marry me," he said, "but everything is uncertain. I've been waiting, trying to decide what to do."

"I'm not ready to get married," she said, and, to herself, *That's a fine way to propose. I wouldn't marry him if he crawled to California for me on his hands and knees.*

"I want to travel," she said. "I want to see some more of the world before I marry."

"Don't go," he said again. He took her hand in his, turned it palm up, and stroked it gently with his other hand, and she was more moved by the gesture than she would have been by a passionate embrace from another man.

But she went. The next day she wired her cousins in California that she was coming to visit them, packed her clothes, made a reservation, and bought her ticket. Kate looked on amazed.

"I can't understand it," she said. "Here you've got him where any minute he's likely to propose, and you run off like a scared rabbit. Just don't be surprised if somebody snaps him up while you're gone."

"Mama, you can take care of my interests," Charlotte said. "I'm depending on you."

"Me!" Kate said. "Me! I have nothing to do with it. I'm just an interested bystander."

Charlotte stayed away six weeks and, while she was gone, wrote Ralph long letters full of news about her relatives and descriptions of the countryside and menus of the dinner parties she had attended. He replied with short awkward notes in his big, straggly hand. In early April the United States entered the war, and, in his last letter, Ralph told Charlotte that he had volunteered, that he was through with his work in Homochitto, and that he would probably be called within a few weeks. He asked her to come home and marry him before he went. He had never said he loved her. She replied that she planned to stay in California for six months, and that they could talk about it when he finished officer's training.

Five days later she got a telegram from him. MARRY ME NOW OR NOT AT ALL IMPOSSIBLE WAIT I LOVE YOU CATCH NEXT TRAIN HOME I LOVE YOU RALPH.

It was exactly what she had been waiting for: Ultimatum, command, and declaration. She caught the next train home.

◈

When the first excitement of Charlotte's arrival was over, when Ralph had gone home and Will, disgusted and bored with "girls' talk," had gone to his room, the family gathered in the dining room.

"Well," Kate said, "I reckon we're going to have to listen to that deafening belly laugh for the rest of our lives." She grinned at Charlotte.

"A wedding, a wedding, we're going to have a wedding," chanted Sarah D. She grabbed her mother and whirled her around the dining room table and into the rocking chair by the fireplace.

"Here, here," Kate said. "Settle down. A wedding is a serious matter."

"Not mine," Charlotte said. "It's going to be the loveliest party in the world."

"Ralph's serious," Sarah D. said. She folded her arms, tucked down her chin, and marched up to the mirror. "Father, dear Father, I've come to confess," she chanted, and then, bowing to herself, answered in a deep voice, "Yes, son, yes."

"Silly," Charlotte said. "If you make fun, I won't ask you to be in it."

"I like him," Sarah D. said. "He has lovely curly hair."

"I think he's *quite* handsome; I've always said so," Sis said. "He's a grand fellow."

"But it's beginning to get a little thin on top," Sarah D. said.

> Oh, he had no hair on the top of his head,
> In the place where the hair ought to grow.

Kate rocked and rocked, and shook her head. "Foolishness, foolishness," she said. "You girls are as frivolous as May flies. But never mind. One day you'll dance to another tune."

"There's nothing like a wedding to perk things up, Mama," Sis said, giggling.

"Now, let's be serious," Kate said. "This wedding is not going to have itself, Charlotte, and we haven't much time. Have you talked to Ralph about it? Do you want a church wedding? Who are you going to have as attendants? When will it be? We've got to scare up a little money, among other things."

Charlotte sat down in the chair opposite her mother, and Sis and Sarah D. settled themselves on the day bed.

"We've decided everything, Mama," Charlotte said. "We want to have it in the church, even if I don't wear a wedding dress and veil. After all, Ralph's family practically built the church, didn't they? It has to be right away, within the next two weeks, anyway. I'd like Sarah D. and Sis to stand up with me, but we don't have to have anything fancy. I know we can't afford a big church wedding. And there isn't time for you to make all the dresses, even if we could afford it."

"Do you *want* a wedding with all the trimmings?" Kate said.

"It would be lovely," Charlotte said. "I've always wanted to wear a veil and be a real bride, but it isn't important."

"We'll manage," Kate said. "Don't worry about it. I've been thinking about it ever since I got your wire. I've figured out the whole thing. Sarah D. has that lovely dress Aunt Ella gave her for Christmas, and I can make Sis one just like it in another color. You can borrow Amelie's wedding dress and use Grandmother's veil. And as for your trousseau, I've been working on that ever since you left."

"If we're going to have it like that, I think I'd like to have Amelie in it, too," Charlotte said.

"Ralph," Kate said. "He'll have to select his ushers and groomsmen. And how can he be sure he won't be called before the wedding?"

"He doesn't think he will be, but of course he can't be sure," Charlotte said. "But, Mama, if you don't think it's too reckless, let's plan it this way. We can change our plans if we have to."

Kate sighed. "I can't believe it," she said. "I simply can't believe you're really getting married." She grinned slyly at Charlotte. "It took a party, a trip to California, and a war to wake him up," she said. "You were lucky. You can't always count on a war."

"Now, Mama, don't start that," Charlotte said.

"He's a good man, and that's the main thing," Kate said. "The Lord knows, Charlotte, you should be satisfied. You're old enough and you've been choosy enough in your day. I was beginning to think I had an old maid on my hands."

Charlotte did not rise to this bait. She knew that her mother had had more reasons than one for so anxiously pressing Ralph's suit. Although Kate would never have married him herself, he had everything she wanted in a son-in-law. At thirty he had made his reputation for stability and was beginning to be successful in his profession. He was "comfortably fixed," as she had said privately to Anna and Sarah D. When he had come to ask formally for Charlotte's hand, he had told Kate that his income was a hundred and fifty dollars a month; and there were young couples in Homochitto, she knew, who were getting along quite well on less than a hundred. Now, poverty was more than respectable in Homochitto, and by its inverse standards the Andersons were the last word in aristocracy. But Kate had had enough of it. After her husband's death, flood had compounded debt, she had lost the plantation where she had spent her married life, and moved back to her mother's house in town. For years she had filled the double wings at the back of the house with roomers, single men of good reputation. With this income and the charity of faraway, wealthy relatives she had supported her family. She had never made their life seem a hard one. The roomers were friends whose idiosyncrasies were endlessly amusing. She had taught her daughters to be proud of their independence when they had to go to work instead of to finishing school. Through her own efforts and supported by the peculiar standards of friends and relatives who were often in the same or worse straits, she had contrived again and again to draw the sting of bitter necessity. But necessity was no less real for that. Genteel poverty is quaint only to the well-to-do. Charlotte knew that her mother had listed and stored in her heart all the things she had not been able to do for lack of money, and that she sought for her daughters a fleshier bedfellow than that specter, Want, whose hard bones she knew so intimately, who had lain down beside her almost before the dent that marked her dead husband's place in the feather bed had been plumped up and smoothed away. It was almost, Charlotte thought, as if Ralph must dower her, instead of the reverse.

His prestige, however, did not depend only on his money. He was a professional man with B.A., B.S., and M.S. behind his name. He had a degree from Boston Tech, and his years in Boston gave him a finish that was pure lagniappe. He had heard the Boston Symphony Orchestra play the works of Wagner and Tchaikovsky and had won the intramural tennis championship. He had spent his *Wanderjahr* in Europe and had brought home chromos of the Swiss Alps, a photograph of the entrance to St. Giles Cathedral with the figure of one of his collateral ancestors in the bas-relief, a bone-handled carving knife from Germany, and a Swiss pocket watch to leave to his son.

As if all this were not enough, Ralph's family met the Andersons' most exacting standards. Kate could relax her vigilance in the knowledge that Charlotte had threaded her way through the hazards of a day when girls were beginning to marry the sons of butchers and plumbers, young men (as she told her daughters) whose fathers had not been permitted to call upon the young ladies of an earlier generation.

The final touch, the one other thing Kate might have asked; Ralph was a Presbyterian. The scales were tipped almost too far in his favor.

But Charlotte told herself that she would have married him if he had been a Mohammedan and a street sweeper; she valued him for himself alone.

"Oh, he's grand, he's grand," Sarah D. said. She had moved from the day bed to the floor and now she lay back so that her head was under the dining room table. She took off her shoes

and put her feet in Sis's lap. "Even Charlotte should be satisfied with him. Tickle my foot, please, Sis."

"I just hope he doesn't turn out to be a night drinker," Kate
said, as if, like a Chinese mother, she were warding off the
envious gods.

"Mrs. McGovern will be coming to call," Charlotte said.

Sis absently stroked the sole of Sarah D.'s foot. "Do you
suppose she *approves* of you?" she said.

"She probably thinks you're fast," Kate said. "If she ever
heard about that expedition of yours to Vicksburg when the
Arkansas was going up the river, there's no telling *what* she
thinks. You know those Henshaw girls were always bluenoses.
Readers. And everything had to be just so for them, too. I
remember when we were girls Julia used to wear white gloves
to a picnic — if she would consent to go on a picnic. She
only went if Mr. McGovern was going to be there. She never
looked at another man. And as for Celestine, she wouldn't go
unless Julia went."

"Do you suppose they ever heard about the time Amelie and
I danced for pennies in the barbershop?" Charlotte said. "You
remember that time, Mama?"

"My God, my God!" Kate said. She clutched her head and
stared wildly about the room. "I thought your reputation
was ruined."

"You better not say *My God* around Mrs. McGovern," Sis
said.

"My dear, I can't change my character for Julia McGovern,"
Kate said.

"I believe that was the last whipping I ever got," Charlotte
said.

On the mantelpiece the clock whirred and hissed as if about
to explode and finally brought out twelve rapid chimes. Across
the street the Cathedral bell began to ring the hour.

"Twelve," Kate said. "We're right on time." She got up

from her creaking rocker and patted Charlotte on the head. "You've turned out to be a fairly nice girl in spite of dancing in the barbershop," she said. "I'm going to bed. You girls can sit up and talk about the McGoverns all night if you like."

As Kate would have put it, the only thing wrong with the McGoverns was, they were so good they were dull. No use to search their past for the skeleton in the closet. They didn't *have* a closet. As far as anyone knew, they had behaved themselves with quiet probity for generations. The first one in Homochitto, a doctor, had ridden across the Alleghenies toward the end of the eighteenth century with his medical books and instruments and his Bible in his saddlebags. He had floated down the river on a flatboat as far as Homochitto, and had set up practice there. He had married the daughter of an English planter named Fleming and had inherited his father-in-law's house and land, ten miles out from Homochitto in the dark woods and stillness where birds call sweetly and foxes stalk the rabbit runs. His sons and grandsons had been preachers, teachers, doctors, Presbyterian elders, and, on the side, incompetent farmers who cared more for hunting and for making catalogues of Mississippi fauna and flora than for cultivating their land. Until the Civil War they had been moderately wealthy, for money came easy in those days in Homochitto; and they had married women who maintained the life of rigid formality that went with wealth. They were strict tithers and did not believe in foolishly indulging their children. But now and then one was born or married into the family in whose imagination many diverse matters fell into place — dark woods, animals, fairies, gentle fathers, martyrs, and Indians — a storyteller; in her generation it was Julia, Ralph's mother. His father, the latest male heir, was an incompetent farmer, a pleasant and convivial gentleman, and little more. Almost in spite of himself he had married Julia Henshaw, a stiff and serious young lady, herself the daughter of teachers and ministers, an intellectual who in that day of female academies had actually gone to college. She had held his life together for him. She had borne him three sons — Ralph, the eldest, Waldo, and James — and a daughter, Celestine, who had died of pneumonia as a child. The boys, except for Ralph, did not go out much in Homochitto. From their father they had inherited a love of hunting that kept them in the country, from their mother a reserve that made small talk difficult, and from both the inflexibility of character that requires only stupidity or obsession to grow into eccentricity. Ralph was the pick of the three. He had his mother's slow, thorough, tenacious intelligence and his father's geniality, his mother's fine straight nose and high forehead, and his father's blond curls. In the poverty of the 1890's and in the partly self-imposed isolation of their country life, Julia McGovern had built her sons' lives. She had kept school for them and for the children of neighboring plantations in the schoolhouse where more opulent McGoverns had once maintained governesses or tutors. Until 1904, the family had lived on the produce of their exhausted land, and a small cash cotton crop, eked out with Mrs. McGovern's teaching fees. Then, suddenly, Mr. McGovern had inherited a great deal of money from a cousin in St. Louis, a maiden lady he had never seen who died intestate. The family bought a house in town, so that the boys could go to public high school. Occasionally they made trips, in the winter to New Orleans and in the summer to the Presbyterian resort at Montreat, North Carolina. There was money for college and for Ralph's trip abroad. Except for these changes, they lived as they had always lived. Mr. McGovern continued to farm ineffectually and Mrs. McGovern did not alter by one jot their formal and reclusive life.

The McGoverns and the Andersons had known each other always: even the McGoverns' excessive goodness was comfortingly familiar to Charlotte and Kate. Cousins had married cousins in Homochitto for a hundred years or more, and, earlier, when Mississippi had been a wilderness, their fathers had been buried together in the little cemeteries of Maryland and Pennsylvania. In Scotland, the bones of their Covenanter ancestors had crumbled to a common soil. But the Andersons had been transformed by Creole intermarriages and town life, while the McGoverns had held themselves apart. They had lived in the deep woods. The women were uncommonly fond of the songs of wild birds, and the men of theology. Their stern Calvinism had been tempered, not by French expedience, but by their own simplicity. In the woods, sufficient to themselves, they had not had much cause to be concerned with the ambiguity of human motives. They were, however, very much concerned with God. Theorists by nature, they were willing thralls to a theory insupportable in practice, and were too bound by their own past to recognize the dilemma. *Judge not that ye be not judged*, Jesus had said, and, *He that is without sin, let him first cast a stone*. But a sterner Judge had said, *Thou shalt not . . .* The McGoverns had not only Moses and Jesus to reconcile, but Jesus and John Calvin. Ralph's mother, and later Ralph, had their ways for dealing with these difficulties. If one could not judge, it was best to keep one's eyes on heaven, in order not to see how often the *Thou shalt not*'s were flouted. Steadfastly they assumed virtue; they failed to see or hear what might disturb them; if it were forced upon them, they forgot it; or, in the last extremity, they erased the offender's name and existence from their memories. The last measure was so seldom necessary, and the first three alternatives were so practical from everyone's point of view that family life was almost always serene. Like skillful jugglers the McGoverns kept the problems of judgment and mercy, sin and grace, predestination and free will, damnation and election forever in the air, having not enough hands to hold them if they all came down at once.

Charlotte learned early that the conviction of being one

of God's Elect has its practical recompenses. She and Kate
could not have been wronger when they thought that Mrs.
McGovern might not approve of her as a daughter-in-law. The
fact that Ralph had chosen her immediately placed her above
criticism. If a McGovern could not fall from grace, it followed
that a McGovern was always right; the only alternative was
to cease to exist. Charlotte also learned how to live comfortably within the limits of the McGoverns' peculiar code. No one
ever told Mrs. McGovern a scandalous story. No one would
have dared lower the tone of conversation to the level of gossip, and everyone knew that if the gossip was true and was
about someone she cared for, the problem of dealing with it
would have been too difficult for her. Perhaps the exact truth
is that she had a method for dealing with unpleasant realities,
and her method consisted precisely in not allowing them.
From herself she demanded honor — virtue, good faith, loyalty
and courage, and in everyone else she assumed it. The act of
listening would have been disloyalty on her part. Years later
even her grandchildren, without being told that they must deceive her (unthinkable! you had to figure it out for yourself
and call it by another name), sensed the necessity for accepting the Sunday customs of their grandmother's house without
saying, "But *Mama* lets us play croquet on Sunday." From
the cradle they knew better than to say anything that might
mar their grandmother's vision of their better selves. The
one large exception to this rule was in the area of public affairs. Here, where one was unlikely to find either relatives or
acquaintances, it was possible to gossip and be scandalized.
Everyone whose name was in the papers was either a rascal
or a hero; and all the McGoverns followed the adventures of
their favorite villains, and rejoiced when they were brought to
justice. But, of course, everyone knows that people like Kaiser
Wilhelm and Aimee Semple McPherson are not *real*.

Perhaps relations between the McGoverns and those who
had been forced to accept their lives on other terms might be

differently described. Hypocrisy is one word for it; courtesy is another. For fifteen years of his life, until he was told he had cirrhosis of the liver, Ralph's bachelor uncle was a drunkard. But the word was never mentioned in the McGovern house. Uncle Bob was "not feeling well today." Julius helped him upstairs and put him to bed, and the surface of life downstairs stayed smooth and unruffled. At two o'clock Julius struck the Chinese gong and everyone sat down to dinner. Mrs. McGovern said her long blessing and enjoined Julius to hand the cornbread, while upstairs Uncle Bob quietly got out of bed and got his bottle out of the armoire and drank himself into oblivion. Then one day he threw away the last empty bottle and bought a tin of green tea to replace it. That was the end of that. Courtesy or hypocrisy or an impossible morality had kept the family from preventing or criticizing; now the same deterrents kept them from commenting on his about-face.

The Andersons, on the other hand, had a livelier if more hazardous relationship with the Deity. To them Election was God's business. Like the sinner who expects to confess again and again to the same sin, they acted as if the final outcome were always in doubt. At the last breath, if he were sincerely shaken by the presence of death, a man might find himself elected and his life of sin swept away. Meanwhile, one must put as good a face as possible on the sins of today, if they were not to be embarrassingly apparent. In short, the Catholic Creoles had corrupted their conviction of rectitude; they not only recognized the other side of the coin, they sometimes saw stamped upon it their own faces. They lived in the world and had never mastered the art of being blind and deaf to its more unpleasant realities.

The insane pride of clan that willed a McGovern out of existence, in the Andersons took another form. Mrs. McGovern courteously refused to see that her own could sin. Mrs. Anderson saw the sin and stared it down. One said, *A McGovern must do no wrong.* The other said, *Right or wrong, an Ander-*

son is an Anderson. Perhaps they all meant to hate the sin and love the sinner. But some flaw, some failure of feeling, intervened; and instead, greed and gluttony, selfishness, arrogance, weakness, and cruelty, were forgiven in the name of individual eccentricity or family loyalty.

◄§§►

The morning of her wedding day Charlotte walked to the church with her mother to see the flowers. "I know I won't look this afternoon," she said, "and I want to see it."

The church was empty except for the organist who was playing scale passages in the choir loft above and behind them. The white box pews stood in empty rows with their paneled doors closed, their slick black horsehair cushions and dark mahogany trim crisscrossing in a precise geometric pattern. A forest of green smilax concealed the high pulpit and curled upward around the short, fat Ionic columns supporting the balconies that ran the length of each side of the auditorium (the old slave gallery where now on Sundays, out of sight of their parents' disapproving eyes, the young folk sat and flirted). Cape jessamine flowers gleamed like stars against the dark green smilax, and the air was heavy with fragrance. Kate and Charlotte tiptoed to their own pew more quietly than if the church had been filled with people, and sat down. The organ breathed and sighed as if it were alive.

"So many flowers," Charlotte whispered.

"We stripped half the gardens in Homochitto, *and* the cemetery," Kate said.

"It's lovely, Mama. It couldn't be any lovelier." And then, "What's that thing you've got over the hot-air register?" Charlotte said.

"A sheet of stiff cardboard. The white carpet will cover it," Kate said. "If the weights on your train got caught in the register, you'd get your head jerked off."

Charlotte giggled.

Kate shifted uneasily on the slippery horsehair seat, and touched Charlotte's knee. "Are you nervous, darling?" she said. "You know, I've never married anybody off before."

Charlotte shook her head. "Nervous? I feel as if I could swim across the river and back."

They sat quietly together a few minutes and then, as they started home, Kate tried again. "I know I ought to advise you," she said. "Is there anything you want to ask me?"

"Don't worry about me," Charlotte said. "I'm not scared."

"Well, you ought to be," Kate said. "You ought to be."

"We have to make our own mistakes, Mama," Charlotte said.

"I wish I could make *all* your mistakes for you," Kate said passionately. "I wish I could have all your troubles."

Charlotte stopped short. "What a thing to say," she said. "You shouldn't ever say a thing like that."

Kate laughed. "I didn't mean it," she said. "I just got carried away." She clamped her teeth together as if advising herself to be quiet and put her arm through Charlotte's as they walked on. "I can't think of anything to tell you, anyhow," she said.

"Never mind, Mama," Charlotte said. "I'm all right."

"Did you pack your raincoat?" Kate asked. "Have you labeled those boxes of linens yet? And has Ralph ever checked to see if your train makes a connection in Memphis?"

"Yes, yes, yes. Yes, to everything," Charlotte said.

"Darling, *don't* send your wash out without counting it," Kate said. "If you do, you'll find yourself without a sheet or a towel within six months. Now remember that, or you'll be sorry. And for goodness' sake, darn the holes in Ralph's socks while they're small. You're not marrying a rich man, you know. He may seem rich to us, but you'll have to live within his income. And if you have a servant, caution her about leaving your silver knives in hot water. You know what it does to the solder."

"*Mama!*" Charlotte laughed.

"Well, I've got to tell you something," Kate said. "I can't send you out into the world without a word."

"Stop worrying," Charlotte said. "Ralph will take care of me, if I haven't sense enough to take care of myself." She looked shyly at her mother, as if wondering how far irony would carry her, and then, feeling for once that she could speak without fear of ridicule, she said, "I know what I want and I know what I have. I want a man who's head of his house, and a pantry full of preserves, and a house full of children. I want to be able to help you and the girls when you need me. Ralph and I . . ." She stopped short. "Mama," she said, "I'm so full of confidence in myself and Ralph this morning, King Solomon couldn't advise me."

Kate sighed. "I know how you feel, darling," she said, "but I can't resist trying to get the last word." She squeezed Charlotte's hand and walked a little faster. "Now, hurry up," she said. "If we dilly-dally much longer, we'll be late for the wedding."

Ralph McGovern

⁊ LIKE many young men of his generation, Ralph McGovern learned briefly in 1917 and 1918 to look with surface equanimity and inward disbelief on the possibility of his own death. But he did not go to France, and he was thirty-three before he had to watch helplessly the suffering of someone he loved, thirty-four before he had to take on himself in his own way, or reject, as every man must, the peculiar burdens of his conscience, thirty-five before he watched at a long death.

1921, then, his thirty-fourth year, was the year of the beginning of his maturity. He stepped without thinking that year into the narrowing tunnel whose walls are consistency, simplicity, virtue, and ignorance of the human heart. Always before that time there had been the possibility that a shock might turn him toward some other tunnel. But never again. Acting from consistency, simplicity, virtue, and ignorance, he was to break through the walls of his particular tunnel more than once in his life, for his weaknesses were also his strength; but he did not know the tunnel was narrow, and so, even at his best and most heroic, he did not appreciate the landscape outside, or feel its loss when it was shut away again.

Already portly and balding, Ralph began that year to be so set in the mold of his life that at sixty-five he would be instantly recognizable as the same man. He would seem then to be wearing, in winter, the same brown, pin-striped, single-breasted suit, the same carefully buttoned vest, watch chain arcing from the same button to his worn gold pocket watch; and in summer the same rumpled brown and white seersucker. Only his straw boater would be exchanged with the passage of time for a panama. Ralph carried his weight with assurance. His stomach, made to seem even larger than it was by his erect, sway-back carriage, was solid, not flabby, and he wore his belt exactly around the middle of it, held miraculously, without suspenders, at the most outward point of its swelling arc. Deep lines ran from the wings of his big, high-bridged nose to the corners of his mouth and almost intersected the deep line that curved above his cleft chin. The lines were stern but when he came home he looked to his children, in spite of them, like a plump Presbyterian Santa Claus, loaded down with a bushel of peaches, a gallon bucket of dewberries or scuppernongs for Charlotte to preserve; or, from his occasional trips to New Orleans, with French sauterne, Edam cheeses, guava jelly, avocadoes, and artichokes. He was inclined in those days to bring pocketfuls of gum and gimcracks to his children but Charlotte pointed out that they had begun to greet him every week-end with "What did you bring us?" Then the present-giving stopped. He and Charlotte agreed they were teaching the children to value him for the wrong reasons.

In July, 1921, Ralph's second daughter was born. When the first child, Katherine, had been born in 1918, he had been away on maneuvers, and he had come home to the accomplished facts of a clean and bawling baby daughter and a wife exhausted but serene. When Anna was born he was at home, eager to share his wife's labor, to support her.

Setting out to fill up the measure of his life that he had made for himself, Ralph had no more idea than any other young man what would be required of him. He had felt his strength well up and had said to himself — or to God — *I wish to be used.* But how could he know the limits of his strength or what lay beyond? How could he know that others must suffer so that he could be used? He did not know it then, and he never consciously knew it. At the beginning he knew only that he was eager; that whatever the use to which he might be put, he would be equal to it. Rooted like a young tree in the receptive soil of his marriage, he had spread his roots and grown strong — ready, he was confident, for anything. Later he refused ever to think again about the two days of Anna's birth, so much more painful to him than to Charlotte; and he felt, although he was ashamed of the hocus-pocus that seemed to him involved in the thought, that perhaps he had dared God too far with his eagerness; that it was better to wait for trouble rather than to run joyously to meet it.

Charlotte had had a hard pregnancy. She had been ill for the first three months, scarcely able to stand the sight of food. And then suddenly she had been hungry, and she had eaten as ravenously as if the child leaping and growing at the cord's end were consuming her life. She could scarcely carry its weight on her thin legs, and the downward pressure of her grotesquely swollen womb made the muscles of her thighs cramp, so that sometimes she woke out of a deep sleep almost screaming at the sudden pain. Her strength was used up.

When she was nearly eight months pregnant, heavy, clumsy, and tired, Charlotte left the little west central Louisiana town of Eureka where she and Ralph had settled after the war and went to Homochitto to have her baby. She took Katherine with her, riding all day in the cindery day coach to get there. She wanted her cousin, Sykes Anderson, to deliver the baby. She had had Katherine alone in California, two thousand miles from her family and with Ralph away. This time, she said, she was going to be surrounded by familiar faces. Ralph joined her a week before the baby was due.

Early the following Sunday morning she woke up lying beside Ralph in the big tester bed in her mother-in-law's guest room, and felt stirring inside her the faint cramping beginnings of labor. She opened her eyes wide with excitement. She lay half an hour waiting, staring up at the satin sunburst in the tester, looking through the haze of her mosquito-netting cave at the big bare room, listening as intently as if she expected to hear a faint cry from the child beginning its struggle to be born. She kept her hands resting lightly on the sheet that covered the mound of her body. After a while, under her hands, she felt the ripple of muscle and, again, the slow cramp. She got quietly out of bed and dressed slowly and happily. Then, remembering how long it would be before she could wash her hair, she undressed, went into the bathroom, lit the big iron tank over the tub, drew a hot bath, got clumsily in, and washed, soaped and rinsed it until the long strands squeaked. Then she put on a bathrobe, sat down by the window in the sunshine and rubbed it dry. When Ralph woke up, she told him she thought her labor was beginning.

He was out of bed in a moment, fumbling with his clothes and stumbling around the room in his excitement, all his customary methodical composure gone.

"Have you called Sykes? Hadn't we better get right down to the hospital?"

"There's no hurry," she said calmly. "Go on and shave and dress. I don't want to rush to the hospital and then find it's a false alarm."

"How are you feeling?" he asked when he came out of the bathroom and found her still sitting by the window, looking out into the sunny morning.

"All right. Just a little pain about every twenty minutes."

"It's quarter past eight," he said. "I'd better phone Sykes. We don't want to let him get away on a call."

"All right," she said. "But don't disturb your mother. I don't want to get everyone excited." Now that the time had come, she was full of the secret, private importance of birth. She had no inclination to call all the friends and relatives she had come to Homochitto to be surrounded by. Just then a sharper pain came and she drew in her breath and bent over to favor it.

"I'm going," Ralph said. "Sit still now, and relax. I'll be right back."

"Tell him I'm going to eat breakfast and we'll be down in about an hour."

"Eat breakfast!" Ralph said. "Are you hungry?"

"Starving," she said.

At the breakfast table, during the long Sunday blessing "And bless our dear Charlotte, oh, Lord, and keep her under thy care, and . . . ," Charlotte felt another cramping wave of pain. By the time the blessing was over, it had passed, and she ate grapefruit, hash and grits, scrambled eggs and bacon, and hot biscuits, and drank a cup of coffee. Katherine sat beside her in a high chair and beat a tattoo on the tray with her spoon and smeared herself with jam. Ralph, at the end of the long table, opposite his mother, looked at Charlotte from time to time very much as he might have looked at a live hand grenade that had suddenly fallen into his lap.

❧

The air in the bare, hot hospital room throbbed to her moans like the inside of a struck drum, and Ralph stood beside her bed in his wilted seersucker suit, sweating, helpless, and anguished. It was almost night.

"Bear down! Bear down!" the nurse said impatiently. "You're never going to have this baby if you don't bear down."

Charlotte, caught in the uncontrollable downward heave of a contraction, ground her teeth with rage. When the pain had passed, she turned to Ralph who was holding both her small, light-boned hands in a grip that would ordinarily have made her cry out with pain.

"Get that woman out of here," she said. "I hate her."

"Settle down," the nurse said. "You're not the only woman who ever had a baby."

"Go away," Charlotte said. "Please, go away. And while you're gone, call Dr. Anderson. I need him."

"Dr. Anderson is on his way back," the nurse said, "and he instructed me to stay with you until he arrived."

Charlotte heaved herself up in the bed and looked at her grimly helpful antagonist. *"Leave* my room!" she said.

When the nurse had gone, she made Ralph lie down beside her on the narrow hospital bed, wrap his arms around her and, when the pains came, press his hands hard against the rippling muscles of her belly.

"Help me," she said, not even hearing herself speak. "Oh, somebody please help me."

When the doctor came again, he found them lying together, fighting their battle, commonplace and unique, for the life of the child.

Together he and Ralph turned her heavy, unmanageable body on the bed, and then he sent Ralph out of the room and examined her, muttering to himself and to her, "Now, lie still. Yes. He's begun to crown. Now. And the dilation is almost complete. We'll have him here in a little while."

He covered her with the clean, rustling sheet and took his watch out of his pocket. "How far apart have the pains been?"

"I don't know," she said. "I'm tired and I've forgotten."

"Where is Miss Ball?"

"I sent her away, Sykes. She's too rough." She smiled at him. "Get me another nurse, Sykes. I can't bear her. You know how notionate pregnant women are."

"Do you really want . . ."

"Here comes one now," she said. "Oh, God. Call Ralph."

Outside the door Ralph had sat down in silence beside Kate Anderson. His hands, clasped together between his spraddled legs, trembled.

"How's she getting along?"

"I don't know," he said. He could not say how frightened he was.

Kate looked down at his hands and then patted his shoulder.

"By tomorrow she'll have forgotten all about it," she said. "Try not to take it so hard."

In a few minutes Sykes opened the door. "She wants you, Ralph," he said. "Come on in. I don't think it'll be long now."

But the little while lengthened into hours. The night passed slowly and the pains came regularly, hour after hour. Charlotte's lips were bleeding and swollen where she had bitten them, and there had been serious talk of a Caesarean, and the advanced degree of the labor had ruled it out, and Sykes was beginning to look as anguished as Ralph when, shortly after noon the next day the baby was born at last.

That was the beginning of Ralph's knowledge of use.

❧

Ralph was standing on a street corner in Eureka one Saturday morning the December after Anna was born, waiting for two friends with whom he was going hunting. His black Buick touring car was parked at the curb and his shotgun in its canvas case lay across the front seat. Two lean, brown-spotted pointer dogs shook their long heads restlessly and watched him from the back window of the car. He had unbuttoned the isinglass window flaps when he got out, so the dogs would not be restless, and now they crouched, blinking in the bright sunshine, their paws on the window frames, while the Negro man who kept them for Ralph sat beside them, shivering in his worn officer's overcoat, his head tied up in an old wool scarf that had once been gray and was now purplish with age. One bare brown hand, gray with a scurf of peeling winter skin, held a dead cigar, the other was thrust into his torn pocket. Ralph leaned on the front window frame and talked to the Negro across the dogs' backs, lapsing into the queer, singsong intonation that he used with Negroes and Cajuns.

"Nah, nah," he said. "I don't care what Fitz says. Ain't no sense going back out there this week. We went over that old pasture last week. Didn' we? Hey? Didn' we?"

"That's right, Mr. Ralph, but he say . . ."

"Yeah, I know what he say, but he wants to make a little money out of us, don't he, George? Ain't that what he wants?"

The Negro looked thoughtfully at the cold cigar, knocked the ash off, and then put the cigar into the inside breast pocket of his overcoat.

"Yassuh," he said. "He do like it when y'all comes out there."

"Le's go out to your place," Ralph said.

"I done told you we ain't got no bobwhites out there," the Negro said, "and that's the truth."

"We could go back, cross the creek, George. I betcha woods back yonder's full of em."

"Over on Mr. Davis' place."

"Yeah, I know, but he don't care. And Martha could feed us. I'd heap rather y'all make a little money than Fitz. You know he's gonna drink it up, if he gets hold of it."

"Fitz going to get it from me if he don't get it from you," George said. "It don't matter."

"George, why don't you make that boy behave?" Ralph said.

The Negro looked at him without expression. "Yassuh," he said.

The old man's blank face made Ralph uneasy. He stood up straight and looked around him. Nothing in his stance indicated that he felt the bitter December wind that flapped the dogs' ears and whirled the dust in the dry, unpaved street. He stood erect, his belt fastened exactly around the middle of the curve of his stomach. He was dressed as properly as if he were to take the part of a hunter on the stage. High laced boots confined his khaki hunting breeches, and his corduroy hunting cap was settled comfortably on his balding head. He thrust his gloved hands into the huge pockets of his khaki hunting jacket, pockets that with luck would hold by evening the stiffening, softly feathered bodies of a dozen quail.

George courteously made conversation to bridge the gap that his look had made between them. "You looking salubrious these days, Mr. Ralph," he said. "How Miss Charlotte and the new baby doing?"

"Oh, they're fine, thank you," Ralph said. "Fine."

"You needs to find you a boy, now," the Negro said. "When you going to find you a boy?"

"One of these days," Ralph said. "One of these days."

"You wants to have a lots of children," the Negro said. "You know what the Bible say: 'Happy is the man that hath his quiver full of them.'"

Ralph looked sharply at him. "You sound like a preacher, George," he said.

"Well, in truth, I has been at one time and another," George said. "I often turns my hand to preaching during the winters."

"I wish they'd come on," Ralph said. "We're going to miss the best part of the day." He looked down the street and saw Dr. Bondurant, the Presbyterian minister, coming toward him, his shoulders bent against the chill and his lips moving concentratedly as he walked and stared at the ground. He stepped carefully and absorbedly, like a child watching the sidewalk and reciting, "Step on a crack, break your father's back; step on a line, break your mother's spine."

"Dr. Bondurant," Ralph said.

The old man looked up. "My boy," he said. "I was thinking about you. I meant to call you today."

In the car George settled his head deeper into his overcoat collar and leaned back and closed his eyes.

"You would have missed me," Ralph said. He nodded at the dogs and the Negro. "I'm going hunting," he said, "but I intended to get in touch with you when I got back. I knew you were waiting to hear from me."

The two men looked shyly at each other. *I'm not ready yet,*
Ralph said to himself. *Don't ask me.*

Dr. Bondurant cleared his throat. "Well . . ." he said doubtfully.

"I was just sitting in the coffee shop reading about all the excitement in Durante," Ralph said, quickly choosing the
subject he knew was most likely to drive everything else out of
Dr. Bondurant's head.

"Yes, yes. It's a bad business. Bad business all the way
around. But the church is within its rights. Anyone would
admit that. It's up to the Presbytery now."

I've got to decide today, Ralph said to himself. *That's all there
is to it. I haven't any more time to think about it.* Aloud he
said, "Will you have to sit on the Board of Inquiry?"

The old man nodded.

"Much as I hate to," he said.

"What do you think about it?" Ralph said.

"My boy," Dr. Bondurant said, "I feel sorry for the man.
He acted according to his lights. He spoke honestly from the
pulpit where another man might have kept his doubts to himself. I can't condemn him for that."

"That may be," Ralph said. "I suppose it did take courage
to speak out, but it would have been better for his congregation
if he hadn't. He should have resigned."

"It would have been more convenient for everybody," Dr.
Bondurant said.

"After all, the Session has its responsibilities. The Session
had to pass judgment on him."

Dr. Bondurant shook his head impatiently. "I'm not talking about the church," he said. "I'm talking about the minister.
Who knows how God is testing that man and what may come
of it all? Out of his doubts and confusion he may emerge a better Christian, and when he does, if he does (God willing), I'll
be the first to rejoice."

"But that's not the question," Ralph said. "That's not the

question at all. He's not responsible just for himself or just to himself. Is he?"

"It's the main question to me," Dr. Bondurant said. "I know the man."

"It's hard for me to sympathize with him," Ralph said. "I keep thinking about the people in his congregation. They're as important as he is. *He's* the one who undertook the responsibility of ministering to them. He knew what he was doing when he started out. And now look at him. There's no telling how much damage he's done."

Dr. Bondurant sighed.

"The Bible says, 'Judge not that ye be not judged,' " Ralph said. "But the church *has* to judge to survive."

"No, no," Dr. Bondurant said positively. "We have to *act* — not judge, *act*."

"But how can you . . ."

"Ralph," Dr. Bondurant said, "I'm sure no one has ever told you it's easy to lead a Christian life. Sometimes you have to act whether you know you're right or not." He paused and looked down at the sidewalk for a long time, almost as if he had forgotten Ralph was there. Finally he looked up. "It's not necessary to *always* think you're right," he said smiling. "Let God worry about that." He paused again. Then he said, "That's one way to take a man's measure. What does he do in the face of doubt? And what does he think about what he does? It's easy enough to choose good over evil. But can he choose between two evils? Do you understand me?"

Ralph nodded cautiously. He had not much experience of indecision.

"Then, yes," Dr. Bondurant said. "If you understand what I mean by that, yes. The church has its responsibility — not to judge the man, but to protect its own integrity. That man has sat at the feet of the Antichrist. There is certainly no doubt about that. He can't be allowed to preach evolution and mongrelization and the social doctrine. He can't be handed on a silver platter the opportunity to corrupt the minds of his congregation (especially the young people — that's where the damage can be done) and distort the doctrines of the church he's supposed to be a minister of. I would have to vote to expel him from the ministry. But that doesn't mean I judge him as a man. The shepherd seeks the lost lamb. His concern is not to the ninety and nine in the fold." He paused and shook his white head sorrowfully. "He was a fine youngster," he said. "I knew him as a lad. His father was superintendent of the Sunday school in the Durante church for thirty years — an active, a dedicated layman. I remember how he rejoiced when the boy got the call. Thank God, the old man is dead. I believe this would have killed him." He passed his veined and mottled hand over his eyes as if he were brushing away a cobweb. "What happened to him?" he said. "What *happened* to him?"

"Didn't he go to school in the East?" Ralph said.

"Yes, he went to Princeton, but he took his ministerial training in North Carolina."

"By then it may have been too late," Ralph said. "I went to Boston Tech for a year, myself. You run into some clever men in the eastern universities. Irreligious men, I mean."

"Perhaps that's where it all started," Dr. Bondurant said. And then, "Yankees and atheists," he muttered. "Yankees and atheists."

The two men stood in silence for a few minutes. The wind blew along the dusty, rutted street and banged the split and peeling board sign that hung above the shoe repair shop across the street. Two Negro cooks on their way to work approached, one gesturing and talking animatedly and the other saying from time to time, "Yes, Lord. Yes *Lord.*" When they saw Ralph and Dr. Bondurant the two women fell silent and passed them silently.

Abruptly Dr. Bondurant laid his hand on Ralph's shoulder. "The Southern church has a mission, my boy," he said. "We must stand for the Word of God and preach Christ Crucified.

We must stem the tide of modernism and turn back the Antichrist. Are you ready?"

"I don't know," Ralph said. "I don't know."

"The time comes when we have to stand up and be counted," Dr. Bondurant said. "And the church thinks that time has come for you. No. Don't interrupt me. You've served your apprenticeship in the deaconate. I couldn't have been more delighted when the Session selected you to fill this vacancy. I know you are young for the responsibilities of an elder, but we're a small church, and we need your fine mind and background and your judgment." He stopped and waited expectantly for Ralph's reply, but Ralph said nothing. "I know you of old, Ralph," he said. "Your grandfather and my father went to the seminary together. Your great-grandfather — I've heard my father talk about him — he was a scholar and a gentleman, and he was presiding elder in the Homochitto church for thirty years, all his life a witness for Christ. He took his five talents from the Master and multiplied them a hundred times. And I needn't remind you that in the days of the persecution one of your ancestors was on the proscribed list of the Covenanters. I've seen his statue above the entrance to St. Giles."

Ralph shook his head and for the first time hunched his shoulders against the wind. "I know all that, Dr. Bondurant," he said, "and I appreciate what you've said, but I'm not sure. In all conscience I'm not sure. That's why I've delayed all week giving you an answer." He straightened up again. "I'll give you an example of what I'm talking about," he said. "Now I've been teaching Sunday school ever since we came to Eureka . . . I can teach Old Testament without any trouble at all. It's nothing but a history of the Hebrew people and their relationship with God. Right? But the New Testament! That's another matter. Something is missing. In me, I mean. I don't feel at home. Sometimes I even feel — " He broke off. "And the questions they ask!" he said. "I can't answer them for myself. How can I answer them for anyone else? I'm not fit to be a spiritual adviser to anyone," he said, "and that's what an elder is supposed to be."

"Ralph, Ralph," Dr. Bondurant said, "Do you think God exempts you from service because you're in doubt? Doubt is the scourge of God. What would your faith be without it?"

"I don't work like that," Ralph said stubbornly. "I've got to be settled in my mind."

"Are you saying that you must understand with *your* finite mind all the teachings of the Son of God?"

Ralph shook his head again, but the words echoed in the cold morning air, giving him the beginning of his own conviction.

Abruptly the minister changed his approach. "Let me ask you a question," he said. "What do you believe about the Bible?"

The wind blew stronger and colder, whipping up the ears of the dogs waiting in the car. The younger of the two whined and yawned and gulped the cold air in his excitement. The Negro still sat motionless in the back seat, hunched down in his coat, but he had opened his eyes and was watching Ralph. He enjoyed listening to talk about God. Ralph saw his two friends turn the corner and approach, guns balanced easily in their hands and pointed at the sidewalk. The bright sunlight glinted off the barrels and the air had the steely smell of hunting weather. The trees and buildings around him reared up in bright, quivering solidity. To answer in, he had the time it would take the two men approaching to walk the length of the block, their heels clicking on the dry concrete sidewalk.

"Here they come, Mr. Ralph," the Negro said.

Ralph nodded.

"We get us *some* birds out to Fitz's."

"No," Ralph said automatically. "We'll go to your place."

Dr. Bondurant waited patiently.

"What do you believe about the Bible?" The question hung like smoke in the cold air. Everything that Ralph had thought

and wondered for fifteen years came into focus as if Dr. Bondurant had held up the tablets of the law before his unwilling
eyes. It came to him that the voice speaking to him was not the
voice of Dr. Bondurant. There was only One who cared what
he believed about the Bible. God had given him his answer
and his answer was a question. With His question God had
said, "You must do it all. You must take My work and the
burden of faith upon yourself out of your own free will, and
support it in the face of every inward doubt and outward
threat."

"I believe the Bible is the inspired word of God from Genesis
to Revelation," Ralph said. "I accept it on faith and I accept
the Lord Jesus Christ as my Saviour."

"Ah!" Dr. Bondurant said. "Then you *are* ready!"

Ever afterwards Ralph considered that moment one of the
turning points of his life. It seemed to him that God had said,
in Dr. Bondurant's quavering old voice, "Ralph, Ralph," and
that he had answered, "Speak, Lord, for Thy servant heareth."

❧

In a small town, on a street dark and deserted since the early
hours of the evening, in a still, dark house where a sober and
industrious man and his wife and two children are sleeping,
if the telephone rings, his heart turns over. Something is bound
to be wrong. He comes fighting out of deep sleep, thinking,
Somebody's died, and then, to exorcise the fear, *Wrong number. Must be the wrong number.*

That night in 1924, roused by the insistent, repeated jangle,
Ralph got out of bed and groped for his slippers and bathrobe.
Charlotte, already beginning to be deaf, was also already beginning to be abnormally sensitive to motion. She was
awakened, not by the sound of the telephone, but by the slight
jarring of the floor under her husband's steps.

"Is anything wrong?" she asked sleepily.

"Telephone," he said, putting his lips close to her ear.

"Oh." She raised herself on her elbow and turned on the lamp by the bed. "Who could be calling this time of night?"

Ralph went out into the hall and picked up the receiver. "All right," he said. "Yes. This is he." There was a brief silence. He raised his voice when he spoke again, and gave it the carrying force that means long distance. "Hello. Mother. What's the trouble?" Another longer silence. Then, "What does Sykes think about it? . . . Oh. I'll dress and start right now . . . No, no, I'm used to night driving. It won't bother me. The roads are deserted . . . Have you talked to Waldo? How about James? . . . Well, try again in the morning. I'll be there, let's see, what time is it?" Then, "I'll be there by seven if I make the six-thirty ferry, or by eight if I miss it."

After he had hung up, he went back into the bedroom. Charlotte was sitting up in bed, waiting. He sat down opposite her on his own bed. "What is it?" she said. "I couldn't hear."

"It's Father," he said. "That was Mother on the phone. Father is sick."

"What's the matter with him? How sick?"

"He's got pneumonia," Ralph said. "She says he's very sick."

"Oh, *Ralph!*" She pushed the covers back and sat on the side of the bed, groping with her feet for her slippers. Ralph had picked up a match from the chest of drawers and was lighting the gas space heater. Then he sat down again. "What are you going to do?"

"Well, I'm going over there," he said. "I'm going on over there right now. She can't get in touch with James; he wasn't in his room at the boardinghouse. And Waldo has gone down on Bayou Teche hunting. They are sending someone down there to find him. I'd better go right on over."

"Can't you wait until morning?" she asked. "Is he that sick?"

"I'd better go right on over there," he said. "She needs one of us."

"Well, I'll get up and fix you something to eat," she said.

"No need for you to do that."

"Yes, I will. Maybe you could drink a cup of coffee," she said. "You don't want to doze off at the wheel."

"All right, sweetheart," he said. "That'll be fine."

She sat looking at him anxiously, and he got up and crossed the narrow space between them. He patted her gently on the shoulder with his big, thick-fingered hand. "I better call Wilcox," he said. "There are some things he'll have to do for me tomorrow."

"Is he in the hospital?" Charlotte asked.

He shook his head. "You know Father," he said. "He's hard to do anything with. Mother said he'd been sick since Monday with flu, and then he got a lot worse a couple of hours ago. Sykes was there when she called and she said he wanted to take him to the hospital, but it upset him so, they decided to let him have his own way. She said Sykes was making arrangements to get a nurse out there right away."

Charlotte shivered.

"Charlotte," he said, "he must be even sicker than Mother said. It's not like her to telephone in the middle of the night." He was still standing over her and she took his hand from her shoulder and kissed it.

"I'll go make you some coffee," she said.

❦

From the beginning it was evident that Mr. McGovern was desperately ill. Sykes told Ralph when he arrived that there was very little hope for his father, and that he should call his brothers' home. Waldo came up from Opelousas the following day, but James was working in Oregon and did not get home until the day after his father's death.

The second morning after Ralph came, he was sitting beside his father's second-story bedroom window and looking out at the sunny October day. He had sat up most of the night. Roused by his mother shortly after midnight to take the second shift, he had, a little later, watched his father fight through such a spell of coughing and choking that he was sure he could not survive it. When the time had come to call Waldo to take his place, he had been unable to go to bed and had stayed, sitting alert and silent in the shadowy room. Mrs. McGovern, as soon as the coughing had begun, had wakened from her own still, deathlike sleep of weariness as quickly as if she herself had been choking, and joined her two sons. And so all three of them had been up most of the night, sitting helplessly by while the nurse and doctor worked over the dying man. Ralph and Waldo had squeezed their big bodies against the wall and pulled their feet under them, as if half afraid the nurse with her armor of professional briskness and impatience would reprimand them for getting in the way; but Mrs. McGovern, hardly aware that the doctor and nurse were present, had sat by the bed holding her husband's hand and drawing every agonized breath with him.

Now Ralph sat by the window and rested his elbow on the sill and his head on his hand, drowsy in the hot room, the gravel of lost sleep scratching his eyelids. Outside in the flooding sunlight grackles were walking decorously among the fallen leaves, bending their shining heads to the insect-swarming earth, calling hoarsely to one another of the death of summer. Inside, propped high in the bed where he had slept for nearly forty years, Mr. McGovern fought, breath by breath, the rising flood in his own lungs that would shortly drown him. But the acute attack was over now, and he was sunk in a kind of half sleep, half stupor. Waldo still sat against the wall with his feet drawn under him, and every now and then his blue eyes, redveined and bushy-browed like his father's, filled with slow, unbidden tears. When that happened, he would bend his head and cover his eyes with his hand as if he were praying, and wipe them secretly away.

Celestine had joined the family in the big bedroom, and now, as was her custom every morning, she was reading the Bible. Sometimes she read to herself, and sometimes she read aloud. Her pince-nez was fixed firmly in the deep red grooves on her nose; its thin chain dropped to the back of a round, gold button on her shoulder. She was dressed, like her sister, in a pastel "semi-mourning" house dress and black leather, pompon-trimmed house slippers. Her short, plump feet in the soft slippers were arched, the toes curled tensely under. Whenever she saw that Waldo, sitting beside her against the wall, had begun to weep, she would close the Bible, marking the place with her finger, and take his hand in hers. She would lift her head, turn her face heavenward, looking like a beaked and wattled bird, and close her eyes and go on from memory with what she had been reading.

"Hear my cry, O God; attend unto my prayer.

"From the end of the earth will I cry unto thee, when my heart is overwhelmed: lead me to the rock that is higher than I.

"For thou hast been a shelter for me, and a strong tower from the enemy.

"I will abide in thy tabernacle forever: I will trust in the covert of thy wings. Selah."

Mrs. McGovern wet a cloth in a bowl of cracked ice on the table beside her and patted her husband's lips. She seemed not to hear her sister's voice, as if it were part of the noise of the house, the ticking of clocks, the creak of warming walls in the sun, the discreet opening and shutting of doors downstairs, all of which was suspended from breath to breath of the dying man. There was a long silence. Then Celestine began again.

"Bless the Lord, oh my soul," she read, "and all that is within me bless his holy name."

Automatically Ralph said the psalm with her in his head: *Bless the Lord, oh my soul, and forget not all his benefits.*

"Who forgiveth all thine iniquities; who healeth all thy diseases."

Her voice, serious and quavering, rising so unnaturally in the quiet sickroom, was almost unbearable to him. He felt himself falling asleep, for he could not bear to stay awake.

The hot, sunny air pressed throbbingly against his ears and his aunt's voice brushed rhythmically and painfully across his heart like whisks brushing a big drum: "Who re*deem*eth thy *life* from de*struc*tion . . ." The doctor stood by the door, his hand on the knob, and his low-voiced instructions to the nurse and her brief replies rattled against Ralph's ears as if the drum were full of pebbles, falling, falling, as the drum turned. *Whoo-oom, whoo-oom* groaned the drum as it turned and turned.

I dreamed I was inside a drum when I had my appendix out. I was inside the drum then, and someone was pounding on it, he said to himself as he slipped into the area between sleeping and waking where dreams act themselves out on a stage before one's eyes, but one is still conscious enough to cut them off at will.

Four orderlies dressed in white jackets stepped forward and lifted him onto a stretcher. "He certainly is heavy," said one as they carried him down a long corridor, bare as the inside of a shoe box. "It's centrifugal force," said another. "The drum does it. He gets heavier and heavier as he goes round and round. It's part of the treatment." "I can't carry him any farther," said a third. "Here, we'll put him in the school room." And they turned aside and entered the little room at home where in the days before the money came his mother had kept school for her own children and a dozen of the neighbors'.

Inside, his mother was sitting at the desk at the front of the room, fresh and proper in her high-necked dress with ballooning leg-of-mutton sleeves. Her beautiful dark, curly hair, piled high on her head, escaped its confining net in little tendrils around her face and at the nape of her neck. She was reading a story aloud to the children and while she read, her everyday austere reserve dropped away and he heard her voice,

charged with excitement, change from the squeaky caw of Mrs.
Crow to the deep Jug-o'-rum of Mr. Bullfrog. She cocked her
small head on one side like a bright-eyed bird and the nostrils
of her delicate high-bridged nose flared in outrage. "Mind your
manners, sir," she said to Mr. Bullfrog, "or I'll peck you good."
The children giggled.

The orderlies put the stretcher down. "Here he is," said
one. "What shall we do with him?" Ralph looked up at them
and saw that they were four erasers with heads and legs and
arms hooked to them like the card people in Alice In Wonder-
land. "Rub him out," said an unknown man's voice behind
him, and he tried to turn and see who it was, but he could not
move his head.

Then his mother began to read again, but this time it was in
Celestine's quavering Bible voice. "For he knoweth our frame";
she read. "He remembereth that we are dust. As for man, his
days are as grass: as a flower of the field, he flourisheth. For the
wind passeth over it and it is gone; and the place thereof shall
know it no more."

Ralph woke up, sat up straight, closed his mouth on the beginning of a snore, coughed, and looked around the room. The
doctor had gone.

"But the mercy of the Lord is from everlasting to everlasting," Celestine read.

"Where is the nurse?" Ralph said, in a voice too low to interrupt his aunt's reading.

"She's gone to get her breakfast," Waldo whispered. "You've
been dozing."

"No, no, I'm awake," Ralph said.

Celestine began to read to herself and for a little while the
room was quiet, except for the sick man's labored breathing.
The pages of the Bible rustled and whispered in the stillness.
"The Lord is my shepherd; I shall not want," Celestine said
suddenly.

Ralph leaned his head on his hand and closed his eyes.

I thought it meant, "I shall not want the Lord for my shep-herd," he said to himself, looking again at the schoolroom where his mother was assigning the memory work for the week. *And the iniquities. I thought visiting the iniquities meant the Lord was paying a call on a family named* The Iniquities. *Nothing makes much sense to children,* he said to himself, and made a note in his mind to be sure to explain their memory work carefully to his own children. *I'll have to remember to tell Mother about Katherine last week asking when she'd be old enough to go to* Christian and Devil *on Sunday night.* He smiled to himself, and then, remembering that this visit there would be no way he could make his mother smile with the sayings of the children, felt himself overcome with drowsiness again.

Father was there. Father came in that day when we were learning visiting the iniquities, and that's why I didn't have a chance to ask Mother about it. But maybe I thought I under-stood it. He looked at his mother through half-closed eyes, where she sat by his father's bed, holding his hand, watching him, breathing with him, deep and then shallow. *Just like Charlotte opens her mouth every time she puts a bite in the baby's mouth, as if she's helping her eat.* He turned away and looked drowsily out the window again. *A day like today and blackbirds, blackbirds, blackbirds . . . in the leaves . . .*

His father came into the schoolroom and Ralph sat at his desk admiring him. He was dressed for a trip, dark suit, high white collar, light overcoat on his arm. "I'm off, Julia." His mother's face lighted up at the sight of him. "Oh, Jimmy, you look so handsome," she cried. "Your suit is lovely."

His mustache had been brushed until every silky blond and reddish hair gleamed separately. His bright blue eyes sparkled with excitement and his narrow face was scrubbed red. "Thank you, my dear," he said with modest dignity.

"When will you be back, Jimmy?"

The children gazed in awe at their dashing father, off for an adventure . . . where? In New Orleans, maybe. "He must have been going to New Orleans on business," Ralph said to himself.

"I don't know . . . in a few days. I'll wire you."

"Take care of yourself, darling," his wife said. "Remember your stomach's easily upset."

"Now don't worry about anything while I'm gone, Julia," he said. "You won't have a thing to think about. Clay can manage everything. And I've told him to slaughter the hogs if we get a hard frost."

To Ralph he said, as he always did when he was leaving, "Look after your mother, son. You're the man of the family while I'm gone."

"Yes, sir," the little boy said loudly, and blushed at the thought of his own importance.

Ralph, sitting by the window, looked at the child tenderly. Then he heard his father say, "Julia, why don't you give the children a holiday for the rest of the week if the good weather holds?"

The little boy sat up straighter in his seat, ready to run for the door, but his mother shook her head firmly. "Regular hours and regular habits," she said. "They have their work to do."

"We could help Clay," the little boy said hopefully, knowing when he said it that school and Sunday school and church and mealtime and bedtime would come regularly, if it were the judgment day.

It did freeze, the grown-up Ralph said to himself, emerging briefly from his dream. *That's why I remember it. That must have been the year of the big freeze. The year the Magnolia fuscata in the front yard was killed to the ground. The freeze of '99. Clay Jr. and I tracked foxes together in the snow. So . . . The hogs. Yes. It was so cold your fingers stuck to the doorknobs. And Mama in her riding habit with a wool scarf over her head and an old overcoat of Father's on over her coat,* out getting the smokehouse ready. Blood on the snow and the pigs squealing and Waldo crying because they were going to kill old Barton. So school must have let out after all. No. I had charge, that was it. I was teacher and Waldo and James wouldn't be quiet and wouldn't stay in their places and study, and I cried. No. Waldo. It was Waldo cried about the pig. He watched a plump, worried child, blond curls falling in his eyes, write on the blackboard, and he seemed to be writing over and over, "Visiting the Iniquities, visiting the Iniquities."

And then the strange man's gruff voice from the back of the schoolroom said again, "Rub it out, erase it," and the four orderlies got up from the desks at the back of the room and started toward him, and he began to cry. Suddenly the door of the schoolroom opened as if blown by a strong wind and he heard voices in the hall. The wind blew the flame in the lamp, for it was night, and he crept to the door of the room and looked to see who was there. His mother in her night gown and wrapper, braided hair hanging down her back, stood holding a lamp and talking to Lucy, the cook. "She took bad, Miss Julia. Midwife skeered. I'm skeered. You gots to come help." "What's the matter?" his mother said. "Won't the baby come?" "Baby won't come, and midwife say the baby dead. Say hit's been dead." "All right. Let's see." The ghostly figure put the lamp down and stoop thinking. "Go quick. Get Clay up. Tell him to saddle Whitey and ride to town for Dr. Shields. No. Tell him to stop by the house first. I'll give him a note for Dr. Shields. Now. I'll dress and come down as quickly as I can."

Ralph shook himself awake again. Dreaming, he thought. I must have been dreaming. The ghostly, white-shrouded figure of an unknown woman moved across the corner of his vision and vanished. That was a hard winter, he thought. We were glad when Father got back. Didn't he stay for Mardi Gras? No, I reckon that was another year. He couldn't have been gone that long. And then, I remember what I was thinking *when I dozed off.* He smiled. *I was thinking about* Visiting the Iniquities. *And I remember that week, when Father took the trip and there was the big freeze, I remember finally asking Mother what it meant, and she explained to me about original sin.* "When people do bad things their children suffer for them as much as they do. Like, for instance, suppose your father were a bad man who mistreated his children. You would suffer from his sin in two ways: you would suffer in your body because he was cruel to you, and you would suffer in your spirit because you would learn cruelty from him. Do you understand? So, you see. Adam sinned, and we must all suffer because of his sin. Because Adam was our first father and we are all his children. But then Jesus came and took our sins on himself and died for us and that is how we are saved and can go to heaven." She had paused and looked down at his troubled face. "But our *father*," Ralph remembered saying. She had interrupted him. "You are a very fortunate little boy," she had said. "You have a wise and just and loving father. But you must never stop working to root the sin out of your heart just as he and I and all good Christians do."

Mrs. McGovern got up from her place by the bed and walked to the window. "He's a little better; I think he's a little better," she said to Ralph. "He's breathing easier."

Ralph nodded. He went over to the bed and took his mother's place. "Go lie down for a little while, Mother," he said. "Go rest. I'll call you if we need you."

But she paid no attention to him.

"Hear my prayer, O Lord, and let my cry come unto thee," Celestine read.

"Hide not thy face from me in the day when I am in trouble; incline thine ear unto me: in the day when I call answer me speedily.

"For my days are consumed like smoke, and my bones are burned as an hearth."

Stop, Ralph said to himself. *Please don't read any more.*

The father turned and muttered on the bed and his deep, rasping breaths were broken by two or three short gasps. Then he opened his eyes and looked sharply around him from beneath his shaggy, sand-gray brows.

"What time is it?" he said, so loud that Waldo, sitting tilted against the wall, brought the front legs of his chair down with a thump.

Celestine read on. "My heart is smitten and withered like grass . . ."

Mrs. McGovern had turned back from the window at the first sound of a change in his breathing and now she stood bending over him. She took his hand in hers. "It's ten o'clock, ten-ten, Jimmy, darling," she said. "You're better. You're feeling better, aren't you?"

He looked about him as if to see who was in the room, and, turning his head with an effort far to the left, saw Celestine and Waldo sitting side by side in the corner of the room.

"What's Celestine doing in my room at this hour of the night?" he said.

"It's morning, darling. You've been sick, you know, and she came in to inquire about you."

He raised his eyes to the long windows. "It's been dark," he said.

Celestine had neither heard nor seen any of this. "They shall perish," she read, "but thou shalt endure: yea, all of them shall wax old like a garment . . ."

Mr. McGovern looked at her again and then turned to Ralph. "I'm dying," he whispered.

Ralph hesitated. Then he laid his hand on his father's and nodded. But Mr. McGovern had looked away, his eyes following his wife as she crossed the room toward Celestine. She put her finger on her lips, touched Celestine on the shoulder, and gestured toward the bed.

Celestine got up, but Mr. McGovern shook his head. "No," he said. "Let her stay. I like company."

Then a fit of coughing seized him and for a few minutes he struggled, gasping and retching, to get his breath.

"Where's the morning paper?" he finally said. "I haven't seen the paper today. I'll just lie here a little while and then get up, but I can read the paper in bed."

"Wait a while, Father," Ralph said. "When you're rested, you can read the paper."

Waldo got up abruptly and left the room.

Mr. McGovern's breath rasped and rattled in his chest. He turned his head to his wife again. "Hot," he said, "I'm getting hot."

Aspirin would not bring his fever down and he alternately shivered and burned. His narrow face was dry and rosy and his red-veined blue eyes turned first to one member of his family and then to another in gentle supplication. Ralph reached out to touch his forehead and a wave of heat struck his hand, as if his father were wrapped in an envelope of burning air.

"Mama, we'd better get the doctor back," he said.

"He'll be here in a little while," she said. "He said he was going to make two calls and then come right back. He canceled his office appointments for today."

Mr. McGovern pushed himself up and gazed out the window. "It's a fine day," he said.

"Lie back, Jimmy. Lie back and save your strength."

"Ralph," he whispered hoarsely, "I went out to the place yesterday and got Clay Jr. to saddle Nellie for me and Pet for him and we rode through the woods there by the creek on the back. Ralph, we saw a fox in there — a beauty. I believe he's the one Belle treed last month. We'll get in there next week and run him, eh?"

"Yes," Ralph said. "We'll do it, Father."

"How about it, Julia?" he said. "Shall we go fox hunting one night soon? As soon as we get a full moon?"

"Yes, darling, of course," said Julia, who hadn't been on a horse in thirty years.

He lay down again and gave Ralph an unmistakable "among us men" look. "Julia won't go unless I'm along, you know," he said. "She won't go to a picnic or a party or a hunt unless I take her. Now, how did I ever get in a predicament like that, I ask you? But it's true. I'll make you a little bet, old man. Ask her if you can come to call. I'll lay you five to one she won't let you. They're few and far between who ask and when they do, they're not welcome."

Ralph looked unhappily at his mother.

"It's because I don't care for anyone but you, Jimmy," she said. But he did not know she was there.

"Excuse my voice," he said to Ralph. "Cold. Can't seem to talk above a whisper." And then, "Well," he said, "you know what everyone says about the Henshaw girls. They're bluestockings. Did you know Celestine and Julia have both been to *college?* That's probably why they're so odd."

"Jimmy, try to be quiet a little while. Rest. The doctor wants you to rest."

"She's a strange girl, there's no denying it," Mr. McGovern said. "Plainly, she's shy, and she's certainly religious. All those Henshaws are too religious for their own good. But there's something charming about her. Something about her appeals to me. You know, I think she loves me. Whatever I do is all right with her." He turned restlessly. "This is the hottest August I've ever felt," he said. "The bottom side of the pillow is hot when you get into bed." He looked at Ralph again and his cracked lips parted in an ironic smile. "Well, I've had my fling," he said. "I'm ready to settle down. I'm feeling my years. After all, I'm over thirty. I'm just like any other man. I want a home and children."

"Jimmy, Jimmy," his wife whispered, and she wet the cloth in the bowl of ice and patted his lips and forehead.

He sighed and turned away from her. "I want to get *out,*" he said. "I can't stand being cooped up. I can't miss October. The woods are so full of bobwhites, you stumble over them."

The rattle in his chest got louder, and he coughed and choked again, choked so long and so hard that while Ralph held him in his arms, his wife had to reach down in his throat and pull out the rope of phlegm that was stifling him.

Afterwards he said, "Where's that damn doctor? Get him out here and make him do something about this damn foolishness. What's a doctor for if he can't get you well?"

"He's been here already, darling. He was here while you were asleep, and he's coming back in a little while."

"Never mind, Julia," he said. "Don't worry about me. I'm all right. Don't worry about me. I've always tried to shield your mother from every worry and trouble," he said to Ralph. "All the years before the money came, when times were hard, I never let her see what a struggle we were having. Ain't that right, Julia?"

"Yes," she said. "Yes. You've always been lovely to me, Jimmy."

"When I used to read the paper aloud to her in the evenings," he said, "I never read about crime and war and all the terrible things in the world. I always read the county news and births and deaths and such."

He looked at his wife. "My dear," he said, "would you go downstairs and look in the drawer of the secretary in the study, and bring me that leather case with the tax receipts in it?"

She shook her head. "You can see about them later," she said.

He raised himself on his elbow. "Go on, my dear," he said. "I'm a sick man. I have to have my way."

She looked anxiously at Ralph and when he nodded she left the room.

As soon as she had gone, Mr. McGovern turned to Ralph again. "Give me your hand, son," he said. "I just sent her out so I could talk to you alone a few minutes." He glanced at Celestine who still sat in the corner, the anxious, bewildered look of deafness in her eyes. She had stopped reading. He nodded and smiled at her encouragingly and then turned back to Ralph. But his eyes filmed over with bafflement, and he shook his head. "I wanted to tell you something," he said, "but it's gone out of my mind." He sighed. "I'm dying," he said in a wondering voice. And then, "It's not so bad, son. When I get to choking like that, it's not so bad. I remember once, when your mother was having Waldo, she said to me, 'It's not so bad, Jimmy, when the pains come. I know it looks awful to you,' she said, 'but I'm not really exactly there.' See? I didn't know what she meant."

Ralph bent his head and held his father's hand in a crushing grip.

"Don't sell the place, Ralph," the old man whispered after a pause. "Whatever you do, whatever happens, don't sell the place. That's what I wanted to tell you."

"I won't, Father."

"But promise me."

"I promise I won't, no matter what," Ralph said.

"It's been in the family a hundred and twenty-seven years this past September."

"I won't sell."

"There are so many things you ought to know. It never has made any money — not in the last fifty years, anyway," Mr. McGovern said. "It won't be easy." He sighed. "But your mother knows all about it. She can help you." He looked out the window at the blue sky where puffs of cumulus were building up from the horizon, and at the dull green October leaves waiting limply for November's frost. "I'd like to wait till the chinaberries turn," he said. "Every year I watch that one in the corner of the yard, and when the sun gets in the branches, the berries are like bunches of gold grapes." Then, "The dogs are spoiling for a good run, Ralph," he said. "Take them out while you're here."

Across a chasm of pain Ralph struggled against his own silence, but he could not open his mouth to say the words he knew must be his last goodbye.

"You're hurting my hand, son," the old man said.

"I'm sorry," Ralph whispered. "I'm sorry, Father."

Mr. McGovern drew his hand away and looked at it wonderingly. "I've tried, Ralph," he said. "I've tried to be a good man. But I'm selfish, ain't I? It's always been hard for me to notice other people."

Later the doctor and nurse came back, but by then he was out of his head again, tossing on the bed, fighting for breath, demanding to be allowed to get up, so that Ralph and Waldo had to hold him down, choking and heaving as if his chest would burst.

When it was over at last, when the moistened rag could no longer ease the pain of his cracked lips, dry and swollen from gasping hour after hour at the dry, unrelieving air, his wife sat down in the brown wicker rocker where she had held his children in her arms and soothed away their pains. She began to rock.

"Oh, oh," she said. "Oh, it hurt him so. Oh, if I could have helped him."

Ralph knelt beside her and laid his head in her lap, crushing her knees against him, and they wept together.

Summer Days

໒ᦓ RIDING south and then east, south and then east through the bright June countryside, Anna watched the straight rows of young corn and cotton flash by, alternating green and black, like the spokes of a great spinning wheel to whose rim the high-riding, black Buick precariously clung, and whose hub lay hidden in the woods on the horizon. She watched until her eyes ached. Dark earth and shining, still dewy leaves blurred to a shimmering gray smear, slipping past the window and at the edges changing again into fields and trees and ditches where red-winged blackbirds darted up and scattered.

Anna felt for the square of mirror in its tissue paper case that her mother had thrown away and that she had put in her pocket for the trip. A little mirror was better than no mirror at all for a long day's ride in the car. She tore off the paper and squeezed the glass until she felt the sharp edges cutting into her palm.

"You can't come out, yet," she said in a whisper. "It's too early." She began to tell herself a story.

They slipped through the jungle like shadows, drifting from tree to tree through the thick undergrowth. "Not a sound," she breathed. "You'll give us away." But the others had none of her skill at woodcraft. A twig snapped and instantly in the distance the soft boom, boom of a drum sounded the danger signal in a dozen native villages. They were surrounded. She knew it. Everything depended on staying hidden. She led them to a tiny clearing that she alone knew about. A trickle of clear water ran from under the roots of an old coconut palm. "Drink," she said, and with the skill of the jungle-born she swung herself into its branches, drew her knife, and cut coconuts for them all. Not for an instant did she let herself be seen. Her keen eyes scanned the horizon for miles and on every side she saw signal fires sending plumes of smoke heavenward.

"Blundering fools," she muttered. "Stupid savages. We'll escape them yet."

They slept there that night, while she kept watch. Once her keen knife found the vitals of a tiger in mid-spring, and she throttled the death scream in his throat. At dawn they started on. But the odds were too heavy. She could not lead them and cover their trail and keep them quiet.

Suddenly out of the steaming foliage tall warriors sprang, their black faces covered with hideous masks, their legs and arms painted in spirals of red, white, and blue. One of her party gave a single scream of pure terror and fell lifeless at her feet.

"Fortunate man," she muttered. "Would God we might all die so easily."

"Mama, Anna's talking to herself," Katherine said. "She's driving me crazy."

"Hush," Charlotte said. "Don't start a quarrel, Katherine. She's just whispering. You don't have to listen."

A dozen alternate plans flashed through her mind in an instant. If she were to make a break for it, deliberately sacrifice herself so that the others could escape in the confusion, it would be useless. They would be helpless without her, even if they managed to get away. Hypnosis might work for a few minutes, but there were too many savages for her to control. Perhaps they should allow themselves to be captured and try to escape later. "I, too, am a fool," she told herself. "There's no escape. We're all doomed unless Carlyle and Marjorie get here with help."

Stoically she allowed herself to be bound with vines, her head high, her face proud and contemptuous. "At least," she said calmly to the others, "let us behave like men."

That night in the village the flames of the council fire, a great pile of logs and underbrush, leapt fifty feet into the air. All day the prisoners had lain bound, without food or water, in a dark, filthy hut. Now and then a low moan broke the silence.

"Courage," Anna whispered. "Courage. All is not lost. If we can hold out even a day, Carlyle may get here." To herself she said, "I know they'll take us one at a time. If I can contrive to go first, it will purchase a few hours." She rolled toward the doorway and lay, quietly listening to the steady beat of the drums.

They came at last, two tall, silent warriors, and pulled aside the straw mat that covered the doorway. As she had expected, they saw her first, lying at their feet. They picked her up and dragged her roughly out into the red light of the council fire. A thrill of courage sent the blood pounding through her heart. She looked directly at the chief and said calmly, "Do with me as you like. I am a match for you." Instantly a spark of respect was lit in that savage breast.

In his own language, which she understood, although he did not understand hers, he said, "Here is much woman. Great princess in her tribe. Let her die the long death. We see if her gods give her courage." A cruel smile lit his painted face.

They drove four stakes in the ground and spread-eagled her, face up, lashing her arms and legs to the stakes. Warriors brought razor-sharp knives and whips plaited of green vines, and the torture began. Again and again the whips rose and fell, but no sound escaped her. As the night crept by, the savages became more and more frenzied. They were conscious of nothing but their victim. Even the sentries on the high log walls left their posts and joined the half-crazed throng around the council fire.

The chief bent over Anna to see if she still lived.

"*I spit on you,*" *she muttered, and she gathered all her strength and spat.*

A scream of mingled rage and admiration broke from a thousand throats. "*Kill, kill,*" *they screamed, and, throwing down their weapons, began to dance wildly around the fire.*

But through the hellish noise she had heard faint sounds in the jungle, sounds that told her Carlyle and his men were on the way. The old war cry, the signal to attack, broke from her lips, "*Ah-eeeeee-eeee.*"

"Mama, I can't *stand* it," Katherine said. "I can't *stand* it." She flopped forward and leaned her arms on the back of the front seat, behind her mother's head. "She's been going on like that for miles and now she's screaming in a whisper. She's big enough to quit talking to herself."

"Anna," Charlotte said. "Anna. *Anna.* (Now, keep quiet, Katherine. Let her alone. You used to talk to yourself sometimes, too.) Anna, I'm talking to you."

"Hmmmm?"

"Come on," Charlotte said. "Let's play Clouds. Look way over there above that cabin. I see George Washington. See his nose and his three-cornered hat?"

"I'd rather play stamping white horses," little Ralph said. "Or counting cows. I bid this side of the road. I already see about a million and a half in that pasture up there."

"You were talking to yourself," Katherine said in a whisper. "Can't you ever stop talking to yourself, *baby?*"

"Hush, Katherine," Charlotte said. "You're getting too big to tease Anna."

Above the pointed tops of the log stockade on every side, the faces of Carlyle and his men appeared, and then Carlyle's commanding voice rang out. "*Release her instantly or die!*"

"*Baby,*" Katherine whispered right in her ear.

"Oh, shut up, Katherine," Anna said. "You make me sick."

"Here, here," big Ralph said. "You children stop that quarreling like your mother told you."

"You've got a long ride ahead of you," Charlotte said, "and you may as well make the best of it. Come on now, who wants to play Clouds?"

❧

Later, when Katherine went to sleep, sprawled beside her, on the back seat, Anna cautiously brought the mirror out of her pocket and stared into it. The round, serious, plump-cheeked face of a nine-year-old girl, her fine straight blond hair cut in a Dutch bob, looked back out of wide brown eyes. In the structure under the healthy flesh of well-fed childhood, broad across the cheekbones, coarsened by the flat nose and spreading nostrils, in the too wide mouth and strong teeth, were traces of the Celtic peasant. A high round forehead shadowed the eyes with its slightly disproportionate bulge, and marked the still half-formed face with intelligence and obsession; and self-obsession looked out from the wounded eyes.

"*Where were you?*" *Anna said to the mirror.* "*You came near losing me that time. Were you afraid? You could of come with Carlyle. It's the least you could of done.*"

"*I was locked up,*" *Marjorie said.* "*I was in prison. I wore my fingernails to the quick. I bruised my head against the bars, but I couldn't escape.*"

"*Convenient for you,*" *she said sarcastically.*

"*You're not fair,*" *Marjorie said.* "*Come, my captain, set me a task. Put me to the test. I am ready to follow you, even unto death.*"

Forbearingly she said, "*You've always been faithful. I'll give you another chance.*"

"*I am strong,*" *Marjorie said.* "*I am tireless. I have just come back from Greece where I won the cross-country mile, the javelin throw, the discus, and the hundred-yard dash in the Olympic Games.*"

"*We must prepare ourselves for a new test,*" *Anna said.*

"These people are about to hold their national games and we have been invited to enter. Weak as I am after my ordeal, I must enter or be dishonored."

She drew a wafer from her leather pouch and broke it in half. "Eat," she commanded. "This is all I have."

A pistol shot rang out and a dozen strong runners sprang forward. A roar broke from a hundred thousand throats as the greatest athletes of two continents pitted their strength and endurance against one another. At first, every step was agony to her, as she felt the ache of old wounds and torn muscles. Then she hit her stride and fell easily into a tireless, steady pace. She passed Sweden, England, Greece. The field was left far behind. Ahead she saw Marjorie, running like a frightened deer. Slowly, inexorably she closed the gap. Two lengths, one length, a few inches separated them. The finish line was only yards away. Her lungs burned and her heart pounded, but she did not falter. With a superhuman effort she pulled abreast of Marjorie, into the lead, and snapped the tape. Momentum carried them both onward, and then they dropped panting onto the sand at the side of the track. Immediately they were surrounded by a crowd of cheering spectators and officials. Someone dropped a laurel wreath around her neck, someone else lifted her and poured wine into her parched mouth. She pushed away the bottle and gestured toward Marjorie who still lay, exhausted, unable to rise. "My friend," she said. "Give it to her. She needs it more than I." Gently she freed herself from the supporting hands and, staggering to Marjorie's side, helped her to rise. Together they took the frenzied acclamation of the crowd.

Katherine stirred and stretched on the seat beside her. She brushed back her tangled brown curls and yawned, her eyes still closed. At twelve, almost thirteen, she was, as her mother said, beginning to have a figure. Already her long face showed traces of poise, sophistication, and self-control that filled Anna with a mixture of respect and envy. Katherine could be depended upon in any situation to know what to do and, even more remarkable, what to say. Her hair was curly and she tanned in the sun instead of turning red and peeling.

Anna slipped the mirror into her pocket and shoved her sister's legs off the seat. "Hey, you're kicking me," she said. "Stay on your own side."

Katherine opened her eyes and sat up. "Aren't we almost there, Mama?" she said.

"We just passed Hard Luck," Charlotte said. "We're on the last lap." She shook little Ralph who was sleeping, blond and fat and rosy, across her lap. "Wake up, son," she said. "Who's going to be the first to see the Catholic Church spire?"

"Bois Sauvage," Anna said. "I see Bois Sauvage." She pointed to a clump of trees far away across the fields on the left side of the road.

"No, that's not it," Charlotte said. "We haven't gotten there yet."

The children sat up, tense with the excitement of arrival, and stared out the windows. The flat delta fields whirled blurringly by. Chickens and geese flapped, squawking, out of the road in the path of the high square car. Cattle and sheep and bearded goats grazed the thistles, clover, and bitterweed on the roadside, and sometimes strolled slowly across, so that Ralph had to stop the car and wait for them.

"A billy goat," Anna cried passionately. "Oh, mother, I wish we had a goat cart."

"A goat cart!" Charlotte said. "I'd just as soon give you a loaded shotgun."

"You had one when you were a little girl."

"Things were different in those days," Charlotte said.

If only we lived at Bois Sauvage, we could have a goat, and horses, and a creek and a boat all our own, and fields full of arrowheads. "You had all the luck," Anna said.

"There it is," Charlotte said.

A half mile back from the road, almost hidden by trees, Bois

Sauvage faced away from them toward the invisible river. The curve of the levee held back the water on three sides. The house, a two-story clapboard farmhouse, set up against flood on a brick foundation higher than a man's head, had no columned portico, no iron balconies, no double curving stairs, no driveway lined with oak trees, none of the accessories of opulence and romance.

"It's not like itself," Anna whispered. "It's never like it should be."

She thought of the other houses she knew in Homochitto, houses that asked nothing of anyone, but were only themselves, crammed with their own lives: étagères with dead, daguerreotyped faces, blurred as old mirrors, on their shelves, and vases of red crystal with fine traceries of gold decorating their jewel-like facets; golden-scaled snakes on the lids of porcelain boxes, snakes that raised their heads and thrust out delicate, forked tongues, as if poised to strike; chests all crammed with stiff black dresses and festoons of cut-steel beads that had decorated the gray shot-silk of a second-day dress; in every room mirrors that had briefly flashed with secrets now hidden in their plumbless depths, and portraits hung so high she had to tip back her head to see them, portraits to whose mystery she assigned a physical cause; there was Jean Dupré, a little boy of four in a full-skirted dress, hanging over her grandmother's parlor mantel; life-sized and full-length in a gigantic gold leaf frame, he sat with one leg under him in a high-backed straight chair, a round straw hat close beside him on the seat; sometimes it was a hat and sometimes it was a third knee with which this ancient child had been equipped by God for purposes natural to a world where boys (her grandmother insisted he *was* a boy) wore dresses and had long curls; and in the dining room of her grandmother's house there was Charlotte Augustin, Anna's great-great-grandmother, her long, elegant, white face and slender neck bent under the weight of brown-paint curls stacked like cordwood in pyramiding layers upon her narrow head, her cream-colored dress below a stiff lace ruff stretched taut over her bosom and molded without a wrinkle to her waistless, slender body. *Gran says in those days the ladies used to wet and starch their dresses when they put them on, and then let them dry on them — sort of stuck down, so they'd be extra smooth and stiff.* Starched and dripping ladies stood waiting for their ball gowns to dry, and then bowed and crackled to equally starchy gentlemen who came to ask them for a dance. *How did they ever sit down?* she thought, recalling the scratchy misery of the high-necked, starched guimpes she had to wear under her jumper dresses in the winter.

All these things and more had been at Bois Sauvage, but none of them were there now. Stripped of its furnishings, it stood like an almost transparent, naked ghost; its life had bled away in chests and chairs and pictures whose new owners — her grandmother, aunts, and ancient cousins — said now and then, as if they were identifying themselves, "This came from Bois Sauvage."

"Who lives there now, Mother?" she asked, as she did every time they passed that way.

"I don't know," Charlotte said. "I never can remember who owns the place."

Empty fields, a dusty turnrow, a grove of trees like any other trees, and a square house where strangers lived.

"Do you suppose they have any furniture?"

"Of course they have furniture. What do you think they sit on, the floor? Sometimes you ask the silliest questions."

"I'd like to go there sometime," Anna said. *I could find it, I bet.*

"Maybe we will some day, darling."

There's a secret stair, hidden in the wall, with a panel door that swings out like in The Cat Creeps, *and it leads to a little room all full of letters and diaries that tell where the gold is hidden.*

The car raised a cloud of dust, the road curved, and the house vanished.

Anna buried the nameless fear that Bois Sauvage did not fill the measure into which she poured it, the measure of her mother's and her grandmother's memories, and plunged into her dream, exploring its limits as a small, brave, translucent fish explores the great aquarium in which it bursts to life. Danger lurks in the sunken castle on its washed white sand, and sunlight glances off the pink and green shell chips scattered over the floor. All around swim others, contained, but unknown, unknowable, unseparated from itself, surrounded by mysterious green, floating forests, pausing sometimes in their constant, gentle motion to stare blindly through the clear glass walls at another world, or, if the light is right, at a graceful, golden image of themselves.

There were all those people then—Gran and everybody. And Billy.

Billy grazed round and round a post in the barnyard, making a cropped circle with the radius of his tether. The house murmured with the voices of her family, some still living and known to her now, some years dead, of whom her mother spoke as familiarly as if they had gone to New Orleans for the weekend and would be back on Monday: her great-grandfather, a foolish, crotchety old man who had nothing better to do than tease the children and sensitive old-maid aunts, and who brought the groceries when he was invited to dinner; Alice Major, the big, yellow, bland-faced, pock-marked cook in her huge basement kitchen, always in the act of prying up the lid to an eye on the squat wood range; Mr. Anderson, her grandfather, reading, or, suddenly, riding through waist-high cotton at a furious gallop; the children, Charlotte, Sarah D., Anna, and Will, who had unexplainably grown up and become parents and aunts and uncles; and last, but best, Gran, rock of practical reality and never-failing source of joy, Gran, who seemed to bear in her own thin, active body the very source and secret of Homochitto, of Bois Sauvage, of her family's life, who never hesitated at tucking up her skirts and wading in the creek, could make an Indian costume out of a torn quilt and a couple of feathers and whistle through her fingers louder than a boy, and who had once by mistake cooked Mr. Anderson's finest gamecock for Sunday dinner.

Stories of Bois Sauvage spun round in the wind of her imagination, blurring as the colored, pie-shaped segments of a pinwheel blur in motion, so that they are sometimes the color of light and sometimes of darkness.

Horses stamped and whispered in the damp, moldy storerooms that smelled like the dark underneath houses where she crawled sometimes to retrieve a lost ball or a sick puppy. Silent children fed them clover to keep them quiet, while upstairs a Yankee captain drank a glass of wine with her great-grandfather, that foolish, crotchety old man, now suddenly young, uniformed, and wounded, who urbanely assured his enemy that all his livestock had long since been commandeered. Gran had told the children this story of her father-in-law, and how, many years later at a dinner party in Baltimore, he had met the erstwhile Yankee captain, and had not told him even then that his last bottle of claret had earned its price a hundred times in horseflesh.

To Anna, Mr. Anderson and his horses belonged in their own category — among the tales of long-dead members of the family, whose names were prefaced by courtesy Sirs and Dons, or by military titles; of men like General McCrae, the staunch Presbyterian with an ingrowing toenail, who had cut off his big toe with an ax because he believed literally in the admonition, *If thine eye offend thee, pluck it out;* and like the first Charles Dupré, a widower whose sister had locked him in the cellar with a barrel of whiskey, as an effective method of curing him of drink: he drank until he died.

Anna saw the grieving widower shut up in the damp cellar where the horses had been hidden, and shuddered at his fate, just as she wept when she read of the little mermaid treading every step for love on two-edged swords. It was a strange, intoxicating, heart-swelling sorrow, evoked by action too intense, too exaggerated for reality, by courage so noble it could exist only in imagination, by capacity for which the world no longer seemed to have any use. The morals were made for a life always in crisis, where one was put to the torture for the true faith or called upon every day to battle dragons and rescue drowning brothers. But, at the same time, they were so seductive that she longed for the time when she would be forced to face her own ordeal.

In a second category were tales that Charlotte and Kate and all the grown-up relatives told about themselves in the days when everyone lived in the country; stories of goats and pony carts and crayfishing and exploring the woods and creek banks, of hayrides in real wagons, of times when there were no public schools and no one could afford governesses, when children didn't go to school at all, but were turned loose in old libraries with no more supervision than an occasional book report to Father.

Anna stared at her parents' backs. *Were you ever really a little girl? Were you ever bad, or sad, or sick like me?* A deep crease marked the base of Ralph's skull with a familiar groove. Charlotte's dark, graying hair was combed in precisely the waves it knew, and no others. There they sat, frozen into the mold of parenthood, her father bald and stout, stern, gentle and preoccupied, her mother corseted and erect, loving and irritable, a refuge and a gadfly. *And mother was there, as little as I am and she had a horse all her own. They all rode horses because there weren't any cars, and they had yards full of chickens and turkeys and ducks and geese and you could chase them, if they didn't chase you first.*

Game roosters strutted in their run, and sprang without a thought to mortal combat, and ducks swam in a round, banked pond with a raft tied to the single, twisted haw tree at its edge.

Gypsies in long skirts and roman-striped blouses, with gold hoops in their ears, drove covered carts into the yard, and asked if they might sleep in the barn; the men, black-eyed and dark-bearded, cracked whips for the bears to dance, while the children shrieked with mingled joy and terror. Every house had its creek or bayou within walking distance, a boat drawn up on the muddy beach and fishing poles leaning in the crotch of a tree. And every day there was the chance that the plow being dragged across the field beyond the turnrow might uncover an arrow head, a string of Indian beads, a shard of ancient pottery, a spent cannon ball, or even a rusty Spanish sword.

Another segment of the pinwheel flew by, and she saw her grandfather riding out into the windy spring dusk. All night long he patrolled a section of the levee. Sometimes he fell asleep and almost slipped from the saddle, but then the faint, deadly trickle of water penetrated his numbed brain, and he shouted for his men to bring sandbags and stop an opening crevasse. In the kitchen his wife and servants kept pots of coffee hot on the stove and made stacks of sandwiches to take to the hungry workers. *Three years of floods,* she heard her grandmother say, *and then your grandfather died. We were wiped out.*

It was as if the very floods had swept Bois Sauvage bare and deposited its furnishings like silt wherever the falling water stood stagnant.

Another bend in the road, and an unmistakable blue line threaded the horizon. Slowly the wooded face of the bluff emerged and seemed, as they approached the still invisible river, to rise out of the cotton fields that stretched to its banks on the Louisiana side. Homochitto, hidden in trees and haze, crowned those distant heights. The children stared with strained attention and picked out in the very center of the far, high town the tiny needle of the Catholic Church spire.

"There it is, there it is," Katherine shouted. "I saw it first."

"We're almost there," Charlotte said, and settled back against the seat.

Anna's heart pounded and she tasted on the back of her tongue the brassy, prickling taste of an excitement so intense it was like fear.

"We're almost there, we're almost there," she chanted in time to a steady bouncing up and down on the back seat.

"Anna," Charlotte said, "*Anna*. Children. Control yourselves."

From the top of the levee they saw the ferry drawing slowly away from the landing. The mile-wide river was so full and strong and self-contained that its brown waters looked higher in the middle than near the shore where small waves escaped the current, sighed, and, on the weedy mudflats, broke and were absorbed. The huge screws that drove the ferry churned the river into a lengthening trail of yellow foam. On the far shore the shale bluff reared up three hundred feet into the sky, steep and green, covered with blackberry thickets and twisted trees that clung to its face with half-exposed roots, and curved upward toward the sun. This strange, perpendicular forest was marked here and there with wide, smooth patches of brown where a slide had carried rocks and earth and a tangle of trunks and branches to the river's edge, to lie half in the water and half buried in silt, bare as a pile of old bones washed over and whitened by the rise and fall of the water.

Charlotte and Ralph looked at each other.

"We just missed it," Ralph said.

"An hour's wait," Charlotte said.

"Tell us a story while we're waiting, Mama."

"Tell about the time Will ran away from home," Anna said.

"You've heard that story a thousand times," Charlotte said.

"We don't care," Anna and Katherine said.

"You'd better draw it out," Ralph said and, picking up his paper from the seat beside him, opened it and began to read.

"You can tell one, too, if Mama gives out," little Ralph said.

"Ummph," Ralph said, and raised his paper a little higher.

"Well," Charlotte said, "one day when Will was about five years old and Sarah D. was six and Sis was nine and I was twelve, Will ran away from home. Of course that wasn't the only time Will ever ran away from home, but I reckon it was the first time. Gran had baked a cake."

"Was Gran your grandmother, too?" Ralph asked.

"No. She was my mother," Charlotte said.

"Silly," Anna said. "How could Gran be Mama's grandmother and our grandmother, too?"

"Why not?" Ralph said. "She could if she wanted to, I bet."

"Anyhow," Charlotte went on, "Gran baked a cake, a big devil's food cake, and put it out on the back gallery to cool."

"I don't like devil's food cake," Ralph said. "It's too black."

"Stop interrupting, Ralph, or I won't tell the story," Charlotte said. She put her arm around him and gently shook him. "You remember the time you ran away, son, inside your playpen, and dragging it with you? I bet you don't. Well, Will was kind of like you. He didn't get very far. But he was a lot harder to find than you were."

Ralph looked up from his paper. "He never gets far," he said. "But he's always hard to find. Maybe he needs a playpen."

Charlotte laughed. "You're not supposed to be listening," she said. "And besides this story doesn't have a moral."

"What do you mean, Father?" Anna said. "What do you mean, he's always running away? Uncle Will doesn't even live with Gran any more. He doesn't have anyone to run away from."

"Now, you all listen," Charlotte said. "When Gran went back to get the cake, someone had eaten *all* the icing, and the cake was ruined.

"Well, you know how Gran carries on. She grabbed her head and began to pull her hair like she was dying in agony.

'My cake!' she screamed. 'My cake! Alice Major, come look at my cake.'

"And Alice Major came out of the kitchen and looked at the cake and she said, 'My Gawd, Miss Kate. It's ruint.'

"And Gran said, 'Will did it. Come here to me, Will Anderson.'

"But Will didn't answer. He knew better.

" 'Now, Miss Kate,' Alice Major said, 'he ain't nothing but a baby. He don't know no better.' (Alice Major always took our part, and specially Will's. He was her favorite.)

"But Gran said, 'He'll know better when I get hold of him.'

"Then she called Sis and me and told us to find him. She knew we were too big to pull a trick like that, and Sarah D. was off somewhere with her nurse. Besides, Will was always the one who got into trouble."

Anna looked into the mirror which she held hidden in her cupped hand. *I never would have ruined Gran's cake like that,* she said silently. Marjorie stared back at her. *Well, if I had, I would have owned up to it. Or I would have gone away and never, never come back until I was a famous explorer and everyone would be glad to see me.*

"We didn't want very much to find him — especially Sis," Charlotte said. "Even then she thought Will and Father were perfect. As far as she was concerned they couldn't do wrong. I knew Will was a devil, but he was so much younger than I, I didn't take him seriously. We knew if we put off finding him long enough, Gran wouldn't be mad any more, or at least not as mad as she had been, so we drew it out as long as we could — looking in all the most unlikely places first. We thought he was probably up in one of the fig trees or the peach trees, because that's where he stayed most of the time in the summer, so we saved them until last. We looked in the pasture and the chicken yard, and then we went in the barn, and we even walked down to the bayou. (It bounded the pasture on the side away from the house and flowed into the river about a mile to the north.) Finally we climbed up in the fig trees and when we saw he wasn't there, we stayed a long time, eating figs.

"Meanwhile, Gran had looked everywhere in the house, upstairs and down. It was two o'clock, dinnertime, and he had never come home. She began to get worried. Not scared. There was nothing dangerous in the country, or rather nothing Gran was afraid of. She never was the kind who wasted herself worrying about snakes or lightning, and she had taught us children to stay away from the river and bayou unless there was a grown person along, but when he didn't come home at dinnertime, she thought he must be lost and frightened.

"Just then Father (that was your grandfather, you know, Ralph) came riding back from the south end of the plantation where he had been all morning. Father had a big black mustache like gentlemen wore in those days and curly black hair, and he was much more excitable than Gran, and his hair and mustache always seemed to get even curlier and his face redder (he had very high color) when he was excited."

"What was he like?" Anna said.

"You've seen his picture," Charlotte said.

"Yes, but I mean what was he like, *really?* Was he like Father?"

Charlotte shook her head. "Not at *all,*" she said. "As different as Creole is from Scotch."

What does that mean? Anna asked the mirror, but she said nothing.

Little Ralph gazed out the window at the cows grazing the sloping levee. "I think I'll go chase the cows," he said.

"No," Charlotte said. "Sit still a little while. The ferry will be here soon."

"Go on with the story," Anna said.

"I always thought he was stern," Charlotte said, "but Sis says he was gentle and indulgent. So you see it depends on your point of view. I think most of the time Sis was so good there was no occasion for him to be anything but gentle, and when she was bad — when she had a temper tantrum — she was *so* bad, he dealt gently out of respect. She was like the little girl in the poem: When she was good, she was very, very good, and when she was bad, she was horrid. I reckon, if you want to know what Father was like, he was like the rest of us. He read a lot. Mama always said he was a *reader*. You know, she never has cared for reading, and I remember she used to say she was surrounded by *readers*. If Father had his nose buried in a book, you couldn't get a word out of him — you know how that is, don't you, Anna? But he hunted, too, and he was a fine horseman. I remember how I used to admire him when he rode up to the house at the end of the day. He had a big gray stallion and he sat straight and came galloping up as if he were in a hurry to get home. Of course, everybody rode a horse in those days; it was nothing unusual. But he was a small man and he rode as if his life depended on it. I suppose he was most like your Uncle Will. Will has his charm and recklessness and his quick mind and his weakness for the ladies."

"What?" Katherine said.

"I mean, when Will and Father were young, before they married, they both liked to squire the ladies around. But Father had something else that Will lacks, and that *your* Father has. You could always depend on him."

"I thought this story didn't have a moral," Ralph said, looking up from his paper again.

Little Ralph squirmed under his mother's restraining arm. "I'd *rather* chase cows," he said.

"I'm going on," Charlotte said. "Where was I?"

What does it all mean? Anna asked the mirror.

"When Gran told Father Will had run away, he had some more horses saddled, and got the hands in from the fields, and they searched the whole place, pasture, bayou, and levee, and rode up and down the road two or three miles each way looking for Will and asking if anyone had seen him. One of the men even went as far as the ferry landing, but no one had seen him.

"About five o'clock Father came in the kitchen. Gran was sitting at the kitchen table, sewing and waiting, and Alice Major was puttering around, whispering to herself, like she always did. I don't know why Gran was sitting in the kitchen, except she was getting more and more worried, and Alice Major was company for her. She even had Alice set the table for our supper in the kitchen, although we almost never ate there. I suppose she couldn't eat and Father didn't have time to eat and that was why.

"Father didn't stay long. He patted Gran on the shoulder and said, 'Now, don't start imagining things, Katie. He'll turn up any minute. He's bound to be some place close, and you know he won't stay out after dark, scary as he is.'

" 'Oh, Mr. Anderson,' Gran said. 'Where can he be? Where on earth can he be at this hour?'

"You know she always called Father Mr. Anderson. All the ladies called their husbands Mr. in those days."

" 'I have an idea he's been playing with Bowles and Billy and we've just missed them,' Father said. (Bowles and Billy were two little colored boys on the place.) 'I'll bet all three of them wandered off the place and ate dinner with some of Bowles's cousins. He's got a million of them between here and town.'

"He just made that up to pacify Mama, because when he left he didn't go toward town, he went toward the levee.

"We were all so scared and sick we couldn't even look at one another. Gran got up and began to get the grits and eggs out of the safe for supper. 'He'll be starving,' she said. 'We'd better get supper ready early.' Sis and Sarah D. and I were standing around the kitchen not knowing what to do with ourselves and feeling very sad and terrible. I remember saying over and over to myself, 'Suppose he's dead. Suppose he's dead.' He got smaller and smaller and more helpless to me as

I thought about him. I saw him wandering along the edge of the bayou and falling in and drifting down the river with his face all white and upturned and his eyes closed and his hair floating around his head like the lady in the illustration for *The Marsh Queen*."

"Aren't you being a little bit morbid?" Ralph said. He had stopped reading and was listening as attentively as the children.

"They like it better that way," Charlotte said, smiling with him in baffling, grown-up complicity.

"Of course," she continued, "I didn't say any of that about drowning out loud; I tried to think of something comforting to say to Gran, but I couldn't. I was tongue-tied.

"Then, all of a sudden, Sis burst out. 'Let us remain inflexible, Mama,' she said.

"She had been standing in a corner of the kitchen for what seemed like hours. I knew she was getting ready to cry, but I couldn't think what to do about it.

"Gran looked at her kind of funny, and then she said, 'What is it, darling?'

"She was breaking eggs in a bowl and Alice Major said, 'Here, Miss Kate, lemme do that,' and took them away from her.

" 'Let us remain inflexible,' Sis said.

"Gran sat down and put her elbows on the kitchen table and put her head in her hands. 'What in the world are you talking about, Sis?' she said.

"I had a cold biscuit that I had been licking the jelly off of, and I began to crumble it up and spill the crumbs on the floor. I knew what she was talking about. We'd read about it in one of the *Little Colonel* books. Do you remember, Katherine? It was Mary Ware or somebody in her family who was always quoting it.

"Sure enough, Sis began to cry." Charlotte screwed up her face, and drew her breath in a hard sob, while the children watched and listened, fascinated. "And then she said to Mama, 'Don't you know /sob/ the Vicar of Wakefield said, "Let us

/sob/ remain inflexible, and fortune will at last change in our favor"?'

"Alice Major took the old crumbly biscuit out of my hand and gave me another one. 'Have another biscuit, honey,' she said. 'You done wore that one out.' She tried to give Sis one but she wouldn't take it, so she gave Sarah D. two, and Sarah D. sat down on the floor and began to eat them, looking first at Sis and then at Mama, as if she'd never seen them before.

" 'The Vicar of Wakefield!' Gran said. 'What do you know about the Vicar of Wakefield?' And then she began to cry, too, and so did I, and Sarah D. stuffed both her biscuits in her mouth and hollered as if her heart were breaking.

"None of us had ever seen Mama cry, never in our whole lives (she's not like me, you know, crying at the drop of a hat) and we were shocked into tears. It was as if she'd said, 'I've given up. He's drowned.' Sis patted her on the shoulder, and kept saying over and over again, 'Don't cry, Mama. Please don't cry. I didn't mean to make you cry.'

" 'You *all* stop it,' Alice Major said. 'You can't cry him home,' and she began to cry, too. 'Where's my baby?' she said. 'Where's Alice Major's baby?' "

"I know where he was," little Ralph said. "I know where he was, all the time."

"Hush, Ralph," Katherine said. "Let Mama tell it."

"Well, of course Gran stopped right away, and got everybody cheered up a little bit, and then, about dusk, Father came back. Will had been gone since noon. There was almost nothing left to think of except the bayou and the river. *Suppose?* But still none of us said our supposes to one another. Father came in the kitchen only long enough to say he was going to town. We children were sitting at the kitchen table eating our supper.

" 'What for?' Mama said.

" 'I need help,' he said. 'If we're going to be looking for him at night, I've got to have some help. I'm going to stop at the Metcalfes' and the Duprés' on the way in, and then I'm going to get as many men in town as I can.'

"Alice Major went outside, to the cistern by the kitchen door, drew a dishpan full of water and brought it in to heat. She heaved the dishpan up onto the range and groaned.

" 'Alice Major, if you can't stop moaning, go home,' Gran said.

" 'I got to wash these dishes,' Alice Major said. 'Why don't you go upstairs and lay down?'

"There was no sense staying in the kitchen any longer, but I don't believe Gran could think *where* to go. You know she's always either working or talking or both. Probably she couldn't sew, because she was too worried, and I'm sure she didn't go and sit in the parlor, because it would have been too much like a wake."

"What's a wake?" little Ralph asked.

Charlotte sighed and thought for a minute.

"It's when somebody's dead," Anna said, "like in *The Bride of Lammermoor* where they all stay up and celebrate and eat and drink a lot and put on their best clothes when somebody's dead."

"That's about it," Charlotte said. "Anyway, I'm sure Gran wouldn't have sat down in the parlor for anything."

She saw his cold white form, Anna thought, *all shrouded in black.* "Gone," *she shrieked.* "Gone. My heart's darling, the fairest child in all the land, gone from me forever." *And in that instant her hair turned as white as snow. She never smiled again.*

"Go on, Mama," Katherine said. "What happened next?"

"Well, we all went trailing upstairs. Between the bottom of the stairs and the top Gran put on a cheerful face, and in the hall she gathered us around her and told us that Will was bound to be all right, and that Father would be coming back with him any minute. We didn't believe her, at least I know

I didn't, but we pretended like we did. Then she told Sis and me to go on and get our lessons (we didn't go to school then, you know, like you all do; but Father assigned us lessons to get) and she took Sarah D. by the hand and started off to put her to bed.

"Sis and I were on the way upstairs to get our books and Mama was ahead of us pulling Sarah D. along, half asleep on her feet, when all of a sudden we heard a knock at the front door."

"It was Will. It was Will. I know it was," Little Ralph shouted.

"We knew it couldn't be Will," Charlotte said, "because the knocker was way too high for him to reach, and this person, whoever it was, was lifting the knocker and letting it fall, *bang* — *bang* — *bang*, very slowly. It sounded like a signal, like someone warning us ahead of time that he had come on a solemn errand.

" 'It's one of the men Father went for,' Gran said. 'Run quick, Charlotte, and open the door.' She sat down on the steps, holding Sarah D. against her shoulder, as if she couldn't stand up any longer.

"I ran and unlocked the door and opened it, and there he was — *Will* — standing on tiptoe with a stick in his hand. He had been hooking it under the knocker and pushing it way up and then letting it fall against the door.

" 'Hey, Charlotte,' he said, 'I bet you didn't know I could knock on the front door like that, did you?'

"Mama left Sarah D. on the steps and ran down and fell on her knees and hugged him and began to cry again.

" 'I'm hungry,' Will said. 'When's supper?'

" 'Alice, Alice Major,' Gran called. 'He's here. He's come home. He's all right. Run tell Alice Major, Charlotte. Are you all right, sweetheart? Ring the bell, Sis, so the men will come in.' She held Will away from her and looked at him. He had on navy blue shorts and a sailor blouse like little boys used to wear in those days, and his blouse was filthy and his hair was full of cobwebs, and he had a long scratch on one side of his face with the blood dried on it. 'Are you hurt?' she said. 'Where have you been, you rotten, good-for-nothing boy? I ought to snatch you bald-headed.'

"Will was a pretty little boy, and he opened his eyes wide, and looked at her as innocently as an angel. 'I been under the front steps,' he said. 'I was skeered, and then I went to sleep.' "

"He was under the steps," little Ralph said. "I knew it all the time."

"Then Alice Major came, and she and Mama began to holler and cry like anything. Sarah D. woke up and came down the stairs and sat beside Will, holding his hand and yawning and smiling proudly at everyone, as if she had found him, and Sis looked at him as if she could eat him with a spoon. Will sat just as quiet through it all, while I was envying him for being the center of attention and almost a hero in spite of having been the one who caused all the trouble to begin with."

"The prodigal son," Ralph said.

"And while they were carrying on so, he looked at me and said, 'It's a pretty good hide-out, Charlotte. I'll let you use it sometime, if you want to.'

"But Mama didn't hear him, and I didn't tell, and I guess that's the end of the story."

The ferry docked at last and Ralph drove cautiously down the levee and aboard. For a few perilous minutes, as other cars followed them into place, the ferry rocked and swayed and the children waited, half hopefully, for the brakes to give and the car to roll into the river. A Negro man came and braced the wheels with heavy wooden chocks. When everyone was aboard, he cast off, unwinding the ropes, thicker than his own strong arms, that snubbed the ferry against the grooved stumps in the edge of the dock. The ferry drifted in the still water near the shore. Then the current, the quiet, endless brown tide, pushing as irresistibly as if it were a live and moving wall, caught the square flat-bottomed ferry, and it yawed out and drifted heavily southward. The engines caught, the boat shuddered as its screws began to beat the water, the cars rocked against their chocks, and the pilot headed northeast and began a crabbing, diagonal course toward the Homochitto dock.

Charlotte stood close by while Katherine and Anna and little Ralph hung over the side rails to stare into the ferry's foaming wake as they moved steadily, throbbingly forward. Ralph threw chewing gum wrappers into the water and watched them whirl away and founder, like boats crashing down Niagara Falls. Ahead, the bluffs reared up, closer and closer. Now they could see the road upward from the dock to Homochitto, steep and narrow and winding, a crack in the bluffs that disappeared into a screen of trees.

Homochitto, looming invisible above her head, filled Anna's whole mind. She saw the great red mass of the Cathedral towering over and shading her grandmother's house, heard the steady drip of water from the fountain in the little park whose round, dense live-oak trees on short thick trunks seemed to have sprung up like a cluster of green mushrooms in the shadow of the church's great flank. The choir sang from far away, from some mysterious, cool, inhuman depths like the bottom of a tideless sea, chanted that strange endless and beginningless music, so foreign and yet so beautiful.

"Mama, why don't they ever sing 'Onward, Christian Soldiers' or 'Here I Raise My Ebenezer'?"

"Who?" Charlotte said.

"You know, in the Catholic Church."

"It's just a different church and they have different music," Charlotte said.

Water spouted from the mouths of iron children clothed in long strands of wet green moss, and dripped down into the round brick pool where ancient goldfish fattened on the crumbs that live children daily fed them.

"It's entirely too confusing to me, Mama," Anna said seriously.

"You mean about churches and things?" Charlotte said.

"*Everything*. And churches, too. Everybody talks too much about everything in this family. Everybody talks about everything all the time and I remember it all in little pieces."

Charlotte laughed. "We all remember in little pieces," she said, "and we all get confused sometimes."

You don't. And Father doesn't. And Ralph's too little, and Katherine doesn't think it's important, and besides she always knows what to think and what to say. Nobody's confused but me.

The sisters from the Catholic orphanage in dark blue, full-skirted habits, their winged white hats standing out stiff and dazzling in the summer sunshine, marched the orphans home from Mass. The Cathedral bell struck every hour. Horses' hoofs clopped on the still morning streets, and the vegetable man called out his long-drawn chant, "Mustard greens, turnip greens, gre-e-en corn, gre-e-en peas, lady peas, butter beans, stringbeans, fresh squash, fresh tomatoes, o-o-okra. B-u-u-y." "Vegetable man, oh vegetable man, wait a minute, please," her grandmother cried. Homochitto invented itself in Anna's mind so lavishly she knew a whole summer would not be long enough to take in all its life.

"It's summer," she whispered to herself. "It's summer, summer, summer, and we're here."

The house sat close to the street behind a wrought-iron fence, crowded on one side against a dark red brick, turreted house of the 1870's with a round tower like Rapunzel's prison, a steep, gray slate roof, and windows with leaded panes of colored glass; on the other side, its yard stretched away to an adjoining three-story mansion of the nineties with jigsaw trim and an octagonal sun parlor; across the street were the Cathedral and the park. Situated thus, surrounded by mansions and churches, the house was small — a little story-and-a-half clapboard cottage, peeling and dingy, the green shutters black with age and dirt. But it was not small — small on the outside and big on the inside, Charlotte called it. It was enormous, the largest house Anna had ever been in. She could wander from room to room and apartment to apartment for hours. At the back, invisible from the street, two-story brick wings faced each other across a brick-paved court, joined to the house by a covered walkway from the latticed back porch to the old outdoor kitchen in the west wing. And quite hidden away behind the east wing was a tiny brick building that had been her great-grandfather's office and was now the children's playhouse.

Anna burst out of the car and threw open the iron gate. The pins and rings on which it swung screamed with such a familiar sound that her very ears ached with happiness. At the corner, in Mr. Tillman's iron and welding works, someone was crashing sheets of tin together, as if a company of giants were celebrating their arrival. She did not stop even an instant to see if the house was the same as it had been last summer, but without hesitation stamped its real image on the one she knew, an image built into an indestructible cubic space in her head, as unalterable as a remembered dream. If it were to burn tomorrow, the fire could not consume those boards. There was nothing she could add to it in imagination, nothing she could edit away, no way she could make it more or less than itself, as she did with the shell of Bois Sauvage, infinitely alterable in its emptiness and mystery. This house was so full of its own life, so specific and so vigorous in its impact upon hers, that the act of taking it in used her whole attention. It was the most formidable, the most interesting, the strangest, the most familiar and commonplace, the most *exciting* house in the world. Everything inside it was as real, as strange and yet familiar, as shocking in its strong unpalatable uniqueness, as castor oil in orange juice, as breath-taking as the first plunge into a cold creek in May.

At the door its smell, compounded of dust and age, of the heavy perfume of a sweet olive tree blooming in the side yard and the fishy breath of the fountain across the street, engulfed her like a warm familiar sea.

"We're here," she shouted. "Gran, Sarah D., we're here, we're here. Charlotte, Sis. Hey, everybody."

Here was the parlor with every piece of furniture exactly where it had been last summer, the rug worn in the same places, the same dust on the gold and maroon Empire urns, the splintery floor still marked with a dark stain where little Ralph had spilled a bowl of mayonnaise. Here, in this shabby house, lived in not with apology but with pride, was the mysterious emotion that was the keystone of her family's life. Here, more than anywhere else, it was clear that there was an instantly recognizable way in which real people acted. The furniture and the peeling walls were saturated with it, as they were with the mist from the fountain in the park. We are different, said the Victorian love seat. No overstuffed chairs for us. Yes, ticked the Seth Thomas clock on the mantelpiece. Here we are. You can see how impossible it would be, how really disgraceful, to be otherwise. We are right-side-up, said the glasses on the china closet shelves. Only common glasses sit rim down on a shelf. It doesn't matter how shabby I am, said the rug, I'm yours and you'd better stand up for me. How lucky you are to have us, said the house. How fortunate you are that we are here to confirm you. It would be vulgar to mention it, but on our account it should be obvious to everyone that you are a real person. You depend on no one but us, said the house. Allow no one else to pass judgment on you. Don't be absurd, said the Empire vases. Who else is there?

Like those primitive people to whom the name of the tribe is the word for The Men, Anna called the limits of her life by a larger name, and joyfully claimed that this prison built of love and pride was the universe.

She ran through the house to the kitchen and dragged her grandmother and Sarah D. toward the front porch, still shouting, "We're here, we're here," dancing around in a frenzy of excitement, and bumping into and hugging her aunt and grandmother over and over. Everyone kissed everyone else; little Charlotte (Sarah D.'s daughter) and Ralph shyly retired to swing on the gate and stare at each other; Katherine began to help her father unload the car. But Anna still jumped up and down, wanting to ask her grandmother a dozen questions, not for the answers, but to re-establish her own familiarity, her own belonging: Are the storerooms unlocked, so we can play dress-up? Is the hammock up? Are there any grapes on the arbor this year? Has anybody climbed out on the gallery roof since we left?

"Anna," Charlotte said, "calm down. You're going to knock Gran's specs off if you charge her like that again."

"Well, Dear," Ralph affectionately patted his mother-in-law on the shoulder and dropped into the bantering voice he always used with her, "what's new in the metropolis?"

"Ralph, everyone in town is agog over old Doc Wells disinheriting his children and leaving everything he had to that woman who married him last summer."

"Where's Sis?" Charlotte asked.

"She's not home from work yet," Sarah D. said. "Did you know poor Jeanne Dupré had another stroke last week?"

"How was the trip, Charlotte?"

"Poor thing," Charlotte said. "I don't see how she keeps on living."

"No flats," Ralph said. "Not one."

"Thank the Lord," Charlotte said. "And the children behaved themselves very well, considering. But we missed the ferry by about five minutes."

"You're looking salubrious, salubrious," Ralph said to Sarah D.

"Come in and sit down," Kate said. "I know you're tired."

"We've been sitting down all day," Charlotte said, turning back to the car and beginning to gather up toys and parcels.

"Where's Kitty Spooks?" little Ralph asked.

"Asleep on my bed," Sarah D. said. "He's worn himself out waiting for you all. Charlotte, you and Ralph haven't forgotten each other, have you?"

"Let's go feed the fish," Anna said.

"I'm going to call Judy and tell her we're here," Katherine said.

"My, you children are practically grown," Kate said. "I can't get over it. Why, Ralph, you've lost a tooth, haven't you?"

Ralph smiled with embarrassed pride and swung furiously.

"Charlotte, take Ralph to see Kitty Spooks," Sarah D. said.

"Come on," little Charlotte said. "I've got a turtle."

"Give your old Auntie a kiss before you go," Charlotte said to little Charlotte. "You haven't even spoken to me yet."

"I've got a turtle," the child said again.

"Horrors!"

"Come in and hear the news," Sarah D. said. "You can't imagine what has happened!"

"Bad or good?" Charlotte said.

"Not exactly either, but exciting. It depends on how serious it is — and other things."

Kate waved her hands palm outward before her face, as if warding off a swarm of bees. "Not yet," she said. "At least let them catch their breath and come in the house."

"Don't keep us in suspense," Charlotte said.

"Sis has a new beau!"

"Grand," Charlotte said. "Wonderful. I didn't know there was an eligible man left in Homochitto. Why didn't you write me about it, Mama? Who is he?"

"Eligible!" Kate said. "Humph."

"Here, let me help you," Sarah D. said to Ralph.

The grownups gathered the luggage and went into the house where they piled suitcases and boxes by the front door and sat down in the parlor. Katherine went back toward the dining room and the telephone. Anna, the park and fishes forgotten, sat down suddenly and quietly on the horsehair-covered Empire sofa with its hard, scratchy, black seat and curving arms like mahogany scrolls. It was so uncomfortable that it had been pushed to the back of the parlor where no one ever sat on it, and she was sure that there she could listen unnoticed to the conversation.

Just like always, she told herself. *Something exciting is happening.*

"We couldn't have written you," Sarah D. said. "It just happened this past week, and in the strangest way. She met him over-the-river in the cafe where she has lunch."

"He's nobody you ever heard of," Kate said. "*I* think she picked him up."

"*Anna?*" Charlotte said. "Impossible. Never in this world."

"You don't know what's been going on," Kate said. "She's simply out of her head. I can't think what's gotten into her. She's had an engagement with him every night for a week and a half. And the way they carry on! You'd never believe it was Miss Touch-me-not. They sit here in the parlor and bill and coo like a pair of turtle doves. I think she's in love with him. In love for the first time in her life, and with that . . . ! But what else can you expect? There's no fool like an old fool."

"It does happen, Mama," Charlotte said. "Remember, you always told us John Sterling fell in love with Aunt Bé the very first time he saw her on the street, not even knowing who she was. You remember? You thought it was the most romantic thing in the world."

"That was different," Kate said. "She was his own second cousin."

Ralph had been sitting upright and uncomfortable on a small rosewood boudoir chair, his legs spread apart, holding his hat between his knees as if poised and ready to go if the conversation took a turn he did not like. Now he laughed. "But he didn't know it then, did he, Dear?"

"Bé was a perfectly beautiful young girl," Kate said. "The prettiest girl in Homochitto. And this man . . . !"

"What's he like?" Charlotte said. "What's the matter with him, Mama? You know if Sis likes him, *you* don't have to. He's not courting you." She leaned forward and touched her mother's arm and smiled. "You may be getting choosier than she, you know," she said.

"Mama's gotten in a terrible uproar," Sarah D. said. "I say it's time for Sis to have a little fling. She's no spring chicken, and she ought to know what she's doing. Besides, she hasn't had a beau in five years. Why should Mama begrudge her a little light romance?"

"Light!" Kate said. "If you call this light, deliver me from heavy."

"What about old Willis?" Ralph said. "He's always willing to squire her around. He's what I'd call a heavy beau."

"Oh, Ralph," Charlotte said. "You know what she thinks of Mr. Willis."

"But he *is* heavy, ain't he, Sarah D.?"

"Why won't you tell us about him?" Charlotte said. "What's his name?"

"His name is Alderan Wheelwright, if you can imagine such a thing," Sarah D. said. "And he's a dragline operator on the levee construction job below Tallulah."

"Oh," Charlotte said.

"Auldron," Kate said, "Like cauldron, I reckon. I don't know how he spells it (if he *can* spell it)."

"Where's he from?" Ralph said. "Has he been in construction work long?"

"He's from Arizona," Kate said. "And God knows what he's been in. Jail probably. We don't know anything about him at all."

"Arizona," Ralph said sadly. And then, "Maybe he's just down on his luck like a lot of folks are these days."

"What's so terrible about operating a dragline?" Sarah D. said. "Your own first cousin is night watchman at the oil mill. And you're lucky you don't have him on *your* hands to feed and house."

"I *said* he was probably down on his luck," Ralph said. "Don't get excited, Sarah D. I don't even know the man. I was just thinking if he had been in the construction business long I might have heard of him."

"What's he like?" Charlotte said.

"*We* never see him," Kate said. "She hustles us out of the parlor like she's ashamed of us — or him. It's 'How do you do, Mr. Wheelwright,' and 'Good evening, Mr. Wheelwright,' and that's all."

"Then how do you know so much about their billing and cooing?" Ralph said.

"Don't tease me, Ralph McGovern," Kate said. "I have *not* been spying on them. You can just *tell* about things like that."

"Poor Sis," Charlotte said. "If she were ten years younger, a new beau wouldn't mean anything to you one way or the other, Mama."

"That's what I keep saying," Sarah D. said. "And you know how Sis is. If Mama cuts up jack much more, she may marry him just out of contrariness."

"Is he handsome?" Charlotte asked.

"He's not like anybody I can think of," Sarah D. said. "He's certainly not handsome, though to tell you the truth I do like him, what little I've seen of him. At least I think I would like him, if he weren't Sis's beau. He needs polishing around the edges a bit, but she could manage that."

Kate moaned. "You talk as if it's all settled," she said. "Think what you're saying, Sarah D. Let someone else polish him. Why, your father would turn over in his grave if Anna married that man."

"He's strange," Sarah D. said. "A stranger, if that doesn't sound too silly. *Different*."

"From Arizona," Ralph suggested.

"Yes, that's part of it. He's kind of leathery-looking, like you would expect a cowboy to be, but small, not rangy. He's wiry, and he acts as if, well, as if he's *waiting*, or as if he's so full of energy he has to sit perfectly still to keep from bursting at the seams. And he calls her Ann, as if he didn't have time to say Anna."

"Nonsense," Kate said. "Foolishness. He's common, that's what he is, a common, uneducated cowboy, trying to better himself. He calls her Ann because he hasn't any better sense than to think that's her name, and, worse than that, he calls a Chevrolet a shivvy. Can you imagine falling in love with a man who called a Chevrolet a Shivvy?"

Sarah D. laughed. "You couldn't be wronger, Mama," she said. "He certainly murders the king's English, but he's got plenty of sense, I *know* he has, and he's not trying to better himself. He hasn't given *us* a thought. The mystery to me is what he sees in Sis."

Sarah D.'s judgment of Mr. Wheelwright had begun to get too complicated for Anna and she was losing interest in the conversation. *I'm waiting for somebody to say something to explain all this,* she said to herself.

She had been sitting straight up on the sofa with her feet drawn under her, watching and listening intently, but as soon as Sarah D. began to explain, her attention wandered. She slid down on the sofa, legs stretched straight out, until she was sitting on her shoulders, and stared at the oval painting on the opposite wall. A dark-haired, naked lady with a large solemn face and long wet hair was raising a dripping arm out of the sea to take the next stroke in a leisurely practiced crawl. The last downward thrust of her other arm had lifted one broad, bare shoulder and half a swelling breast above the white-tipped green waves.

Where is she? Anna asked herself for the dozenth time in her life. She never asked anyone who knew. It was a fixed and comfortable mystery that left room for infinite conjecture. She was certainly *there* on the wall, wherever else she might be. On the étagère in the corner below the swimmer, another lady, this one in miniature, painted on ivory and set in a frame hardly larger than the bowl of a tablespoon, occupied her accustomed place. Her black hair was looped back on either side of a center part like carefully arranged draperies, and her startlingly red face looked out between cascades of long corkscrew curls, as clean and expressionless as a parlor window. Her white lace dress fell in a graceful décolletage from sloping maroon shoulders. *And the Indian lady, too,* Anna said. *Where was she, to be dressed up like that? Maybe she went to England like Pocahontas.*

Ladies certainly don't swim naked around here. But they're both bound to be members of the family or Gran wouldn't have their portraits. The dignified swimmer challenged her slightest disrespect. *I bet you she's a famous cousin who swam the English Channel years and years ago, and that's a picture of her swimming it. Do you suppose they do it naked? The water's terribly cold, isn't it? But maybe it didn't use to be in the olden days.*

"It's after five," Sarah D. said. "We'd better get off the subject before Sis comes in."

"I don't care if she hears us," Kate said. "She knows we're talking about it."

"Mama," Sarah D. said, "it's none of our business."

"None of my business who Anna marries!"

There are lots of strange things to think about — lots of things I don't understand — and half the time, if you ask questions about them, they laugh at you. And then they tell about it afterward, when you aren't supposed to be listening. But if you sit around waiting for someone to say something important it gets so boring you forget to listen. All they do is talk,

talk, talk — never play games, or even just climb a tree, except Sarah D. At least she'll climb a tree sometimes when the figs are ripe. And Father looks like he's getting ready to run away. He doesn't want to hear Gran say something bad about Sis. But he wouldn't climb a tree. She giggled at a vision of her portly father looking dignified as always among the sagging branches of the fig tree. *He likes to talk as much as they do, but it's all about the president, or the price of cotton. No one could listen to that.*

And now somebody else coming around every night instead of Mr. Willis, she thought. *That won't be so bad. Mr. Willis came up the gallery steps in his brown seersucker suit, enormously tall and stooped, towering over them all, his black-rimmed glasses slipping down a little bit on his nose, his long yellow teeth exposed in a painful smile that said, "I know I'm ugly and dull, but please like me." Ha, ha, ha, ha. Ha, ha, ha, ha, he laughed, like a chattering machine gun, no matter what anyone said. I don't like you,* she thought. *You're so ugly it makes me sad. Nobody likes you, and Sis doesn't either. She makes us stay on the gallery to keep her company when you come.*

"Of course you care, Mama," Charlotte said, "but whatever you say, you certainly ought to think about it ahead of time. Suppose he leaves town at the end of the job and Sis never sees him again. If you've said anything ugly, you'll be sorry. Or suppose she decides she doesn't like him. No matter how things turn out, there's no point in antagonizing her."

You could never be a member of the family, Anna said to Mr. Willis. *Why did Sis let you keep on coming to see her? If she picked out somebody on purpose to make her sad, it would be you. Nobody has to be as ugly as you are.* "I'm sorry," she said graciously to Mr. Willis. "I would not hurt you. But true love has come to me at last. I only hope we may part as friends." Anna shivered. *I don't even want him for a friend,* she thought. *And neither does Sis. He'll just have to go away and never come back. The best thing about Mr. Wheelwright is, Mr. Willis will have to go away.* She stared thoughtfully at the naked swimmer. *Sis loves Mr. Wheelwright. Gran says so. So he'll be a member of the family, too — like Sarah D., and Gran, and me. And like you, too,* she said apologetically to the swimming lady. *I didn't mean to leave you out. And you,* she said to little Jean Dupré in his full-skirted dress, *And even you,* to the Indian lady in the miniature. *If he likes to play games, I'll teach him to play casino,* she thought.

The front gate creaked. "Here she comes, girls," Kate said. "Behave yourselves."

"*Us* behave ourselves!" Sarah D. said.

Sis came in in a hurry, pulling off her round, brown straw hat, walking with quick, light steps, smiling and greeting everyone in a gentle, controlled voice. The child recognized the quiver in her voice, the tension in her eager crooked smile, and knew them for what they were, in so far as they applied to her. *I'm her favorite,* she said, the new lover forgotten. *She loves me so much she can't even say so.*

Sis was small ("the aunt I'm named for only weighs eighty-nine pounds," Anna proudly told her friends, as if any exaggerated quality had an incontrovertible value); her thin, fine brown hair was cut short and waved in beauty parlor scallops against her small head. Her hair, as a matter of fact, was the kind that never grew. She could not have worn it long if she had wanted to, and this had to Anna the same peculiar distinction as her weight. As to what she looked like, the child did not know. Sometimes she asked herself if her mama and Sarah D. and Sis were pretty, but she had never been able to decide. She had seen their pictures as children, soft-eyed and trusting, their hair in carefully brushed ringlets. They had certainly been pretty then; but now — now they were different people and she found nothing in those round and lovely faces that had survived into a grown-up and graying reality. They were simply themselves: brown hair, brown eyes, thin, white skin that freckled in the sun, and small hands and feet that testified to a frailty their strong chins and erect carriage denied. Their faces were scarcely more real to her than her own. Sis's face was narrowest, and she was bony to hug, while Sarah D. and her mother were soft and bosomy; Sarah D. was fattest and her mother's mouth was biggest. She imitated their characteristic slue-footed walk because she thought all ladies were supposed to walk like that; but when she tried to look at them as if they were strangers, it was as if she had commanded her own fat grubby hand to detach itself and act alone. They were no more and no less than extensions of herself.

She jumped up to greet Sis, feeling in the hug she gave her aunt's thin, tense body the specialness of the bond between them. They bore the same name, and its syllables, the same vocative addressed to them both by all the world, made it necessary for them to be alike. She knew their alikeness and she knew that Sis knew it, too, that perhaps she even thought they were more alike than they really were. Already she felt that in her family's eyes, everyone's except Sis's, she was odd, that she sometimes overflowed the vessel they had made to contain her. She had heard her mother say it in a dozen different ways: "Anna's the demonstrative member of the family. I don't know where she gets it." "Calm down, Anna. You'll knock Gran's specs off." "Don't take things so *seriously*, darling." Prudently, wherever they found intensity, they advised moderation; where she turned inward they drew her out, and where she turned outward they blocked her. But her oddness was acceptable in the same way the worn rug on the parlor floor or the red lady in the miniature was acceptable: because it belonged to them all. Only occasionally and with sudden, intense, irrational pain did she find their judgments unjust; and that, perhaps, was only when she felt herself made by her own excessiveness to appear foolish. Sis alone claimed her uncritically. They took long walks together in the late summer evenings. Sarah D. was more fun, and Mama was Mama, but

Sis was a special person in whose seriousness and intensity and single-mindedness she saw reflected her own most private and dangerous impulses.

Everyone sat down again, Sis on the sofa beside Anna with an arm around her. They all began to talk at once, no one listening, and then suddenly all hushed.

"Well," Ralph said.

Silence.

"Charlotte, did you know Jeanne Dupré had another stroke?" Sis said.

"Yes, Mama told us," Charlotte said.

Silence.

"And how's your corporosity segashuating, Sis?" Ralph said.

"I'm fine, Ralph, just fine."

Silence.

"Did you get a good report this term, Anna?" Sis said. "Where are the other children?"

"Yes," Anna said. She was beginning to be unhappy, as she was when her mother fussed at her father for being late to dinner. "Ralph and Charlotte have gone to see the turtle," she said. "And Katherine's talking on the telephone."

"Well, I think I'll take the children and go out to Mother's," Ralph said, but he still sat on the boudoir chair, holding his hat, as if waiting for something.

Charlotte grabbed the question with both hands and everybody sat straighter. "We're anxious to meet Mr. Wheelwright, Sis," she said. "Mama and Sarah D. have been telling us what a rush he's giving you."

Anna felt Sis's body stiffen and draw into itself, as if she would become smaller.

"He's very pleasant," she said in the blank, courteous voice one uses with a stranger. "Someone to pass the time with."

"Humph," Kate said.

Sis jumped up like a shot, as if it were a signal she had been waiting for. "All right, Mama," she said. "All right, all of you. Charlotte brought him up and all of you are sitting around as solemn as if you were waiting for a baby to be born. You want me to say it, so I will. I'm in love with him. I can't think of anything else. I loved him the instant I laid eyes on him. I didn't rest a minute until I found a way to meet him. I'm going to have him if it's the last thing I ever do. Now. Put that in your pipes and smoke it."

Ralph got up. "I think I'll take the children out to Mother's," he said.

"Calm down, Sis," Sarah D. said. "Don't get so excited about it."

"Anna, go find the other children," Ralph said.

"Why not?" Sis said. "Why not? I *am* excited about him, and I intend to stay excited about him." She turned and left the room with her quick, light, decisive step, her heels striking the floor lightly and sharply, like the blows of a tack hammer.

Kate followed Ralph and the two girls out to the car.

"Now, Dear," Ralph said. "Take it easy, Dear."

"I'm going to keep my mouth shut," Kate said. "I'm not going to say a word. I didn't say anything, did I, Ralph? I was sitting there as silent as the grave, and she turned on me. Isn't that true? Not a word have I said from the beginning."

Ralph patted her shoulder. "Go on and get Ralph, Anna," he said.

"Oh, oh, oh," Kate said. "It's awful. It's disgusting."

"Now, Dear," Ralph said.

"But she'll change her mind. She'll come to her senses in a few days. It's nothing but a tempest in a teapot."

⋅⋅⋅

Alderan came to call that first night, and the children liked him immediately, even Katherine who at twelve was beginning to be choosy about the grownups with whom she associated. The pattern of Anna's and Katherine's relationship to the lovers was established as soon as the children understood that the parlor was forbidden to them in the evenings. They invented a game of spying, hiding in the dark enclosed staircase that opened into the dining room downstairs and into Sarah D. and Charlie Dupré's low, slant-ceilinged apartment upstairs. The staircase, hidden away in the chimney space between the dining room and parlor walls, had always been a playhouse to them. Doors shut it off from the house at top and bottom, and it was dark, narrow and steep. It had been at one time or another their jail, their clubhouse, and their ship. Now it was headquarters for a new game. As soon as Alderan arrived they gathered notebooks and pencils and hid there, whispering and giggling. Alternately they crept out, slipped to the parlor door, and peeped in at Sis and Alderan, sitting on the love seat, talking or gazing raptly at each other. Sis wore her best summer dress, a beige pongee with soft gathers in the yoke that made her small bosom look a little fuller, and Alderan always had on a stiff, navy blue suit. His sandy hair was brushed back, exposing two V's of encroaching baldness. He had a straight, sharp nose, small, bright hazel eyes, and leathery skin. Deep laughter lines marked the corners of his wide mouth, and fans of squint lines radiated from the corners of his eyes. Sometimes his arm lay along the back of the sofa and he watched Sis as brightly and intently as a bird or leaned forward to say something in his animated, unselfconscious voice. Sis listened, open-faced and vulnerable. To the children she had never looked less herself. Anna did not think the lovers heard her or Katherine as they eased open the heavy, creaking parlor door and peeped in, or that the rest of the family, sitting in the dining room, had any idea what the game was. She would look through the crack for a few minutes and then run as if pursued by wolves back to the dark stair and make a hysterical, giggling report to Katherine. Appropriate notes were made: "A. holding Sis's hand. This looks serious." What it was that made it serious they could not have said, but that it *was* serious and mysterious they were sure.

"It's your turn now," they urged each other. And each replied, "No, you go. I'm scared she'll see us." None of the grownups paid the least attention to them.

One night Alderan came early and Sis was not dressed. He stood in the doorway, stiff in his tight double-breasted suit that would never look like any suit they had seen their father or their uncles wear. No matter how often he wore it, it succeeded in looking only like a new suit that he had just put on for the first time. He held his hands uncomfortably behind him and looked at Anna with an eager conspiratorial grin.

"Where's Sissy?" he said.

"Who?" Anna asked.

"Sissy. Sissy. Where's your sister?"

"Here I am," Katherine said from the sofa where she had lain reading until he came in.

He brought his hands from behind him and held out a squirming kitten. "I brought you girls a present," he said.

"Oh," Anna cried. "Oh, oh. A kitten. A beautiful little kitten. Is he really for us?" She held out her hands for the frightened little animal, cuddled him against her face and crooned softly to him. "Now, kitty. Kitty, kitty, kitty." She stroked down his ruffled, striped gray fur and held his paws to keep him from scratching.

"Look," Katherine said. "He has three white feet. We could name him Three Socks."

"And call him Socks for short," Anna said.

Katherine, at once mindful of her manners, conscious that Mama and Gran might not be so pleased as they were with the new pet, and eager to hold him herself, nudged Anna and said, "Thank you, Mr. Wheelwright. Here, let me have him, Anna. Go tell Mama to come see him." She explained to Alderan, "We'll have to ask her if we can keep him."

Remembering herself in a sudden access of shyness, Anna said, "Yes, thank you, Mr. Wheelwright," and turned away to call her mother.

"Wait a minute," Katherine said. "Maybe we better ask Gran instead of Mama. If Gran says we can keep him, Mama probably won't say no."

Alderan touched Anna gently on the shoulder. "Here," he said. "Don't run off so fast. I'll tell you where I got him, and then we'll figure out a way to persuade your granny to let you keep him."

The children, unused to grown-up complicity, stared at him in astonishment, but he sat down on the sofa, unaware that he had said anything surprising, took the kitten from Katherine and began to scratch under its chin. "I was walking down by the levee this afternoon," he said, "and I saw something moving inside an old towsack. When I opened it, there he was. Someone had thrown him away down there. Now, who would do a thing like that? They could've thrown him in the river, couldn't they? So he'd drown quick, I mean, instead of leaving him to starve. Well, I couldn't leave him there, and I haven't got a place to keep him, so I brought him to you. Do you like cats?"

"Oh, yes," Katherine said. "We'll take good care of him — if Gran and Mama will let us keep him."

"They won't care, will they?" he said. "I bet your granny likes cats. And I bet she lets you do whatever you want to when your mama's not around."

Neither Anna nor Katherine could think what to say to this. It had nothing to do with their understanding of Gran, who had always treated them with tender ruthlessness, as if they were responsible grownups with a few irritating but tolerable idiosyncrasies.

Katherine decided to stick to the first subject. "Everybody in this family likes cats except Mama," she said. "She doesn't care much for any kind of pet. She says she likes people better." She paused, uncertain whether he would be amused, but he laughed properly and said, "Well, people are more interesting most times, but then you get to where you wish they didn't talk so much, and then a cat is better. I always did like a cat more than a dog. Dogs don't have any pride, do they? But a cat can get along on its own any time, if somebody don't shut it up in a sack."

"I thought all men liked dogs better," Anna said, to be saying something, because she was embarrassed by her own silence. But then she was embarrassed by what she had said.

"I'll tell you," he said, "one time I had an old striped alley cat, a tom, and he gave me more trouble than half a dozen children. He was always out courting, getting into fights and coming home half dead. But one night I was in my room, and some way — maybe I was smoking and went to sleep — the bedclothes caught on fire, and that old cat jumped up on my chest and waked me up, and ever since that day I been mighty fond of cats." He held out his hand and showed the children a long, white, crepy scar on the back of it. "That's where I got burned," he said.

The children examined the scar with respect. "I should think you would have waked up when your hand got burned," Katherine said.

"I was sleeping mighty heavy, I reckon," he said. "No telling how long that cat had been trying to get me up before he got right up in my face and meowed in my ear and scratched me till I woke up. The room was full of smoke and I was half suffocated. I had to drag the mattress outside and shoot the hose on it."

Gran appeared in the doorway. "How do you do, Mr. Wheelwright?" she said. "I see the children are entertaining you."

The children instantly recognized, although they could not have communicated its quality or meaning, the cold formality in Gran's voice. This was not the time to ask if they could keep the kitten. But there he was in Mr. Wheelwright's lap.

"Anna will be out in a minute," Gran said. She drew out the syllables, *An-nah,* and little Anna remembered what she had said that first night: "He calls her Ann because he hasn't any better sense than to think that's her name." *He looks to me like he's got good sense,* she thought.

Mr. Wheelwright, still holding the kitten, stood up.

"Oh, Gran," Katherine said, "look. Look what Mr. Wheelwright brought us. May we keep it? May we, please?"

"Please, please," the children chanted together.

The kitten meowed softly as if adding its voice to the plea.

Alderan held it out to her tentatively. "I didn't mean to put you on the spot," he said. "Somebody threw him away tied up in a towsack. Cute little fellow, ain't he?"

"Threw him away!" Gran said. "Threw him away!" She took the kitten warily and looked him over. "He's filthy dirty," she said. "He needs a bath and he looks half starved."

"I give him a saucer of milk this afternoon," Alderan said.

"We'll bathe him, Gran," Katherine said. "And we'll feed him and take care of him and everything. Please let us keep him."

Torn between pleasure in the children's excitement and resentment at its source, Kate hesitated. "Do you think he'll get along with Kitty Spooks?" Then, "All right," she said. "It's all right with me, darling, if your mother doesn't mind. Did you thank Mr. Wheelwright?"

"It was very kind of you to bring him to us, Mr. Wheelwright," Katherine said formally.

"We just love him already," Anna said.

Alderan laughed. "Don't mention it," he said. "They already thanked me, Mrs. Anderson. In fact they been mighty nice to me. And I was telling them about one time a cat saved my life."

Kate gave the kitten to Katherine and sat down on the love seat, still stiff but obviously determined to be pleasant. Alderan sat down beside her and when he had finished repeating his story, she raised an eyebrow and looked at him skeptically. "You must have been sleeping soundly, Mr. Wheelwright," she said.

"I was *stupefied* by the smoke," Alderan said solemnly and they both laughed.

Anna was listening attentively. *That's another one of those jokes grownups have,* she thought.

Alderan examined Kate carefully, as if he could assess the degree to which she had thawed. "Say, Mrs. Anderson," he said, "I wish you and the kids wouldn't call me Mr. Wheelwright. I'm not used to it and it makes me uneasy. Just call me Aldrun, if you don't mind."

Kate sat up a little straighter and declined to give him a direct answer. "That's an unusual name," she said. "I don't believe I've ever heard it before. How do you spell it?"

"Well, I'll tell you," he said, "when I sign, I spell it A-l-d-e-r-a-n. But that's not really my name, it's kind of an abbreviation."

"You mean it's longer?" Kate asked. "What else is in it?"

Alderan stretched out his legs and thoughtfully examined the ceiling. Then he pointed upward as if at something pasted there. "It's a star," he explained. "You see, my daddy was crazy about stars. That's one thing I know about him, and one of the few things. He had a little telescope and some charts of the sky, and he used to watch the stars. He knew all the names and everything. Another thing I know about him is, he had an itchy foot. He liked to wander, and I understand that, because I took after him. But I'm wandered out, you might say — through with it. He stayed with my momma long enough to get us and name us, and then he put his telescope in his pocket and went on his way, and we haven't seen him since. But he named us after stars. My sisters are named Vega and Capella. Ain't that absurd? The last one was born after he left, and Momma named him Sam. She didn't have much use for stars or fancy names. My name is really Aĺl-dy-bá-ron. That's a real bright star in the constellation Taurus, The Bull

— the bull's eye, it says somewhere. I looked it up one time. But that's too fancy for me, and so I cut it down to size and call myself Aldrun."

Kate laughed appreciatively. There was no place she was more at home than in the world of picturesque peculiarities.

"How about us, Gran?" Katherine said. "Remember Selah and all those crazy names?"

"We're just as bad," Kate said. "One of my grandmothers liked Bible names, and she called her daughters Bathsheba and Selah, and her sons Ezekiel and Daniel. Ezekiel and Daniel were side by side, like the books in the Bible — twins, you know. And Selah was the youngest. Grandmother said she wanted to name her Amen, because she hoped that was the end, but she couldn't be sure, and besides Amen wasn't much of a name for a girl, so she took Selah and hoped it meant there would be a pause, anyway."

"How about Bathsheba?" Alderan said.

"Bathsheba," Kate said. "She was gone before I was born. I never knew her, and my grandmother never talked about her. But one of my great-uncles told me — he was an old man who had no more sense about what to tell young girls than I have — he told me she ran away with a drummer."

"I know who Bathsheba was," Anna said. "She was that lady King David liked."

"My grandmother was a good Presbyterian, although she married a Frenchman," Kate said. "I can't think why she picked Bathsheba for a name. I reckon she liked the sound of it."

"Did she marry him?" Alderan asked.

"Oh, yes. I reckon she did. I've heard there's a whole family of them living out west somewhere."

"Then why did your grandmother get so upset?" he asked in a puzzled voice.

Kate was abruptly recalled from telling the myths of the past to considering their truth, and she gave him a blank look.

"You can see how she would feel," she said vaguely. She got up. "I'll go see what's taking Anna so long," she said, and wandered out.

Alderan turned to the children. "Do you see why Bathsheba's mama got so upset?" he asked.

"I reckon it was because he was a drummer," Anna said. "Gran seems to think that was what it was. Maybe she didn't like music."

"Not *that* kind of drummer, silly," Katherine said.

"Ann," Alderan said. "Ah, here's my girl. Run along, kids, and feed your kitten."

From that night on, Katherine and Anna loved Alderan and were perfectly at home with him.

To Anna, afterward, that was always the summer Alderan and Sis were married. Other summers had their own distinguishing marks, events that rescued them from the rush of days forgotten as they passed: the summer Ralph was born; the summer Aunt Carrie died and the coffin sat two days in Gran's parlor; the summer little Charlotte had malaria; the summer Gran stepped in the quicksand. But this one had a long, continuous, coherent differentness, as if a live story were being slowly made by actors separated from the child by a wall of thick distorting glass through which their voices could be faintly heard and their bodies seen, slowly and curiously moving with exaggerated gestures she had never seen before and could find no place in her mind to classify. From the beginning, from the moment Gran said, "I think she picked him up," and evoked in Anna's mind a vision of her tiny aunt hefting the weight of a large, protesting man, she knew that the grown-up members of the family were not editing for the children's benefit. Whatever was missing had been left out, not out of that usually dependable, grown-up concern for "little pitchers" but because Gran and Mama and Sarah D. and Sis already knew and so did not have to talk about some things that persistently escaped her. Except for these unintended omissions, except for the distorting wall and the limits of her own attention, no boundaries were drawn. They all behaved as if, for once, they were too absorbed to care what she saw or heard or thought. And although she thought very little, she saw and heard and remembered a great deal.

But if, afterward, it seemed that the marriage had taken up everyone's time all summer, her life then was more complex. It was only because the complexities were constant and the marriage was a variable that the latter loomed so large.

Daily the children plunged into other worlds, equally fascinating to them. At the Andersons' they played games of Movie Stars or Ladies, scrambled over the roofs and in and out of the peach and fig trees, rooted through the storerooms, sat for hours with candles and matches, making wax patterns on the courtyard bricks or on their own hands and arms, or, among the roots of the oak trees in the park, built doll houses with twig beds, leaf quilts, and acorn tea sets.

Anna was the accepted leader of the gang that consisted of herself, Ralph, and little Charlotte. She ordered the younger children about, and ruled with absolute power until one or the other of them revolted and ran off yelling, "I quit, I quit; I'm not going to play any more."

At night Anna and little Charlotte slept together upstairs in Sarah D. and Charlie Dupré's apartment; Ralph had a trundle bed in the room with his mother; and Katherine slept on the day bed in Sis's room in the wing. Charlie was away that summer, working in Monroe, and came home only for an occasional weekend.

Mrs. Anderson had turned the upstairs into an apartment for Sarah D. and Charlie when they had first married, and when Charlie was at home they lived entirely apart, but when he was away Charlotte and Sarah D. ate downstairs with Kate and Sis. The little apartment upstairs was a wonderful retreat to the children. The very act of climbing to it by the narrow enclosed staircase was an adventure. The apartment itself, two slant-ceiled rooms and a tiny doll kitchen and bath, was made for children and lovers. Outside the dormer windows of the bedroom three laurel trees made an impenetrable dark green forest and here the flat roof of the downstairs gallery jutted out, so that the children could climb from the windows onto the roof and from the roof into the trees. Ralph and Charlotte dared not try the breathtaking swing from the roof up into the trees, and watched Anna with awe and envy as she swung upward, shouting down instructions as she climbed. "Furl the tops'ls, men. The wind's freshening. Hard aport there, pilot. There's a pirate craft off the starboard bow. Break out the guns, boys. Rake her decks. Fire, now! Fire! Fire, Charlotte — don't just stand there with your mouth hanging open. Come on, Ralph, are y'all playing or not?"

Occasionally the children went to their Grandmother McGovern's for a few days, changing the color of their characters like chameleons for the duration of a visit. For life was different at Mrs. McGovern's. Where poverty, gaiety, flexibility, gregariousness, worldliness, and cruelty characterized Kate Anderson's house, Grandmother McGovern ruled in another way: with wealth, joy, rigidity, seclusion, piety and kindness. Kate's poverty was frank, for it was not worth concealing; Mrs. McGovern would live by the schedules of wealth long after the butler's last uniform was too threadbare for another day's service; she would will him into an imaginary uniform so that a visitor might afterwards describe it down to the last button. The Andersons were gay because they saw that people, themselves included, were ridiculous. The McGoverns were joyful because they saw that man's chief end is to glorify God and enjoy Him forever. Kate was flexible and gregarious and worldly because it was native to her to be so, and because she had learned young that she could charm a bird out of a tree, and never thereafter failed to find pleasure in exercising her charm. And she was cruel because she was arrogant and innocent of her own arrogance. Mrs. McGovern was inflexible, reclusive, and godly, because it was native to her to be so, and because she had learned young that she could not sustain her vision outside her own domain. And she was kind because she was arrogant and innocent of her own arrogance.

For the children the daily concrete effects of their Grandmother McGovern's character were these: breakfast was served at eight-thirty. Julius struck each of the three graduated Chinese gongs that hung from the stag's antlers just inside the dining room door, and the rising ting, ting, ting drifted up the stair well. Grandmother's bedroom door opened immediately, and she started down the wide upstairs hall with its worn scatter rugs and massive, varnish-blackened bookcases and armoires, knocked at the door at the end of the hall, opened it, and said inquiringly, "Sister? Teen?" Miss Celestine, the children's "Aunt T.," who could not hear the bell or the knock, was waiting. She pinned her pince-nez to her bosom, and the sisters, clinging to each other and to the mahogany balustrade, started cautiously down the wide stairs. The day had officially begun. In the dining room the children sat at the oval table with bowed heads through two long blessings, one by Grandmother and one by Aunt T. From every wall stern and ancient faces looked down at them, as if alert to the slightest irreverence. Dr. McGovern, who could easily have passed for Andrew Jackson, and his wife, a lady so frighteningly severe of expression that one could only be thankful one did not know her, hung above the sideboard. Dr. and Mrs. Henshaw faced them from the opposite wall, one like an ancient, wizened Dickens clerk, the other stout and florid with ropes of auburn ringlets. On the wall between, as apologetic as if she had gotten there by mistake, hung Aunt Anne, vague and pretty behind her steel-rimmed spectacles, her reddish hair carelessly piled high, a look of bewilderment in her shy eyes, her hand raised to her chin, as if she intended to cover her mouth with the classic gesture of sorrow and rejection. Followed by all these dead eyes, Julius passed the biscuits while Grandmother warmed the cups for coffee with steaming water from a silver pot. After breakfast Grandmother conferred in the pantry with Julius and Rosa regarding the order of the day while Aunt T. inspected and watered the house plants, gently wiped the dust from the leaves of the rubber tree, and speculated with the children about what was one of the great events of the summer: when the night-blooming cereus would bloom. The children knew they could not romp in Grandmother McGovern's house. The drawing rooms were furnished with great pier glasses above marble stands, fiddle-backed chairs with frail, mended legs, and Victorian sofas with carved rosettes in the backs that fell off if you breathed on them. Crystal pendants hung from the candelabra and the chandeliers; fragile étagères held breakable ornaments which they might examine but not touch, and even the music box, which they were allowed to wind and play, had to be treated with respect. Only the great hall through the center of the house between the parlor and the double drawing rooms was theirs; here they spent hours playing on the scatter rugs, pretending they were boats; or jumping from one to another as if they were ice floes in a river. After the morning plant inspection, the two old ladies went upstairs to read their Bibles for half an hour and the children played outdoors. The car was called for nine-thirty and Grandmother went to market. One could go along if one liked. Grandmother carried her money and her market list in a white linen reticule and she never touched a coin without putting on her gloves. At home from ten-thirty until dinner at two one could visit with Julius, the butler, who was also the yardman, chauffeur, and housekeeper, or come in for a story from Grandmother about talking animals, fairies and cruel old aunts, or from Aunt T. about Indians, tarantulas, boa constrictors, and the persecution of the Covenanters. At four o'clock Julius closed and locked the shutters downstairs and went home. Just when life at Gran's house was beginning to stir and become its most exciting, Grandmother's house closed up as tight as a day lily at dusk. Supper, a game of casino, evening prayers, and the day was over.

⋘⋙

In church on Sunday morning these two innocent worlds met and acknowledged each other. Church was like the market place of olden times where the isolated inhabitants of embattled keeps and walled cities met at an open crossroads to exchange greetings, goods and news, and to make truces with each other.

All across the rooftops of the town the church bells rang, solemn, slow, and joyous, their heart-swelling summons. At nine-fifteen Julius brought the ancient Cadillac around and held the door for the ladies. Anna and Katherine held their Testaments, won for reciting the Child's Catechism, in white-gloved hands and sat in the jumpseats in front of Grandmother and Aunt T. They wore their Sunday dresses of thin, pastel voile with intricately smocked yokes, and round straw hats with curled-back brims and grosgrain bands in which tiny bunches of flowers were caught. Grandmother and Aunt T. were dressed, as always, in the black of some half-forgotten period of mourning, with mesh gloves and white linen lace-trimmed reticules. Little Ralph, the man of the family in his father's absence, already enthusiastically assumed his role, and sat beside Julius on the front seat.

"Do you know your Sunday school lessons?" Aunt T. would ask, and the girls would nod.

"Anna, what is God?" Grandmother would say, smiling gently at her Sunday joke, for Anna had always been the family prodigy at Catechism and, when she was only three, could say, "God is a Spirit, infiniteeternalnunchangeable in his BeingWisdomPowerHolinessJusticeGoodnessnTruth."

After Sunday school there was church. The McGovern pew was third from the front of the church, because Grandfather McGovern's grandfather had been deaf. Now Aunt T. was deaf, and its location again served a practical purpose.

"It's fortunate in a way that the old gentleman was deaf," Grandmother said. "Otherwise, I reckon we would have had to change our pew on Sister's account."

At five minutes to eleven the usher deferentially pushed open the tall, paneled oak door and led the McGoverns down the aisle. Gran and Sarah D. and Sis and Mama and Little Charlotte sat in the back of the church in the old Hunt pew ("where I can nap in peace if the sermon's too long," Sarah D. said) and Sarah D. winked at Anna when she trailed by behind Aunt T. When the children were seated, Aunt T., the last one in, closed the door of the box pew, settled herself and pointed her ear trumpet (which she used only in church where it was important not to miss a word) at Dr. Falkner, as if signaling him to begin. Sure enough the choir in the loft at the back of the church began to sing:

> Praise God, from whom all blessings flow;
> Praise Him, all creatures here below;
> Praise Him above, ye heavenly hosts;
> Praise Father, Son and Ho-o-o-ly Ghost.

Outside, parked in the shadiest spot he could find, Julius sat patiently behind the wheel of the black Cadillac and waited.

"I believe in God the Father, Almighty, Maker of Heaven and Earth, and in Jesus Christ, His only Son, Our Lord . . ."

The organ sighed and the music swelled out again.

> Glory be to the Father
> And *to the Son—*

When the familiar excitement of making an entrance was over, when the Creed had been recited and the Doxology and Gloria sung, the Lord's Prayer said, the offering taken and

the announcements made, Dr. Falkner, tall and thin, in striped
trousers, dark morning coat, and ascot, leaned both hands on
the pulpit, elbows out, as if bracing himself to keep from top-
pling over, and examined his congregation. His deeply sunken,
light blue eyes moved accusingly from face to face in the
rustling silence, as if he searched out the blackest sinner and
commanded the devil to depart from him. He drew his hand
across his high, shining brow and down his sunken cheek
and long, clean jaw, and touched the bridge of his large thrust-
ing nose, while he waited for the congregation to attend him.

"Pride," he said.

"Pride is your besetting sin.

" 'Pride goeth before destruction, and an haughty spirit
before a fall.

" 'Better it is to be of an humble spirit with the lowly, than
to divide the spoil with the proud.' Proverbs 16:18-19."

He stepped from behind the lectern, clasped his hands behind him and altered his tone from oratorical to didactic.
"Webster defines pride as 'inordinate self-esteem,' " he said, " 'an
unreasonable conceit of superiority in talents, beauty, wealth,
rank, et cetera,' and as 'proud or disdainful behavior or treatment; insolence or arrogance of demeanor; haughty bearing; disdain.' " Dropping his voice to a stage whisper, he leaned
forward again. "But I tell you that God defines pride not as
an *unreasonable* conceit of superiority, but as *any* conceit of
superiority, as any thought or word or deed by which a man
puffs himself up and pretends to himself and to the world that
he is not a miserable hell-bound sinner in desperate need of
God's grace."

Again didactic, "I shall consider three points in my sermon
this morning: First, how are we proud? Secondly, why are
we proud? Thirdly, how can we become humble before God
and before man?"

Anna's attention wandered. She knew quite well from long
experience that she could not listen to a sermon. She did not

believe she could *ever* listen to a sermon. Like talk of politics
and crops, it was beyond the limits of any imaginable change
that growing up might bring. She had a number of ways of
passing the time in church. In the winter in Louisiana where
her resources were fewer, she had to content herself with
reading the selections for responsive reading in the back of
the hymnbook, or with napping inconspicuously against her
father's rocklike shoulder or holding his hand and smoothing
the thick blond hair on his fingers or counting the planes of
corrugation on his thumbnail. Here, she entertained herself
in other ways. First she pulled off the bamboo binding of the
palmetto leaf fan lying beside her on the pew seat and straightened it. Then she broke off a segment of the fan and carefully
split it into narrow slivers of equal length and piled them on the
seat. Little Ralph, rosy and drowsy, had already begun to doze.
Katherine, sitting between Anna and Grandmother McGovern, as dignified as if she were really listening to Dr. Falkner,
saw what Anna was doing and frowned. Anna turned away
from her, sat sideways in the pew and bent her head as if she
were praying. Using the fan binding as a rake, she began a solitary game of jackstraws. But at last, weary of this, she gazed
at the ceiling.

"In the vanity of our possessions we are proud. I say to you,
look on your dearest possession, and if you have ever prayed
that God would not take it from you, then go home and offer
it up to Him as a sacrifice, even as Abraham bound Isaac and
laid him on God's altar."

The ceiling was patterned with curious paneling that
looked like row on row of tiny doors, just large enough
to squeeze into, and through her particular door, above and
slightly to the left of Grandmother McGovern's pew, Anna
entered the tunnel.

In the back of the church, sitting in a row in the old Hunt
pew, the three sisters and Kate composed themselves to attention. There were no men with them. Ralph, after settling

his family in Homochitto, had gone back to Louisiana, and Charlie Dupré was still out of town. Kate gently flapped her palmetto leaf against her bosom and felt the air lift and dry the damp hair at the back of her neck.

. . . *to spend this morning praying for Sis. Can't listen to the sermon. But, oh, God, don't let her marry him. Please don't let her marry him. You know how unhappy she would be. And I'm afraid of him, God. What is he? Why does he want her? And I know he's all right, I don't mean that, I'm not being proud. But not for us. Oh, God, don't take this wrong, because I trust Thee and I'm not afraid, really, but I know, so please don't let her. Please, please, please.* She bowed her head and closed her eyes.

When she looked up again she saw Anna's bent head and her protective arm stretched along the back of the McGovern pew. . . . *playing jackstraws, I'll bet a nickel. She'll tear up half a dozen fans before the summer's out. . . . time for the children to come back. We haven't had a picnic yet. We could go out to Cole's Creek one day this week and take lunch and go wading. Have a good time.* She looked around the church and nodded and smiled to friends and cousins, steadily flapping the fan against her bosom. The ceaseless whisper and twinkle of fans all over the church made her eyelids droop, she nodded briefly and then sat up straight and looked around for something to keep her awake. There was a familiar bulbous-nosed, broken-veined profile and scarlet neck to her right and four pews nearer to the front of the church. . . . *and there's Jimmie McGee, the old reprobate. Haven't seen him in church in a year. Another empty pew. Those lovely McGee boys all dead now but him. And what's he doing here? He must be on the wagon again.* Kate smiled. *Ah, wasn't he a handsome lad? Used to waltz like a prince.* She looked down at her mottled, crepy hands. *You're no beauty any more, yourself, dearie. And as for that, what are you doing here, if we're going to talk about reprobates. You're a sinner, if one ever lived. God,* she said to herself, *it's a good thing you're so far away. You couldn't stand us, if you had to live with us — me, anyway.*

"Are you proud in your righteousness and do you say like the Pharisee, 'God, I thank thee, that I am not as other men are, extortioners, unjust, adulterers, or even as this publican?'

"But, dearly beloved, the publican stood far off and would not lift up so much as his eyes unto heaven, and smote his breast, saying, 'God, be merciful to me a sinner.' "

Dr. Falkner paused and looked down on his flock with infinite pity in his light blue eyes and a sad smile on his small, clearly defined mouth. Then he struck the pulpit a thunderous blow.

"I tell you," said Dr. Falkner, "this man went down to his house justified rather than the other: for every one that exalteth himself shall be abased; and that humbleth himself shall be exalted."

All around the high, cool, square auditorium the gentlemen sat erect and stern, the ladies fanned the air rhythmically, *whish-whish, whish-whish,* and tried to think about God, and the children squirmed and dreamed. Upstairs in the old slave gallery the boys and girls giggled quietly at each other's jokes and held hands and passed notes.

Sis like the rest of her family could not carry a tune, but the Doxology still rang in her mind's ear in perfect beauty:

> *Praise God, from whom all blessings flow;*
> *Praise Him, all creatures here below . . .*

She gazed upon her world in serene beatitude. The sun shone through the clear, chaste glass of the windows and turned three threads of her graying brown hair to gold. Surreptitiously she drew the threads through her fingers and admired them. *I'm still young,* she thought.

"*I'm afraid we're lost in here,*" Marjorie said to Anna. "*We've been crawling for hours, the air is so close I am choking, and still not a ray of light.*"

"But we followed the map," Anna said. "Two right turns, and then take the long curving tunnel to the left. Mark the broken board across the passage. Forward fifty feet and then feel for the hinged panel in the ceiling. We should be getting to the broken board. Then we'll reach the upper level, and we ought to see light."

"Air, air," Marjorie muttered. "Air or I die."

"Lie down and rest," Anna said. "There is more air close to the floor. Lie down and breathe lightly."

They lay trapped in the close passageway with scarcely room to turn. "I'll never give up," Anna said between clenched teeth. "I'll find the treasure."

"We'll die before we find it," Marjorie said. "We never should have tried to escape. Let the treasure rot."

"Shhh," Anna whispered. "Footsteps. The guards have missed us."

"They'll never find us here," Marjorie said. "Only Carlyle knows the secret passageway, and he will never give us away."

Aunt T. leaned forward and pointed her ear trumpet at Dr. Falkner in a passion of attention. A ringlet escaped the invisible net that confined her steel-gray curls, and fell coquettishly on her temple. Her pince-nez dropped on her bosom, leaving a deep red indentation on either side of her nose. Aunt T. had what was called in the family "the Henshaw nose," and it rivaled Dr. Falkner's in its arched severity, its flaring, high-strung nostrils, its unmistakable importance.

"Wash a just man be proud of his justice?"

Wash?

"An honest man of his honor? Why, my friends, why askew dewey thus perfect God's will?"

Askew dewey? Ah: Why, I ask you, do we? But I've missed some.

". . . shore up our human ruins with the rotten sticks of pride? This sinful pride in our accomplishments, in our virtues, in our . . ."

He always drops his voice at the end of a sentence and I miss the last word.

"Why do we set ourselves up and temptor justify ourselves . . ."

The temptor justifies . . . no; that's wrong.

"Here," Dr. Falkner said. "Here, friends. Here is the answer. Here is the devil that rides us. Pride is the outward sign of here."

Of what?

"Fear," Dr. Falkner shouted, as if in reply. "Fear."

I'm not afraid, Aunt T. said. Yea, though I walk through the valley of the shadow of death I will fear no evil, for Thou art with me.

Dr. Falkner's shout fell into a breathless silence. The fans stopped whispering. The young folks in the balcony stopped courting and guiltily dropped each other's hands. Sarah D. started up from the half sleep that always took her irresistibly in the middle of a sermon, and banged her heels on the floor. Mrs. Clark across the aisle looked eagerly around as if she hoped someone had fainted. Sarah D. smiled sweetly. *It's just me, you old busybody,* she silently said. *I went to sleep, that's all.*

I think, Sarah D. said. *I'm almost sure. Two weeks late now, and that never happens.* She bowed her head and smiled to herself, remembering old devices for making things come true. *If he pounds the pulpit twice before I count to a hundred, it'll be true. One, two, three, four — Bang. That's too easy. And when I write Charlie tonight I'll tell him. Can't wait. A boy . . . wouldn't a boy make a difference to him? He'd settle down. Yes. He'd settle down. Things would be different. He'd come home, wouldn't he? Got to find a job here to come home. Oh, it's hard on him, yes, he wants to be so successful, he's trying for us, yes, it's true for us; but, no don't think it, waste time to think it . . . but, he's slow, yes, he can't help it. So lovely he is, so hmm, yes, and it's true, he loves us . . . isn't that enough? I'd go, I'd go if it would do any good. But . . . give up my job? And then, suppose he loses his? And, Mama said, 'There's more to marriage than dancing all night.' But no . . . can't . . . if I tell, it won't be. . . . Wait. Wait a little longer.* She looked straight at Dr. Falkner. *What do you know about it, old man?* she said. *You're a dull, hateful old man. You never should have been a preacher. I bet you never made love in the daytime in your life. And this time,* she said, *this time I'll be so careful. I'll do everything right. Dear God, let him be all right this time.* Her heart turned and contracted at her touch, and she shook her head, thinking of the tiny mound in the cemetery: Charles Augustin Dupré IV, b. April 3, 1929, d. April 6, 1929. *This time I'll try not to want him so hard.*

Anna, dragging herself feebly forward, felt a stab of pain and hope as a long splinter raked and tore her bare leg. "The broken board," she muttered, and, gasping, fainting, with her last ounce of strength she pulled herself forward. "Is that fifty feet?" She reached up and felt frantically over the surface of the panel above her head. Her hand touched the button, a spring clicked, and the catch was released. She pushed the panel up and life-giving air poured into the tunnel.

Marjorie had fainted. Anna reached back and dragged her friend's limp body to the trap door and pulled her into the upper level, where the air slowly revived her.

They looked around them. The great bell hung directly over their heads.

"We're in the belfry," Anna said. "If we don't get out of here before the hour strikes, the vibrations may deafen us for life, drive us mad, or even kill us."

"But look," Marjorie said.

All along the wall were trunks with curved lids, marked with strange characters like hieroglyphs; some, so full the lids could

not be forced down, had spilled part of their treasure on the
floor — golden chains, rubies and diamonds as big as her fist,
and a dagger with a jeweled hilt.

She thrust the dagger into her belt. They filled their pockets
with jewels. ("Found, found at last, the lost treasure of my
house. I, I alone have found it, and I will restore it.")

"Now, quick," she said, and clinging to the vines that grew
on the tower wall, they painfully made their escape.

Katherine poked Anna in the ribs and whispered, "You're
talking to yourself again, silly. Be quiet," and Anna, who had
been careful to keep her lips closed until the sight of the
jewels had swept away her caution, whispered back automatically, "I am *not*."

Grandmother McGovern looked at the two children in
astonishment. "Are you ill?" she whispered to Katherine.
Katherine shook her head, and Grandmother laid an admoni-
tory finger on her lips. Katherine turned scarlet at this in-
justice and Anna gleefully stuck out her tongue.

"Go home, read your catechism and live by it," said Dr.
Falkner. "We are all lost in Adam's sin. Even as little children
we are taught that because Adam violated the Covenant of
Works, all mankind are born in a state of sin and misery. Still,
in our pride and our fear we think to make ourselves acceptable through works. We set ourselves up and attempt to justify
ourselves before God and man. I tell you that none can be
saved through the Covenant of Works. But in the Covenant of
Grace Christ represents us before God, us, his elect people,
us poor miserable sinners who no longer need live in pride
and die in fear. In the Covenant of Grace God has promised
our redemption, and has undertaken to justify and sanctify
those for whom Christ should die."

His voice dropped to a carrying whisper. "How long, sinner, since you have read those words?"

Slowly, resonantly, and impressively: "In the wisdom of
your fathers, in God's holy Word, find your salvation."

At Dr. Falkner's imperious gesture the congregation rose. The organist struck a chord. The choir chanted, "May the words of my mouth and the meditations of my heart be acceptable in Thy sight, oh Lord, my strength and my redeemer."

Dr. Falkner stepped down from the pulpit and strode rapidly to the back of the church. There he threw out his arms and held them out, rigid, in the attitude of the crucifixion, and his head fell forward on his chest. "Now may the God of peace that brought again from the dead our Lord Jesus, that great shepherd of the sheep, through the blood of the everlasting covenant, make you perfect in every good work to do his will, working in you that which is well-pleasing in his sight, through Jesus Christ; to whom be glory for ever and ever. Amen."

The congregation poured sedately out into the sunny, columned portico. At the entrance to the church Dr. Falkner stood, as was his custom, shaking hands with and calling by name each member of his congregation. "Good morning, Mrs. Anderson; Miss Carrie, you're looking well; good morning, Miss Sarah. William, stay a few minutes. I'd like to talk to you in my study. Thank you, Mrs. Wheeler; Mr. Wheeler; Mrs. McGovern. Ah, you have your grandchildren with you. Anna; Katherine. And here's the young man. Is he named for his father? Shake hands with me, Ralph; no, the other hand. Another elder in the family! Ha, ha, ha. Mr. McGee. It's a joy to see you here, sir, a joy. God bless you and bring you back."

Sarah D. cringed. *He'll run him off again, if he's not careful,* she thought. She exchanged a pained glance with her mother.

"Jimmie!" Kate held out both arms to Mr. McGee. "Where have you been, you old devil? When are you coming to see me?"

Groups formed and broke, as cousins greeted cousins and exchanged the week's gossip, dinner invitations, and plans for the day. Dr. Falkner, his duty done, vanished into his study, followed by several of the deacons and elders. The quiet, deserted Sunday street echoed with conversation and laughter. The children stood with proper Sunday dignity, beside their Grandmother McGovern.

"Such a lovely sermon," Aunt T. said to old Mrs. Wheeler who stood, trembling, waiting for her daughter to help her down the steps.

"G-o-o-od morn-i-n-ng, Te-ee-en." The old lady's voice shook and her chin waggled until she put up her hand to keep it still. "I wanted to speak with you. Are you going Wednesday?"

"What's that?" Aunt T. said.

"I said, are you going Wednesday. Are you going to the Home?" shouted Mrs. Wheeler in her quavering voice. She and Miss Celestine taught weekly Bible classes at the Presbyterian Home for Unmarried Mothers.

"Of course I'm going," Miss Celestine said. "I'll call for you at a quarter to four."

"Send Julius up the steps to get me," Mrs. Wheeler said. "You know I can't get down alone."

"Wait a minute, Jimmie," Kate said. "I want to get my children from Julia." She touched Charlotte on the arm. "Don't you think the children have been with Julia long enough?" she said.

Charlotte nodded and Kate joined Julia and two or three old ladies who were earnestly discussing the sermon. She put an arm around Katherine and patiently waited until there was a pause.

"Aren't you getting weary of these good-for-nothings?" she said. "Send them to us for a while."

Mrs. McGovern looked anxious. "I'd planned dinner for them," she said, as if this were an insurmountable obstacle.

"Let Julius bring them down this afternoon," Kate said, "or Charlotte can come get them."

"We don't use the car on Sunday except for church, you know," Mrs. McGovern said. "But if Charlotte can arrange . . . Would you like to go, children?"

Anna and Katherine squirmed with embarrassment. They wanted to go, and they particularly wanted to go because it was Sunday. At Grandmother McGovern's, croquet, casino, the funny papers, and a number of other fascinating occupations were ruled out on Sunday. But they would not for the world have said they wanted to leave.

"I don't care," Ralph said. "I'd just as soon stay or just as soon go." He could not read yet and didn't know how to play most games.

"You need a rest, Julia," Kate said, covering the children's dilemma. "You mustn't wear yourself out."

Just then Mr. McGee joined the group. "Miss Julia," he said. "Miss Celestine. How are you?"

The two old ladies smiled benignly at him.

"Why Mr. McGee, how nice to see you," Miss Celestine said. "Have you been away?"

"Yes, I've been gone, off and on," he said. "But you two. I can always count on your being here when I come back. And you're the same as ever. Still just as pretty as you can be."

When he had moved away to pay his respects elsewhere, Mrs. McGovern turned to Kate. "Such a lovely fellow," she said in a low voice. "The McGee men have always been charming. But he doesn't look well. My, if my color were as high as his, I'd see a doctor. I wouldn't have asked him for the world if he'd been ill. Has he, Kate?"

"He has chronic indigestion," Kate said.

"Too bad. Too bad. Poor fellow, he looks as if he's on the verge of apoplexy," Mrs. McGovern said. She shook her head. "We're all getting along," she said. "It doesn't do to indulge in rich foods any more." She looked at her watch. "Twelve twenty-five," she said. "And Julius is waiting. We have early dinner on Sunday, you know, so that he can go to church in the afternoon." She raised her voice. "We'd better go, Sister. Goodbye, my dear," she said to Kate. "Come, children."

Kate followed her to the steps. "The children," she said.

"Would it be convenient for Charlotte to get them this afternoon?"

"Of course," Mrs. McGovern said. "Of course. Whatever suits you, my dear."

Julius held the door. The ladies settled themselves in the car. The children pulled up the jump seats and sat down. Aunt T. put her ear trumpet in its case.

"Home, Julius," Grandmother said.

Church was over.

◦§◦

A few days later Sis announced her engagement to the family and took Alderan to call on the cousins and aunts and uncles, who would have been bitterly offended if they had not been among the first to know. Rusty bank boxes were opened and family silver was discussed and sorted and cleaned and wrapped and presented and exclaimed over.

"Sis, I want you to have the tablespoons Aunt Charlotte gave me for a wedding present. They belonged to your Great-grandmother Shields."

And — "Anna, these are the last J.D.J. knives of the set your great-grandfather had made in Philadelphia. See the monogram? They used J.D.J. for Josephine and Jean Dupré, instead of her initials only. Isn't that a lovely thought? I'll bet Sarah D. and Charlie have some of this same silver from his branch of the family." "No, Josie, Charlie is descended from the *Charles* Dupré branch, don't you remember? That's a generation back."

And — "Darling, I brought you these sheets for your trousseau. They were woven on the old Hunt place in Maryland. See the date here in the corner — 1797. That was just two years before the Hunts moved to Homochitto. For God's sake, don't put them on your beds. They'll fall to pieces if you wash them. But I do want you to *have* them."

Wednesday, after the engagement was announced, Aunt Annie Hunt Jordan, Kate's sister-in-law, came in from the country to call. She was a short wiry old lady in her early sixties, with unruly pepper-and-salt hair, an abrupt manner, and the force of a man. One eye was gone and she wore spectacles with a dark glass over the sunken, empty left socket. At the time the eye had been removed, she had not been able to afford a glass one, and after a little reflection had declared she wouldn't have one if she could afford it. Aunt Annie Hunt had married late, at fifty-seven, and she had an old maid's passion for her brother's children, tempered and made tolerable by her brusque, casual manner, and, lately, by absorption in her new husband. For years before her marriage, she had lived alone and farmed a small plantation a few miles outside Homochitto, and her contact with her brother's family had been confined to long, almost daily telephone conversations with Kate, and to weekend visits in town. After she had married, suddenly and without apology or explanation, a gentle, aging, ne'er-do-well bachelor on an adjoining place, there had been no change in her life except that she came to town less and less often, and that, under her husband's management, the farm was yearly less productive and her clothes more threadbare and purplish-black with age.

Kate had telephoned her to say that Sis was getting married, but the news was no shock to her, as, indeed, by that time, it was not to any of the connections. Every morning Kate had reported the progress of the courtship by telephone to Annie Hunt, to her two nieces and her intimate friends, and they in turn had relayed the news to their close relatives and intimate friends. From the beginning everyone had felt that it was unexplainable and disastrous, but inevitable that Sis would marry this strange man. There was not a member of the huge connection who had not felt at one time or another the weight of Sis's intensity, whether in love or in anger, and they were all convinced that what she determined to do she would do.

Without knocking, Annie Hunt came out of the bright July morning into the cool dusk of the parlor, and walked with the caution of the near-blind to the middle of the room. "Kate?" she called inquiringly.

"It's me, Aunt Annie Hunt," Sis said, coming in from the dining room. "Sit down. I'll call Mama."

"Come here," Annie Hunt said. "Let me see you." She took Sis by both arms and frowned at her, tilting her head back and peering upward, as if she still hoped she could catch a glimpse of the world from beneath her sunken eyelid. "My good eye's none too good any more, you know," she said, and gave Sis a dry peck on the cheek. "Well, sit down and tell me about it. I want to hear all about it."

"Mama," Sis called. "Aunt Annie Hunt is here." She guided Annie Hunt to the love seat and sat down beside her. "Sarah D.'s at work and Charlotte and the children have gone swimming," she said.

"And you? Why aren't you at work? Have you quit your job?"

"I have a few days off to get ready for the wedding," Sis said. "But I'm so up in the air I can't think what to do."

Annie Hunt took off her round black straw hat and fanned herself with it. "My God," she said, "it's uncivilized to get married in this weather."

Sis laughed. "Don't add the weather to Mama's list of objections," she said.

"Mama's list of objections to what?" Kate said, coming in and sitting down opposite them.

"I, for one, wish you all the happiness in the world, dearie," Annie Hunt said. "At least you didn't have to wait as long as I did. God bless you and give you as good a husband as He gave me when He finally got around to me."

As all the family knew, she loved her lately acquired husband as passionately as if she were a bride of seventeen.

"Thank you, Auntie," Sis said.

"Well, where is he?" Annie Hunt said. "Bring him on. I want to see what he looks like."

"He's not here," Sis said. "He had to go out to Arizona to make some arrangements with his family before the wedding."

"Well, *good*, good," Annie Hunt said. "We'll all feel more at home with him when we've met his *family*. Is he going to bring them back with him or are they coming on later?"

"He's divorced," Kate said. "I didn't tell you over the phone because I didn't know it myself until yesterday."

"Divorced!" Annie Hunt said.

"He has two little girls, Aunt Annie Hunt," Sis said. "One ten and one twelve. They are with their mother, and he has gone out to see them and tell them about us."

"Well!" Annie Hunt said. "That puts a new light on it."

"Now, don't you start acting as if I'd told you he was a cannibal," Sis said. "People do get divorced, you know. Your own cousin Amelie has had three husbands."

"Harley's cousin," Annie Hunt said. "That's different. Marriage is just a hobby with Amelie. But it does put a different light on the matter. Where are you going to be married? Surely under the circumstances you won't plan to have a big church wedding."

Sis and Kate looked at each other. They had not yet discussed the wedding arrangements. Kate had held back, as if afraid of each decision that laid another brick in the wall separating her from her daughter, and Sis, avoiding anything that tied her love to practical reality, had seemed incapable of the smallest practical move. The fact that Alderan was divorced had been as much a surprise to Sis as to Kate, although from the depth of her entrancement she did not consider it important. Now each one thought that she would be less threatened if they talked in Annie Hunt's presence, as if Annie Hunt could unconsciously take on herself the responsibility of commitments that neither — one out of fear and the other out of love — could bear to face. With the help of a strong, practical, uninhibited moderator, they would be guided through the crisis and would avoid an open and irretrievable quarrel.

"I haven't ever wanted a church wedding or a big reception, Auntie," Sis said as decidedly as if all the arrangements were firmly fixed in her mind. "We simply haven't the money. And if I'm not going to have a reception, I'm certainly not going to let people give me a lot of parties. We'll have a simple home ceremony with no one but the immediate family."

"How about his family?"

"His mother's dead," Sis said, "and he doesn't know where his father is. Besides which, he ran away from home when he was fourteen and has seen very little of any of them since. His sisters and brothers are scattered and couldn't afford to come, and he doesn't even write to some of them."

Kate muttered to herself something that sounded like "Poor white trash."

"What'd you say, Kate?" Annie Hunt said.

"Nothing. Nothing. I haven't been consulted."

"Mama, you know I haven't had time to consult you. I haven't even consulted myself. We'll plan the wedding right now, if you like, and I'll do anything you want, within reason."

They began to make a list of the members of the family who would have to be invited.

"How about Cousin Dalton?" Kate said, after the sisters, brothers, aunts, uncles, first cousins, and nieces and nephews had been listed. "He's always been like a member of the family. He'd be crushed if we left him out."

"If we go outside this list, Mama, we'll have to add a hundred names," Sis said.

"But you've already gone outside it," Kate said. "You've got Caroline Bell on here and she's not even a cousin, much less a member of the immediate family."

"Mama, she's my closest friend. You know I have to have Caroline."

"I don't see how you can have her without having Dalton," Kate said.

"Just because Cousin Dalton has been trying to marry you for twenty years I don't have to have him at my wedding," Sis said. "It *is* my wedding, isn't it?"

"Besides," Annie Hunt said, "if you invite Dalton, there are at least fifty other people whose feelings will be hurt because they weren't included, too."

"All right, all right," Kate said. "I suppose you're right, Annie Hunt. The parlor isn't big enough to hold them all. But I don't know what I'll tell Dalton. I suppose the best thing to do will be to telephone everyone in that class and explain to them why they aren't invited."

"If it will make you feel any better, Mama, I can ask Caroline to stand up with me. Then there would be a good reason for her being here, and no one's feelings would be hurt."

"What about the minister?" Annie Hunt said. "Who's going to marry you?"

Kate looked up from the list. "Why Dr. Falkner, of course," she said. "Who else?"

"Dr. Falkner doesn't marry divorcés," Annie Hunt said.

"I'd forgotten that," Sis said. She got up restlessly, wandered around the room, and then sat down again. "To tell the truth, I've been so excited I haven't thought once about any of it until this morning. Maybe it would be better for us to get in the car and get the first preacher we can find to — "

"No," Kate said. "That's where I draw the line."

"It's probably the sensible thing to do," Sis said. "We haven't the money for a wedding. You know it yourself, Mama. Once you get started, there are all sorts of things you haven't thought of. Announcements. Are we going to send announcements? A reception. Even with only the family, a reception will cost twenty-five or thirty dollars. And it seems mean to get them all here and not even give them a drink. Flowers for the altar. There's no end to it."

"Oh. Oh. Oh." Kate put her face in her hands and began to rock herself back and forth on the love seat. "Can't somebody stop her? She's ruining her life, Annie. She's breaking my heart."

Annie Hunt pushed her glasses up on her nose and looked sternly at her sister-in-law. "Now, Kate," she said, "every mother feels that way when her last chick and child marries. You can't expect Anna to stay with you the rest of her life and if she's ever going to be old enough to choose a husband, she is now. Shame on you."

"I'm not that kind of mother," Kate said. "I've always wanted the girls to marry. I've welcomed their beaus. But this is different. I know it is. I *know*."

Sis stiffened and drew into herself and lowered her voice, as she always did when she met opposition.

"We'll have the wedding, if you want to, Mama," she said. "We'll go on and have it. I'm sure Mr. Wilson will marry us."

"A *Methodist* wedding!" Kate said.

"You certainly don't have to send announcements if you don't want to," Annie Hunt said. "And you know Ralph and Charlotte will want to do something for you. Let them have the reception. And I'll send Harley in with all the smilax you can possibly use to decorate the parlor."

"No one in the family has ever been married by a Methodist preacher," Kate said.

"Aren't you ashamed of yourself, Kate!" Annie Hunt said. "The idea!"

"Mama, I'm trying to plan it to satisfy you," Sis said.

"We can bank the fireplace with greens and borrow some of those tall standing candelabra from the church," Annie Hunt said. "The parlor will be lovely. What will you wear, Sis?"

"I think that pale green linen suit I bought last spring," Sis said. "I've only worn it two or three times. It's just like new."

"It's no use," Kate said. "Nothing we say is any use and we

may as well face it. Sis and I have been polite to each other until we're both ready to scream. For a month, ever since Charlotte and Sarah D. bullied me into keeping my mouth shut, we've been acting as if everything were all right between us, and I can't stand it another minute."

"Kate, don't say something you'll be sorry for," Annie Hunt said.

"That's what they all tell me. But suppose I'm sorry I *didn't* say it? Look at her, Annie Hunt. She's thirty-five years old, and you say she's old enough to choose a husband. But she's not. She's as innocent as a child. She's never been in love or had a serious beau in her life. She hasn't the least idea of what it means to live with a man for thirty years. Oh, I'm not talking about sex, although I could. To *live* with a man. She thinks love is something that happens to you instead of something you make happen. She thinks everything will always be the same. Every one of us knows her as well as we know our own aches and pains; we know how careful you have to be not to step on her toes. Nobody would ever do anything to shake her idea of what we're like — or what we *ought* to be like. Still, at thirty-five, when any fool has better sense, she thinks you can love folks like that. If you have everything on your side, marriage takes more patience than anyone but God can give you. Just a *man* is a stranger, any man. If you've known him all his life and understand all his faults and virtues and he understands yours, you find he's not what you thought he was, once you're in the same house, sleeping and eating together, poor, or sick, or well, or drunk, or sober, or faithful, or philandering, angry, or silent, or full of some joy you can't understand or share. What does a woman do, a woman who's meant all her life to be a wife, to have children and make a home, what does she do when those things happen? Even if she's meant for it, what does she do when she has to care for someone like she does for herself? She's laid more on herself than she ever understood at the beginning, and it's only because life comes one day at a time, and because necessity is too much for her little private self that she can sometimes grow bigger. But what does Anna know about all that? When will she ever understand that over and over again you have to choose wrong and live with it? She thinks she's made her first, last, and infallible choice. She thinks she's seen the light and that she's strong enough to keep the window open. But a passion and will are the last things she needs and she'll never understand tolerance and content."

Kate stopped short and began to rock again, holding her temples with her palms. Annie Hunt and Sis sat stunned, unable to speak.

"They might have a chance, if she didn't love him so hard," Kate said. "But she hasn't even *seen* him yet. All she sees is the reflection of her own passion. I know. I *know*. She's having the love affair she should have had at sixteen when she was young and helpless and could have been prevented from doing anything about it. *Look* at him, Anna. *Look* at him. He can't even speak the King's English. What will you feel toward him after the thousandth 'I *seen*'? How will you like watching him eat a poached egg on toast in four bites the thousandth morning? How will you feel when you begin to see him and *hear* him in your children? What will you think when he brings home his drinking companions, when he introduces you as 'the little woman,' when he gets involved with the first woman who encourages him and doesn't even bother to conceal it from you? He's as different from us as it's possible to be. He'll never know what you're angry about."

Sis had gotten up while her mother was talking and walked to the mantelpiece where she stood with her back to the room, one hand clenched at her side and the other holding the base of the heavy Empire urn so tightly her knuckles showed white. Now and then, as her mother's words poured out into the hot stillness of the shabby room, she looked up with blank eyes at dead **Jean Dupré** in his golden frame.

Now she turned around, still holding the urn with her left hand. "*I seen!*" she said furiously, "*Poached egg on toast!* I'm talking about love."

"You don't know what you're talking about," Kate said.

Down the block at Mr. Tillman's metalworks, sheets of iron crashed like cymbals. On the front porch roof a squirrel said, *chick, chick, chick,* and above him in the trees angry jays called to each other as harshly as if they were dying of asthma. The fountain wept. *Tick-tick,* said the parlor clock. *Tick-tick. Get out, get out, get out, get out.*

"I've been waiting for him twenty years, Mama," Sis said. "For twenty years I've known how I would feel when he came, and I've known nothing else would do. Don't *dare* talk to me about his grammar or his manners. Let Charlotte marry for security if she wants to. Let Sarah D. marry for somebody to dance with. Let Will marry for admiration. That's their business. I'm marrying for love and nothing but love. The more he's different from everyone I've ever known the better I like it. I want to love a man for himself, not for his manners or his grammar, or his school, or his money, or his tailor, or even for how much he loves me. I'm getting *loose.* I want everything to be possible for us, and it only can be when love is more than all the rest put together."

"You're a child," Kate said. "Everything you say makes me more afraid for you."

Sis leaned forward. Her voice was no more than a whisper. "Then God help me to stay one," she said. "At least I won't be the kind of child I've been to you all my life." She straightened up. "I won't have to forbear when I know you're thinking, 'Poor Anna. She never has a beau.' I won't have to support for another day your sympathy for my inadequacy. I'll go free, under my own colors, and if it's a mistake, I'll pay for it with my life because I'll put my life into it."

"I know you will," Kate said. "That's what's breaking my heart."

"Here, here," Annie Hunt said. "Now, *you* hush, Sis. Don't talk to your mother like that. Shame on you."

"It's true," Sis said.

"Don't do it, my darling," Kate said. "For God's sake, for my sake. Don't break my heart."

"Hush, Kate," Annie Hunt said. "Lots of things are true, Anna. Sit down. Stop towering over us. And let go of that vase. I thought you were going to break it on Kate's head."

Sis let go of the vase, but she did not sit down. Instead she turned her back and leaned her head on the mantel.

"Lots of things are true," Annie Hunt said again. "It's true that you love your mother and she loves you. It's true that one way you love her is by tolerating her sympathy and one way she loves you is by being sympathetic. That's what Kate is talking about, Anna, when she says love isn't all will and passion. You ought to understand that as well as anyone."

"I won't have it any more," Sis said without raising her head. "I won't have it."

"You'll have what the good Lord gives you," Annie Hunt said. "And so will you, Kate. Now both of you settle down before somebody says something nobody can explain away, not even me."

Kate got up and went over to Sis and timidly touched her shoulder. "I'm sorry, darling," she said. "I'm sorry I spoke out like that."

Sis shook her head as if to say *no*, but instead she said, "It's all right."

"I shouldn't have," Kate said. "I wouldn't have if I weren't so upset. Forgive me."

Sis turned around, and went back to the love seat. She did not touch her mother, but sat down again by Annie Hunt. "I'm sorry, too," she said. "Try not to worry about me any more. I *know* I'm right."

The three women stared at each other blankly, as if they had just met and could think of nothing to say. Sis's hands trembled slightly in her lap. Kate straightened her shoulders carefully and drew a cautious breath, as if expecting a stab of physical pain from her broken heart. Then Annie Hunt thumped the floor with her cane.

"Now, listen, girls," she said. "I really came to town today to find out what Sis wants for a wedding present." She paused, and then said as solemnly as if she were giving away the crown jewels, "You can have your choice between the Hunt sideboard and the Anderson Hepplewhite desk."

"Oh, Auntie," Sis said, "you shouldn't. They're both too grand for me. I'll feel as if I'm taking your furniture right out from under you."

"Never mind that," Annie Hunt said. "You're my last niece and you were Brother Will's favorite child (don't ever say I said so) and I want you to have one of them. If Brother Will were here, you wouldn't be going into marriage empty-handed, and since he isn't, Kate and I have to make up for it. Ain't that so, Kate?"

"Yes," Kate said. "It's true. We'd all be different if he were alive."

⋘§⋙

They were married August 11, 1931. Will and his wife Eunice, who lived in New Orleans, drove up for the wedding. Will was tight when he arrived and drunk when he left. Only the immediate family attended the wedding: Kate, Will and Eunice, Charlotte and Ralph and their children, Sarah D. and Charlie, little Charlotte, Aunt Annie Hunt, Harley, and Kate's two nieces, Mary and Alice Dupré. Caroline Bell stood up with Sis, but Alderan stood alone.

Charlotte and Ralph paid for the announcements which Kate insisted be sent out afterwards.

The parlor was dark, the shutters closed against the August heat. Candles were not used because they would have melted and fallen over before the ceremony was finished. Harley's smilax was banked in front of the fireplace and Alderan had sent a bouquet of stiff white gladioli for the mantelpiece.

Kate stood on the bride's left, not beside her but against the wall by the mantelpiece; Will stood beside his mother and the rest of the family stood in a semicircle around the room.

When the minister said, "Who giveth this woman to be married to this man?" Kate said, "I do," without moving from her place, and Sis put her own hand in Alderan's.

They all looked small and wintry that hot afternoon. In the dusky room their summer dresses were gray. Alice and Mary wore black, as they were still mourning the death of their father some years earlier.

Afterwards, when she remembered the scene (and she never forgot it), Anna's feeling for it was one of surprise. Perhaps she had grown that summer, for everyone except her father and Eunice (who was two inches taller than Will) looked small to her, scarcely larger than children. They stood around the room, those small, dark people, like so many sparrows on a telephone wire, alert and bright-eyed, their bodies tense against the shifting breeze.

> *"Who killed Cock Robin?"*
> *"I," said the sparrow,*
> *"With my bow and arrow,*
> *I killed Cock Robin."*

And afterward, twittering, they pecked Sis and Alderan on their cheeks and flew away home.

Sarah D. had a box of rice, and she and Charlotte and the children threw it at Alderan and Sis as they ran down the steps and through the creaking iron gate, and climbed into Alderan's Model A Ford.

Kate smiled and waved and called, "Goodbye, darling. Goodbye, goodbye."

When they were out of sight, she put her head down on the

iron fence, her body bent and her stomach drawn in as in a sudden severe cramp, and wept.

Anna had never seen her cry before.

Charlotte took Kate into the house, while Sarah D. invited the rest of the family to come in and share the champagne Will had brought. The screen door banged behind the grown-ups as they went in, chattering again.

Anna and Katherine sat down on the front steps together and the sparrows from the rain gutters on the roof flew down and began to peck up the scattered grains of rice.

☙

At night showers of falling stars brushed across the dry August sky. Meteorites hurtled into the earth's thick atmosphere, dragged through the hot restraining air, and were consumed. The sun and the moon rose in the east and travelled round and round the world.

Like the world, the child, Anna, spun in her place. Her grandmothers' houses, her family, the lovers, the summer days, flashed by in circular succession. Strange astral bodies flew off in unforeseen directions and collided with one another and exploded, but she observed everything with godlike interest and detachment, and the unconscious conviction that, whatever the new orbits into which they finally settled, she would still be at the center of the universe.

Christmas Holidays

◆§ SIS AND ALDERAN had already been divorced in the winter of 1935 when Anna spent part of her Christmas holidays with her grandmother. Sis was at home again in the evenings after supper when the family gathered in the dining room for the day's "visiting"; Sis, and Gran, and Sarah D., and Charlie Dupré who was working in Homochitto that winter, and little Charlotte and the baby, four-year-old Billy.

The dining room was unchanged by the five years that had passed since Sis's marriage, except that it was dingier, the floors more splintery, the upholstery stained and worn in a few new places. The Empire day bed still stood against the wall below the huge mirror that still seemed about to fall and crush whoever happened to be lying under it; the big platform rocker still sat by the fireplace where anyone who passed might bruise his shin on it; the mayonnaise stain still marked the floor by the parlor door. The one change that had taken place in the house was that it no longer belonged to Kate. Unable to keep up the mortgage payments, the family had lost the house to the Building and Loan Company and now rented it. Sis had lost Alderan, the family had lost the house, and Anna, too, had suffered a loss. Marjorie was gone. She did not look for her in the mirror because she had a new love. Sometime during the winter of her eleventh year she had begun to read with the voracious absorption of childhood and Marjorie had gone away, replaced by Mowgli, Tarzan, Bomba the Jungle Boy, Jo

March, Elsie Dinsmore, and the Little Colonel. The first winter she had been struck by this new passion she had read the *Book of Knowledge,* all twenty-four volumes, straight through, unselectively, and she had been so obsessed that if she were in the bathroom she would read all the fine print on the Lysol and milk of magnesia bottles. She wanted only books for Christmas, and the year she had gotten ten she remembered as the most satisfactory Christmas of her childhood. She was too shy to look for what she wanted in strange places, and so she did not discover the Public Library until she was in high school. In her grandmothers' houses she was limited to the curious collections in their tall glass-fronted bookcases. The McGoverns, of course, had an overweening passion for theology and religious history; even Anna's obsession was balked by the multi-volume *History of the Reformation,* Foxe's *Book of Martyrs,* the collections of sermons, and the *Decline and Fall of the Roman Empire.* When she was thirteen, she read straight through the four volumes of *The Rise of the Dutch Republic,* but that was a dull summer. At Kate Anderson's house she had to choose among an ill-assorted collection of remnants. Will was a reader, and he had taken the sets of Dickens, Thackeray, Scott, and Cooper to New Orleans. All that were left were a few of her great-grandfather's medical books, a set of Presbyterian moral stories for children called *Line upon Line, Precept upon Precept,* the Rollo books for boys, and some odds and ends, mostly popular novels, acquired during a brief period of prosperity in the 1890's.

This particular night, although she was scornfully conscious that she was too old for it, she was lying on the day bed, reading *Rollo at Eton.* Sis had gone to a movie with Caroline Bell; Sarah D., sitting by the fire in the platform rocker, was reading *The Delineator.* Charlie and Gran had drawn two straight-backed chairs up to the dining room table and were cracking and picking out pecans.

But Anna did not read as absorbedly as usual. Something

was going on in her family, something that made her restless
and excited, something fascinating and tragic that she did not
understand. She could not have kept her attention even on
the climactic scene of *Elsie Dinsmore*, the moment when Elsie
faints at the piano because her father has forced her to play
profane music on Sunday. As for Rollo, she had always had a
feeling that he was a sissy, although the author did not seem
to know it, and now she read of his difficulties with his wicked
cousin Basil abstractedly, chiefly out of the habit of having a
book in her hand. In another part of her mind she examined
snatches of conversation and tried to understand what her
family's trouble was.

It's like the Lysol bottle, she thought to herself. *There's
something about the label on the Lysol bottle that I don't understand. Now what is it?*

"Feminine hygiene," the advertisements said, and there was
the worried lady in the picture, holding the Lysol bottle and
frowning unhappily. What was she worried about? And how
would Lysol solve her problems?

Mama thinks she's told me all about it, Anna said to herself,
*and I understand what she said about babies and menstru-
ating and all that, but where does the Lysol come in?*

"I don't know what to do about her," Gran was saying.
"I'm at my wits' end. Do you know how much she weighs
now, Charlie? *Seventy-eight pounds!* I don't see how she stays
alive."

Sarah D. looked up from her magazine. "What worries me
more than that is she's quit going to church," she said. "Now
if it were *me*, that would be one thing. But for Sis not to go
to church! That scares me."

Charlie bent over the nutcracker that was screwed to the
edge of the dining room table, swung the handle rhythmically
back and forth and dropped the cracked nuts into a bowl in
his lap. His words were punctuated by the creak of iron and
the explosions of pecan shells.

"Now, let me tell you something, Mrs. A.," he said, "and you, too, Sarah D. I've had a lot more experience of the world than you all have and I've seen this kind of thing happen before. Why, I could have told you after ten minutes' conversation with Alderan how this thing would turn out." He laughed a rueful women-are-like-that laugh and put a pecan in his mouth. "Sis has had *me* over a barrel a couple of times," he said. "I know her. She ain't an easy woman to live with."

Kate shook her head impatiently. "Damn him," she said. "God damn him."

Shocked, Anna looked at her grandmother sadly. That was the sort of thing Elsie Dinsmore would have to pray over for weeks. But then, hearing the slow sound of the words ringing in her ears, she realized that her grandmother was not cursing thoughtlessly. It even sounded as if she might be praying. At any rate, she meant it. She meant, *God damn him. So he must be awful*, Anna said to herself. *Even if I never thought so.*

"Now, Mrs. A.," Charlie said again, "let me tell you something. In the first place, she'll get over him. She'll pull out of it. Mark my words. She thinks she's never going to be the same again, but she will. She may even think she's going crazy, or that she's going to kill herself (goodness knows, you're right — she acts half crazy), but she won't. All you've got to do is be patient and give her time to settle down. She'll start going to church — in fact, I'll betcha she'll be going to prayer meeting within six months."

Sarah D. had gone back to her magazine and Charlie lowered his voice and nodded at Anna who sat cross-legged on the day bed, bent over her book. "Anna's the best medicine Sis could have right now," he said to Kate in a low voice. "She makes a big effort to be cheerful for her."

"Sometimes I almost hate her for making herself suffer so," Kate said half to herself. She pressed her lips and teeth together as if biting off an invisible thread and ran her hand through the wispy gray hair that was twisted into a knot on top of her head. Then she sighed. "I remember when she was a little thing, how she used to shut herself up in the closet to pray after she'd been punished. I feel now just like I did then. I want to rip open the door and shake some sense into her."

Charlie was pursuing his own thoughts. "I know one thing about it," he said. "If Sis had a little passion in her nature, it probably never would have happened." He shrugged in a half-embarrassed, half-superior way. "After all," he said, "a man wants a *woman* when he marries. Why do you think Alderan took up with this little gal in Maraisville? Sis just ain't made for marriage and she'll be better off without him — without any man, for that matter."

Kate looked at her tall, balding, paunchy son-in-law, and Anna watched her watching him. Then she looked at her uncle to see what it was Kate was looking at so fiercely. He was bent over the nutcracker, a half smile of tolerant understanding on his face. His small chin disappeared into the roll of fat around his jowls, and the long strands of black hair that he usually brushed carefully over his bald spot had fallen down on his high, shiny forehead. He put another pecan in his mouth, and his face, still handsome in repose, seemed to vanish into layers of moving fat, as he chewed it thoughtfully.

Anna knew that something had happened. She moved restlessly to a new position on the day bed, hanging her legs over the side and leaning back against the cushions at the head. She wished that Charlie would not talk so much and hoped that Kate would talk about something else. Although she wanted very much to hear everything they had to say about Sis and Alderan, she had the constricted feeling in her chest that came when grown people were angry with each other.

Kate continued to look at Charlie as if she had just remembered something unpleasant that she had failed to take into account. She watched him cracking nuts and her face was controlled and contemptuous.

At last she said, "You're eating all you pick out."

Charlie continued his exposition. "So you see," he said, "Alderan wasn't all to blame. You have to think about his side of it."

"*His* side of it!" Kate said. "I don't *care* about his side of it."

Charlie looked up at her. Then, "Oh, I'm not saying he wasn't at fault," he said. "Alderan's a little bit stupid, or he would have known Sis — known you *all* for . . ." He broke off. "Alderan's a good fellow," he said. "He's a good man to take on a hunting trip or — or a stag party. But he never had a clue about you — about *us*. About our kind of people. Especially the women."

Kate got up and got the whiskey bottle and the sugar bowl from the sideboard and brought them to the table. She put them down with a thump. "We ought not to talk about it," she said. "I get too mad. When I think . . . When I *think* what he did to Ralph and Charlotte, and then you say, *his side of it* . . ."

"As for Ralph," Charlie said, "Ralph has always been as naïve and trusting as a preacher. If he'd had his mind on his business, he'd have kept his warehouse locked up."

Kate silently sprinkled sugar on a few pecans in a glass and poured in some whiskey. She shook her head warningly at Charlie. "Do you want me to fix you some whiskey and pecans?" she asked.

But Anna had heard. "What are you talking about, Charlie?" she said.

"She's old enough to know," Charlie said. "It can't hurt her."

"You already know, darling, don't you?" Kate said. "You know that Alderan stole some money from your father last year and he had to fire him. And you know Sis and Alderan just got a divorce and Sis is living here now. You know all that."

"Oh," Anna said. "That. Give me some pecans and whiskey, Gran."

But I never did understand it all, she said to herself. *I never did know why he did it, when he was working for Father and everything. When Father gave him the job when he was broke. And he and Sis were living right there in the house with us and we were having such a good time. And he was right in the middle of teaching Katherine to drive. If it hadn't all happened he would have taught me to drive this year.*

A picture flashed into her mind, as vivid as that old picture of her grandmother saying in the parlor just before Sis and Alderan were married, "I could never marry a man who called a Chevrolet a Shivvy." Was it so important what you called a Chevrolet? A yawning abyss opened at the edge of her mind and she gazed into it, shivering and unhappy. Alderan stood on the bank of Lake Jackson with his hands on his hips looking at her and laughing. They had been fishing all day, she and Alderan and Sis and Katherine; he had just dragged the boat up on the bank ready to go home. Some time in the course of the day they had decided to go through a narrow channel between the upper and the lower parts of the lake, a little twisting canal choked with brush and rotting logs and jutting cypress knees. Halfway through, the boat had stuck on a mudbank and Alderan had climbed happily out, knee-deep in mud, to shove it through. Sis had sat rigid in the boat, muttering admonitions from time to time about water moccasins, while the children giggled with excitement.

"Hey, girls, the water's fine. Won't you join me?" he had said, as he strained and pushed and sweated and rocked the boat, stirring up whirlpools of mud-black water.

Sis had said over and over, "Look out for holes, darling. For God's sake, don't step in a hole," for Alderan couldn't swim and wouldn't wear a life preserver.

"We'll save him," Anna and Katherine had shouted joyfully. "We'll save him if he steps in a hole."

The boat had rocked and swung and scraped across the mud, and finally slipped into deeper water, and Alderan had climbed back in, his old, oil-stained khaki pants and ragged tennis shoes clotted and rank with slimy black mud, his shirt torn across the shoulders by a thorn branch; and they had gone on fishing.

Now, in her mind, Alderan stood on the bank and looked at her. The black mud had dried to a crust on his pants and shoes, and a long smear had dried across his cheek and forehead. His shirt was dark with sweat stains across his back and under his arms, and he smelled like sweat and fish. He was smiling at her, the low, western sun striking into his eyes and making him screw up his good-natured, leathery face. She must have said something to him and he had said in reply, "I'll bet you never saw your *father* look like this in your whole life." At twelve she had laughed, and he had laughed and that was the end of the scene; but at fourteen the surface of her memory of it was pierced by doubt, by the beginning of a painful understanding, and she felt her heart contract in embarrassment.

For already there was beginning to work in Anna the combination of qualities that were always to torment and support her. She had a sure sense of the reality of the action that went on around her and an unfaltering memory for its climactic moments. The fabric of events, the content of scene after scene in her life, stuck persistently in her mind whether or not she could assimilate it and understand it. Far from forgetting or transforming the painful moments that children are generally supposed to suppress, she could *never* forget them, and year by year they collected to themselves whatever understanding she could bring to them at a given time. They gathered like the fallen leaves of autumn after autumn, and pressed each other down at the bottom of her mind. But they were *there*, articulated and remembered, ready for her understanding when it was ready for them. It was as if she were riven from the top of her head to the ground she stood on, and pinned there with the sharp, unbending stave of reality. She could not even turn her head to look away. Already, at ten, at twelve, at fourteen, she could not look away; she could not make her world seem other than it was. She was an accurate transcript of the surface of all she took part in. She did not yet know how to use her reality. Even the pain of her embarrassment was without value to her; she was simply unable not to see.

Charlie had declined the pecans and whiskey, and now he got up and went into the kitchen. She heard the sounds of the icebox door opening and closing, and then the creak of the hinges on the kitchen safe. "Can I fix you a sandwich, Mrs. A., Sarah D.?" he called.

"No thanks."

"I just can't mix whiskey and sugar," he said. "It ruins good whiskey for me."

"Every man to his own taste," Kate said, "as the old lady said when she kissed the cow."

"What's that?"

If I asked Gran to explain it all to me, Anna thought, *I reckon she'd try. What I don't see is, if they all think he's so awful, why aren't they happy now he's gone.*

Another fragmentary memory stirred in her troubled mind and she heard the telephone ringing as she had drifted into sleep one night, and her father's slow, gruff "All *right,*" as he answered. *That must have been the year before Sis and Alderan moved in with us, or it would have happened in Eureka,* she thought. "Charlotte," she heard her father say, and she knew he must have his hand on her mother's shoulder, shaking her to rouse her, holding her hearing aid ready in the other hand. There was a murmur of conversation, and then her father raised his voice, and she heard him say clearly, "I said, she said Sis has had a miscarriage." And then her mother's distressed voice answering, "Oh, *Ralph,* not *again.*"

That was all. Somewhere in those brief memories lay buried the secret of what had happened.

And then there was that other time, about the telephone, she thought, *when Sis cried.*

It rang again, this time late in the afternoon while she and Sis were sitting together in the living room reading. Sis answered and it was Alderan calling long distance. "Do you *have* to?" she heard her say. And then, after a silence, "But, darling, couldn't you drive home late? Even if you didn't get here until ten or eleven, it would be better than not coming." And then, "Yes, yes, of *course* I understand. It's just that I miss you so."

But after she had hung up, Sis had begun to cry, sitting, little and huddled, in Father's old green easy chair, and Anna, in a passion of sympathy and bewilderment, had flung her arms around her and said over and over again, "I love you, Sis. Please don't cry. *I* love you."

Had Sis known even then that Alderan loved another lady? That was a long time before they got the divorce.

"I just missed it," Charlie was saying. "If I had been able to convince Will Strickland that it was a good thing, we'd have picked up five or six thousand dollars, just like that." He snapped his fingers. "Just like that."

Kate sighed. "Um-hum," she said, and worked out an embedded bit of pecan with her nut pick. "Sarah D., come help us, you lazy sinner. My fingers are giving out. And you, too, Anna."

"Let us finish our stories, Mama," Sarah D. said. "We'll come in a minute."

"I never yet met a banker who could see beyond the end of his nose," Charlie said. "They'll hang on to their money till hell freezes over." He stuffed the last bite of his sandwich into his mouth and chewed slowly and thoughtfully. "Curious thing about bankers," he said. "They don't seem to realize they're in business to lend money. You'd have thought I was asking him to do me a favor, instead of putting him in the way of a little business."

"Well, there's not much loose money to hand out, these days," Kate said.

"Oh, he's *got* it," Charlie said. "Don't you worry, he's got it. He just doesn't know when to turn it loose." He put his hands in his pockets and tilted back in the frail dining room chair.

"Tilt down, Charlie," Kate said. "You'll break that little chair."

Obediently he tilted forward onto four legs. "Now, something just struck me," he said thoughtfully. "Ralph's got plenty of credit. If I could put this thing across to him, between us we could probably scare up the money." His face lit up happily. "Just think, Mrs. A.," he said, "we could buy back the house, at least make a start on it."

Sarah D. closed *The Delineator*, got up, came over to the table, and leaned on Charlie's shoulder. "We can't ask Ralph for money, Charlie," she said, "not even for a good investment. We can't ask Ralph for any favors."

"Favors!" Charlie said. "I'd be doing him a favor if I let him in on this. Come on, baby, and help us."

Sarah D. sat down and picking up a pecan examined it thoughtfully. "I don't think Ralph can stretch his credit any farther than it's stretched," she said. "You forget how many places his money has to be put. It's a miracle he could get the credit to get started again, after Mr. Wilcox took bankruptcy and they had that trouble with Alderan."

"I know exactly how old Ralph gets his credit," Charlie said. "Have you met Rife McKay, the president of the Farmers' Trust over there?"

Sarah D. shook her head and Charlie laughed delightedly. "Well," he said, "when they met, it must have been love at first sight. He's Ralph all over again. Presbyterian elder, on the school board, loves to hunt. He even has that 'Ha, ha, ha' belly laugh like Ralph's. And he's the only man I know besides Ralph that I'd be ashamed to tell a dirty joke to. (Not that they'd refuse to listen, mind you. I don't mean that. They're just too — too pure.) Anyway, after the way Ralph behaved in that bankruptcy proceeding, I betcha old McKay'd lend him the whole bank if he asked for it."

"What's a bankruptcy proceeding?" Anna asked.

"Charlie, you shouldn't talk like that in front of the child," Kate said.

"She's not a child," Charlie said. "She's a half-grown woman. Aren't you, sweetheart? And I haven't said a word about her daddy I wouldn't say to Charlotte or to anyone."

"Charlie," Sarah D. said, "I don't know whether you know it or not, and it's strictly in the family, but Ralph has had the whole support of Miss Celestine and Miss Julia ever since the Hibernia Bank failure. And he's so hardheaded he won't get them out of that huge, expensive old house and into a sensible little apartment, so he's pouring money down a rathole out there. I guess Waldo sends his mother a little something when he can, but James is hardly able to take care of his own family, and I know the McGovern place is just barely paying its taxes. Besides that, Ralph sends Mama thirty-five dollars every month. He has a wife and three children to support, he's up to his ears in McGovern and Wilcox debts, and he's trying to get a new business started. We simply can't ask him for anything else."

"What's a bankruptcy proceeding?" Anna asked again.

"Besides which," Sarah D. said, "it was Alderan's shenanigans that finished off McGovern and Wilcox. I think we'd better give Ralph a little breather as far as in-laws are concerned."

"Are you putting me in the class with Alderan?" Charlie asked, "when I'm sitting here faithfully picking out pecans and minding my own business?" He grinned at her.

"No, sweetie, I'm not. I'm just saying Ralph has got enough *family* to choke a horse. Have you forgotten that Sis doesn't even speak to him if she can help it?"

"All right, all right, I give up," Charlie said, "but you mark my words, somebody's going to make big money out of that."

"What's a bankruptcy proceeding?" Anna said.

"When your business fails," Sarah D. said, "and you don't have any money to pay your debts, the law lets you do something that's called 'taking bankruptcy.' That means that the people you owe money to can divide whatever you have, what are called your assets, among them, and then they can't try to make you pay any more. It's a way for people who are hopelessly in debt to get a new start."

"Did Father do that?" Anna asked.

"Anna," Kate said, "haven't you heard your mother and father talking about all that? Didn't you ask *them* about it?"

Anna shook her head. "How could I ask them when I didn't even know what to ask them about?" she said.

Sarah D. laughed. "They probably never even thought about telling you," she said. "I don't guess they thought you'd be interested. But I'm sure your mother would tell you if you asked. What happened was that Mr. Wilcox took bankruptcy, and since he was your father's partner, your father was liable for his debts. Do you know what I am talking about?"

Anna nodded.

"But your father didn't want to do that. In other words, he didn't want to say that he wouldn't pay all his debts as soon as he was able to pay them. Under the law there is nothing wrong with it, but it seemed wrong to him. So he'll have to pay all the debts of the partnership."

The front door banged and they heard Sis's step in the parlor, quick and firm and light. She came into the dining room, pulling off her gloves and hat and smiling her small, crooked smile. She said hello to everyone in her quiet, controlled voice, and then hovered over the fire, shivering. "It's too cold for any use," she said.

"How was the movie?" Sarah D. said.

Anna did not need Sarah D.'s warning glance to know that

the subject of conversation would be changed, that they were not to mention what they had been talking about. *You'd think she would look different, wouldn't you?* she said to herself. *You'd think it would show.* She examined Sis carefully, her slight, frail body, her neatly waved, short, graying brown hair, the tiny wrinkles in her soft, dry skin, her wide, thin, sad mouth, her worn tweed suit and shirtwaist, fastened at the collar with an onyx brooch. She looked just as she had always looked.

I'll bet you never saw your father look like this, Alderan said.

Oh, Ralph, not again, her mother said.

I *love you,* she said to Sis, weeping by the telephone. I *love you.*

Anna came back to the dining room and heard Sis say, "We didn't go after all. Caroline wanted to call on Miss Lucy and Miss Sally and take their Christmas presents, so we went down there and visited awhile."

"How are Lucy and Sally?" Kate asked.

"Poor old things," Sis said. "Shut up in the house together, and you know they never have gotten along. Mama, Miss Sally is pitiful. She's getting blinder by the day, and Miss Lucy is so cross with her — even when we were there, she was cross, so you know when they're alone, she must lead her a dog's life."

"Come on, Sis, and help us pick out pecans," Charlie said. "Mrs. A. and I have been trying to get your lazy sister to help us for an hour."

Sis sat down at the table and began to shell nuts. She sat straight and worked rapidly and with every nutmeat that dropped into the bowl the tension in the warm, smoky room grew tighter.

Sarah D. got up restlessly. "All right, all right, I give up," she said. "Come on, Anna, you help, too. We'll get them all picked out tonight, and then, Mama, you can get them wrapped and in the mail tomorrow."

"Have you made the list?" Kate said.

They all began to talk at once.

"Well, we want to send some to Jane Richardson. And then there are Ralph and Charlotte's, and Will and Eunice's, and I'd like to send Carrie a box. You know she always sends my Charlotte something handsome for Christmas."

"How about Bill Dupré, Charlie?"

"And the Harper girls, and — "

"I'd like to give some to Caroline."

"Hey, wait a minute, wait a minute," Charlie said. "I've already worn my hands down to the finger bones. We'll be picking 'em out for another week, at that rate."

"Never mind about Caroline," Sis said stiffly. "I'll pick some out for her."

"Come on, now, Sis," Charlie said good-naturedly, "I was only kidding."

"Well, it's the most brilliant idea we ever had for Christmas," Kate said, looking around anxiously at her family and then smiling encouragingly at Sis. "Look how many we've got, and the tree is still loaded. I can get a little nig to thrash it tomorrow for a quarter and we can pick up another twenty or thirty pounds. We shouldn't have to buy presents for anyone but the children."

"Have you seen the sweater Sis is knitting for little Ralph, Anna?" Sarah D. said. "Let me show you."

Sis continued to shell nuts, her head bent over the bowl so that her face was hidden.

"She hasn't seen the scrapbook you made for him, either," Kate said. "Get that."

Sarah D. started into the front bedroom and Charlie cautioned her, "Shhh. Don't wake Charlotte and the baby." In a few minutes she came back with an almost completed sweater and an enormous scrapbook made of bright red Indianhead, the edges pinked and the back fastened with a silk tassel. RALPH'S BOOK, the cover said in big letters cut from newspaper headlines, and below the title was a picture from the cover of a *Saturday Evening Post* of a little boy gazing passionately into the eyes of a dirty, feisty-looking dog. She laid it on the table beside Anna. "Now, you mustn't tell when you get home," she said. "It's a surprise."

"Oh! it's just like Ralph and Bo," Anna cried. "Won't he love it?"

Inside was the story of Ralph's life in pictures out from old magazines, accompanied by silly poems composed by Sarah D. Anna giggled over the pictures and poems, and then began to examine the sweater.

Sis looked up. "I dropped a stitch in there, and it's a little bit messy," she said, pointing to the waistband with her nut-pick.

"I think it's beautiful," Anna said.

"Just wait till you see what I have for you, dearie," Sis said. "You'd never guess what it is in a thousand years."

Creak, crack. Creak, crack. Creak, crack. The nutcracker groaned and the pecans exploded rhythmically into the bowl in Charlie's lap. Sis shelled her pile faster and faster. Everyone was quiet for a few minutes, and then the nervous compulsion to talk, to draw Sis out of herself, struck them all again.

"Well, Sis, what did Caroline have to say for herself?" Kate said. "Did she know any gossip?"

Charlie got up and started for the kitchen again. "Anybody want a drink of water?" he said. "Sis, can I get you a glass of milk?"

"No, thank you," she said. "No, Mama, she didn't know a thing."

The door from the dining room into the front bedroom opened slowly and they all looked up. Billy Dupré in a drag-gled cotton nightgown, his cheeks rosy with sleep, an old piece of blanket clutched in his round baby arms, stood there, blinking in the light.

"Did I hear someone call me?" he said in a businesslike voice.

Charlie, on his way to the kitchen, stopped, burst into a roar of laughter and went to pick him up. "It was me, Billy Boy," he said, holding him tight and kissing the top of his head. "I just couldn't live without you another minute."

"I thought it was Santa Claus," he said. "Isn't it Christmas yet?"

Charlie sat down at the table with his son and gave him a pecan. "Next week," he said. "You've got another week to wait."

"You're going to give that child a stomach-ache," Kate said, "feeding him pecans at this time of night."

"Don't worry, Mama," Sarah D. said. "His stomach's made of cast iron."

Sis put down her nutpick and shoved aside the bowl of pecans. "Come to me, Billy," she said, holding out her arms. "Come, sit in Sis's lap a minute."

Charlie let him go and he climbed into Sis's lap and lay back sleepily against her shoulder. "Is it tomorrow?" he asked.

Sis put both arms around the child and laid her cheek against his soft hair. "Just about, baby. Why don't you shut your eyes and take a little nap, and in a minute it'll be tomorrow."

The child sat up and frowned at Sis. "You're too bony," he said. "You stick me awake." He climbed down and went over to his mother.

Anna opened her mouth to laugh, but then she looked at Sis and saw the expression on her face, and closed it again. Sarah D. picked Billy up and began to pat his back and sing softly.

> The sons of the prophet are brave men and bold,
> And quite unaccustomed to fear,
> But the bravest by far in the ranks of the Shah
> Was Abdul the Bulbul Amir.

Charlie got up again. "Well," he said, "I'm still thirsty. Water, anyone?"

"Why don't you drink a glass of milk, Sis?" Kate said. "You're getting entirely too thin."

"No, *thank* you, Mama," Sis said, "I'm not hungry." She had begun to work again, and she spoke without looking up.

"That's a funny song to sing to a baby," Anna said. "Does he like it?"

"He's *crazy* about it," Sis said. "Isn't that absurd?"

"But you ought to eat more," Kate said. "You really should."

Sarah D. frowned at Kate and shook her head, still patting Billy and singing softly.

> Vile infidel, know, you have trod on the toe
> Of Abdul the Bulbul Amir.

In the kitchen Charlie began to hum, "Ta tah, *dum*, tah, *dum*, tah, *dum*," and then to whistle clearly and penetratingly above Sarah D.'s soft tuneless voice a popular song a few seasons old, "In the Valley of the Moon." Anna was leaning on her elbows watching Sis's quick fingers. "I just wish I could shell pecans or peel shrimp as fast as you can," she said.

Sis did not look up, and Anna, watching her fast-moving hands, had the curious sensation that they were the only part of her that was alive. She looked at Gran and Sarah D. and they, too, were as motionless and tense as statues. Sarah D. had stopped singing. Billy was asleep.

Everyone seemed to be listening to something, but the only sound in the house, except for the loud ticking of the clock, was Charlie's whistling in the kitchen. He began to sing, over and over the only line he knew, "Tah, tah, dum, tah, dum, tah, dah. In the valley of the moon."

Gran and Sarah D. both started talking.

"Sis, I wish you would . . ."

"Mama, when you go to market in the morning . . ."

"Excuse me," Sis said quietly, politely. She got up and without looking at anyone started up the stairs, not walking fast and lightly as she always did, but slowly and carefully, looking down at each riser as if she were expecting to stumble over a monster or a pot of gold.

When she was gone Sarah D. and Kate looked at each other, and then Kate closed her eyes, rested her forehead on her hands, and sighed.

Charlie came back into the room, still singing.

"Hush," Sarah D. said sharply. She sat quite still so as not to disturb the sleeping baby.

"Huh?"

"Shhh."

He stood in the doorway, bewildered. "What's the matter with you?" he said. "What's going on?"

Kate did not even open her eyes.

Anna picked up Sarah D.'s magazine and looked down at it unseeing, pretending to read. Her heart pounded with anxiety.

"Charlie, how *could* you?" Sarah D. whispered fiercely. "How *could* you?"

"Honey, I don't even know what you're talking about," he said.

"That *song*," Sarah D. said. "Don't you know that was Alderan's song?"

Charlie looked around and saw that Sis was gone. "Well, for God's sake," he said. "Of all the damn foolishness. If she can't listen to a damn song!"

"Just try to be careful, Charlie," Sarah D. said. "When you're around her try to be careful, will you?"

Charlie turned ruefully to Anna. "You see how it is, honey," he said. "I'm snakebit. I can't *ever* do anything right."

"Oh, *Charlie*," Sarah D. said.

"But I was just trying to help. How was I to know she'd get upset? I was just trying to cheer us up. That's all. I'm getting so I'm scared to open my mouth around here."

Upstairs they heard the water gurgling down the drain in a flood.

"What's she trying to do, wash herself away?" Charlie said.

Kate picked up a piece of newspaper and braced it stiffly against the side of the table for a dustpan. She swept a pile of loose pecan shells into it and dumped them into the paper under the nutcracker. "Go to bed, all of you," she said. "Go on to bed. I'll clean up." She touched Sarah D. lightly on the shoulder. "Maybe tomorrow will be a better day," she said.

Oh, to Die
for Love

ANNA accepted without further question her family's verdict that Alderan was a bad, *common* man, and that he had ruined Sis's life. The only person she never heard mention Alderan was her father, and as she had never heard him talk personally of anyone, she did not notice his silence. In fact, she dismissed Sis and Alderan and their troubles from her mind. More and more self-absorbed, she hesitated at a brink in time, poised to dive into her own life, and she could waste herself no more thinking about anyone else's.

She was a sophomore in high school. She had moved, the year before, from the intimacy of a small grade school to the echoing vastness of the huge high school that served the town of Eureka and the surrounding farm lands. For a year she had been absorbed in getting over the change, for she was shy among strangers and could establish herself only gradually in a comfortable niche. Besides, she was taken up with new feelings that were beginning to stir, and with the commonplace, passionate desire of a young girl to be beautiful and popular. Sometimes, alone in her room, thinking of a green-eyed boy who had once taken her to a movie on Saturday afternoon and held her hand in the intimate darkness, she threw her arms around the fat post of her bed and tenderly kissed it. She anxiously examined the two or three reddish pimples that appeared from time to time on her face; and on Saturday mornings she submitted without a murmur to the elaborate facials and egg shampoos which her mother administered, even though on Saturday afternoons she might take to the trees to play Tarzan with little Ralph and the neighborhood children.

She studied geometry that second year in high school, and for the first time her teacher was a man.

She had been falling in love with her teachers every year since she had walked into the first-grade class room her first day in grammar school and had seen a gentle expectant face above a pile of dog-eared *Baby Ray*'s. In every case the sequence was the same. To begin with, the new grade was a nightmare, a threatening world where everyone else had the skill and self-confidence in human relations that she lacked. Shy and inarticulate among strangers, she suffered for days and weeks in silence; the effort to make friends, to step outside herself, was beyond her. Then the teacher's kindness drew her slowly out of the nightmare, charmed away her self-obsession, and opened a new door to her.

She always gave the teacher credit. When she began to be able to read well, in the third or fourth grade, and the language of books burst on her, she gave the teacher credit for opening to her a marvelous new world. Of course, the teacher deserved it — she had opened the door. But the homage she received in payment was exaggerated.

Anna never knew how to communicate her love and gratitude. She was never the teacher's pet, because she was too quiet, too dull. But she was "smart." The more she loved her teachers, the harder she studied, all the while vaguely hoping they understood that the perfect lessons were a gift. She knew no other way to make them love her back. At fourteen, she had still discovered none.

Mr. O'Malley, her geometry teacher that year, was a slight, handsome man in his early thirties, with paper-white skin that flushed easily and burned brick-red in the sun, an upturned Irish nose, a crooked, sorrowful smile, beautiful, wavy black hair, thinning above the flat plane of his white forehead, and a soft, light, flexible voice. His smile seemed to Anna charged with understanding, as if it said, *I've been there; I know what it's like.*

His classroom was on the fourth floor, high above the campus, and, as she climbed toward it each day after lunch, the metal stairs clanging and thundering with hundreds of feet, her heart pounded, not from exertion, but from a mysterious excitement and elation that she recognized from other years and other loves. For a year she climbed the steps to class each day. She did not *think*, but her heart beat with the knowledge that something was going to happen. Every day she entered the classroom and sat in the third row, silent and anonymous. The one-armed desks were arranged in orderly ranks, just as they were in the other rooms; but at the front, on either side of Mr. O'Malley's desk, were two empty seats. About the third week of the semester he moved the two noisiest boys from the back row to the seats on his left, appointed one of the girls roll-keeper, and moved her to a place on his right. The roll-keeper, Marthe, was small, animated, and French, one of those girls who come into the world knowing how to make a man pay attention. Anna envied her all year. She responded with such poise and gaiety to Mr. O'Malley's gentle teasing, and besides, she had curly hair. Sometimes she stayed after class to go over the roll with him, or even helped him grade papers.

Anna knew she lacked the glamour that attracted Mr. O'Malley to her curly-haired rival. Her face was round and broad-nosed, without form or distinction; her fine, ash-blond hair never stayed combed, no matter how she struggled with it, and was inclined to frizz when she had a permanent; she wore a little pale pink lipstick, but somehow it was always eaten off ten minutes after she left home. In the mornings before school and after Katherine was out of the way, Anna looked into the bathroom mirror, drew in her cheeks, drooped her eyelids, and tried to look sultry, but she could never summon the courage to look sultry at school. It did not seem to come naturally, and she was afraid Mr. O'Malley might think her ridiculous.

As the weeks passed, the air of her geometry class seemed to her more and more charged with excitement. She sat still and tight as a coiled spring, and every word he said turned a screw in her heart and wound the coil tighter. She tore the corners off all the pages in her notebook and rolled them into tiny cones. Sometimes, when she was sure no one was looking, she peeped at him through her paper spyglass, catching his face for a moment and framing it in the tiny circle of light; but it slipped immediately away.

She studied. Mr. O'Malley learned that he could count on her for a correct answer, and at midterm he even asked her to help him grade the examination papers. But the unidentifiable *something* did not happen. Toward the end of the year she began to worry about how she was going to hang on to him, for she knew that until it did happen they could not part. He did not teach any of the courses she had to take the following year, but he was adviser for the math club. Desperately, since she could think of no other way to hang on to him, she decided to join the math club. She had never been a talker, but she imagined herself lecturing, soft-voiced, brilliant, and enthralling (like Mr. O'Malley), to a fascinated gathering of the nation's greatest minds. And so, timid and silent as ever in the presence of the juniors and seniors who made up the majority of its membership, she joined.

Here, in a high school club room furnished with knife-scarred desks and cloudy blackboards, the *something* happened. Here a door blew open for Anna that let in the winds from all the ends of the world.

Mr. O'Malley began his lectures with the Greeks, and the syllogism:

> All men are mortal.
> Socrates is a man.
> Therefore, Socrates is mortal.

Or, to give it the false twist:

> All men are mortal.
> Socrates is mortal.
> Therefore, Socrates is a man.

From Aristotle and Pythagoras, he moved on to the relationship between mathematics and philosophy and logic, to numbers as the repository of absolute truth. He gave an elementary course in logic, touching lightly and confidently such matters as *a priori* and *a posteriori*. He talked of Roger Bacon and Francis Bacon, of Descartes, Einstein, and Whitehead.

Anna was fascinated. She forgot in her excitement that Mr. O'Malley was her reason for being there. Without recognizing exactly what was happening, she learned that it was possible to generalize. She had never before dreamed of the power of human reason, or of the excitement of learning to use her mind as skillfully as a carpenter uses his tools. She began to grope toward a yet unarticulated conviction about herself, a dawning knowledge that she would always need to bring order to the chaos of experience, to view her life whole from a position outside it, to understand and put to use all the layers of remembered experience that lay like the strata of geologic time beneath her life. She was never to forget that year, when every idea was new, and a blinding radiance broke over all the wondering, unselfconscious past. The incoming tide had begun to wash into her rock-bound pool, and joyfully she felt herself drawn out of it into the sea.

And besides all this, Mr. O'Malley had exorcised her most haunting fear — the fear of not being accepted, of being inadequate to a situation, the peculiarly adolescent fear of inadequacy that has to do not with worth but with charm. She had always been afraid that she could not make herself beloved, that she would be alone. She was never again to feel that fear in all its self-obsessed, destroying force. Mr. O'Malley had released her from it, and she would have walked over hot coals for him. It never occurred to her that he was not perfect, that he might need to use *her* as she had used him.

Mr. O'Malley was a marvelous adviser. He had the combination of qualities that makes a successful high school teacher — a quick mind, an ability to enjoy functioning at the adolescent level, and great personal charm. His students worked for him without stint, and the harder they worked, the more exciting the results. When they were stumped, he could supply an answer; more important, he could help them find an answer for themselves without making a judgment on its right or wrongness.

The school year wound down to its end, slower and duller, but Anna was perfectly happy. She had secured her future. When she said goodbye to Mr. O'Malley the last day of school, he laid his arm across her shoulders for a moment and smiled at her. "Parting is such sweet sorrow . . ." She almost wept.

The summer went by. She scarcely thought of him. Instead, she bought a *History of Western Art*, the Modern Library edition of *War and Peace*, and Vincent Sheean's *Personal History*. She read all three and a great many other equally ill-assorted books, whatever came by chance to her attention, understanding almost nothing of any of them, but confident that she understood them all.

The first day of school in the fall Anna went confidently to the math club room. Now, instead of living in the twilight of Mr. O'Malley's attention, she knew she was one of the chosen few, the Inner Circle, as they called themselves. She even learned like the seniors, to call Mr. O'Malley "Paul." For months she stayed in a state of ecstatic, intoxicated excitement. At the beginning of Activities Period each day she would walk into the math club room and look around with possessive pride at the long tables covered with notebooks and card files, the shelves of reference books against the walls, the lectern at the front of the room, the blackboards scrawled with outlines, stick men, initials, formulas for trisecting the angle, attempts at fourth-dimensional figures, and snatches out of Shakespeare. Her new friends would be sitting at the tables or tilted against the wall in attitudes of negligent confidence and ease, talking or working as they chose, looking up to say, "Hi, Anna," as she came in, or "Hey, come here; I want to ask you something," or "How about a date Friday night?" It didn't matter what they said. She would be overwhelmed with joy. She would stand watching her new friends, wanting to climb onto a table and shout for joy.

I belong, she kept telling herself. *I belong.*

Her happiness was so new and lovely that not two months of the fall had passed before half the boys in the senior class thought they were in love with her. With characteristic single-mindedness she settled immediately on Taylor Kelly to love back. Her life was complete. Beginning the journey where loneliness waits hungrily at every empty station, she mistook the beginning for the end. She had arrived at the city of bliss.

She began to go out with Taylor in November of that year. She was a junior, at the age when a girl says to herself, Juliet was only fourteen. Taylor was a senior, the most important man in the senior class. The acquaintance, begun after work sessions in the math club room, was casual enough at the beginning for Anna to carry her end of it. If she had thought when he first began to tease her and walk her home from school that he might ask her for a date, she would have been paralyzed with timidity. But he walked her home as if it were the most natural thing in the world and it became so.

Taylor did not displace Mr. O'Malley in Anna's heart. She had not the least difficulty giving them both as much of herself as they could possibly manage. It never occurred to her that there might be a conflict, because she did not call her devotion to Mr. O'Malley being *in love,* and never thought of falling into the amorous daydreams about him that kept her at a pitch of excitement about Taylor. Instead, she credited Paul with giving her Taylor. After all, he had brought them together.

But childhood's habit of silence and secrecy were still strong in Anna, and it never occurred to her to tell Paul how much she owed him or how godlike he was in her eyes. She knew well enough that her most serious thoughts, if she made the mistake of confiding them, might be considered amusing even by those who loved her most. But she had to put her happiness somewhere, and so she began to keep a journal.

January 16

I have just begun to realize what life is all about. Dear Journal, *I believe I have grown up!* The influence of serious people like Paul and Taylor is changing me so fast I hardly know myself from one week to the next. When I think about all the things I used to believe were important and all the things I used to think I'd do, like be a missionary and go to Africa, and the silly games we used to play, like rubber guns, and tree houses, and digging a cave in the back yard, it's so embarrassing I don't think I can be the same person. I'm *not* the same person. There's a dividing line between child and woman and sometime this fall, without knowing it, I stepped across the line.

"When I was a child, I spake as a child, I understood as a child, I thought as a child: but when I became a man, I put away childish things." (I Cor. 13:11.)

The long afternoons after school in the math club room, working and talking together. ("Every item derives its truth and its every meaning from its relevence to the background which is the unbounded universe." You could think about that for years.) The picnics on Indian Creek with Paul and the crowd lying on the pine needles loafing the afternoons away; the ride home from Clayton, Taylor and me sitting on the front seat, Paul driving, talking, his voice quiet in the darkness, his quick mind penetrating, analyzing, recreating, serious and then joking, talking on and on in the quiet darkness, with the rush of the car through the still air murmuring beneath the sound of his voice, until I feel half hypnotized.

This brings me to something new, Journal, something I have held back for weeks because I couldn't believe it myself. *I'm in love, and he loves me.* It's Taylor, of course. Who else could it be? I will append a short character sketch of Taylor. He is brilliant, *brilliant,* a fine speaker, has read everything. He's ugly, I suppose — mouth too big, nose too long and turned up a little at the end, but beautiful brown eyes. He is erratic, and irresponsible, funny, entertaining, gay, fascinating. He's editor of *The Spyglass*, number one debater, etc. Anyhow, that's all words, *words*, and what's happened to us makes words seem inadequate and useless.

Paul approves!

This brings me to the unpleasant items in tonight's entry. *Approval!* Why can't people let you alone? Why can't they let you go when the time comes to let go? Why can't they understand when you are old enough to run your life and make your own decisions? I won't do my children like that. They'll be *free* when they're grown. I won't try to hold on to them past my time.

Can you believe it when I say that Mother is sitting in the room as I write this? I could reach out and touch her, and yet she's as far away from me as if I were on Christmas Island. She knows nothing of my thoughts, nothing of the hot seething of my soul that I feel sometimes will reach such a pitch, I will burst like an exploding star, and little bits of me will go whirling through cold black space forever. Her experience is so limited, her life so bound by conventional formulas of behavior that have nothing to do with reality . . . How can she or anyone know what is happening to me? I have the feeling that no one, *no one* has experienced this. Even the classical lovers, Romeo and Juliet, Tristan and Isolde, and who was it swam the Hellespont . . . No, that's not right; other people fall in love, maybe not with this terrible intensity, but they do fall in love. Then they grow old and forget what it was like. She sits there, little and shrunken . . . Have I ever characterized my mother, Journal? No, I suppose I think you're her child, too, but you're not. Like Paul and Taylor, you belong to me and to no one else. Anyhow, she sits, reading. She's always reading — some bourgeois book about Edwardian England or something like that. She has the squarest jaw in the world and believe me, she lives up to it. Between her and Father, who is less *vociferous*, but more *immovable*, my life around home is *pure hell*.

Like the other night. Taylor and I walked out Jackson Street to the little bridge that crosses Rattlesnake Bayou. We sat on the bridge, swinging our feet over the side, a long time. It was the dark of the moon and the world was black as the Styx all around us. As far as you could see down the bayou, the fireflies bloomed and vanished, thousands of them, beautiful and silent in the silent night. Taylor told me he loved me, and I won't write about that, I can't, but later we walked home and were standing on the front steps kissing goodnight when father opened the door.

"Eleven o'clock, Anna," he said, and slammed it shut again.

When I went in, I told him I couldn't stand being treated as if I were doing something shameful when I was consummating the most sacred experience of my life. I told him that I loved Taylor, and that we were going to marry some day, and that I intended to kiss him whenever I wanted to.

"Grummph," he said, and went back upstairs.

If you cut him open, you'd probably find a T square, a slide rule, and a Biblical Concordance inside. Well, he can't measure me with his slide rule or guide me with his Concordance. He'll have to find something better than that. In fact, the best thing for him to do is to sit back and take it easy and let me manage from here on in.

But I have gotten off the track (not really, since *approval* is my subject). To go back to Mother, I suppose she doesn't approve of Taylor because his family is Catholic (and even worse, he's not anything) and because in her limited, snobbish way, she doesn't think he's from "a good family." I can just hear her saying *Shantyboat Irish* (I couldn't marry a man who called a Chevrolet a Shivvy), although at least, to give her credit, she doesn't say it to me. She just *snipes, snipes, snipes* all the time. Only one date a weekend with Taylor, be in by eleven o'clock, etc., etc. My God, how can I stand it?

Actually, I can understand a little about their not liking Taylor. I know they think I'm too young to be seriously in love, and I *am* too young. God knows I wish we were five years older. But that can't be helped. I could no more help loving him than I could stop breathing. I see their other objections, too. He's wild, not wild in the conventional sense, I don't mean drinking or anything like that, but a real wild man, and they sense and fear his wildness, his fearlessness, the quality in him that is most his own, and most attractive. I suppose they think the world will beat it out of him, and they don't want me to suffer with him (if they even think or understand that instinctive fear, I mean); but the world couldn't beat anything out of him — destroy him perhaps, but not defeat him. As for the family business, of course that's not even worth mentioning. Anyhow, I know all that about Taylor, and I even understand a little how they feel. They're old and I don't suppose they can help it.

But *Paul!* Why do they dislike *him?* I mean it's absolutely un-fathomable to me. How could anyone not like Paul? I sometimes try to figure out what makes them tick, Father and Mother, I mean. I *want* to understand, I *want* to be reasonable; but I haven't a glim-mer of what they're thinking. Surely they don't begrudge him the affection I have for him. But their attitude toward him is faintly suspicious, and more than faintly contemptuous. I'm going to *con-front* them with it one of these days. Maybe they can justify them-selves. Maybe they can tell me *what* it is they suspect him of. Kid-naping? Murder? Bigamy, maybe? So far, I've been making deduc-tions about what they think of Paul. They don't criticize him openly; it's more a change in tone of voice or expression when they speak of him or to him that they think I don't notice.

I get the craziest ideas. Sometimes I think they're trying to put the hex on him or something, just out of pure spite, just because I love him — not by saying what they think, but by planting a faint doubt in my mind. And they're not the only ones, incidentally. Plenty of the teachers don't like Paul either. They're all jealous, jealous of his ability, of his charm, his popularity with the students, of our loyalty to him. Surely Father and Mother couldn't be jealous of him. I keep beating my brains out trying to figure what it is, what they're afraid of.

The truth is, instead of putting him off they should try to imitate him once in a while. If they could just once try, as he does, to see things from my point of view, maybe we would understand each other. He treats us as if we were intelligent adults, endowed with our normal share of judgment. He knows I love Taylor; he accepts and respects our love. He is so far above the pettiness of the other teachers that they really hate him. He's a grown person, and they're just grown-up children, jockeying for position in a graceless battle for a five-dollar raise, hemming us in with stupid rules and prohibitions whose only purpose is to shore up *their* precarious dignity.

In fact, the long and short of it is, Paul is *on our side*. What else could we ask?

Maybe Mother thinks he lets us be too free with him. Could that be it? But the wonderful, magic thing about it is the freedom. Maybe she thinks he is too young to be a proper chaperon; he's not much more than thirty. Does she think no one *ever* grows up? *She* grows older and older, hoary with years and experience (she thinks!), and everyone else is arrested at some stage of childhood, never very far from the cradle.

But honestly, I, *I* feel like the little girl who said she couldn't walk when she was a baby because she had no feet. All of a sudden I've grown a fine pair of feet, and all I want is to walk, walk, walk, to walk and run all the time.

Spring comes to Eureka in February — the jonquils and paper-white narcissus and flowering quince and Confederate jessamine bloom, and the first trees trust their buds to the sun. Frost is unheard of after the beginning of March. Anna bloomed with the jonquils, as unconscious of the future as they of the gardener's snips. The young birds sang their love songs, the air hummed with millions of flies and gnats and mosquitoes and tree frogs and bees and wasps and locusts, all crying over and over again, *Here we are, here we are. The world has just been made and here we are.*

Anna and Taylor spent long afternoons swimming or walking or reading together, or sitting at The Fountain Terrace drinking cokes and gazing at each other. Neither of them had much money to spend, but they didn't care. It was 1937 and you could buy a coke and a hamburger for a dime. A date cost twenty cents, plus maybe twenty cents worth of gasoline. If Taylor was *really* broke they walked, or sat on the glider in the side yard and drank lemonade.

Everything about Taylor was bathed in the light of Anna's growing obsession with him. He was homely, as she had written, but his ugly face had in it the beginning of the beauty that was all she really saw. Potential strength and gentleness marked its high, wide cheekbones and eager, intelligent brown eyes, and when he came loping along the sidewalk, almost running in his eagerness to see her, every straight brown hair of his head, every awkward gesture of his young body, was precious to her. He was the answer to her need to begin a new life — courageous, careless of convention, moved by the conviction that he would put a mark on the world. She did not think it ridiculous when he said that at seventeen Alexander had conquered the world.

Every afternoon during the spring and summer of that year Taylor came to see her. The Episcopal Church clock was within hearing distance of her house, and when it struck five, Taylor started home. He always said, "Walk part way with me," and holding hands and swinging their arms they set out. The way was three blocks. At one end of the walk was Anna's house, tall and severe New England Colonial, with narrow clapboards and a gray slate roof that would last forever. At the other end was Kelly's, ramshackle, fifty-year-old Victorian bastard, big enough for all the nine members of his Irish Catholic family. The blocks were all side streets. The houses along each backed up to the alley down the middle. No one ever looked out of those side windows to see them walk by every afternoon, hand in hand.

"Look at us, look at us," Anna wanted to say. "We're in love. You know Taylor Kelly, don't you? Everyone knows who Taylor Kelly is. Well, he's in love with *me!*"

They passed the fence that hid one back yard, weighed down and sweet with honeysuckle, and stopped to pull the stamens through the trumpets and suck the drop of honey that swelled out at the base. Then they crossed the street, and walked by the bishop's garden with its cloister and shrine.

When they reached Taylor's house, they sat down on the curb to finish whatever they had been talking about, and then Taylor walked halfway back with her. In the middle of the second block they sat down again, by this time giggling at themselves. But the game never flagged. Anna walked half of half with him, and then he walked half of half of half with her, and by that time it was five-thirty, and they both knew they *had* to go home. Taylor walked back to the true halfway mark in the middle of the second block, and there they said goodbye.

For almost three years that stretch of sidewalk meant Taylor to Anna. If he had telephoned and she knew he was coming, she sat on the front steps, waiting for him to turn the corner with his long, loose-jointed, hurrying stride, swinging his arms and grinning for joy. If he was late, she played a game with herself. *The third person who comes around the corner will be Taylor,* or *I'll see him before I can count to two hundred.* He was often late. He was not systematic, and he was so full of life and health and intelligence and enthusiasm that there was never enough time for everything. When he finally arrived, it was always with, *I can't wait to tell you what I've been doing,* or, waving a book, *Just wait until you read this.* Whatever it was, Anna thought that it was brilliant, and that Taylor was the first person who had ever thought of it. He swept her into the current of his life and the water was fine.

But afternoons together, and one evening date a week can't fill the twenty-four hours of the day. Anna was still at home, a member of a family, although there were times when she would have wished them all out of existence if she could have. She stayed furious with her father and mother all that year and the next. This was because she saw her own life in a way peculiar to sixteen — as if everything were happening once and forever. One life, one love, one joy, one sorrow, one rage. The idea of protecting herself from pain, of saving herself for another round or another match, of finding her adversaries suddenly transformed into allies, would have been repugnant to her even if she had had experience enough to formulate it. She was hopelessly ignorant of the sources of her own motives and emotions; she could not possibly understand anyone else's.

She believed without question that only her parents' interference prevented her getting to a happy ending. She did not know that real stories cannot have happy endings, only happy beginnings, that there are no endings except parting and death, and even these are beginnings for someone. And, thinking to arrive at herself, she had thrown away everything that had been given her, all the credit stored up during a childhood spent among people who had been content to let her find herself slowly, undisturbed, in the green forests of her imagination.

The trouble began the following year. Taylor went off to a small college upstate where he had a scholarship. He came home weekends, hitchhiking both ways, but the days between were a torment of waiting. During the week, at school, Anna continued to spend her study hall and activities periods in the math club room. She worked and studied harder than ever, not only because she loved the work, but because it made the weekdays pass more quickly. She was a senior now, and she had commitments and responsibilities that she took seriously. She stayed late after school almost every day, enjoying her own importance, and also, more and more, Paul O'Malley's companionship and flattery.

She was walking up the stairs toward the math club room one afternoon after school when she heard the clang of footsteps on the empty stairs. The building was almost empty, echoing strangely in her ears. The loud steps broke into a run and she looked back. Paul was hurrying to catch up with her. She stood waiting between the second and third floors until he came even with her and stopped, breathing hard. He caught her hand and they climbed on together. He held her hand with his thumb on the back and the tips of his fingers against her palm, and squeezed it abruptly two or three times, as if he were giving a secret grip of some kind. Anna looked at him for a minute, puzzled, and then decided to pretend she hadn't felt it.

"Why don't you stay and help us this afternoon?" she said. "Louis and I are going over the talk he's going to make next week."

He laughed. "You're a funny little girl," he said.

"What do you mean?"

"Don't you know what this means?" he said, and squeezed her palm again with the tips of his fingers.

For a second the old uneasy feeling that she was not going to make the right response rushed over her. But she *didn't* know.

"No. What?"

"It means, *Will you?* And you're supposed to squeeze back."

She knew he was joking, and she groped for an amusing, sophisticated answer. They left the stairs and turned down the hall toward the math club room. She could see Louis sitting just inside the door, his desk tilted back against the wall, scribbling furiously on a three-by-five file card. Mrs. Gladden, her Latin teacher, dish-faced and stern, passed them with a curt nod and a disapproving stare. Anna knew she was thinking that Mr. O'Malley had committed a breach of dignity by holding her hand, and for once she was inclined to agree. She wanted to pull loose and make an excuse to follow Mrs. Gladden down the hall, but she did not. She looked down at her hand, still held tightly in his, as if it did not belong to her, and left herself time, before they were in the math club room, only to say "Silly," in an incredulous voice. She couldn't think of anything else to say.

Mr. O'Malley stopped in the doorway. "I can't stay this afternoon," he said. "Faculty meeting." He walked down the hall toward his own classroom.

One afternoon about a week later Anna had stayed after school quite late and was gathering her books to go home when she heard Mr. O'Malley's familiar step echoing down the empty hall. He came in and sat down.

"I'm tired, Anna," he said. "Come sit here and talk to me a little while."

Her heart began to thump as it had used to when she climbed the stairs toward his room her sophomore year, thinking, *Something's going to happen. Something's going to happen.*

"What's the matter?" she asked.

"These fools around here," he said. "It's like swimming in molasses to try to get anything accomplished. If I were principal for about six weeks, I could set a lot of things straight."

"What's the matter?" she repeated.

"Oh, it's a long story, Anna," he said. "I won't burden you with it. Matter of fact, it's a pretty trivial, shabby matter, rooted in a conspiracy against me by several teachers who shall remain nameless. Jealous cats who can't stand the thought that if old Sexton ever dies the school board will probably make me principal. They're always trying to undermine me one way or another."

"You ought to be principal," she said, "except what would we do then?"

"Oh, you'd get along all right. Out of sight, out of mind. At least that's the way I've always found folks are."

"I'm not like that," Anna said softly. "I'll *never* forget you."

"You're not, eh? And how about old Taylor? Hmmm? You think he's being true to you?"

"I hadn't thought about it," Anna said. "But I know I miss him and he misses me."

"So you miss old Taylor. Tell Paul about it."

She shook her head. "You know," she said.

"Anna, I don't know what I'd do without you," he said. "Nobody in this whole damn school, in fact, in this whole damn town, cares whether I live or die, except you."

"Everybody loves *you*," she said. "I just wish I thought

someday I could make people care for me as much as they do for you."

He slipped one hand under her breast, and with the other lifted her face and kissed her.

"You're a sweet thing," he said. "You know I love you."

"I love you, too, Paul," she said. Her body was rigid, and his soft, wet kiss was still on her lips. She felt the alternations of a great pressure against her ears and then a rushing away and a vacuum, as if the empty, creaking building were breathing for her in huge, unhappy sighs. He pressed his hand against her breast and drew her closer.

"I've got to go," she said. "It's nearly five."

He let her go at once and stood up. "Can I take you home?"

"Thanks. I've got my car."

They walked to his room together, and she waited while he gathered his books.

Outside the building he looked at her and smiled his crooked, sorrowful smile. "You're not mad at me, are you?" he said.

"How could I be mad at you?"

It happened again the next time he found her alone in the math club room. Terrified every minute that someone might come in on them, feeling not the least quiver of desire, but instead, a sickening revulsion from his hands and his wet kiss, she nevertheless let him kiss her and touch her. She did not break away until she was sure she would not offend him.

After the state-wide scholastic rally, he contrived to take her home last, and when they were alone, parked on a quiet side street to "talk." They had worked hard all day and driven a hundred miles home. Anna was tired and sick at heart as she waited for what she knew would happen. But she could not extricate herself from the situation. She *did* love him and she could not have borne to lose his favor. She could find neither the time, the place, nor the courage to say "Stop. I don't like this," or even to use the easier but equally true excuse that she wanted to be true to Taylor. She must have been transparent to him. He could not have failed to see her for exactly what she was — a child and a willing slave, struggling to deal with miserable, bewildering circumstance. But he never told her what he felt.

Without ever being quite sure what she was avoiding or how she was doing it, Anna was too much a product of Presbyterian moral rectitude to be seduced; and she was also enough a woman to avoid seduction without openly offending. But all the time she went through the motions of responding to and at the same time warding him off, she was so lonely and guilty and confused, it seemed as if her whole life had been pushed awry, like a finished jigsaw puzzle with its pieces just out of line, so that the roofs are on the houses crooked and all the limbs have joints in the wrong places. One trivial incident made the puzzle begin to fall apart.

Mr. O'Malley and Mr. Miller, the football coach, were quite friendly. In fact, Mr. Miller was one of the few teachers Mr. O'Malley had anything to do with. He was a young bachelor, just out of college, but Anna did not think of him as young. To her he was of an age with all the other grown-up people in the world. He wore his trousers below his flat stomach, hanging precariously on his hipbones; he always walked as if he had on tennis shoes; he had heavy shoulders and still, passionate, heavy-lidded eyes; and she was afraid of him. He and Mr. O'Malley had a private joke on the world. It always seemed as if they broke off their conversation when another teacher or a student joined them. They looked at each other with knowing smiles; sometimes they even winked. Anna knew Mr. O'Malley had told Mr. Miller that he had tried to make love to her, that he was still trying. She knew, because when she came up to them in the hall or in the math club room, Mr. Miller looked at her and smiled and winked. With that knowing, salacious smile, he made her their accomplice. It was hateful to her. That sly look made up her mind for her. She would not, she *could* not rebuff Mr. O'Malley, but she found a substitute. She avoided him, without allowing him to see that she avoided him.

During the next few months, the location of Mr. O'Malley's room became painfully important to her. His room was two doors to the right of the central stairwell, and on the same side of the hall. Across the hall and three doors to the left was the math club room. Beyond Mr. O'Malley's room, taking up all the end of the fourth floor, was the oversized classroom that served as a senior study hall. Anna could not reach the study hall or go from study hall to the math club room without passing Mr. O'Malley's door. She had always spent her activities periods in the math club room and now, as a senior and honor student, she was privileged to sign out from the study hall to the math club room. But Mr. O'Malley quite often stood in the doorway of his room to lecture, and sometimes he would set his class a quiz and, following his policy of treating his students like adults, would leave them at work unsupervised while he wandered down to the math club room to chat with whoever happened to be working there, or to the study hall to visit the teacher in charge. He was always wandering the halls of the fourth floor, and, to protect herself from him, Anna followed a rigid set of rules. She never signed out from the study hall to the math club room unless she was sure someone else would be there. She never stayed alone after school. She always contrived to take one of the other students when she went to his room to visit. On her way to study hall every day, she stopped at the head of the stairs and peeped out to see if he was standing in the entrance to his room, before she made a dash past his door.

All her life, school buildings, the smell of chalk dust, the clang of feet on metal stairs would bring her back in an instant to those spring days when she stood, drawn completely into herself, while people stamped and shouted around her; when she stood at the head of the stairs, her heart aching and constricted, peeping down the hall, feeling herself both dishonest and dishonored, before she scurried into the study hall.

She wanted to tell Taylor about it, but she could not. She felt that perhaps, if she told no one, it would stop happening, would turn out not to be true any more. She would avoid him, she would pretend it wasn't true, and perhaps it wouldn't be. Besides, she was ashamed. She knew that her own part in the affair had been shameful, and she was afraid if she told Taylor, he might say, "But if you really loved me, you would never have let him touch you." She knew he might force her into action, and that if he did, it would be just. But she could not act. She could not think of what to say or do. She would lose them both.

All this time Anna did not once stop to think how Paul O'Malley felt. She did not wonder about his wife. She never asked herself if he were using her thoughtlessly for a moment's excitement. She loved him. That was all she felt. She loved him and she did not want to hurt his feelings. She did not wonder at his foolhardiness even in the moments when she was terrified that they might be discovered. Everything he did seemed inevitable to her, and not once did she see the tragic absurdity of his risking his job, his future, perhaps even his marriage for a stolen kiss from an unwilling sixteen-year-old child. If one of his faculty enemies, or worse still, the principal, had walked in on them when Anna was caught, unwilling, in his arms, the knowledge would have been the lever to bring about his ruin. But she did not think about that. It never occurred to her that *he* might be vulnerable. Her attention was all on herself, on keeping his favor, on avoiding his warm, wet kiss, his hand on the body she was saving so confidently for Taylor.

Her misery dragged on all through the spring.

Then, just before graduation, he caught her watching for him. She was on her way to study hall. She was late and the hall was empty when she reached the fourth floor. She knew that if Mr. O'Malley was standing in the doorway of his room, he would leave his class and ask her to come down to the math club room to talk. She stood at the top of the stairs, as she had done dozens of times before, hidden by the jut of the wall, and eased out just enough to look down the hall toward his room. The doorway was empty. He must be busy with his class inside. She stepped out, ready for a dash to the study hall. But he was coming out of the math club room behind her and he had seen her. He had seen her pause, look out furtively, and then slip into the hall. He walked quietly up behind her (she still had not seen or heard him) and put his hand on her arm. Her heart turned over.

"Why are you trying to avoid me, Anna?" he said.

"I'm not," she said. "I'm not. I was just standing here."

"I can't understand it," he said. "I thought you cared about me."

"Ah, Paul," she said, "I do. But I'm so miserable."

He smiled with infinite tolerance. "You, too," he said. "They all leave me, finally — and now you, too."

Anna's eyes filled with tears and she looked down at the floor and shook her head. She wanted to speak out, to tell him how much she loved him, how he had betrayed her, how she had betrayed *everyone*, even herself, but it was beyond her. She wanted to say, "Don't you know that's not the way things are? Don't you see I couldn't bear for you to make them less?" But she thought it would only make him angrier.

He stood and waited for her to speak.

"I've got to go," she said. "I'm late to study hall." She rubbed at her eyes and smeared the tears across her face.

"Never mind," he said before he turned away and left her standing there. "It's all right. I don't suppose you can help it."

Praise God, from whom all blessings flow;
Praise him all creatures here below;
Praise him above ye heavenly hosts;
Praise Father, Son, and Ho-o-o-ly Ghost.
A-men, Ahh-men.

*. . . to think. I have to think. Is it true? Nobody to ask.
How long can I wait to find out?*

*Did we? So close, and then, that . . . Like gold, like
flecks of gold in your blood.*

Anna gripped the rounded top of the pew in front of her
and began to recite: "I believe in God, the Father Almighty,
Maker of heaven and earth: and in Jesus Christ his only Son
our Lord: Who was conceived . . ." She closed her mouth
and stared at the dark, downward slanting church floor.

She looked at her father standing calm and solid beside her,
and then away from him, across the church, at the window
where a long-faced, effeminate Jesus, robed in white and royal
blue and crisscrossed with heavy leading, sat on a rock and
held a lamb in his arms. An inscription was lettered at his
feet: Sacred to the Memory of Mary Elizabeth Stowers/1901–
1917/"Weep not; she is not dead, but sleepeth."

*1901–1917. Sixteen. If I could go to sleep. Sleep and
sleep, wake up and it wouldn't be true. A nightmare.* She
looked down at her bare arm and surreptitiously drew a long
hard scratch across it with her fingernail, watching the skin
draw and turn white for a moment behind her finger. Then
she closed her eyes. *For God's sake.*

The minister's voice, hoarse and deep, penetrated her absorption, and she realized that with the rest of the congregation she had sat down.

". . . Hold your peace, let me alone, that I may speak, and
let come on me what will.

"Wherefore do I take my flesh in my teeth, and put my life
in mine hand?

"Though he slay me, yet will I trust in him; but I will maintain mine own ways before him.

"He also shall be my salvation."

She stared distractedly at the strange minister, not recognizing him, scarcely hearing him. Then she looked again at her father sitting beside her, his face intent, his arms folded across his chest. She looked at his big familiar hands, the bloodstone ring on his little finger, the familiar queer corrugations on his thumbnails, and wanted to reach out and touch him. *Please. Please.*

She turned away.

There must be someone — some stranger who would help me. The preacher?

I know you, she said. *Strange man, I know you. What you would say: Sin, sin, sin. We all sinned in Adam. Dark scary eyes and tufted eyebrows, dark rosy face. Who is he? Dr. Shaw away?*

What difference does it make? Like all the rest. He wouldn't, couldn't help me.

What was it Mother said? The McGoverns are always good. If a McGovern is bad, he ceases to exist. Joking, yes, but . . . Will I cease to exist when they find out?

I'm not one of them. Me.

Is it true? Can it be true? Dumb! If I weren't, I'd know. That book, flowers and tadpoles, girls in white dresses with big sashes smiling at boys in knickers. My God, it's not like that. All fire and night, and your heart . . . Pain and desire.

And even if the book is right, how can you be sure . . . Even just kissing. If you're close enough, how can you be sure it wouldn't happen? And if it didn't, then what's the matter with me?

"There was a man in the land of Uz whose name was Job; and that man was perfect and upright, and one that feared God and eschewed evil," the preacher said.

"I have to think. What to do? They say you can go to some-

one and . . . Yes. And they take a long sharp thing, like, like a
knitting needle, and . . . Yes. You can do that. But how do
you find one? Who tells you where they live? Taylor? No!
Because, if he knew, he would think he had to . . . And it
wouldn't be for me. Everything ruined. I can do it all, alone.
And besides, what a child, *if it turned out not to be true.*

". . . And the Lord said unto Satan, Whence comest thou?
Then Satan answered the Lord, and said, From going to and
fro in the earth, and from walking up and down in it. And the
Lord said unto Satan, Hast thou considered my servant Job, that
there is none like him in the earth, a perfect and an upright
man, one that feareth God, and escheweth evil? Then Satan
answered the Lord, and said, Doth Job fear God for nought?
Hast not thou made an hedge about him, and about his house,
and about all that he hath on every side? Thou hast blessed
the work of his hands, and his substance is increased in the
land. But put forth thine hand now and touch all that he
hath, and he will curse thee to my face. And the Lord said
unto Satan, Behold, all that he hath is in thy power . . ."

If he would let me think . . . Everybody sitting, looking,
pretending to listen, and who cares? Feathered hats and Sun-
day suits. Square ugly church, ugly yellow pews, and dressed-up,
ugly people. And the fans turning, turning. Cool and comforta-
ble. I hate . . . Can I do it? The needle, long sharp needle.
But, if I don't . . . Go away. I couldn't go away without telling
Taylor. Alone. All alone.

The man in the pulpit looked, it seemed to Anna, straight
at her. He raised both hands and rumpled his already unruly
hair. "*Hear* me," he said. "Do you remember what Job said
to his wife when she told him to curse God and die? 'What?
Shall we receive good at the hand of God and shall we not receive evil?' Do you remember what he said to the reproaches
of his friends, to Eliphaz the Temanite who said, 'Remember,
I pray thee, who ever perished, being innocent?' and to Zo-
phar the Naamathite who said, 'If iniquity be in thine hand,

put it far away, and let not wickedness dwell in thy taber-
nacles'?"

I'm not wicked, old man. And God is dead. No one hears me.

"In Job's answer, in the passion of his song, is the secret of
love and prayer:

> . . . will ye contend for God?
>
> Is it good that he should search you out? or as one man mocketh
> another, do ye so mock him?
>
> He will surely reprove you, if ye do secretly accept persons.
>
> Shall not his excellency make you afraid? and his dread fall upon
> you?
>
> Your remembrances are like unto ashes, your bodies to bodies
> of clay.
>
> Hold your peace, let me alone, that I may speak, and let come on
> me what will.
>
> Wherefore do I take my flesh in my teeth, and put my life in
> mine hand?
>
> Though he slay me, yet will I trust in him: but I will maintain
> mine own ways before him.
>
> He also shall be my salvation . . .

"Out of the dark Job spoke, out of the earth of his soul,
where the roots move and draw life from the rain and from
the cold springs that water the roots and crumble granite to
sand. As the oak tree knows, with the cells that draw its leaf's
edges, so he knew. As the vine that twists round the branch,
turning with the sun's motion, so Job turned toward God.

"Past sin, past belief or doubt, past the limits of desire, where
death alone was welcome, Job still looked toward God. Hold
your peace, he said. Let me alone that I may speak, and let
come on me what will. And he made a lament for man's mor-
tality and a song for his passing, a song for the just man and a
song of grief at his destruction; for the lives of the wicked he
sang, who sleep in the dust with the innocent; for God who
treads a path which no fowl knoweth and which the vulture's
eye hath not seen, who putteth forth his hand upon the rock;

he overturneth the mountain by the roots. Job shook off the death of pride and suffering, and God's life flowed through him and washed away his mortal limits. Who dares stop his voice or admonish him?

"The tree groans to the ax and the rabbit shrieks in the fox's jaws. But out of rotting wood and the marrow of dry bones is the soul fed."

He was silent a long moment under the turning fans. Then, "On Sunday morning I hear your children's voices singing, 'love Him, love Him, all ye little children. God is love. God is love.' And I tremble for them in the day they understand what they sing; when they learn that no man buys life or love but with the willingness to die. Do we ever sing that song ourselves — the song we teach our children? Or do we even in our most desperate hours live for vengeance, triumph, or despair?

"Beloved, let us give all things to each other and to God — our loneliness and absence and defeat; our doubt — that other name for death; and pain and sudden joy. And all these gifts accept from Him and from each other. For all that a man can know of God is that love and trust are his human form.

"Trust Him to give thee a voice with which to pray, for He is thy prayer. Trust Him; for trust is the instrument of His love, and the opening lock that lets through the torrent of His life.

"In God's name, Who made us quick, and made us know we die."

And if they take the needle and . . . Then I've killed my baby. Mine and Taylor's. Like I'd killed little Billy, all rosy and brown, running to meet us when we go to Homochitto in the summer. Only mine.

So I swear, I swear I'll never do it. And if they won't help me, if it makes them hate me, I'll go away, and no matter how hard it is, I'll keep the baby and love him. Yes, I'll love him no matter what he ever does.

Vanish. Can't I go to one of those homes like where Teen

teaches Sunday school on Wednesday afternoons? You have to stay a long time afterwards, until you're well. So, I'll be learning something all the time, like to type and take short-hand. And afterwards I'll go far away to a strange city and get a job and take care of him myself. Yes, I could do it. It would be possible . . . Awful. That's what it would really be. Oh, God. Awful.

Can't waste myself thinking how awful . . . First, find out where. Memphis? New Orleans? I couldn't ask anybody. Thirty-five dollars in the bank. Get on a bus and get as far away as it will take me. Maybe Memphis. They're bound to have one there. Somebody can tell me. I'll go to the Salvation Army when I get there. Give a false name. No one will ever know. Vanish.

"But this is not the end of the Book of Job," the preacher said. "No man's life is reaped and sheaved with one heroic deed. His triumph runs through his hands like water and is spilled. 'I know Thou wilt bring me to death,' he says, 'and to the house appointed for all the living. Howbeit he will not stretch out his hand to the grave, though they cry in his destruction.'"

. . . and one day I'll be walking along the street in a strange city, all thin and tired with working so hard, and lonely, with nobody but my baby, and I'll look, and there, coming down the street with that bouncy, loping walk, swinging his arms . . . and I'll think, Taylor, like I do sometimes when I see someone far off who walks like that. And it will be Taylor. And when he sees me — ohhh. He's been looking for me everywhere. Ever since I disappeared he's been wandering from one town to another, looking for me, never giving up. Maybe even two or three years have gone by, but he's still looking, looking. Then, then it'll be different. "Why did you do it?" he'll say. "Why didn't you tell me?" And I can't explain to him how it had to be free, how I've always known he would come, would find me, and everything would be all right at last.

"At the end it almost seems that God is not pleased with Job for the right reasons, and that Job does not respond to God in the right way. Poetry lapses into prose. The burning hour is consumed; the sound of a falling leaf, the cry of a dying child are mysteries still.

"Was it an illusion then, that triumphant loss of self?"

What is he talking about?

"Ah, sufferer, expect nothing from God except one hour in his light, nothing except the water of life, the fire that marks thee His. Trust in these and God may show himself to thee. But afterward thou art still a man.

"To his last day Job must grieve for his dead children. When the wind blows from the wilderness, his soul will still be crushed, and he will be bowed to the dust as he hears the walls crash in and drown their dying shrieks. Who could forget that mortal sound?

"The Lord blessed the latter end of Job more than his beginning; for he had fourteen thousand sheep and six thousand camels, and a thousand yoke of oxen, and a thousand she asses. He had also seven sons and three daughters. And in all the land were no women found so fair as the daughters of Job: and their father gave them inheritance among their brethren. After this lived Job an hundred and forty years, and saw his sons, and his sons' sons even four generations. So Job died, being old and full of days.

"In all the land were no women found so fair as the daughters of Job. They grew fair in the mild light of their father's face, who had once known despair and had put his trust in God.

"And now may grace, mercy, and peace from God the Father, God the Son, and God the Holy Ghost, rest and abide with each of you, now and forever more. Amen."

Stand up. Time to go.

The pulpit steps creaked as the minister came rapidly down and walked toward the back of the church. The organ rang out gustily, and a sigh swept across the congregation, as if they turned away from a troubling dream. A general, cheerful conversation began, as they made their way decorously out into the brilliant summer noon.

"Good morning, Mr. McGovern."

"Good morning."

". . . Mrs. Harding."

"Hello. How do you do?"

"Wasn't that an odd sermon, Mr. McGovern? And so short, too."

"But no one knew Dr. Shaw was going to be away."

"Where did he . . . ?"

"Called out of town. His father is ill."

"But this man . . . Who is he?"

"I don't know. I'd never seen him before in my life."

"Shall we introduce ourselves at the door?"

"Such an odd sermon, Mr. McGovern. What did you think of it?"

"*Job*'s a hard book to take a text from. I know my grandfather always said he would never preach on Job."

Out. One step at a time. One minute at a time. One day at a time.

"Well, what did you think of it?"

"He's not too well grounded in doctrine. I'd say he was a bit unorthodox. I wonder where he was educated."

"I like a longer sermon, myself, something you can get your teeth into."

"And he was such an odd-looking man. I never saw a Presbyterian minister who looked like that. Do you suppose he is a foreigner, Mr. McGovern?"

"He's dark, all right."

One step at a time. One minute. One day

"Mr. McGovern."

"Good morning, Mrs. McGeehee."

"Did you arrange for the substitute this morning? And where did that man go?"

"No, I thought Dr. McGeehee had made the arrangements."

"He didn't even know Dr. Shaw had been called away."

"It's most irregular. And now he seems to be, gone. He didn't even wait to meet the congregation."

Oh, the sky is bright with summer, and see, in the east, pale thunderheads whirl up like steps to heaven, and somewhere drowned in brightness, the stars are shining, and in my ears the air rings like someone struck a bell bigger than the world. Whatever it is, however it comes, I'm waiting.

Journal: August

This has been a strange and terrible summer. Two things have happened to me, and I can write about one, but I must keep the other locked in my heart forever. All through June Taylor was home. Of course, we couldn't see each other every night. Mother still lays down her niggling rules. I went out with Louis and Frank, etc., to please her, and they're all right and we had a good time. But Taylor and I did see each other every day almost, and it seemed as if things got tighter and tighter, as if we couldn't stand being apart, more and more every day. Then that other terrible thing happened, the one I can't talk about. But it wasn't true, and Taylor says I was silly, it doesn't happen that way.

Well, toward the end of June we had a date one night, and everything was like always, and then the next day he didn't call. And the next day he didn't call. And the next day. I was lonesome, crazy, wondering what could have happened. Finally the fourth day I called his mother. I couldn't help it, I had to find out what was the matter. I had thought everything. Maybe he had amnesia; maybe he was in the hospital delirious; maybe he had fractured his skull and was in a coma; maybe he was dying. And Mrs. Kelly said that that morning after the night he'd had the date, he had gotten up, evidently very early, and had left her a note saying he was going away, and that he would write to her, not to worry about him. That was all she knew. She hadn't heard from him since. She would call me if she did. Two weeks, two centuries went by. The postman comes every morning about ten. I'd get up in the morning, already waiting for him. I couldn't tell anyone how it was. No one asked me where Taylor was, and I didn't tell. After breakfast I would sit in the living room trying to read and waiting for the postman. If Mother or Katherine were there when he came, I'd sit, looking at the book I held in my hand, seeing the letters, the words, as if each one had a separate existence, no connection with what followed or what went before. I wouldn't let them see my misery. Mother would go to the door and bring in the mail and look through it, and when she didn't say anything I would know that another day had gone by and still no letter. The day was over. All that was left to do was to get through the twenty-four hours until he came again. At night I'd crawl into bed and put the pillow over my head so no one could hear me cry.

And then, if the phone rang, I would force myself not to answer it, I wouldn't let them see me eager, waiting for a call. I wouldn't let Mother *dare* to look at me with pity, to think I allowed Taylor to treat me as she would never have let anyone treat her. I would wait, pretending I hadn't even heard the phone, hoping it was for me, hoping I would hear his voice saying "Here I am," having a reasonable explanation for what he had done to me. And if it were for me, it would be Marian, wanting to go to the show, or Frank or Louis, wanting a date, and every time it was like dying. "Yes, I'd love to." "Sorry, I have a date tonight." Hearing my own voice as if it were coming out of a cave, a dark cave I'd never been in, would be afraid to enter. By then it was the middle of July. My birthday had come and gone and I'd hardly noticed it; everybody pretending nothing was wrong, pretending it didn't matter.

Then one day the postman brought a letter from him. He still loved me. He was coming home. He had hitchhiked and ridden the rails to West Virginia. He didn't know why he had done it. Something had just come over him. He had been broke, had lived on stale bread from the back doors of bakeries, had been picked up for vagrancy in the rail yards of a little town in West Virginia, had spent ten days in jail. He hadn't had a penny to send me or his mother even a penny postcard. Now he had a job and was going to work a week to get a little money and hitchhike home. He loved me, he'd never realized how much until he was gone and couldn't even write.

Then he was back and everything was wonderful again, but the separation had only made the year ahead even more of a nightmare. I keep waiting for life to begin and it seems as if it never will. We can't go on like this very long . . . A year? Two years? How long can we stand it? I want us to be married, to live together, never, never to be apart again. All our life together has been looking forward to one agony of separation after another. And when we're apart, more and more it seems as if I'm dead, or walking around on feet that are asleep, not able to feel if they touch the floor or not.

Taylor came back, as Anna had written, around the corner by the honeysuckle-covered fence, past the bishop's cloister and garden, grinning and swinging his arms, one day about ten days after she had gotten the letter from him. The rest of the summer was as idyllic as the first part of June had been. He did not need to explain himself. Anna was so glad to see him, she simply listened to everything he said, and agreed that it was all inevitable. From him she would have accepted without question the most monstrous lie. Not that he lied to her; he never did, if he could avoid it, and like her he tried to give everything to their love. But they were both so young they knew nothing about themselves and less than nothing about each other. He could not have given anyone a believable account of his reasons for going away or for coming back. And all the while they were both sure that they were in control of their destiny.

Out of youth and pride Anna did not tell him how much she had suffered. She quarreled with him for a few minutes — until she thought it respectable to make up, and then she abandoned herself to joy. They decided before the summer was out that Taylor should double up on his courses and finish college in three years; then he could get a job and they would marry. They gathered their strength to face two more years of suffering.

For their part, Charlotte and Ralph were determined to send Anna as far away from Taylor as possible. Charlotte kept saying reassuringly to Ralph, and to herself, "Just let her get away for a year; with a change of scene and new interests, she'll get over this." But she was terrified that the two children might marry before she could get Anna away. Charlotte in truth thought about the affair everything that Anna imagined she did — and more. She could not sleep at night for seeing Anna and Taylor setting out one evening to find a justice of the peace. Nothing about the affair pleased her — its intensity, Anna's single-minded agony, the boy's background and religion, or his behavior. She had spent the month of his absence and silence in a rage. The idea that any young cub should treat her daughter so! And when Anna took him back without a question, she ground her teeth. She could scarcely be civil to him. Hopefully she bought the long sweaters and plaid skirts, the saddle oxfords and swirling evening dresses that were supposed to make a college girl of Anna; Ralph borrowed another couple of thousand dollars from the bank; and with the two girls now in college Charlotte let her maid go to economize; and they saw Anna off to Virginia.

She could have gone anywhere she liked — Charlotte and Ralph would have managed to send her to Vassar or Smith or Barnard, for they thought she was brilliant and were determined to give her whatever education she wanted; but she chose one of the women's colleges in Virginia, indifferently, sure that wherever she went she would be miserable. She let her fine, straight hair grow long and wore it twisted into a straggly, little blond knot on the back of her head; she made no effort to enter into the life of the college, which seemed to her incredibly childish — a tug-of-war between the freshmen and sophomores, indeed! She retired to her room and pretended she had forgotten to go. Indifferently she joined her sister's sorority and went through its initiation in silent embarrassment. She was the despair of her sorority sisters, who reassured each other from time to time that at least she brought up the pledge class average. She attended her classes conscientiously, eyes big and attentive behind their round tortoiseshell rimmed spectacles, hair dragged back behind her ears and escaping in wisps at the nape of her neck.

Afterward Anna remembered very little about that miserable year except getting off the train at home for the Christmas holidays and running first into her father's arms and then into Taylor's. The months of separation did no good from Charlotte's point of view. She was more in love than ever. The whole world was nothing to her except a projection of her obsession, and that was to a degree true even of Taylor. She thought of him only in relation to herself.

From the beginning he had been, like Paul and like her parents and their world, an extension of her life. Although *she* had deceived him — about her trouble with Paul, about her suspected pregnancy, about everything she thought might be unacceptable to him, it never occurred to her that *he* might have to deceive her, any more than she would have expected her own arm to deceive her. She thought she was thinking always of him, but she never thought, did not know how to think, of the enormous pressures on his young life, of the formless weight of ambition and uncontrolled energy that was all he had to bring to bear on a world that expected more of him every day. When she had talked to his mother on the telephone a few days after Taylor had disappeared, it had not once occurred to her to wonder if Mrs. Kelly was worried about him. She had been thinking only of the humiliation to herself of calling a boy's *mother* to find out where he was, a thing she had never before dreamed of doing. Mrs. Kelly had said, "Don't worry. You'll hear from him. I'm sure he is all right." It had not crossed Anna's mind that his mother must be half crazy, that she was reassuring herself, too. Once she knew he was gone, she had not wondered if he was dead, or hungry, or sick, or in trouble. She had only thought over and over to herself, *Why, why, why did he leave me?* She could not separate herself from him enough to understand that the answer might not even include her. And when he told her how he had been broke and in jail, she only thought of his story as at least an adequate excuse for not writing her. She did not understand that the qualities she found so attractive in him were at the root of his restlessness, his growing desire to find out what the world was like.

The Christmas holidays were over before she had drawn breath. She spent most of them holding hands and kissing Taylor. Afterwards she could not believe she had even been home, so nightmarish and seemingly eternal was the life she led at school.

Then in the spring, when the year was two thirds over, he appeared one day at her dormitory without a word of warning. He had quit school, he said, and hitchhiked to see her. He had decided that school was a waste of time. He was not learning anything he could not get by himself. In fact, he knew a good deal more about some of his courses than his professors. He had decided to go to New York and get a job on a paper and get started. They would be able to marry all the sooner, and meanwhile he would not be wasting his time and spending money that his parents could not afford to give him. Anna was delighted. For the first time it seemed to her that they were getting somewhere. If he was lucky, if he got a decent job, perhaps they might even be able to marry before another year was out.

He stayed two days and then left for New York, broke, still hitchhiking. He had his pride, too. She did not know until the following summer that he had been broke, did not know that the reason he used her cream and his, too, in his coffee at the College Inn, plus heaping spoons of sugar, was for the extra nourishment. He had dinner both nights at the dormitory dining room as her guest, and very little else to eat. He told her he was staying at an inexpensive boardinghouse near the school, but the truth was he slept out both nights. He had fifteen dollars in his pocket, and he was saving it to finance him in New York until he got a job. When he told her all this afterwards, she said, "Why didn't you tell me? I would have lent you some money." But he didn't know. He only knew vaguely that he hadn't wanted to involve her in his confusion.

He had been gone three days when Anna got a letter from home, from Mrs. Gladden who had taught both her and Taylor four years of Latin, and had been the faculty sponsor for the school paper of which Taylor had been editor. She was a childless widow, a solitary, dedicated schoolteacher whose husband had died in the influenza epidemic during the first World War, and who had never considered remarrying. Anna liked her with the reserved but passionate respect one has for a good teacher. She could have been nothing but entirely reserved with her, because she was so formidable. She had a New England face, although she was a South Carolinian — an over-articulated jaw, thin stern mouth that bit off a smile before it had a chance, and small, sharp, intelligent eyes. She laughed with her mouth almost closed, as if she were afraid someone might think her truly amused. Anna was at home with her for two reasons. First, she had recognized in her immediately the same uncompromising moral code that she had never known her father to deviate from, what was coming to seem to her that damn nuisance, a Protestant conscience. Second, Mrs. Gladden was a good teacher and Anna was a good student.

But Taylor's friendship with this middle-aged, stern-faced Latin teacher was another matter altogether. Mrs. Gladden loved him with all the stifled passion to which her thin mouth and its bitten-off smile gave the lie. Son and lover come far too late, he was her protégé. All through high school she had fed him and nurtured him and fought his battles and listened to the outpourings of his teeming young brain.

Now Anna had a letter from her, written in her small, round, precise hand, with a broad-nibbed pen.

Dear Anna,

I am writing to you because I know Taylor loves you, and I believe he needs your help. I am not a talebearer, and I have thought a long time before writing this letter, but, unpleasant as it is to me, I have decided that it is necessary. I presume Taylor has been to see you. If he told you the same thing about leaving school that he told me, he lied to you. Taylor did not leave school. He was expelled. He left me with the tale that he could not live without you any longer and that he was going to New York to get a job, so you two could be married. I was very much disturbed by his decision, I was even more disturbed when I learned that, because of some kind of financial trouble, he had been expelled from school. As I understand it, from sources sympathetic to Taylor, he allowed one of his friends to "borrow" several hundred dollars from the treasury of the school paper. The friend was unable to repay the money, Taylor refused to tell the authorities who the friend was, and, as the finances of the paper were his responsibility, he, of course, had to take the blame.

Taylor is at a difficult place in his life. He has always found it hard to set a course and follow it, and to set a course that meant drudgery and wasted time must have seemed impossible to him when he left school. So far he has managed to charm his way out of most of his difficulties, but now he has run head-on into a situation where his charm is useless. I think he justifies his running away through the mistaken notion that it would be wrong to expose his friend, who was undoubtedly in some kind of need. I have an idea that the friend had gotten in debt gambling, and had to pay up immediately or be exposed to his family. But if Taylor chooses to shield his friend, he must also assume his friend's responsibility. I think, too, that he says to himself that he will get a job, make a great deal of money, and repay the school in a year or two. But I know that such a point of view is disastrous. He *must not* run away from this trouble.

As you know, I have been fond of Taylor for several years. I know him very well. He is a boy of unusually fine intelligence and of great good will. He has a tremendous store of energy and vitality, and I believe his difficulties usually result from his inability to channel and control his energy, and from his outgoing good nature with people, many of whom may seem like interesting characters to him, but may also in the course of their acquaintance with him need to use him. Like most young people, he is impatient for his life to begin, and he jumps from one project to another in the belief that today, or to-morrow, or next week, he will find the answers to all his dreams and questions. I know that all young people are impatient with the advice of their elders, but believe me, I have brought the sincerest good will and most honest thought to bear on Taylor's problem, and I *must* advise you.

It is out of character for me to advise, and even more out of character to beg, but I *beg* of you that you read what I have written and am about to write, and act upon it.

You are the only person who can influence Taylor. Write to him. Tell him you have heard what happened. If you like, tell him I wrote you of my great concern. Tell him he *must* come home and pay back the money he owes. He cannot put it off with the notion that next year or the next he will have the money and can pay it back without the pain of facing his disgrace. He will never find a convenient time. He must come home *now*, live at home where he has few expenses, get a job, and send all the money he can spare to pay on his debt. If he does not do this, he will have put his foot in a path from which turning back is not easy. It is a path made more natural to him because, with all due respect to his family, they have made him accustomed to it; and it is a path the pleasures of which will always be his greatest temptation. You are the only person who can block his entrance into this path. I do not know you intimately, Anna, but I know your father, and I know that if you can say to Taylor, "You will never have my respect unless you can meet your just responsibilities," you will be acting on the standards by which your family lives.

Now that I have brought myself to write this letter, I find there are many, many things I would like to tell you, but perhaps it is best to stick to the business at hand. I will only say, in closing, that I believe Taylor is worth the pain and anxiety he brings to those who love him. Perhaps you cannot believe it matters that he is so very young, but give him time, and give him the steadying hand he needs. I know I put upon you a hard necessity, but I cannot avoid it.

Your friend,

MILDRED GLADDEN

Anna had gone to pick up her mail during the fifteen-minute break between nine-thirty and ten-forty-five classes. She stood in the hall outside the post office and read the letter. She started blindly for her room, the class forgotten, and met her professor coming down the hall. She must have looked as distressed as she felt, for he stopped her.

"Why, Miss McGovern, what's the matter? Aren't you coming to class?"

Anna shook her head and tried to brush past him, but he laid a hand on her arm. "Are you ill?" he said. "You'd better stop by Dean Farr's office and tell her. You don't want an unexcused cut."

Anna shook her head again. She felt that she could not speak, but she opened her mouth and said in a calm, low voice, "I'm not feeling very well. I think I'll go lie down." Then she walked calmly to the dean's office, reported herself ill, and went to her room. She closed the door and stood in the middle of the room, looking at the wall.

"I'm dying," she said aloud. "I must be dying."

Immediately, almost without thinking, she wrote Taylor the letter that Mrs. Gladden had told her to write. Then she began to wait. She had waited for Taylor before — all the nights he had been late, the long month he had been in West Virginia, and all the months they had been apart; but this was the worst time of all. Day after day at ten-thirty and three-thirty she went to the post office, and day after day her box was empty. At last, after two weeks, she got a letter from him. He had thought it over, he said. At first he had been hurt and angry. He had never dreamed that she was capable of limiting their love by laying down conditions. But he was over that now. He had decided to go to Alaska. There were plenty of jobs in Alaska and the pay was high. He would make a lot of money in a hurry and pay his debt. He would never love anyone else, but she would not hear from him again until he had paid his debt.

Anna knew it was the end, that she would never see him again. In dumb misery she went conscientiously to class, and methodically prepared her work. After class in the afternoon and on the weekends she sat in the window of her third-story dormitory room and watched spring come on. But not one flower bloomed or one leaf turned green for her. She was wrenched loose from the world that she had thought a year ago had been created with her and in her and for her. She sat leaning on her elbows looking out her window those long spring afternoons with the light, flowery wind in her face, and whispered to herself, "I'll kill myself." She thought about jumping out of the window, but she knew it would be messy and might not even kill her. "I'll kill myself," she whispered, and waited for it to happen. And when she did not, she was outraged and ashamed of herself. "I can't live without him," she said, but she *was* living without him. How could that be, if all she had felt and said were true? It never occurred to her that she would some day grieve any less for him; she knew her life was over, that she would always be as miserable as she was minute after minute, day after day, all that spring. But even so . . . She held on tight to the sill of her window and stared at the concrete walk thirty feet below. "I can't stand it," she said. "I'm going to kill myself." And the knowledge that she did not mean it stared mercilessly back at her from the gray concrete.

Six weeks went by and then one day she heard from Taylor again. This time the letter was from Helena, Montana. He had worked his way north and west across the country. When she saw the battered, dirty envelope, so thick he had had to put two stamps on it, she knew, even before she turned it over and looked at her name written in his hand, in pencil, that it was from Taylor. No one else wrote her such long letters. He would cover eight or ten big pages, both sides, writing as fast as he could in a smallish, sprawling hand — what he thought of everything he was reading: Spengler, Marx, Nietzsche, Veblen, Dostoyevsky; all the music he had heard and how it had affected him; lively accounts of his friends; and long declarations of love. The letter from Helena was not different from the rest. He jumped into it with both feet. *Sweetheart,* he wrote, *I am going home. I've run away as long as I can.* She leaned against the wall of the post office hallway and read those two sentences over and over, her heart pounding in her ears. She was so happy she thought she might explode for joy. The rest of the letter was an account of his trip, how he had worked and traveled alternately, had slept in barns and flophouses, hitchhiked when he was broke, and ridden the bus when he had enough money. (He had not tried hopping freights since his trip to West Virginia.) He had taken with him besides what he was wearing only an extra pair of underwear shorts and an extra shirt, a sweater, and his limp-backed Shakespeare, on India paper and in fine print, not so large as a standard three-dollar novel. Sometimes it had been so cold he had worn all his clothes — both shirts and both pairs of shorts, sweater, jacket and trench coat. He wrote how he had stood on Brooklyn Bridge the day before he left New York and thought about jumping off. *I had to get down from there in a hurry,* he said, *or the temptation would have been too great. (Never mind,* she thought. *I know all about that.)* At last in Helena he had come to himself. He felt as if he had been sleepwalking for weeks. *What are you doing going to Alaska?* he had asked himself. *Are you crazy?* He had realized what he was doing to her by not writing. Could she ever forgive him? Whatever she decided, he knew he had to go home and pay his debt, and if she still loved him, she would find him waiting when she got home.

Forgive! It never crossed her mind that there was anything to forgive. From beginning to end she never thought Taylor meant to hurt her. It was in the nature of things and unavoidable.

At home Taylor stuck to his job the rest of the spring and all that summer. He made twenty-five dollars a week, and sent twenty of it to pay on his debt. By the end of August he had paid it out. He decided to go back to school and finish. For Anna that meant another two years of waiting, as he had lost the second semester of his last year, but she was willing if he wanted it that way.

Even so, her reservations had begun to be formulated when she left for school that fall. She could not stand another year of misery. She did not think about it, and if she had, she would probably have told herself in the old dramatic terms that she was willing to stand anything. But that second year she went to a co-educational school, and she set out to make a bearable life for herself. For the first time since she had been accepted by Paul's Inner Circle she thought in terms of dates and dances and houseparties. She wanted to make friends and drink beer at the College Inn and lead a frivolous life. She cut off her long hair and got a permanent, and she stopped wearing her glasses except in class. She had a passable figure and she did her best to make the most of it and of her shining ash-blond hair and big, trusting brown eyes. She would never be a beauty, but she was attractive as most young girls are attractive, because she was young and excited and because she wanted to be attractive.

For two months she and Taylor corresponded faithfully. Then, in November, he struck her the last blow, jarred her with the shock she could not absorb . . . This time, ironically, he acted out of increasing maturity and the desire to realize his own potential. But she saw it only as a final instance of his inability to set a course for himself and for them. She got a letter from him saying that he had changed his mind again. He did not want to get a B.A. and then a job. He wanted to study law. He intended to change schools at midterm, get into pre-law (it would take him a year to complete the requirements for entrance into law school) and then enter law school. Law school took three years.

For Anna that was all. She was through. She could not stand any more. All her capacity for waiting, for accepting was used up. In one moment she closed her heart and it was all over.

She had a wonderful time the rest of that year. She looked back on her affair with Taylor with the contempt of the very young for themselves when they were a little bit younger. And no matter how attractive she thought the boy she was currently dating, no matter how pleased she was when he called, she said to herself, if he seemed a bit overconfident, *I can get along without you, buddy. Don't worry about breaking my heart. I can get along without anybody, and I can get over anything.*

At home the following summer Anna thought a great deal about her past, and it seemed to her that it was very long and full of experience — of events that had given her what she was sure was a genuine maturity. She thought about Paul, and for the first time she saw herself as she had been the year he had tried to seduce her. A *child*, she said to herself, and cringed with embarrassment. *What a child I was.* For the first time she was angry with him. She saw him coldly — a selfish man, with his petty vanities, his thinning black hair, his intramural quarrels; a man who would make love to an innocent, helpless, loving child, who without a thought for anyone but himself clutched at the youth that was slipping away from him.

One day that summer she happened to meet him on the street, and he asked her to have a cup of coffee with him. He still looked the same, not a day older. She joined him for politeness' sake, and, to put their conversation on a formal plane, asked about his family. He dismissed them, as he always had, with a sentence. Two young girls came into the coffee shop while they sat there, high school juniors or seniors, with unmarked faces and not-quite-finished bodies. She savored her own poise and felt that she was centuries older than they. They said hello to Paul, and on some transparent pretext came over to the table where he sat with Anna. She watched him as he gently teased them and smiled his sorrowful, understanding smile. Finally they went out, and he turned again to her. Her anger died in a moment, and she felt a familiar movement in her heart. In spite of herself, she wanted to speak out, to tell him what he had meant to her and how he had betrayed her, how cold she found the world he had helped to give her.

"Why don't you ever come to see me any more when you're home?" he said.

She still could not give him a straight answer. "I was coming," she said. "I haven't been in town long."

"The others come," he said. "Louis and Marian and Cliff. They haven't forgotten me."

But they didn't love you like I did. "I really didn't know you were in town," she said.

"You've forgotten me, Anna," he said, "and it hurts." He put his hand on his heart. "You, of all people, have forgotten me."

She thought, too, that summer, of Sis and Alderan and the ruin that Sis's single-minded passion had made of her life. How could Sis at thirty have been so naïve? How could she not have already learned the secret that Anna knew would be thrust like a bare sword between her and everyone to whom she might ever again try to commit her life?

She thought about Taylor, and talked about him to Charlotte. It was the first open conversation she had had with her mother in more than three years.

"It'll be a cold day in August when I fall in love again," she said. She could talk of herself with detachment. "Loving is like getting born," she said. "Once it starts, there's no stopping it, and when it's over, you find you're alone in a new world."

Charlotte did not smile. "I suppose so," she said.

"You don't get born but once," Anna said.

"That's not true about love," Charlotte said, "and one of these days you'll thank the Lord it's not."

But Anna did not believe her. She had moved one giant turn around the wheel, and she knew for the first time that her motives were separate from the motives of everyone else in the world. Her second self had been born — the dissenter who would always stand by, detachedly watching from the wings, making ironic reservations. She had not named the dissenter or pointed at him yet, but her life loomed up, and she felt that she could never be involved again. What man could make her forget that love dies? Every word she ever spoke in love again would remind her that she had spoken it before, once and forever, with her whole soul, and it had proved untrue.

The sidewalk that Anna had waited so often for Taylor to appear on, and had walked with him so often in the late afternoon was the last thing in the world she ever felt she owned. It belonged with the houses of her grandmothers, the Presbyterian Church in Homochitto, the ferry churning its brown wake on a fair June day, the nuns and orphans walking home from Mass, the cry of the vegetable man in the early morning; among all those places and sights and sounds that were pieces of herself, that had formed like crystals in the structure of her life, coexistent with her, one piece with the bones that held her up. She never saw or heard any of them without the wrenching pain of loneliness and separation.

Now their separateness spoke clearly to her: "We were here before you," they said, "and we will be here when you are gone. There is nothing in the world from which time and change will not part you."

And when the Episcopal Church clock struck five on a summer afternoon, the hour that had always meant the end of her day with Taylor, it said to her, "You cannot die for love. Love dies for you, but you can never die for love."

A Weekend
in New Orleans

⌐⌐ IT WAS NOT until the summer of 1941, six years after the divorce, that Anna heard the story of the end of Sis and Alderan's marriage. Once Alderan had gone, once the violence of Sis's grief had been spent, the rest of the family stopped talking about them. They had nothing more to say to one another; they had worn out their responses and were sick of their own thoughts. Perhaps they were waiting for the children to grow up, patiently cultivating new reflectors for their lives, and especially for that violent period that had baffled them all.

In the same way, someone who had almost drowned might keep in his mind an image of his confrontation with death and terror, going over and over it to himself, saying to himself with surprise in the middle of the night, *But what did it* mean? *After all, what did it* mean? until at last he turned away from his ordeal, not in horror, but in boredom. Yet, if he met a stranger, the impulse would be almost irresistible to try out again that hard, unmanageable memory, to say again what he had said to himself a thousand times: *I was so surprised,* surprised. With a new audience, the old story is no longer boring. He watches the stranger's face, watches the interest, the horror, the envy, looks again and again into his face for assurance that it really happened, for the meaning he cannot find alone.

So, Charlie Dupré and Will Anderson, and eventually Charlotte and Sarah D., used Anna — the ideal stranger for their purpose. She was young and uncritical, and there were many things they could tell her, things she had never heard, things she might even feel had been kept from her. They knew she was bound to be interested — that was a condition of her being Anna McGovern. She was a member of the family, and therefore she had a right to be told all they had marveled at, all the dramatic, tragic, private truth that they would never have told an outsider.

In a way, too, the telling of their stories was like a family puberty rite. "Here are our secrets," they said. "Here are the hidden springs that have seen us through seasons of drought. Here is how we have lived. The pain of which we tell you, you must understand, is the price of survival. It is true no one else would be interested in what we say, but to you the information is vital, because you have no choice, no other place to begin. Take as much of our wisdom as you can and use it to grow up. Above all, listen to us, receive us, and be like us. You are our mirror and our future; in you we see ourselves made clear, and for a moment can almost think ourselves immortal."

Charlie Dupré and Will were the first to begin the accounting, by accident it seemed; for it was an accident that Anna was alone with them that night in New Orleans; and they would never have talked so freely if Charlotte had been along. Everything that preceded the evening she spent with Will and Charlie — a whole strange summer of change — had set her nerves humming with expectancy, her mind quivering under the impact of fresh appraisals. And the afternoon's adventure, the accident that had ended by separating them from Charlotte and had cleared the board, so to speak, for an evening of confidences, had been a great deal more than she could begin to take in. After all, it appeared, circumstances were as bewildering, as baffling to grown people as they were to children. When would the world keep still long enough for anyone to find a place to settle himself? Thus it happened that she heard from Will and Charlie the end of the family's great romance. But she would certainly have heard it later, and not much later, regardless of accidents. Too many people were waiting to tell her about it. Afterward Charlotte and Sarah D., when she questioned them separately, added new fragments and whole new episodes to the story. But they had less need to try to sum it up than the two men, one of whom was a talker and the other, at least when he was drinking, a philosopher. Charlotte and Sarah D., on the other hand, simply *knew*; they had always known. To them the meaning was implicit in the ending, as the end had been inevitable from the beginning. Only Ralph kept steadily to his silence. His part in the affair sank like a stone into the sea. No diver could have brought it up. Years later Anna heard him mention Alderan in another context, and the shock of hearing his name on her father's lips, the shock of a new, a strange and completely unexpected point of view (for she questioned him, too, once the name had been mentioned) toward events she had long since explained to her own satisfaction, shook her once more to a recognition of the intractibility of reality. Nothing was exactly what she had thought it. So many memories brought to bear on the same events. Who, even among the principals, was to say what really happened?

None of these private family matters had come up at Katherine McGovern's June wedding, an occasion for which, of course, all the family had gathered. Nothing, it seemed, had happened at the wedding, except that Katherine had gotten married. The gathering had been like a pause, the drawing of a deep breath, as at the caesura in a long, rising and falling line of poetry. The pause was filled with music, and with the restless voices of celebration. It was as if they all — Charlotte and Ralph, Sarah D. and Charlie and little Charlotte and Billy, Gran and Grandmother McGovern and Teen, James and Waldo and Will and their wives and children, Sis and Anna and little Ralph, and Katherine and her handsome young doctor — as if they had all come together like dancers in a figure, to nod and bow and smile, with eyes full of the promise of later, more intimate meetings. "The things we could tell you," their eyes said to Anna, as they met and parted and met again. "Just wait. Just wait."

For Anna the summer of 1941 had been charged from the beginning with a vague restlessness, related intimately not only to her sister's marriage, but to larger wonders. She had been waiting for events both terrible and passionately desired, waiting once more for life to begin, but this time with the frightening and exhilarating certainty that it was beginning all around her, that for her it was only a matter, perhaps, of minutes. At home the roads were choked with convoys, truckload after truckload of young, khaki-clad men among whom one might suddenly catch sight of a familiar face, a schoolmate not thought of for months, waving gaily and hopelessly as he flashed by to — what? Familiar roads and pastures disappeared around Eureka, and desolate cities sprang up in their places; streets lined with windy gray barracks and bleak office buildings roofed with gray corrugated iron and set precariously on gray concrete blocks above a sea of gray mud in wet weather or dust in dry. Barbed-wire fences appeared, enclosing what had been the poorest cut-over pine timber land and barring the roads to the best picnic spots. What did it all mean? It was as if a sick giant were shaking himself under his bedclothes, to the consternation of the swarms of midgets who, while he slept, had made their homes among the folds of his blankets.

A small headline on the inside page of the local paper one night summed up for Anna all that terrible, exciting strangeness: SOLDIER DIES HERE OF SNAKE-BITE. What, in his or his parents' lives, could have prepared them for his death? Snatched from a middle-western city street and set down in a Louisiana swamp to be bitten, to be killed by a tiny, gaily striped and deadly coral snake, the like of which he had never seen or heard of in his life.

But everyone went quietly about his business, as if it all meant nothing. What else could they do? "We're bound to get in it," they said. "We'll be fighting within a year." But no one believed himself when he said it. Katherine and Charlotte went on addressing wedding invitations; Father set off for the liquor store to buy the sauterne and champagne for the punch; and young Ralph, insufferably bumptious at fourteen, clutched his heart and fell on the living room floor, muttering, "No, no, I'm too young to die."

The wedding itself, the boys, some already in uniform, equal at last in the weight of their lives and responsibilities to their fathers, the girls as inexhaustibly gay and frivolous as butterflies on the first cool autumn day, had contributed to Anna's troubled preknowledge that cold winds would soon be blowing. *It scarcely seems possible,* was what she said to herself, *but we're all grown up. After years of thinking so, now it's really true.*

After the wedding, Anna and her mother had gone to New Orleans together to put things in order for Katherine and Mac while they were on their honeymoon. And in New Orleans the first thing that happened had intensified Anna's almost unbearable vision of the expanding, limitless world of maturity. She had turned the big key in the lock and opened the door of Mac and Katherine's apartment — two high-ceilinged dusty rooms in an old house in the French Quarter. Huddled together in the middle of the floor, as if taking comfort from one another in their strange surroundings, were boxes, trunks, suitcases, stacks of books, tables, chairs and chests. As she and Charlotte stood hesitating at the threshold, the sight of so many familiar things in an alien setting made Anna's heart pound against her ribs.

The family had gotten together enough furniture to make do for the two years of Mac's internship, and, with Katherine and Mac's own possessions, here it all was, waiting to take up a new life. Katherine's marble-topped parlor table, left her by a cousin, dominated the room with Victorian self-confidence. It stood in the middle like a great, squat mother monster surrounded by her brood. Four lions' heads snarled from the curves of its four heavy, graceless legs, peering out from festoons of rosettes and acanthus leaves. Its white marble top supported several stacks of medical books, a corrugated cardboard box, and a new luggage rack. Beside the table was an old washstand that had been brought in from the storeroom in Grandmother McGovern's garage to serve as a sideboard. Four cane-bottomed chairs were stacked on top of each other on the other side. Sarah D. and Sis had each given Katherine two of them for wedding presents — gifts beyond evaluation, for they were the old Anderson chairs from the dining room at Bois Sauvage. Behind them was the ruffled dressing table from Katherine's bedroom at home, and in the room beyond, already set up by the movers, was the sturdy round-posted tester bed that Waldo had lent them. Anna knew quite well that all these things (except the ruffled dressing table) had a use quite apart from their beauty or ugliness, or their function as objects to put things on or in. To her mother they were the indisputable hallmarks of "background." Their significance surrounded them like a shimmering aura, and blinded their successive owners to everything else about them. And here they were, ready to set the seal of family blessing on Katherine's new life. Charlotte walked through the living room and into the bedroom. She laid a hand on the heavy, smooth bole of one of the bedposts.

"This bed was made on Golden Quarter from walnut cut on the place," she said. "Old Waldo Henshaw brought it down the river with him on a flatboat when he settled in Homochitto."

"Certainly does need refinishing," Anna said. "It's perfectly black."

"Your father says his Grandpa Henshaw used to varnish

everything in the house every spring," Charlotte said. "I reckon it's got a good bit of varnish on it."

In the living room they looked around again, at the un-painted chest and the couch that Mac and Katherine had bought together.

"I've always wanted a sofa like this," Charlotte said, sitting down on it. "My, isn't it comfortable!"

"Why haven't you ever gotten one?" Anna asked.

"Well, you know, your grandmother gave me that big Victorian sofa from Walnut Hill," Charlotte said. "I had to use it."

"I don't see why you couldn't have put it upstairs."

"Oh, I don't know," Charlotte said. "I never thought of that; and, after all, it doesn't seem quite right, does it?"

Anna laughed. "Mama, you're a case," she said.

"They can paint their own chest of drawers," Charlotte said. "That's where I draw the line. Look here, Anna. This luggage rack will make them a nice coffee table, with that tole tray the Merediths gave them." She looked around again, at the stacks of Mac's medical books and the boxes of wedding presents. "I suppose most of these books were his father's," she said. "But his sister must have gotten all the furniture."

"He wouldn't have had much use for it," Anna said.

"Well, anyway, this is a nice, comfortable easy chair. I suppose it was his father's, too."

"Come on," Anna said. "Look at the cobwebs. This is the dirtiest place I've ever seen. We're going to have to stir around to get it decent."

"What do you reckon they're planning to eat on?" Charlotte said.

"Card table, I reckon," Anna said. "No use buying a dining room table until they're settled some place."

"*Buying one!*" Charlotte said. "Of course they won't buy one. We'll just have to scare one up when they decide where they're going."

As they dusted and scrubbed and put away clothing and presents, Anna kept the sense of fluttery, loving excitement that had struck her when she opened the door and saw the big, hideous, claw-footed, marble-topped table. She was half in love with Katherine's new husband, herself — the shy, charming young doctor with his cap of shining, blond hair, who had seen already so much of the world's pain and irony, but who listened with respectful interest when she talked, groping toward an understanding with him. "You are ours," she wanted to tell him. "Oh, how we all love you." But it is true that she was half in love that year with every attractive man whose look or attention told her that he found *her* attractive. The idea of being married was irresistible and the thought of Katherine's new life wonderfully exciting. Even the fact that they were poor, that Katherine would have to work until Mac finished his internship, was grand, a proof, like holy poverty, of the purity of their vows. To be married! To live in New Orleans! To come home in the evening to an apartment in the French Quarter — great, high-ceilinged rooms opening on a brick-paved courtyard; to cook dinner and then afterward sit together by the open window and listen to the French Quarter coming to life outside. To sleep every night in the arms of your beloved. Nothing else was worth desiring.

Anna and Charlotte worked hard all day, mopping the floors, scrubbing out the kitchen cabinets and arranging the shiny new pots and pans and dishes, brushing down the walls and washing the woodwork, and finally beginning to arrange the furniture and put away the clothes. At four o'clock, grimy and weary, but pleased with the results of their efforts, they sat down to talk over their plans for the evening and the next day. Will had called at noon to say he would like to take them out to dinner, that Eunice was out of town, but that he would get in touch with Charlie Dupré who was working at the time in New Orleans, and they would all go to Galatoire's.

"There's not much left to do," Charlotte said. "They're going to rearrange everything anyway, you know. Just so it's clean, that's all that matters."

"We can easily finish tomorrow," Anna said.

"Well, my dear, I'm weary," Charlotte said. "I'm going to take a bath and a little nap before Will gets here."

"I wish I had a beer," Anna said.

"Why don't you go down to the corner and get some?"

Anna had gotten her purse and started for the door when someone knocked. Then, before she could answer the knock, the door swung slowly open. Will stood in the doorway, swaying, peering cautiously into the shadowy room, as if he half expected someone to jump out at him.

"Charlotte?" he said. He was wearing a rumpled seersucker suit; and the panama pushed back and sideways on his balding head gave him a slightly battered look, as if he'd been caught in the crush of a bargain basement sale. He opened his big, brown eyes wide, like a small, but cheeky owl, and rocked backward and forward, as if he were about to fall off his perch. "Charlotte?"

"It's me, Will — Anna. Hi."

He had something — a towel or a piece of a sheet — wrapped around his left arm, and he held his left elbow carefully in his right hand, blinked and then grinned at her.

"Light behind you," he said. "If you aren't the breathing image of Charlotte. But fair. That's Ralph. Where's your mother?"

Charlotte had gotten up when the door opened, and stood staring at him. "Hello, Will," she said coolly.

He took a careful step forward. "Ha! Charlotte. Didn't see you in the dark. Le's have a little light on the subject." He let go of his left arm and snapped the switch by the door. "There."

Charlotte had crossed the room to kiss him and to examine him more closely, and now her expression of cautious distaste gave away her immediate perception that he was drunk.

They stood not a foot apart just inside the door and looked at each other. In spite of their utterly disparate lives, Charlotte and Will looked more alike every year. Fair-skinned and dark-haired, they were of the type that shrinks rather than spreads, like shriveling ripe figs hanging in the sun, concentrating their mysterious essence as they age. They carried themselves with straight backs and unslumped shoulders, both products of a mother who had said again and again, "Hold your shoulders up. If there's anything I detest, it's poor posture." Will was scarcely two inches the taller of the two, and his small, straight nose, wide mouth, and almost honest brown eyes were like a blurred image cast from the same mold that had defined Charlotte more clearly. Only the skin of their faces marked the difference in their lives. Charlotte's was beginning to acquire the delicate, dry, paper-thin quality imparted by fifty years of regular habits and quantities of soap and water — cool, silky, and translucent as a wilting petal; while Will's was marked by dissipation — sagging, red-veined, and mottled.

"We weren't expecting you until seven-thirty," Charlotte said. She glanced at Anna, and with one grim, outraged look signaled her, *Wouldn't you know it. Now what are we going to do with him?* Then, as a way out struck her suddenly, "Wouldn't you like to come in and take a nap?" she said hopefully. "You look worn out."

"Things have happened," Will said carefully, taking hold of his left elbow again. "Things have happened." He swayed, and without letting go his grip on his own arm, took one step sideways and leaned against the door jamb. He raised his voice. "A crisis has arisen," he said.

By now Charlotte and Anna were both staring at the dark stain on the towel wrapped around his arm.

"Will! You're bleeding," Charlotte said. "What's the matter with you?"

"Bleeding?" He looked down. "Oh, yes, I forgot. I'm bleeding." Keeping his left arm tight against his side, he tipped his hat and bowed. "Wounded on the field of honor, madam," he said. "Gentleman to the last."

"*What* are you talking about?" Charlotte said. "Come in and shut the door, you fool. Anna, help me get him in. Here, take his hat."

"No, no. Halt. Don't tush, *touch* me. M'allright. *Quite* all right. Ladies." He bowed again. "Am I the man, the contemptible cad, to involve an innocent maiden, an untouched virgin in my trouble? I go."

"Come *in*," Charlotte said. "Shut the door. Anna, help me get his coat off." Together they helped him to a chair, and Anna gently unwrapped the towel from his arm and sharply drew a breath when she saw the torn and bloody sleeve under it.

"What happened to you?" Charlotte asked. "Have you been to a doctor?"

"Sot. *Shot*," he muttered. "Wounded on the field of honor. I go."

"I knew somebody would eventually shoot you," Charlotte said. "It was just a matter of time. What's the name of the nearest doctor?"

"Didn't know Anna was here. Forgot Anna was here. Sorry."

"All right, all right," Charlotte said. "Anna's a grown woman. She'll live through it. Now, what doctor shall I call?"

Will looked up and Anna, catching his bright brown eyes looking sharply at her, thought, *He's not so drunk, after all.*

"Can't call doctor," he said. "I'm *shhh-ot*. See? Can't call doctor. Doctor'll call police. Can't have that. Protect family name."

Anna had gotten a pair of scissors and was cutting away his shirt sleeve. Clearly, he *had* been shot. There was a small hole in the fleshy part of his upper arm, and on the other side a larger, messier one where the bullet had come out.

"Will, you *have* been shot," Charlotte said, "Anna, he really has been shot. What have you been up to, you devil?"

Will carefully bent his arm at the elbow and then opened it, stretched it out, and flexed the fingers, whistling through his teeth once at a sharp pain. "See, it's not broken," he said. "Just a little flesh wound. Didn't touch the bone."

"Mama, we've got to do something about it," Anna said. "We'd better call a doctor."

Will was looking down tenderly at his mangled flesh. "Other fellow's dead," he muttered.

"*Dead!*"

"Shot a fellow down on Canal Street. He drew first. Couldn't be helped. It was *in*-evitable."

Charlotte looked at him, and every line of her bent shoulders and bewildered face expressed her inadequacy to the crisis. "He's such a liar," she said. "How can you possibly believe him? But obviously somebody has shot him." A more comfortable explanation occurred to her and she began to look happier. "Maybe he was cleaning his gun and shot himself. But why doesn't he want to call the doctor?" She did not lower her voice as she argued the question more with herself than with Anna. "The *police*. Mercy. *Mercy*."

Will had leaned back in the easy chair and closed his eyes.

"Fooling around with somebody's wife, I'd bet my bottom dollar on it, and somebody got tired of putting up with it," Charlotte said.

"Field of honor," Will said without opening his eyes.

"Or he got in a barroom *brawl*." She stared at him a moment longer and sighed before she straightened her shoulders and said to Anna, "Well, I suppose you'd better go to the nearest drugstore and get some gauze and adhesive tape and a bottle of alcohol and some merthiolate. Hurry up, now."

Will got up and picked his hat up from the washstand. First he put it on his head and looked around the room. Then he tipped it and bowed again. A tear trembled in the corner of his eye and rolled down his cheek. "I came to you," he said. " 'Charlotte's made of steel,' I said to myself. 'Little stick of steel. Loyal to the bone. Succor me in my distress.' But *you* — you afraid of law. Law-abiding citizen. Never mind if I'm your only brother. Reject, cast me out. There are others, *others*, loyal friends, take me in. If I don't bleed to death first." He looked down at the last trickle of blood drying on his arm.

"I can't think when you talk so much," Charlotte said. "Hush."

"Forgot about innocent virgin. I go."

"Sit down," Charlotte said. She followed Anna to the door. "It's the truth," she said. "It could be the truth. Do you reckon the police are after him?"

"I guess we'd better bandage him up and not worry about the police," Anna said.

When she came back with disinfectants and bandages, Charlotte had gotten Will into the bathroom and was washing his arm.

"The pain was intense," Will said, "but not a word of complaint passed his lips. *My God, woman, you're killing me!*"

"I wish you wouldn't take the name of the Lord in vain," Charlotte said.

"*Hellfire and damnation!*"

"Shh," Charlotte said. "The whole neighborhood will hear you. Fine way to start Katherine and Mac off in their apartment," she said to Anna. "Harboring a criminal."

"Field of honor," Will said.

"Hand me the alcohol," Charlotte said, nervously holding his arm up and away from her. "Don't get blood on me, Will."

"Alcohol. Oils joints," Will said, "if in*ject*ed into *pro*per *ori*fice. But not on the outside. *Jesus.*"

"You'd better finish," Charlotte said to Anna. "I'm feeling a little sick."

Will steadied himself on the basin as Anna wound the gauze around his arm.

"What really happened, Will?" she asked him in a low voice. "Who shot you?"

"He drew first," Will said. "I had to kill him."

"He'll probably die of blood-poisoning," Charlotte said meditatively from the sofa in the living room where she was lying down with her eyes shut. "Did you use plenty of merthiolate?"

"Um-hum."

"If you get blood-poisoning," Charlotte said, "just don't expect me to take you to a doctor. Wouldn't we have a sweet time explaining ourselves then?" She sat up and opened her eyes. "Did you *really* shoot somebody? Who was it?"

"I brought you some aspirin," Anna said. "You'd better take about three of them, don't you think?" She put them in his good hand. "Come on, put them in your mouth, and then drink this."

Will gulped down the water. "I forgot to tell you, Charlotte," he shouted. "Don't worry about publicity."

"Shhh," Anna said. "Go in the living room and talk to her."

"Stop managing me, child," he said. "I don't like managing women. Ran me away from home young. Got to curb that." He sat down on the side of the tub and continued to talk to Charlotte through the door. "Ran into Dix Coleman right after it happened. Wasn't that lucky? Good old Dix. 'Hush it up, Dix,' I said. 'We don't want Mama to have to go through a murder trial, do we? At her age.' Dix is a Homochitto boy," he said to Anna. "Good old Dix. Went to school with me. He's assistant district attorney." He raised his voice again. "I know the right people," he said. "Homochitto boy makes good."

Charlotte had lain down and closed her eyes again. "What about the body?" she asked. "Did you just leave it lying in the street?"

"Dix'll see about the body. Nothing to worry about. Influence. A little influence makes all the difference." He looked down at the tub he was sitting on. "What'd you sit me down here for?" he said. "This isn't the most comfortable place in the world for a *dying* man to sit. Come on, my dear, help me up, now. I'm feeling a little dizzy." Leaning heavily on Anna and gripping her shoulder with his right hand, while he half suppressed several low moans of pain, he came out of the bathroom. "Take a little nap," he said. "Got to take a little nap if we're going out to dinner." He let go of Anna, swayed, and waved his arm at the scattered bloody rags, the torn shirt and coat, and the scraps of gauze. "Dispose of the evidence," he said grandly.

Charlotte sat up suddenly. "What about the gun?" she said. "Where is your gun?"

"Threw it in the river." He demonstrated, waving his good arm and rolling across the room. "Had to get rid of it. Clear head. Made my way to the river, wounded and bloody, and *threw* it in. Then I thought, Charlotte's loyal to the bone. Find Charlotte. And here I am." He went into the bedroom, laid himself carefully on the bed, and closed his eyes. "Nap," he said, and in a few minutes began to snore softly.

"Mercy," Charlotte said quietly from the sofa. "Mercy."

Anna looked at her mother and began to giggle. Then, "What shall I do with these things?" she said.

"What do you reckon really happened?" Charlotte said. "Do you think he really shot somebody?"

"He *couldn't* have, Mama. He couldn't have killed anybody, could he?" She looked around the room, transformed so suddenly and violently from a honeymoon retreat to a den of crime. "What shall we do with all this stuff?" she said again. "We can't send it to the laundry, can we?" She began to gather up the bloody towels and rags, the shirt, and the seersucker coat. "They're ruined," she said. "He can't possibly wear them again."

Charlotte got up. "Give them to me," she said. "We'll put them in the trash. She found a piece of newspaper and wrapped them in it. "Dix Coleman, indeed," she muttered. "Dix Coleman is going to hush it up! Did you ever hear anything so absurd? I don't believe Will has a grain of gumption."

"Well, he's certainly drunk," Anna said.

"There must be an incinerator downstairs somewhere," Charlotte said. "I believe it would be safer to burn all this stuff. You bring along that box of trash out of the kitchen." Her shoulders were bent again, as if she hoped to make herself so small that she would disappear altogether. She walked toward the door on tiptoe and opened it as cautiously as if she were expecting to find a policeman waiting for them outside. "Come on," she said in a loud whisper. "Hurry up, let's get this over with." She looked cautiously out into the hall, and then turned back. "I don't see anybody," she said. And then, "I guess you know we're probably accessories after the fact. Do you realize that? We could get put in prison for this."

"Oh, Mama," Anna said.

"That fool," Charlotte said. "If I had a gun, I'd shoot him again."

❦

At seven o'clock Will sat up, groaned, and swung his feet over the side of the bed. He looked disgustedly at the bandage on his arm, stood up, yawned, moved his arm up and down carefully, opened and closed his mouth twice as if wondering what tasted so bad, and walked soberly to the door between the bedroom and the living room.

"Time for dinner," he said. "We're supposed to meet Charlie at Galatoire's at seven-thirty. Turtle soup. Trout marguery, crêpes suzette, and so forth."

Charlotte sat reading on the new sofa while Anna, bathed and dressed, dozed in Mac's easy chair.

"No, I thank you," Charlotte said. "If you're out of my bed for good, I'll just get in it."

Anna woke up. "I'm starving," she said. "Come on, Mama."

"Are you sober enough to navigate?" Charlotte asked Will.

"Sober! Of course I'm sober."

"Well, then, go on and take Anna to dinner. I'll take a rain check. I'm really not hungry." She looked him over as he stood there. Two or three drops of dried blood and a smear of merthiolate stained his wrinkled seersucker pants. Above the neck of his bloody undershirt sprouted half-a-dozen straggly black hairs. "I don't suppose you're going like that," she said.

"He could wear some of Mac's clothes," Anna said. "They're all here."

Charlotte went to the closet. "Will couldn't possibly go to Galatoire's in Mac's coat," she said. "The sleeves would be six inches too long, and the tail would come down to his knees." She pushed the hangers aside and began to look on the shelves. "Here," she said. "You can put on this sport shirt and go home and get a suit of your own." She hesitated. "We burnt up the things you wore over here."

Will stared at her, as if he were thinking, as if he had not heard what she said. Finally he said, "I don't have my car with me. Eunice took it to Mobile."

"Well, Anna can drive you over to your place," Charlotte said. "You oughtn't to be wandering around by yourself with that bad arm, anyway. To say nothing of . . ." She let the question hang, but it stayed unanswered.

"We'd better get started," Will said. "We're going to be late as it is, and old Charlie has to go to work early."

❧

Anna set out to dinner with Will, as excited as a girl to her first dance. She was delighted that her mother had chosen to stay at home, because she felt that Will would be more himself without Charlotte. She was sure that this first party undertaken with her uncles as three grown people together would be — what? She could not say, but there was something to be learned, to be understood in a new way, of that she was certain. The promises of revelations that she had sensed all around her at Katherine's wedding were to be fulfilled. Besides, Will's curious escapade had already set the tone of the weekend. Everything was certain to be new and different.

She drove carefully through the narrow streets of the French Quarter, first to Will's apartment on St. Ann, and then from the apartment to Galatoire's. Certainly, she knew, it would be impossible ever to understand even so much as she could see and hear on this one short drive. Mysterious strangers, hurrying from work to stop at the neighborhood bar, swarmed on the sidewalks, men wearing the New Orleans uniform of wrinkled seersucker and jaunty panama, and calling to each other or to girls in light summer dresses, using the soft, slightly effeminate, Creole-touched New Orleans accent; and, jostling them, chatting on the corners, other men in work pants and khaki shirts pursued their secret errands, shouting occasionally in the unmistakable Brooklynesque language of the Irish Channel. The utter strangeness of the French Quarter, underlined by the unmistakable air of neighborhood, brought her to the thought: somebody knows and understands or tries to understand them all. Maybe something strange and incomprehensible happened to him, too, this afternoon, or to her. So — there's a key, there must be a key. If I can learn enough, even about one thing and one person, maybe I could begin to fit everything else into the picture. Maybe I could finally decide what to think.

She glanced quickly at Will sitting beside her in the car, and grinned to herself. *It's a hell of a note to have to decide what to think about a character like you,* she thought; but hidden under the wry young cynicism was another feeling altogether.

She had had from childhood a certain conception of Will as a man that would have taken harsher treatment than it had taken that afternoon. In the closed constellation of childhood to which everyone clings (and some for their whole lives) with a tenacity born of love and ignorance, he had occupied for her a peculiarly exalted spot. Father could recognize Tchaikovsky's Fifth Symphony and the Beethoven Third, and could still translate Caesar with ease; so, obviously, he knew more about music and Latin, as he did about everything, than anyone else in the world. Mother had spent a winter in Washington and made her debut there; she had visited in New Orleans and could speak with modest confidence of An-twine's, Solari's, the Carnival Krewes, and the Ver-sigh Oaks; so she was the most cultivated and widely traveled woman in the world. Gran had midwifed a Negro baby all by herself; so she was the most experienced and courageous. But Will! She remembered, as a little girl, telling her friends that she had an uncle she hadn't seen in seven years. Perhaps he came that year, the eighth, the year she first missed him, or perhaps the magical number seven never changed, no matter how many years elapsed. At any rate, her first memory of him was a flashing one of his face, one night in the winter after she was twelve. *Charlotte*, she heard him shout, and she saw his slight figure, his bright face, as alert as a vigilant squirrel's, and his gay, quizzical smile. That was the whole memory. But even then she had known a great deal about him. *That is to say*, she corrected herself, *I knew a great deal about what the family* thought *about him*. She had seen his picture as a dark and handsome lad of sixteen in his World War I private's uniform, and had heard in the guttural sound of her grandmother's voice — "The darling, the devil" — how passionately she loved him. She had heard her parents talk of his childhood pranks, of where he was or where he had last been heard from (if he happened to remember to send his mother a postcard) — La Paz, London, New Orleans, New York — seaports and cities in foreign lands. When he had settled in New Orleans, working as a clerk for one of the big wholesale importers of antiques she had heard how in spite of the fact that he had not bothered to finish high school he had risen quickly to a fine position. She had heard her mother, returning from a weekend in New Orleans, say ruthlessly to her father, "How on earth can he hold down a responsible job, drinking like he does? If I were his boss, I'd fire him in a minute." In Anna's gallery of childhood superlatives, Will had the distinction, when she had never seen a man drunk, of being able to drink more than anyone else in the world. All these memories made up her notion of what he was like — gay, charming, and irresponsible, a drunkard who had made a successful career for himself by sheer wit and brilliance, a free agent who lived his life as he pleased, who had dared when he was no older than she to cut himself loose, to think what he chose, and live as he pleased. Mysterious and wonderful, he moved confidently in a world so foreign that it touched hers only at the point where he passed easily from one to the other.

When she was seventeen, at just the age when she most needed an outsider to test herself on, he had been available, the one person in the world who could view their mutual circumstances with the understanding of a participant and the detachment of a god. She had been then at the farthest point in her orbit away from the central facts around which she revolved, straining with all the strength of her own weight and gravity to break loose from that private constellation and take a flyer through the universe. Neither Ralph nor Charlotte could possibly have told her anything to which she could have listened. But Will: there he was in New Orleans, embodying in himself, so she thought, all the ingredients of successful revolt. She was sure, too, that he had heard all about her, that she would have with him her own respectable status as a rebel. By the time she was a senior in high school, he knew that she was "brainy," and "serious," that she was involved in a desperate romance with a young man whom Charlotte and Ralph considered unsuitable. Ten years earlier he would have known nothing at all about her except vaguely that Charlotte

and Ralph had a child named Anna. But Anna did not notice
his changing attitude toward his family, much less consider the
implications. Will, moving in his orbit, had flung himself out
as far as he could go, and had begun to move down the far side
of the revolution of his life, inward, closer and closer to the
center that she was escaping. That, perhaps, was the reason
why, just when she needed him most, the summer she finished
high school, he and Eunice had invited her to spend a week
with them in New Orleans. Taylor had arranged to go at the
same time to visit his relatives, the "shanty-boat Irish" for
whom Charlotte supposedly had so much contempt. The week
had been a joyous idyll for the two young people. They had
spent their days wandering the French Quarter and the river-
front wharves, and riding the Algiers ferry; in the evenings Eunice and Will had taken them to dinner at Antoine's and Galatoire's and Tujacques' and The Court of the Two Sisters. Will
had been everything Anna could have wished for in a rebel
uncle. Charming and attentive, he had made her feel immediately that her life was her own. He had taken a liking to Taylor, and during their evenings together in the French Quarter
restaurants, had listened respectfully while Taylor put before
him a lively picture of himself and his view of the world. He
had had just the proper degree of tolerant and affectionate
scorn for Ralph's and Charlotte's limited ideas and unshak-
able conservatism, and he had amused the two children with
tales of his own wild youth in the army, in the merchant ma-
rine, and as a young man making his own way in the New Orleans world that Sherwood Anderson, William Faulkner, and
the other young intellectuals of his generation had already
made legendary.

But that had been a very special time. Anna, absorbed in
her obsession with Taylor and in full flight from her family,
had missed many things in Will that she was now ready to see
and hear. Now, three years older and surer of herself, and at
the same time cut loose from her dependence on Taylor to set

the tone of her life, she was both shyer and more open-minded. She, too, out of the dawning sense of her own individuality and independence, had begun to be able to allow herself to feel the first light tugs of the strands of family life, as the centers of family passion were defined before her eyes and found over and over again a point in time to express themselves. She had been to her first marriages and funerals and she waited trembling and confident before the approaching inevitable pressures of wartime, of births and christenings, anguished separations and joyful reunions. She was sometimes even able to imagine herself drawn into that same but always shifting pattern of love and likeness. When all those disparate individuals gathered from their separate lives — Will and Eunice, Charlotte and Ralph, Sarah D. and Charlie, Waldo and James, her grandmothers, Katherine and little Ralph, little Charlotte and Billy, and, as they added themselves, new husbands and wives and babies of her own generation, and the cousins and great-aunts who also had, each one, a fixed relation to the somehow homogeneous whole — she felt a dawning, yet unidentifiable wave of excitement. Gathering, separating, gathering again, they came together with glad cries of recognition; and almost without pausing to say hello, to touch cheeks in the accepted gesture of reserved affection, began anew old conversations, old quarrels, the settling of old problems, the retelling or finishing of jokes and stories that had patiently awaited these occasions through months of separation. And all of it, every word they said to one another, rested lightly on the mysterious base of shared experience, layers and layers, hundreds and thousands of years of shared experience, changing imperceptibly from generation to generation like the mysterious changes in a living, growing language, the ambiguous liveliness of words that hold in their roots and affixes, in their very concrete appearance, in their shifts of position and meaning, the whole mysterious, trembling, changing life of a nation.

It would not have surprised Anna, even at twenty, to hear

that Schliemann found the site of ancient Troy by reading Homer literally. She knew then that all she wanted to discover was *there* if she could only find the key to the language.

As for the afternoon's adventure, she was already beginning to forget it. Afterwards, looking back, she realized that she hardly wondered all evening if Will's arm was painful. He seemed to have forgotten it himself, and did not mention the wound or the incident to Charlie when they met at Galatoire's. In fact, he never mentioned it again, either to her or to Charlotte, and it was to remain for her what it had been that afternoon, an incomprehensible and absurd piece of violence that had no connection with anything. No, it was not quite true that it was without significance. She did feel that it marked a beginning. It stood up like a signpost on a tree-lined country road, not native to the landscape certainly, but having its own use. At last she had taken part in concert with her elders in an action where nothing was concealed, where she was not protected at any point by the superior strength and knowledge of others. She did not phrase it that way, or even think of it so clearly, for the thought would have involved admitting too much about the past, but she did see the signpost. Her sense of this new equality and responsibility was that "those others," whom she had always regarded with awe and struggled to be independent from, were as bewildered by their circumstances as children; and that "maturity" might consist simply in *having* to deal, bewildered or not, with whatever resources one had. This conviction and one concrete image of her mother imprinted for good and all on her memory were the profit of the afternoon's work. Charlotte, bent over and scared, making herself smaller, standing in the doorway and saying "I guess you know we're probably accessories." When it came again to her mind, she giggled uncontrollably. There were loyalties that Charlotte could call up, loyalties overriding conscience, caution, habit, distaste, inexperience, and fear; and *Will*, Will of all people, had been able to put them to his service.

The strange trio — the excited young girl with her shining sandy hair and her alert and trusting brown eyes, and the two middle-aged men, one small and for the moment subdued and obscured by his habitual sober response of gentlemanly self-effacement on entering a restaurant, the other huge, towering six-three, and carrying his two hundred and twenty pounds on light-stepping dancer's feet — followed the headwaiter as he walked ceremoniously among the small, white-clothed tables, and settled themselves at a table near the bar. Will ordered highballs for himself and Charlie and an old-fashioned for Anna, sighed, and leaned carefully back in his chair, unobtrusively favoring his wounded arm. Anna, who had learned to cover excitement, uncertainty, or anger by smoking, lit a cigarette.

To begin with, the conversation was stiff. Charlie, particularly, appeared ill at ease before the indisputable evidence that Anna was no longer the round-bellied, towheaded little girl who, summer mornings a few short years ago, had crawled into bed with him and Sarah D. for a game of Push-the-Button. Except at the wedding, he had had no more than a glimpse of her for several years. And Anna was not much help. Usually responsive to the advances of others, she still had her old difficulty in making the advances herself; and now her shyness had the appearance of a silent, somewhat enigmatic poise. She sipped her drink and waited.

"Recovered from the wedding yet?" Charlie asked, a little too heartily.

Anna nodded. "I hope I have as much fun at my own."

"Ha! Never," Will said. "Weddings are fun for everybody but the bride and groom."

"But where is Charlotte?" Charlie asked. "Didn't she come down with you?"

"You know Mama wouldn't have missed fixing up Mac and Katherine's apartment," Anna said. "Although, joking aside, they would have had a struggle doing it all themselves, with

Katherine working. We've really put in a day." She paused and glanced at Will, but he stared dreamily over her head and said nothing. "Mama was just too tired to come," she said. "She sent you her love, Charlie."

"Well, Mac seems to be a fine young fellow," Charlie said. "I was delighted with him, weren't you, Will?"

"She couldn't have done better," Will said. "He's just like a member of the family."

Anna tried to put her attention on what the two men were saying, but something else was tugging at her mind. "Mama kind of got carried away," she said irrevelantly. "I believe she tried to drink too many toasts." *It's their voices,* she thought. *It's the way they talk. Isn't that queer?* "You and Charlie talk alike, Will," she said suddenly. "Isn't that funny?"

"Not very," Will said. "I'd recognize a Homochitto accent if I heard it in Timbuctoo."

"No, I don't mean *that,*" Anna said. "I'd recognize that too. But Father doesn't talk like you all. It's . . . It's . . ."

"Ralph lived in the country," Will said. "He didn't talk to anybody but his mama and Clay Jr. until he went off to college."

Anna laughed. "You ought to hear him talk to Clay now," she said. "You can't understand a word either one of them says." Into their laughter she added, "I like the way you all talk. It's something about a certain kind of man. New Orleans men have it, too. I know a boy at school who has it, a boy from New Orleans." She glanced at Will shyly. "It's like, well, this is kind of dumb, but like you know when you hear it that the roughness has been smoothed out, that . . . that the person doesn't have to feel superior to anybody."

Will shook his head. "My dear," he said, "you can't imagine how many people Charlie and I have to feel superior to."

"You see?" she said. "You prove it when you make fun of yourself like that." *But that's not what I really mean,* she was thinking. *They do have to feel superior to all kinds of folks.*

I can't say it, but it's a little bit effeminate, I guess, if you aren't used to it, and there's an air to it, a manner that says, even if they never got through grammar school, "I'm secure in my cultivation and good manners."

"All it really means," Will said, "is that we were raised by strong-minded women who corrected our grammar and made a little education go a long way."

"But so was Father," she said.

"Your father's been associating with those Frenchmen around Eureka too long," Will said. "He may not speak Cajun, but he's acquired a Cajun accent."

"Old Ralph had a mighty good time at the wedding," Charlie said. "He was as excited as if it were his own."

Will chuckled. "Anna, did you know he paid all the servants twice after the wedding? Wasn't till he got round to the preacher that he found somebody too honest to take his money again."

"Ralph didn't come down with you?" Charlie asked.

"No," Anna said. "He's gone to a Presbytery meeting."

"Your father is a remarkable man, Anna," Will said solemnly. He shook his head as if in wonder and amazement. "Ah, those McGoverns! You know what Mama always says about 'em. They're too good. They just ain't human." He smiled slyly at her. "But I forgot. You're one, too, aren't you? The product of a formidable line!"

"Half, anyway," Anna said. "But I'm half the product of exactly the same thing you are."

"Presbyterians!" Will said. "Yes, I know we've got our share, too. But the Augustins and the Duprés give them a little trouble. You might say our Presbyterianism is adulterated. Or that's what the Presbyterians would say about the Creoles. They never have learned to occupy the same body in peace and comfort." He raised his glass and then set it down again slowly, as if against his will. "You see," he said, "dead or alive, they never give up. Every time the Creole wants a drink, one of those old Presbyterian elders is standing behind him tugging at his elbow or trying to tip the glass over. It's an endless battle. And they have health, clean living, and longevity on their side."

Anna laughed and picked up her own glass. "The Creoles seem to win a good part of the time," she said.

"Oh, but it's a struggle. I have to keep fit. Can't give an inch," Will said. "If I relax, the Presbyterians'll get me yet." He finished his drink and beckoned to the waiter to order another.

"Now your mother," he said, "anyone can see *she's* given up. Outnumbered. Can't cope with her Presbyterians and Ralph's, too. Or maybe it comes from being married to an honest man. *Ruinous.* And, young as I was, I saw it coming right from the beginning." He started to tilt his chair back, remembered where he was, and leaned forward instead, putting his good arm on the table and keeping his bad one carefully immobile. "I'll never forget it," he said. "It was during the war — you know I lied about my age and joined the army when I was sixteen — well, Ralph and Charlotte hadn't been married long, and they were on their way to Ralph's station, out in San Antonio, I think, and they stopped off to see me. I was at Camp Beauregard, out from Alexandria. I was in some kind of trouble at the time and couldn't get a pass. But I managed to get hold of a lieutenant's uniform and dressed myself up in it and slipped off the base to have dinner with them. Had to put on a good appearance, you understand. Ralph and Charlotte were really impressed. A lieutenant already! They've always credited me with more brains than I have. Can you believe it? Charlotte actually thought I'd been promoted — brevetted on the field of battle, so to speak. She wrote home about it. Well, I paid for that prank — paid and paid. But the point of the story is this: I think she'd already fallen under Ralph's influence so thoroughly, she'd lost her sense of proportion. That's the drawback for the liar when he's dealing with honest people. They begin to trust him, and then he doesn't get credit for his ingenuity."

"Mama manages to get along," Anna said, a little stiffly.

"One thing about being good," Will said. "You can always afford the luxury of honesty."

"Maybe, but when you say that, after all, you're being honest yourself. So what's the difference?"

"Only because it suits my purpose tonight," Will said. "What I really mean about Ralph and Charlotte is, they confuse innocence with virtue. But once you lose your innocence, you can't condemn a sinner without condemning yourself. I don't think Charlotte and Ralph will ever do anything bad enough to acquire the virtue of humility."

Anna flushed with anger. "You ought not to say things like that to me, Will," she said.

"You all are going to get in a fuss if you don't watch out," Charlie said. "Drink up, Will, and let's order."

"No hurry," Will said. "Take our time. Anna doesn't get to New Orleans very often, and we're just beginning to get reacquainted. Would you like another drink, sweetheart?"

Anna nodded.

"Well then," Charlie said, "order me one, too, and stop philosophizing, will you?"

"What's the news from home?" Will said to Charlie when the drinks had been ordered, fresh cigarettes lighted, and everyone had settled down again. "Have you heard from Sarah D. this week?"

Charlie shook his head. "I'll be going home for the weekend," he said. "They're probably still recovering from the wedding."

"I thought Mama and Sis both looked grand at the wedding," Will said. "And of course Sarah D. is always on top of the world." He looked deliberately at Anna as if consciously launching them on a new and complex topic of conversation.

"Sis was in better spirits than I've seen her in for a long time. Her own sweet, loving self."

"Sis is all right," Charlie said. "I always said she'd get over it, if they'd let her alone and give her time."

Anna began to shiver with nervous excitement and anticipation. She clamped her teeth together and turned her sweating drink round and round with icy hands.

Now Charlie leaned forward, looked around as if he thought someone might be eavesdropping, and said in a low, conspiratorial voice, "I didn't get a chance to tell you at the wedding, Will, but I ran into Alderan a couple of weeks ago."

"You did! Where?"

"I'd gone over to New Iberia on business, fellow over there's got a proposition we're working on, and I saw him in a bar. First time I'd seen him in years. Since before the divorce, in fact. It kind of gave me a turn, I'll tell you. Walked into one of those little old dingy French night clubs, dark as a cave on a sunny afternoon, and there he was."

"Did you fall out with Alderan like everybody else?" Anna asked. "Do you speak to him?"

The taut skin of Charlie's forehead shone in the shifting light as he rocked back in his chair expansively, hitched one arm over the back, and meditatively patted his rib cage.

(*Tilt down, Charlie*, Anna heard Gran say sharply.)

"I'll tell you, Anna," he said, turning his long, heavy-jowled face toward her and nodding with an air of confiding wisdom. "I was the only person involved in that fracas didn't get mad with anybody. Now, I'm not saying I won't fight, if a man crosses me. I never try to get out of a fight. But that wasn't my fight. I kept my mouth shut and minded my own business."

"What was he doing down there?" Will asked. "Did you talk to him?"

"Certainly I talked to him. He and his wife were down there visiting some of her relatives. You know those Cajuns are all related to each other. But he was drunk. I couldn't get much sense out of him. He'd gotten sick of cousins and he was really tying one on. He did say, poor fellow, that his wife wouldn't let him drink at home."

"Out of the frying pan into the fire," Will said. "You'd think he would have picked a wife who didn't have so much family, for a change."

"You know, Will, I told him," Charlie said, rocking forward with a thump and wagging his finger at Will, "I couldn't help telling him. 'Alderan,' I says, 'do you know how the police go about looking for somebody who's pulled a vanishing act? If he's an insurance salesman from a town of thirty thousand people, who liked to bowl, who deserted a thin, blond wife in a five-room house, they simply check all the new insurance salesmen in towns of thirty thousand, and they find him living in a five-room house with a new thin blond wife. He's probably already joined a bowling team. You can't change human nature.' But he didn't listen. He was too drunk.

" 'All-dy-baron,' he says to me, 'Charlie, you know my name's All-dy-baron? My daddy named me for a star,' he says, 'and then he took off and he ain't been seen from that day to this.' He looks at me, bleary-eyed and head waggling, and actually, *actually*, he's got tears in his eyes. Then he says, 'My mama didn't like his ways. He left, and all she said was "Good riddance! Good riddance to bad rubbish. Men." And I say the same. Only I say, "Women!" '

" 'You got to persist in getting tied up with a house full of women,' I said. 'What do you do it for?' "

"I can see Sis and Sarah D.'s faces if they heard you putting them in the class with the Couvillions and Gremillions," Will said with his staccato, deprecating laugh.

But what about Alderan, Anna thought. *Did he have it so rough? Crying because his daddy named him for a star.*

"Humph, I'd just as soon stick my head in a tiger's mouth as mention his name to Sis."

Anna gripped her glass tighter to keep her cold hands from shaking. "What really happened?" she asked. "I've always wanted to know what really happened."

"Honey, you've come to the right place to find out," Charlie said, "because I'm the one who can tell you. I was there. I saw the end of it." He cocked his head on one side as if a thought had struck him. "But I reckon your daddy's told you all about that," he said.

"Father's never mentioned Alderan to me in his life," she said. "Oh, Mama told me that after he and Father fell out, Sis stuck by him a while longer, and then finally when he kept on seeing that girl down in Maraisville, she gave up and got a divorce. That's all I know about it, except that you can't mention his name in front of Sis."

"You mean!" Charlie gave a grunt of incredulity and tilted back again. "So he never told you. Probably never told Charlotte, either. If that don't take the cake."

•§•

It all began when your father got that levee job down by Maraisville, Anna. Do you remember? Rough! Rough ain't the word for it. Now, I don't know anything about building levees, mind you, but I can tell you, he slipped when he contracted for that job. There was a bed of quicksand along the river there, any farmer who'd lost a cow in it could've told him, I'll bet you, and as fast as they poured dirt onto the levee, it sank. That's why they were working down there so long. Over a year. Ralph lost his shirt on it. 1933. The state of Louisiana was bankrupt. There was no construction work going on. No roadbuilding anywhere, just the federal government building levees and so forth. And that quicksand! Looking back, it seems as if we were all in quicksand then. Shoveling ourselves in and getting sucked under and wondering if we'd ever hit bottom. Eh, Will? And it looked like we never would.

Well, that job was the beginning of the trouble between Alderan and Sis. Rather, the beginning of the end of the trouble. Mind you, I realize there must have been some trouble before, but Sis never opened her mouth against him, and he certainly wasn't going to tell tales on himself, not even to me, although he did feel easier with me than with anybody else in the family. I wouldn't say Alderan had a wandering eye — I don't know. I never saw him up to any monkey business. But — ha — he's a *man*, ain't he? Now don't look at me like that, Anna. You've got a lot to learn about the world. And *Sis!* Sis expects too much of a man, don't she, Will? She's not one to take a man easy. Oh, I don't mean she wasn't devoted to him. She was crazy in love with him, and that's a fact. But living with a woman like Sis, and a woman, to boot, who adores the ground you walk on, could get to be — tiring. And, if you'll forgive me, Will, there were other drawbacks, from his angle. Miss Kate can be mighty ornery, if she takes a notion. I sometimes wonder . . . wonder if he didn't realize . . . if he didn't get to knowing for the first time that he was nothing but po' white trash. Seeing how other folks live can be — broadening. But the trouble was, Alderan didn't want to be improved. He couldn't take advantage of it.

So there they were, staying with you all. Ralph had given him a job when he was down and out, the third year they'd been married. Before that they'd lived a year and a half with Mrs. A. In fact, they hadn't lived alone, except for that little while in Texas. Well, it was the depression, don't forget that. Pear summer and rabbit winter. Everybody was doing what he could, but things could have been better. Alderan and Sis weren't any worse off than the rest of us. Not many folks had more than a piddling job they might lose any day. Take me, for instance. You know I've always been willing to take a long chance, to gamble on a good thing. Well, the chances that were there for the taking in the early thirties would have made your mouth water — the property to be had for nothing but taxes. And I *knew* it. I knew things had to go up. They couldn't go down any more. Why, if I could have gotten hold of a little capital then, right now I'd be the richest man in Mississippi. But all I could do was manage to keep eating. Bankers!

I'm getting off the subject. All I meant was that Alderan and Sis weren't any worse off than lots of other folks — living with relatives, taking what came to hand to do, and damn lucky not to be hungry.

Now nobody but a fool would ever have thought your mother and daddy could get along with Alderan, much less live in the house with him; but necessity is the mother of some hellish inventions, and Sis and Alderan were broke. What else could anybody have done? I'd have given him a job if I could've, Will would have. Anybody would under the circumstances, if they could. To make it harder on everybody, I can't believe Ralph was paying Alderan much, because he was in one helluva mess himself, with the levee sinking in the quicksand fast as they piled the dirt on it.

The reason I say all this is because I see Alderan's side of it, up to a point. I couldn't live with 'em. You ought to know, Anna, you're a grown woman, there's a certain rigidity there . . . Charlotte, for instance, thinks I'm a no-good bastard and she'll go right on thinking so if she's forced to nurse me back from death's door. And mind you, if she had to, she'd nurse me. I know that. And also mind you, in a way she's fond of me, as I am of her. And how about Will here? Her own brother? I know she loves him, but still she thinks he's a bastard, too. She can't understand why everybody in the world isn't just like Ralph except not always late for dinner, and not quite so stubborn and hardheaded. Maybe, maybe it's something about luck. They've been too lucky. You reckon, Will? They have no patience with failure. I realize I keep getting off the track, but there are things about what happened that you can't see on the face of a violent quarrel, things that trigger one man's hatred and another man's courage. That's what I'm trying to get at, talking about Ralph and Charlotte. They want to be charitable, I reckon (to the *deserving* poor, to those on whom a misfortune beyond their control has fallen, like, say, blindness), but they just can't understand how people can do bad things and still not be bad. And it's all because they're so damn lucky. They're lucky; I'm unlucky. I've had some good ideas in my time, but I've been unlucky with them, while Ralph — he's even lucky at cards. You know yourself, Anna, he's a wild bidder. But he just can't lose; he always holds all the cards. If he were a serious gambler, he could make a fortune. Now take Will here. Will's lucky, too, but his character holds him back. Combine luck and character, and you have a man who finds it mighty hard to understand failure.

So: lucky old Ralph — he's got a contract with the federal government. He's managed to borrow the money to keep on financing his operation even though everybody knows the levee is on quicksand, probably managed it because the bank president liked his looks, I can't think of any other good reason. He hires his poor brother-in-law (who never got a chance to charm a bank president in his life) to run a dragline and foreman a section of his levee crew for him. Do you wonder there was trouble?

How do you think Alderan felt, living in Ralph's house, rescued from the bread line by his righteous and prosperous brother-in-law? He hated it from the beginning. I think he got to where he got a kick out of stealing from Ralph just to *show* him. I think he might even, crazy as it sounds, have taken up with the girl in the beginning just to prove he was a man. Well . . . it's all pretty complicated, but give the poor bastard his due.

Anyway he did take up with her — a cute little nineteen-year-old French girl from Maraisville. Now don't let anyone tell you an arrangement like that is all fun. It costs money — a lot more than Alderan was making. So: so, somehow or other he began to make a little extra off your daddy. The way it was, I think (now Alderan never told me this; he never admitted it was true; but your mother told Sarah D.), he was taking a little tractor fuel whenever he needed money, and selling it on the side. Just a drum or two when he needed some cash. Ralph found out about it. He must have practically caught Alderan red-handed, because I can't see old Ralph nosing around *looking* for something to use against Alderan. He wouldn't do anything to upset the family apple cart unless he felt like he had to. Of course, you have to take into account the fact that Alderan had this woman down there and Ralph knew it. In fact, everyone knew it, even Sis, because he got where he hardly ever came home. And Maraisville is a small town. Folks down there could see what was going on. That kind of thing doesn't go down with Ralph. He's one of those freaks of human nature — a natural monogamist; and he had no patience with it. Oh, in a way it wasn't any of his business. But they *were* living in his house; Sis *is* his sister-in-law. I expect it was hard for him to take. I think myself that he would have let Alderan steal him blind if it hadn't been for the woman.

Now, if it had been me, if I'd caught him stealing from me, I'd have handled it different. I'd've fought him. Yes, I would. I'd've let him get in a couple of licks to salve his pride, and then I'd've beat him to a pulp. He would have understood that. He could have gone on working for me if he wanted to; but he would have known who was the boss, and he would have had to keep his nose clean while he was in my territory and living in my house. Sis wouldn't have had to know a thing about it. When you get right down to it, it wasn't a woman's business to know anything about it.

But that wasn't Ralph's way. He fired Alderan. And he told him why he was firing him. Alderan told me *that* the day he got so drunk. "I told the s.o.b." (excuse me, Anna), he says, "I told him I wouldn't steal from him if I was starving. I told him what he was, a Christer, a mealy-mouthed, hypocrite Christer. And he didn't even answer me," he says. "Coward.

The bastard didn't even hit me. I'm gonna make him hit me, if it's the last thing I do."

Talk, all talk, so it turned out. And I must say I took it with a grain of salt when he said it. I can size a man up.

Sis was in Homochitto when Ralph fired him. She'd gone home on a visit, probably because Alderan's staying down in Maraisville had gotten too embarrassing — certainly not because she'd quit him, not by a long shot. So Alderan hightails it to Homochitto. He was stone-broke and had to eat, I reckon. From all that happened afterward, I'd say by that time he was already beginning to think about a divorce. Maybe the girl was already pregnant. No, that came later, the following year.

I was working in Homochitto along through there, so I was home when he got there. Lord, you can't imagine what a mess it was. Sarah D. and Mrs. A. were in a state. Charlotte had written and told them what happened. Sis wasn't saying a word. She and Alderan shut themselves up in their old apartment in the wing and stayed there. They could have been dead for all anybody in the house saw them. That lasted about two days. God knows what Alderan told her. I can hear his voice now, when he'd come home in the old days right after they married. You know he has kind of a quick, light, scratchy voice, like two days' growth of a stiff beard. "Here's my girl; here's my baby," he says to Sis. And he looks at her like they've got a secret between em. I felt it. Lord, yes, anybody would. It was hardly decent. Sarah D. tells me he's real sexy, so maybe that's what it is — I wouldn't know. I don't think that skinny, wiry type would appeal to me, if I were a woman. But whatever it is, he got around Sis. Told her he'd quit the girl, I reckon, and that Ralph had accused him of stealing, and that he'd been insulted and quit. And she swallowed it, hook, line, and sinker. Took him right in, shut the door, and didn't come out for two days. But he was bouncing around like a drop of water on a hot skillet. He couldn't stay shut up long. He was mad, and before long he was drunk. Got some money out of Sis, I reckon, and for all I know she may have gotten it out of Sarah D. It was when he got drunk that I got involved. I'm not much of a drinking man, myself — a couple of highballs at a party and a glass of beer on a summer evening, fine, but I can take it or leave it, so it seems I'm the one who takes care of drunken friends and relatives. You know there's always got to be somebody to drive home from the party. Ain't that right, Will? Anyway, the fourth day I went out with him. He'd stumbled in late the night before, waked up everybody in the house, and by eleven the next morning he was at it again.

He was mad with himself. Someway or other he'd gone off without fighting Ralph, and he couldn't understand how it had happened. Someway, he'd come off second best, and he was really mad. I could've told him, in fact I did tell him, Ralph would be a hard man to fight if he didn't *want* to fight, and he don't ever want to, far as I know. Not that I've ever tried, mind you, never had the occasion. But look at Alderan. Be like a little old feisty dog jumping on a bear. A feist has got plenty of guts, now, and I've seen one jump a bear just for the sheer hell of it, and get his belly laid open for his trouble. But Ralph . . . He'd just stick out his paw, I reckon, and hold Alderan off. Well, I shouldn't have told him Ralph was too big for him to fight, because then he decided he'd kill him. He went and got him a gun, and he made me take him to the bus station and he bought a one-way ticket to Eureka (he was running out of money) and he was on his way. I went in the bus station coffee shop and thought it over. To tell you the truth, I was feeling a little bit uneasy. Hell and high water wouldn't have kept Alderan from getting on the bus, and I hadn't even tried. I'm not one to stop two grown men from killing each other if they want to. I wouldn't appreciate any interference under the same circumstances myself. And I knew Alderan well enough to be pretty sure he wouldn't shoot Ralph in the back. No indeed, he was going to call him out. And I figured

that was between him and Ralph. But still, there were Sis and
Charlotte to think about, and you kids. It struck me Sarah D.
would be pretty mad at me if I didn't at least try to keep Alderan from fighting a duel with your daddy. So I got in the
car and went to Eureka. Burned up the road. I made it in two
hours and forty-five minutes, and had to wait for the bus to
come in. I was hoping Alderan would have sobered up and
changed his mind, and I could take him back to Homochitto.
I knew he only had about one drink left in his bottle when he
got on the bus, and no money. He'd sobered up some all right
by the time he got to Eureka, but he was still as mean as a blind
snake in the spring.

"I'm gonna kill him," he says, and that's all he'd say. "I'm
gonna kill him" — pardon me, Anna — "the son of a bitch, the
mealy-mouthed Christer." Well, Anna, I'd say he never did
understand your father a-*tall*. From the beginning he never
knew what made him tick, and he never found out. I'd say he
thought your father had had his fling when he'd wanted to,
that he just wasn't *open* about it. I'd say he couldn't possibly
imagine the kind of folks the McGoverns are. You understand?
We — the Andersons, I mean, and me, a Dupré — we were
hard enough for him to take. But your daddy! Alderan just
assumed, I reckon, that your daddy was through with whoring,
and self-righteous about it to boot. And as for the other, the
tractor fuel business, I think . . . Well, I don't know what I
think about that, but I know he wasn't going to let himself be
made out a thief for a few measly drums of tractor fuel taken
in a good cause.

Anyway, the upshot of it was, he sent me to find Ralph
and tell him he was gunning for him. I remember Ralph was
playing tennis out at the city courts that day. Does he still
play tennis every afternoon in the summer, Anna? I went
by the house and they told me where he was, and I went on
out to the tennis courts. There he was, red as a lobster and
sweating, in his white tennis slacks and green eyeshade and

his belt right straight around the middle of his stomach.

Well, he looked at me like he thought I was crazy, and to tell you the truth, I felt a little bit silly. "I can't help it," I told him. "I came over here to try to stop him. He came on the bus himself, and he's down at the bus station now."

Ralph whips the grass a couple of times with his tennis racket.

"Is he drunk?" he says.

"He was," I say, "but he's pretty sober now."

Ralph goes over to the drinking fountain and gets a drink of water. He pulls his handkerchief out of his pants pocket and wipes the sweat off his head and face, and then he stands there a minute like he's thinking, and finally he pulls his watch out and looks at it. Then he comes back over to me.

"I'm playing *tennis*," he says. "I'll be out here another hour. You tell him how to find the tennis courts, and tell him if he wants to see me, I'm out here." He shrugs his shoulders and pokes out his lower lip. "Does he think I'm gonna come down there and shoot up the bus station?" he says. "Tell him I said put up his gun and go home."

So off I went. Last I heard was the ping-plop of balls on rackets and courts, and Ralph and the fellow he was playing with calling out to each other.

"Add out, isn't it?"

"Right."

"Ready?"

"Serve."

I knew I was taking fuel to Alderan's fire, and sure enough he turned green with rage when I told him what Ralph had said.

"I'm gonna kill him," he says, "if it's the last thing I do."

That was before they built the new bus station in Eureka, when the buses used to leave from that big old bare terminal down by the city carbarns. Buses warming up and coming and going, and folks shouting and banging boxes around, and

all the niggers in town going off to the country for the weekend, and all the niggers in the country coming to town. The
noise bounced off those hot steel girders and bare corrugated
tin plates in the roof, and hit the hot, greasy concrete floor, and
bounced back. It was like a cave in hell. Made me right sick
to look at Alderan standing in the middle of the hot shouting
and coming and going, with his mouth getting littler and thinner, and his eyes glaring round, like he expected one of these
hollering folks to insult him — to give him a chance to knock
somebody down.

"Come on, old buddy," I say. "Let's go get a drink and get
comfortable." It had struck me, if my money held out, I might
get him drunk enough to pass out.

But he won't. He makes me go to the coffee shop next door
and we sit there at the counter awhile, looking at two hot cups
of coffee, and him stirring, stirring. I was waiting and he was
boiling. That's what it looked like. The sweat poured off him
like he was a kettle boiling over. He didn't say much at all, and
what he said, I couldn't make any sense out of it, and I've forgotten most of it, like you do if you've gotten in a tight and
afterwards feel sick.

I remember he did say, once, just out of the blue, looking
straight at me, "I gave you all the room I could, but you've got
to back me into a corner."

"Me?" I say. "*Me?*"

The sweat was dripping off his eyebrows and running into
his eyes and he wipes his face and kind of chuckles. "Yes," he
says. "All of you. You're all alike."

A man can go on trying to think he's right when all the evidence is against him.

He gets up and puts a dime on the counter. "Come on,
Charlie," he says, "I can afford to buy you a cup of coffee."
And then, when he's leaving, putting his money, two or three
quarters and some nickels, back in his pocket, and walking
through the café door out into the bright afternoon where

the niggers are running to catch the next bus to Paducah, dragging their kids, and hollering for the driver to wait, "I'll *make*
him," he says, just as quiet, conversational. "He'll stop playing
tennis, all right."

The upshot of it was that he made me drive him to
Maraisville and he holed up down there. At least he had sense
enough not to go out to the tennis court and make a fool of
himself. Or maybe he was already beginning to lose his nerve.
But he didn't act like he was losing his nerve. He was spoiling
for that fight.

I reckon the girl gave him some money when he got down
there. I didn't have any to give him. (You know, by the way,
the girl's family are respectable people, even if they are
Frenchmen, and she was supposed to be a nice, quiet, well-
behaved young woman until Alderan got to her. The family
didn't know anything about the affair until she got pregnant.
But I'll tell you about that in a minute.) I let Alderan out by
the hotel in Maraisville and he sent me back to Eureka with a
message for Ralph. I didn't try to stay with Alderan, I can tell
you. By then I was sick of fooling with him. Damn crazy man.
Let him manage his own affairs. He said tell Ralph he was in
Maraisville. He was armed, and he was going to shoot Ralph
on sight. He knew Ralph had to come down there to work
every day, and he figured that would force his hand. I went
back to Eureka and gave Ralph the message. And then I went
home. Alderan was sober and Ralph knew what to expect. I
figured the rest wasn't any of my business. And I was sick of
it, *sick* of it.

But at least the scene was set for Maraisville — for St. Alicia
Parish, where neither one of them would get into any trouble
with the law, as they certainly would have in Eureka. Those
Frenchmen don't believe in sticking their noses into other people's family quarrels. Not that everybody in town — everybody but the girl's family — didn't know what was going on.
Alderan had his friends down there, and believe it or not, so

had Ralph. He knows how to get along with those folks. In fact, I believe he talks their lingo a little bit. *Keska say ka sah* and so forth. Then, too, Ralph had been working on that sinking levee for nearly a year already, and the town had a certain amount of sympathy for a man who was so obviously behind the eight-ball.

So: there it was, all set up, and Alderan figured if Ralph came down there with a gun, they would shoot it out, and if he didn't come, that would prove he was a coward and a liar, too. But I don't believe he ever figured for a minute that Ralph would come. He'd lived in the house with him a year and worked for him. He saw him going about his business every day and to church on Sunday, quiet as could be; he never heard him tell a dirty joke or saw him get drunk; he knew he didn't even own a pistol. He saw him every day on the job, always wearing his single-breasted suit, never going without a vest, and staying as clean as a bank clerk when he was standing on top of a bed of quicksand; and if you'll excuse me, Anna, he probably heard your mama raise hell with him occasionally and saw that he never answered back. He thought Ralph was a coward. He *knew* he was a coward. *I* never would have done what Ralph did. I would have found Alderan right then and there, while he was mad as hell, and shot it out with him. I wouldn't let any man think I was a coward for longer than it would take me to get to him. But I see how he (Ralph, I mean) did it. The fact about him that Alderan never did understand, that made him turn tail at the last and run, is that Ralph can't be budged. He's gonna *do* what he's gonna *do*. Your mama can fuss, Alderan can wave his gun, the country can go to the dogs, the gates of hell can yawn right smack in front of him, but once he's decided what he's gonna do, he just calmly goes ahead and does it, as calmly as if he were blind, deaf, and crazy.

I heard a good bit about it afterward from Joe Laborde who runs the café down at Maraisville. Here comes Ralph, the next morning, heading for his job. He stops at the edge of town at Laborde's coffee shop like he does every day to get a cup of coffee and a piece of pie. (You probably don't know it, Anna, but your daddy always has been crazy about pie for breakfast, and your mama won't give it to him, because she knows he's got a tendency to get fat. She ought to know better. He's gonna have his pie, if he wants it.) So in he comes and sits down at the counter and orders his pie just like he's used to doing every day.

You ever been down there? Joe's café is right on the edge of town to the left of the road coming in from Eureka, set back off the road with a gravel parking lot in front and great big live oak trees all around it. The bayou runs behind it, and Joe sells fishing tackle and has a little dock back there where he rents out a few boats. And he's got a barn of a dance hall hooked onto the side of the café, a great big bare place with Spanish moss hanging from the rafters like dusty rain — that's for decoration. You take your life in your hands if you go down there on a Saturday night.

Joe Laborde's a good man, and a big man, for a Frenchman. He's about five ten and he's got a belly on him big as a good-sized watermelon and tight as a drum skin. Solid. He may eat too much, but you could break your fist on that belly. He sports one of these little black mustaches like so many of 'em wear, and on him it kind of droops down like it's trying to hide his mouth — so you'll think he's mad sometimes, when mostly he can't help being in a good humor. His face is so round and red and his belly so big, I reckon his mustache thinks folks would take him for a clown if it didn't give him a serious look. Joe runs his café and his boats and his dance hall, and he used to bootleg a little during prohibition, and he doesn't bother anybody. He's fished plenty of folks out of the bayou when he's had to, and he looks like he's known for a long time that he can handle most anything comes along. He keeps a gun there in the café to kill the moccasins and rattlers that like his old rotten dock in the back, but Saturday afternoon he takes his gun home for the weekend. Anybody makes trouble on Saturday night he can handle em with his bare hands.

That morning Joe is waiting for Ralph, worried. He knows what time Ralph comes in every morning, and he's screwed up in a knot waiting to hear his car pull up. He's gotten to like Ralph in the year he's been getting his pie there every morning — you know, the queer stand-offish liking where a man says to himself about another, *If there weren't so many things in the way, we could be friends.* But he doesn't ever step across a line that he's drawn himself, or put his mouth on the feeling, so to speak. Of course, Joe knows Alderan's gunning for Ralph, everybody in town knows it; and he feels bad about the whole dirty business. He likes Alderan, too. Truth is, nobody except Mrs. A. could keep from liking Alderan. Joe's already been talking to Alderan about the fight — not to back out, he wouldn't think of suggesting that, but to shoot for the arm, not to try to kill Ralph when he's got a wife and three kids to take care of, and so forth and so forth. And now Joe's waiting to talk to Ralph. I reckon he's the only man in that dark, tight little town would interfere in a fight. Maraisville's one place left in the world where a man's still supposed to be ready to defend himself and his own. But Joe doesn't want to see anybody get killed. You know, he told me in confidence one time (I can tell you all; you'll never see him) that he faints at the sight of blood. How about that? That tough Frenchman. I told him, taking everything into consideration, I thought he could afford to faint once in a while and not lose his reputation. But to get back to the story, Joe had made up his mind he was going to approach Ralph — step across the line, so to speak. Now Ralph's a hard man to approach on a personal matter, but Joe's gonna do it or bust.

Well, anyhow, like I said, Ralph comes in and says good morning and orders his pie and coffee and Joe brings it. You know how Ralph has a different way of beginning a conversation with different people, kind of a ritual that he uses all the time? Like with Mrs. A. it's, "Well, old Dear, how's your corporosity segashuating?" With Joe he'd always say on Monday morning, "Ah, Laborde, bonjour, bonjour," and then look around like he's looking for evidence of a fight and say, "Place get raided Sat'dy night?" And then, "Ha, ha, ha." It was a standing joke between them, because of course the place never got raided. In fact, the humor of it probably escaped Joe, but he always went along. Today, he says, he didn't. He stands in front of Ralph with his hands on the counter, looking down at him and concentrating on what he's gonna say, and when he doesn't answer, Ralph looks up.

"Eh?" Ralph says.

Joe plunges right in. "Mr. McGovern," he says. "I tell you *this*. Listen. In Maraisville everybody know Wheelwright will fight you. You know *that*? Everybody know, but nobody say nothing. I, Joseph Laborde, I speak. I tell you what I think."

That kind of sets Ralph back. His face settles. You know how a man's face kind of settles in when he gets a shock?

"That right?" he says, and he begins eating his pie.

"Listen to me, Laborde, Mr. McGovern," Joe says. "I like you. I tell you for your good. You kill Wheelwright, then you get trouble. Nothing but trouble you get from it. Too much killing. Always down here, too much fighting and killing. And for what? Money and whiskey and women. When a man is dead he cares no more for money and whiskey and women." He stops and waits, but Ralph doesn't say anything, just goes on eating his pie with a frown on his face like maybe he bit down on a rock.

Joe starts again. "I got no right," he says, "but I tell you. I regard you highly, my friend. So I tell you, you shoot for the shoulder, the right shoulder, the right arm. You save yourself trouble, and you still give satisfaction."

Ralph puts his fork down and he looks real friendly at Joe,

and then he says, "Don't worry about it, Laborde. I'm not gonna shoot him a-tall."

"Ah," Joe says. And he's thinking to himself he'll tell Alderan that. Alderan won't kill a man he knows isn't even going to aim at him.

"I don't like shooting," Ralph says. "And I'm certainly not gonna shoot my wife's brother-in-law."

"That's right," Joe says. "You shoot over his head. Aim high."

"I'm not talking about that kind of foolishness," Ralph says. "I save my shot for birds." And that's all he'll say about it. He starts talking about hunting, and a good bird dog he's thinking about buying, and he eats his pie and drinks his coffee, and out he goes. It's plain as the nose on your face he hasn't even got a gun with him.

Well, I guess that was the last thing Alderan would have expected to hear. He would never even have thought about that. "Either he'll come and we'll shoot it out and get it over with, or he won't come like the coward I know he is, and I'll have faced him down." That would be the way he'd have figured it.

But we'll never know what he thought, because he didn't wait to find out that Ralph was unarmed. He was gone when Joe called to tell him. Somebody, one of his friends, the desk clerk said, had just gone up to his room, and they'd come down together and left. Now, I think Alderan, knowing Ralph's habits, probably had somebody posted in Laborde's when Ralph came in, somebody who was supposed to come and tell him if he did show up. The way I figure it is, the friend, whoever it was, went on down to the hotel to tell him Ralph was there, and at the last minute Alderan lost his nerve. Lost his nerve at the end, feisty little man, though I never would have expected him to. The bear came, and he ran. Didn't wait to hear that the bear had clipped his own claws.

They say down there that Ralph parked his car and walked the main street of Maraisville from one end to the other. Can't you see him, Will? With his coat straight, not a wrinkle in it, and his hat on his head, and his white shirt right fresh from the washwoman, walking down that gloomy street, brisk and sway-back, like he was a little late for Sunday school. And all the curlyheaded, blackheaded Frenchmen standing around watching him and waiting for the shooting to begin.

Maraisville's a spooky little town, anyway. The gray moss hangs low in your face. Down there, it grows even on the telephone poles and the wires if they don't keep clearing it away. The bayou runs round one side and joins the river right below town, so it's almost an island. Water everywhere you look — the bayou, black as death and still, where there's open water, and so choked up in places with water hyacinths you can't get a boat through; and the river and the quicksand on the other side. A man could disappear down there, and who would know what had happened to him? In town there are so many trees it's like dusk of a rainy day on the main street at noon. Nobody ever needed to cut one down to make room for a building; the stores are just squeezed under 'em, not much bigger than packing crates, and the hotel looks like it's been there since the trees were acorns. Out from the north edge of town, coming down from Eureka, you drive through a palmetto swamp as treacherous and barren as a desert, green spiky fans sticking up everywhere out of rotten-smelling mud. No farm land to speak of. I don't know how the town ever got started. It's like they just got there and couldn't get any farther. And everywhere there's an open sunny spot you see rows of frames all hung with gray moss where they're drying it for mattresses.

So Ralph walks in the shade and the gloom past the packing-crate stores, through the smell of magnolia trees and Cape jessamine and honeysuckle, like a funeral, looking for Alderan and not looking for him, with the Frenchmen leaning against the store fronts watching. He tips his hat and he walks along. "Bonjour, bonjour." He goes to the hotel and he buys some stamps and mails a letter. He even goes in the bar and orders a bottle of beer and drinks a couple of swallows. No Alderan. So he walks back to Laborde's and gets in his car, and goes back to the business of dumping rocks into the quicksand, and never says another word about it to a soul, as far as I know. Probably forgot about it.

That's the end of his part of it. He never saw Alderan again. But what he did that day, what he had guts and luck enough to get away with, I admire him for it, Anna. He took a line I never would have taken, but just the same, I see it.

The way it ended . . . Alderan got a job in Lake Charles and Sis went down there with him. She pawned her rings that her daddy had left her to get them down there. Nobody knows where she took them, and of course she never got them back. Sarah D. tried to find out where they were because Charlotte wanted to redeem them, but Sis wouldn't tell. They settled down in Lake Charles, and Sis had another miscarriage down there, her third; but it wasn't long before Alderan was going back to Maraisville to see the girl, and within six months he got her pregnant. Then her family found out. He told Sis the girl's father was going to kill him, and for all I know he may have threatened to. Oh, Alderan was a slick one. He told Sis, too, that he knew he had done wrong, that the girl was young and respectable, and that he had to do right by her. That's the way he worked the divorce.

For the rest . . . Sarah D. had the brunt of the rest of it. I know Sis never mentioned Alderan to Mrs. A. again, never spoke his name in her presence after she came home to get the divorce. She couldn't have, because she knew Mrs. A. had the upper hand. God, how she'd hated Sis marrying him. She'd gone on her knees and wept and begged her not to marry him, and she'll never forgive Sis for that. To give her credit, she never said, "I told you so." But sometimes you can hear it in her voice when she's mad at Sis.

As for Ralph, Sis told Sarah D. to keep him away, she never

wanted to see him again. Somehow or other, even after it was all over, she still blamed him. Do you reckon she never believed Alderan took the tractor fuel? I don't know, but I know she put it all on their going to live in Eureka. Ralph had destroyed Alderan. So Sarah D. told Ralph he better not come to the house any more when he was in Homochitto. Sis didn't want to set eyes on him, and under the circumstances Sis had to be humored. He thought that over all one day, and along about four-thirty in the afternoon, he stopped by and picked Sarah D. up at work to take her home.

"Now, Sarah D." he says, "I come over here once or twice a month. I'm fond of your mother, and of you and Sis. I've been in the habit of coming to see you all every time I come to Homochitto, and I've been coming for twenty years, and probably I'll be coming for thirty more. I'm going to keep on coming to your house, and I'm going to act toward Sis just the same as I've always acted. She'll just have to make up her mind to put up with me."

And that was the end of that, as far as Ralph was concerned.

Oh, Lord, oh, Lord, that was a winter. Part of it I was working at home, and I'll tell you, my dear, I was not in an enviable situation. Those three women were as touchy as torpedoes. Scratch 'em and they popped. I sang to 'em, and I cooked for 'em, and I joshed 'em, and I babied 'em. (Try to baby an Anderson, sometime. It's like babying a wildcat.) But finally spring came and Sis began to dig in the yard again. She dug up the place like she was looking for buried treasure. She worked until five in the afternoon, and then she dug until dark, and all day on Saturday and Sunday. (She quit going to church altogether for a while.) She dug and she dug all that spring and summer, and someplace in the dirt she found what she was looking for. She gave him up at last — just like I'd said she would from the beginning.

"You were betting on a sure thing," Will said, turning his glass around with one hand and looking at Charlie with gentle tolerance. His face bore the stamp of a particular drunken frame of mind, an infinite sentimental tenderness in his eyes and, about his mouth, a forbearance that said quite plainly, No one has suffered as I have, and therefore, no one can understand human suffering as I can.

"She *had* to give him up," he said. "She couldn't get him back. And she's too hardheaded to die." He said it over thoughtfully, liking the sound of it. "Too hardheaded to die.

"Order us all another drink, Charlie," he said.

"How about a little dinner?" Charlie said. "Aren't you hungry, Anna? I didn't mean to go on so long." He looked at Will with worried calculation. "Why don't we order one more drink for you, Will, and dinner at the same time? O.K.? I don't want another. Do you, Anna?"

Anna shook her head. The seat of her chair felt hard, and she pressed her back against its hard slats to orient herself. The clatter of silver and the buzz of conversation were as strange in her ears as if she had been suddenly transported to the seashore and heard for the first time in her life the hollow crashing of the waves. Her head seemed to be floating in the smoky air. She looked around at the passing waiters and the scores of diners methodically lifting their forks to their lips and rhythmically moving their jaws. The restaurant was hazy with cigarette smoke; she saw and heard everything, so it seemed, not so loudly and clearly as she should have, but as if she were looking and listening through a dirty windowpane. She licked her lips and they felt numb.

I'm a little tight, she said to herself. *I'd better not drink any more. Will's enough for one evening.*

"You order for me, Will," she said. "You know what's best, and I like everything."

Charlie glanced at her gratefully. Good girl, his eyes said. Let's keep him busy.

Anna had listened to the whole of Charlie's story in astonished silence, and now as the men ordered dinner, she sat taking tiny sips of the sweet dregs of her old-fashioned, and trying to sort it all out in her mind. Did her mother even know what had happened in Maraisville that day? Probably not, if she had to depend on Father to tell her. And Father! She thought of him walking down the street, going into the bar and into the hotel looking for Alderan, risking his life and then never even mentioning it to anyone. If Charlie hadn't been involved, no one in the family would ever have known about it. Yes, her head throbbed with the thought, he had justified his whole life in that one refusal. He had turned away from violence, from the role that everyone expected him to fill, and had quietly gone about his business. He had not even been afraid to be thought a coward. And Alderan had not faced him. Alderan had run away. For a moment a nagging doubt caught at her mind — what made Alderan tick, after all? Did they understand him any better than he understood them? She pushed the doubt away. There was no other explanation. He had been afraid and he had run away.

I want to think clearly, she said solemnly to herself. *I want to understand it*, and she licked her numb lips and frowned in concentration.

Father. He had sat alone in his office that morning before he set out for Maraisville and had made up his mind that he would not lift his hand against Alderan, that he would risk his life before he would break the Sixth Commandment, and then he had set out to get it over with. *In that day's work . . .* she thought. *I want that, too. To have the chance to bring everything to bear, everything; to be justified. How many men wait all their lives to be tested, and in the end are cheated even of the knowledge of their own deaths? I want to know*, she said to herself with innocent self-confidence.

But the picture of her father sitting behind his desk in the rough little office in the empty building, the picture of him pacing to and fro through the corridors of the warehouse, looking up at the stacks of oil drums, listening to the hollow echo of his own footsteps, looking out the window in the gray early morning at the skeleton of a dragline waiting to be repaired, while he weighed his principles against his life, that lovely picture had no reality to her, and she saw that it must have been another way. In her father, thought and action were so inextricably one that it was as if he did not think at all, as if his thoughts were buried in the very muscles and tendons and bones of his body and lived themselves out without assistance from his brain. He had gone on playing tennis; he had come home to supper a little late, as usual; he had read the evening paper and played a game of Russian Bank with her mother; he had gone to bed and to sleep, and in the morning early he had gotten up and driven to Maraisville. He had drunk his coffee and eaten his pie and showed himself on the street; and then he had gone to work. And afterward, if anyone had asked him about it, he would have been surprised. "Carry a gun? What would I want to shoot Wheelwright for? It never occurred to me to take a gun down there." If you knew him well, you might have recognized, when he said Wheelwright instead of Alderan, that he had taken everything in and knew what it meant. That was all. Except, feeling perhaps that some further explanation might end the conversation, he would add, "I knew he wasn't going to take a shot at me. He wasn't that crazy." And later, years later, if one asked him about it, he probably wouldn't even remember that it had happened. "He just left town after I fired him," he would say. "I never saw him again."

"Lack of experience," Charlie was saying. "I put it all down to lack of experience. She never in her life let herself *get* any experience, if you follow me. Why, I could have told her . . . But she wasn't going to listen, not Sis."

Will smiled kindly at him. "Now, don't get me wrong, Charlie," he said, "don't take offense, but there are some things about Sis that you are not equipped . . . *equipped to* discuss. You know that? I been on that train. Oh, Lord, I hoed that row. I know about it." He picked up his knife and shook it in the direction of the other two. "Let me make myself clear," he said. "You got a man here, like this," making a mark on the tablecloth, "and over here you got what he wants. See? All he wants is a wife and a couple of kids, enough money to get along and the freedom for an occasional fling. That's not much, is it? He's a simple man and a realist. Shoot an arrow from the man to his heart's desire and it goes straight. See? But he marries Sis. Now Sis thinks she's got a simple idea, too. All she wants is him. That's all. Ha! But it's not that simple. Oh, no. Here goes her arrow. Bang. First thing it hits is a picture of Father, and it goes skittering off to the left. Bang. Collides head-on with the *Waverly Novels* and goes skittering off to the right." He squinted at the tablecloth. "I believe that was old Nathaniel Greene it hit. Wasn't he an ancestor of ours?" He laid down the knife, shook his head, and sighed. "Here's a good old Southern recipe," he said. "Take a little failing status, add a pineapple-post tester bed and a couple of authentic family portraits, fold in the Ten Commandments, and place in a casserole alternating with layers of *Ivanhoe, Kenilworth,* and *The Bride of Lammermoor.* Bake at 500° for fifteen years, and what do you get? Explosion! One way to avoid consequences of that life — get out young and stay out."

"Mama and Sarah D. haven't exploded," Anna said.

"Look out!" Will said. "Just look out! I been 'specting Charlotte to explode for years." He raised his hands as if to ward off flying fragments. "Look out," he said. "Look out." And then, "No, no, Anna. Your *mama* and Sarah D. didn't *follow* the recipe. You remember I said bake at 500° for fifteen years? They left that part out. See? Old Charlie here and Ralph kind of cut down the heat in the oven. See? Ha, ha.

"That's all joking," he muttered in a low voice when the

other two had smiled politely at his joke. "In slightly bad taste, too. No joking matter. Sis had a rough time. Poor Sis. Always loved me hard, too, just naturally loves too hard. You know what ruined Sis, Charlie? You wouldn't know what ruined her. Too much love, that's what it was. You know she was Father's favorite? Everybody knew it. I was too young when he died to know the difference; but I saw a letter he wrote Mama one time when he was away from home. You know how Mama keeps letters. 'How is my darling Sis? Tell her her father sends her a thousand kisses. And give the others my love, Kate. Your affectionate husband.' I saw it. I saw it in Mama's desk, long time after he was dead. Well, it was nothing to me. I hardly even remembered him. But *Sis*. She was fifteen when he died. You 'member what it's like to be fifteen, Charlie? Lost love of her life when she was fifteen. We all had to pay for that, every man she's ever looked at, including me. Just been waiting all her life for another man to throw herself away on. Look at that business of pawning — pawning the rings. What's it tell you about her? Throw 'em away. Throw 'em all away for him. The rings that Father left her. And he probably never even *understood* what they meant to her." He tilted back in his chair and opened his owlish big eyes wide. "I would have redeemed them," he said. "Charlotte's not the only one would have bought the rings from her. She knew she could have come to me. Didn't she? Didn't she?"

"Sure," Charlie said. "Of course she did, Will."

"No." There was a long silence, as he seemed to be searching his mind for some elusive, final statement. "She had . . . no . . . reason . . . to hesitate . . . to come . . . to me. But . . . But here's the subtle point to . . . my argument. Here's the crux of the matter. She *wanted* to throw them away. She was proving that *he* meant more to her than Father. Am I right?"

Anna nodded. *You?* she thought. You *would have bought the rings? Now, come off it.*

Will drank down half his highball, while Charlie and Anna began to eat.

"Come on, Will," Charlie said. "Your dinner's going to get cold."

"Ah, the capacity of human beings for self-deception," Will said meditatively, staring into his glass. "Ish . . . infinite, infinite." Then, "She . . . see here. I'm not so sober," he said slowly. "I didn't quite finish sobering up this afternoon."

"Yeah, I see," Charlie said. "Don't let it bother you."

"Drink," Will said. "Drink clarifies the . . . perceptions. But has certain . . . inconvenient . . . side effects. Physical side effects. The speech centers . . . the function of speech . . . is shumwhat . . . impaired . . . impaired. But the brain! Brain contin-ues to work. Fact. I find the brain works even better. The . . . prejudishes . . . extra baggage . . . get thrown overboard. You don't believe that? I see by your . . . ex-pression you have reservations. You not with me. But ish true. Wide experience convinces me ish true."

"Yeah, but you get mad," Charlie said. "I don't feel like settling any quarrels between you and the waiters tonight."

"You see?" Will said to Anna. "He doesn't believe me. He thinks I'm going to get mad. But I'm not going to get mad. Uh-huh. All men are brothers. I see it. I see it. Now wait a min-ute. Right on brink of . . . All men are brothers. See? True family is the human race. That's profound truth. Nobody sees it. Nobody sees it but me. Love. That's what the world needs. Less moralizing and more love."

"I thought you said Sis's trouble was too much love," Anna said.

"Ah-hah." He shook his finger at her. "My point. Exactly my point. Wrong kind of love won't do."

"As for me," Charlie said, "I've got all I can do loving the folks I've got to live with."

Will continued without listening. "Now," he said briskly,

"let's look at these folks one at a time, and see what caused all the commotion. Order me another drink, Charlie."

Resignedly Charlie beckoned to the waiter.

"One," Will said. "Ralph and Charlotte. Blind. Don't see the el-e-mentary truth. Man's got a right to live according to his own lights. Is that right? Do they see it? Everybody's got to be like them. Convert the heathen idol worshipers. See what I mean?

"Two. Mama. Gentlemen *only* welcome. Only gentlemen.

"Three. Sis. Can't understand why Alderan didn't turn out to be just like Father.

"Four. Alderan. Gonna have his way, come hell or high water. Don't give a damn whether he's welcome or not.

"Now, there's a simple truth . . . ele-men-tary truth to be . . . learned from all this." He looked intently at his new drink for a long time as if he expected to find the elementary truth floating on its surface. "It's . . . it's . . . wait a minute, it's . . ." He laughed. "I forgot," he said.

"Love," Anna said. "It was about love."

"That's right, love. Nobody got an undershtanding heart. That what King Solomon prayed for? An understanding heart. That's love."

"Seems to me it's gonna take more than love to get all those folks to understanding each other," Anna said.

Will shrugged. "Got to try," he said. "They going to resign from the human race?"

He picked up his drink and as he lifted it a passing waiter brushed against his arm, and he spilled a little on his tie and shirt front.

"Hey, look out there," he said. "Watch where you're going."

"I'm sorry, Mr. Anderson," the waiter said, turning and deftly mopping up the mess.

"Fritz," Will said, "you do that on purpose?"

"Come on, Will," Charlie said. "Eat your dinner. It's getting late and I've got to go to work early in the morning."

"It's all right," Anna said to the waiter. "Don't worry about it."

"Not all right," Will said. "Damn carelessness."

The waiter quietly slipped away.

"Where'd he go, damn coward?" Will said loudly, and then, "My cross. Fight, fight, fight. Got to fight all the time to keep people from taking . . . advantage . . . of my size." He stood up. "You see," he said, "I'm a small man. No denying it. Five-four."

"Come on, Will," Charlie said good-naturedly in his low, deep voice. "Come on, sit down. You don't want to embarrass Anna."

"I thought you said all men were brothers," Anna said.

"That's right," Will said. "Exactly what I was talking about. But they don't know it." He shook his head sadly. "You think if he knew he was my brother, he'd have made me spill my drink?" He sat down and picked up his fork. "All right, Charlie. I'm going to eat right now." He began to eat slowly and methodically while the other two, who had finished their dinner, sat and watched him. "I don't want to eat," he said to Anna, "but I'm a reasonable man. I cer-tain-ly don't want to embarrass you."

"You're not embarrassing me," Anna said. "I'm having a good time."

Will chewed thoughtfully. Then he put down his fork and, leaning across the table, said in a low, conspiratorial voice, "You s'pose that waiter was one of those Presbyterians . . . you know, always pulling my elbow? I'll bet . . ." He sat back and squared his shoulders. "I ask you, isn't that carrying things too far? Bad enough when you can't see em, but to *materialize*, come right out in the open, and, and . . ." he brushed at his tie and shirt front, "spill whiskey all *over* you. Too much, little too much."

Anna giggled.

"Boy," Charlie said, "I'm telling you this for your own good.

Best thing you can do is get that food inside of you and straighten yourself out. Eunice'll be home day after tomorrow, and she's going to be mad at you."

"Look out!" Will said. "Here he comes again," and he hitched himself in closer to the table as the waiter passed behind him carrying a loaded tray. He craned his head over his shoulder and watched intently as the waiter passed and, setting the tray down on a serving table, began to serve the diners next to them. "I tell you how I could find out," Will said thoughtfully. "Foolproof method of finding out." He fumbled in his jacket pocket. "I got a tip . . . You see? If that waiter's real, he'll jump at the chance. You watch. I'll . . ."

"But suppose he isn't," Anna said. "Maybe it would be better not to find out."

"If he isn't, he just better let me alone, that's all," Will said. "Wait a minute, here he comes. Be quiet now, Charlie." He tilted back on his chair, teetering precariously, and grabbed the waiter's arm as he was returning to the kitchen with an empty tray. "Hey, Fritz, wait a minute. I got something to show you."

The waiter stopped and stood looking warily at Will. "Yes, sir, Mr. Anderson," he said. "May I help you?"

Will rocked forward with a thump. "Maybe he's not," he said. "He knows me. But . . . those others, *they* probably all know you, too. Wouldn't you think so? Or how could they keep up with you all the time?" Laboriously he pulled out his wallet and extracted a crumpled slip of paper. He looked cautiously around and then lowered his voice. "Got a sure thing in the third, Monday, Fritz," he said. "Want to see?"

The waiter's expression changed from cautious and irritated boredom to delighted attention. "Yes, *sir*," he said.

"Ha! *Proved* it," Will said. "*Proved* it. They're not getting away with anything yet. Old man's still pretty sharp." He began to unfold and smooth out the paper, but paused as a certain reservation seemed to occur to him. "I don't mean to be personal," he said carefully to the waiter, "I certainly don't mean to be personal, but what church do you attend, if I may ask? No offense intended, none at all. Just tell me your preference in churches."

"I'm a Catholic, Mr. Anderson. I thought you knew that."

"I did, I did," Will said. "It just slipped my mind. *Now*. Here we are," and he handed over the slip. "Remember, not a word about this to anybody, not a word."

The waiter hastily turned over his order pad and wrote the name of the horse on the back. "No, *sir*, not a word. And thank you, sir, thank you very much."

"Really, it's nothing," Will said. "Don't mention it. Glad to oblige. In fact, you might say, you're doing me a favor."

He turned to Anna as the waiter left. "The *acid* test!" he said triumphantly. "Diabolically clever, eh? No Presbyterian ghost I ever knew would claim . . . No self-*respecting* Presbyterian ghost would claim to be a Catholic. Ha!"

"Will, you're grand," she said. "You're simply wonderful."

"Oh, he knows I'm reliable," Will said. "He's been pretty lucky from time to time, following my advice. Charlie, you want a tip on the third?"

"I might. Who you got there?"

Will passed over the slip. "Order me a drink, Charlie, will you? Anna, how about a liqueur. Brandy? Crème de menthe? You all want some coffee?"

"Let's all have coffee, Will. You don't have to press your luck."

"Too late," Will said. "Too late. I already turned the corner. Got to keep on down the road." He half closed his eyes and smiled tenderly, as if another vision of truth trembled dazzlingly behind the fluttering lids. "I know a fellow," he said, "a colored fellow, roustabout. You know those boys? They load and unload down at the docks, and they're . . . they're uncanny. Like . . . like most of 'em can't read or write, and they memorize the symbols on all the crates and bales we handle. Maybe they've got a thousand symbols in their heads. Know what everything is and where it goes. And strong! My God, how strong. And . . . what was I going to say?"

"You know this roustabout," Anna said.

"Yes. I know this fellow, and we were talking one day in the morning, down by the docks, sitting and looking at the ships loading — all noise and confusion, shouting and sweating, cranes creaking, fog just lifting off the river, ships loading up to ship out for Rio and God knows where else in the hazy morning. What I wouldn't give to go . . . to go again! And I said to him, 'Phin' (Phineas is his name). 'Phin,' I said, 'How you stand it all time down here, seeing 'em go, loading 'em up and seeing 'em go? Don't you want to go too? How you keep at it so long?' And he says to me, 'Whiskey, Mr. Anderson. Whiskey keeps me happy. You see?' 'Yeah,' I say. 'It helps.' And he leans back against a crate and looks up at the crane swinging up there over our heads, creaking and moaning, and at the line of stevedores steady shifting crates and bales around the dock, and he says, 'Yes, sir, Saturday noon you gits paid off, and you feels your money in your pocket, and you walks the streets, thinking of foreign lands. And then you sees the girls in they flowered silks, and you spend all afternoon choosing lands to go and girls to love. And Saturday night you pushes the tables together, and you dreams you rich. Ain't that right?' 'That's right,' I said. 'That's right.' 'And then,' he says, and he lets his breath out, like he sees the girls vanishing and the ships slipping off down the river, 'then,' he says, 'it's Monday morning, and you wake up cold in hand.' ' "

Somehow, unobtrusively, with Will's sudden, blundering cooperation, they managed to leave Galatoire's and get into the car. Charlie drove them to Katherine and Mac's apartment, and as they drove with Will slumped down between them, they decided across his inert body to put him to bed in the living room there. It would be best, they agreed, if Anna and Charlotte could get some food into him in the morning and try to get him off to work. Charlie would leave the car and get a taxi home.

As they stood in the shadow of the apartment building, Anna fumbled in her purse for the key while Charlie with an arm around Will easily supported his light, wavering body.

Will roused at the pressure of Charlie's hand against his left arm. "Ouch. Look out, boy. Got bad arm there."

Charlie shifted his hand downward and Will, slumping against him, began to laugh. Anna, still looking for the key, turned toward him.

"I trust," he said, leering out at her from under the crazily tilted brim of his panama, "I *trust* you under no mistaken impression I am . . . laughing . . . at *you*."

"Oh, no," she said. "You've got the key, Will. Remember? I gave it to you when we went out."

"I am laughing," he said, and then he frowned in concentration, as if he felt the thought slipping away from him, "I am laughing, yes, generally speaking, under the circumstances, I am laughing . . . at the *human* condition."

"Oh."

"Come on, Will, the key," Charlie said.

"Key. Tha's shignif . . . shignif . . . Ha. Iss comical, is-n't it?"

"I reckon so," Anna said. "It's gonna be comical if we can't get in."

"Iss comical, but iss pathetic. I see that. You see that?"

"You're right," she said, giggling. "It's pathetic."

"I want key, too," Will said. "Want to understand *all*. Nobody got key. Can't get in. Old Charlie. You got key, Charlie? Po-o-oor Charlie. I take care you, Charlie, Anna. Find key in minute."

Anna began going through his pockets.

"Got shumpin say, first," Will said. He straightened up and pushed them both away. Taking off his hat he held it over his heart.

> Out of the . . . night . . . that covers me,
> Black . . . as . . . the . . . pit, from pole to pole,
> I . . . thank . . . whatever gods may be
> For my un-con-quer-able soul.

"Is't comical?" he said, "or is't pathetic?" He slumped back against Charlie again, dropping his hat; he reached out his hand and moved it aimlessly up and down the rough surface of the brick wall. Then he raised his head to the wide, dark, starry sky, and howled like an old, sick dog. "Iss traaaa-gic," he said.

"Hush, Will," Charlie said. "Shh, there's a policeman coming. Have you got the key, Anna? Get his hat. Come on, let's get him inside."

Will straightened up again. "P'liceman knows me," he said. "Everybody in Quarter knows me. Person of consequence. Nothing worry 'bout, Charlie. Everything . . . I got *every-thing . . . under . . . control.*"

The Late-Blooming Patriarch

⤳ THREE YEARS later Charlie Dupré came home to stay, home to his mother-in-law's house, his wife's table. He was only fifty years old. But he had always wanted so passionately to be more than he could be — richer, stronger, more intelligent, a man of large affairs — that it was as if he had lived his life twice. Once, working at the succession of jobs that had kept him alive, and again, anxiously, day and night, in waking and sleeping dreams of wealth and power that kept his slow mind whirling at a speed too great for it, his heart beating wildly for the success of one doomed venture after another. His blood pressure had always been high, his dark face ruddy, a vein beating visibly in his temple. But no one in the family had worried about his health. Rather, at each new venture, they had worried about his failures, the inevitable prospect of Sarah D. having to extricate him again and support him until he found another job.

"A great big, strapping man like Charlie," Charlotte McGovern would say to Ralph. "He ought to be ashamed to come home to Sarah D. again."

And Kate privately to Sis, "My God, he'll eat us out of house and home."

What they meant, of course, what made them feel frustration and therefore moral outrage, was, "Why can't he *just once* put a sensible value on himself? Why can't he settle down and do what's he's able to do?" But he could not. He must kill himself with his silly dreams.

For the anxious heart gave out. First there were warning attacks of slight nausea and pains in his arms and shoulders for which he did not bother to consult a doctor. He had never believed in doctors, and had his own superstitions about health that he loved to expound at length to anyone who would listen.

"Why," he would say, "I'd no more let one of those quacks go poking around in my insides than I'd eat rat poison. A good dose of Epsom salts now and then to keep the system cleaned out, and (you may laugh, Charlotte, but it's the truth) a course of iron and sulphur in the spring will keep anybody fit. Barring a broken bone, of course, or appendicitis. I don't say I wouldn't have a bone set. I'm no Christian Scientist. And I *have* had my appendix out."

This would send the Andersons, who came of a family of doctors, into fits of silent rage.

When the indigestion came, and the pains in his arms, Charlie took his iron and sulphur and Epsom salts, and kept doggedly at his job, this time at the port terminal in Greenville, a hundred miles up the river from Homochitto. On weekends he rode the bus home. It was wartime, and gas was rationed and besides, his tires were too bad to make the trip in his car.

"I don't like to ride the bus," he would say every weekend. "When I'm in a car I like to be behind the wheel."

And Sis would say, "You *are* a good driver, Charlie, it's true. You're the best driver I know. But you do go too fast."

"It's not speed that makes the difference," he would say. "It's caution and control. I always keep my mind on the road and I'm always in control."

He was at home for the weekend when he got sick — not with the stroke the family might have feared if they had paid any attention to his ruddy face and the vein beating in his temple, but with a severe heart attack — heart failure and edema.

For days he was not expected to live. When the worst was over and his long convalescence had begun, the family congratulated each other again and again that he had been at home. If he had been in Greenville, Sarah D. would have had to take a leave of absence from her job, and that would have have meant a loss of two months' salary at a time when they were desperately in need of money.

"Besides," as Sis said, "to have doctors you trust! That makes all the difference." They ranked their doctor (a cousin who they were convinced could have been one of the country's leading heart specialists if he had wished) above the minister and only slightly lower than the angels.

"Yes," Sarah D. would say, "it was God's providence he was here. That's all there is to it."

As for Charlie, the minute he was convinced that he was "a sick man" he forgot his former attitude toward doctors; he listened with avid attention to everything they told him about his condition and promised enthusiastically to follow the regime they laid out for him. But even before he came home from the hospital, his resolution flagged. One day he would be a stickler for the letter of his treatment and berate the nurses for neglecting it; the next he would demand to be allowed to get up, and would tell everyone who came to see him that there was nothing wrong with him. His attitude fluctuated with his physical well-being. He could not stay convinced that he was well, for he was not. To complicate the heart condition, the pathologist found that his blood sugar was high, "not very high, mind you, but there's an indication there that things are not just right," and he was put on a rigid diet. In accordance with current medical practice he was not allowed to eat salt because of the high blood pressure. To make meals even more unpalatable, every ounce had to be weighed and the calorie intake calculated; and the sweets he had always loved, the apple pie à la mode, the blackberry cobblers, and the tall glasses of iced tea with an inch of sugar in the bottom, were denied him.

He hated saccharine and said that it tasted as though someone were trying to poison him. For as long as a week at a time he would stick obsessively to his diet, hanging over the cook before dinner to see that she measured his food, and trying out new salt and sugar substitutes. Then one day, "Nonsense," he would roar. "It's all a bunch of damn nonsense. Be damned to them all, I'll eat what I please." And no matter how much Sarah D. pleaded with him, he would shake salt over everything on his plate, and finish off his dinner with an enormous slice of cake. So it went, back and forth, for as soon as he began to feel ill again he would go back to his diet.

In spite of these lapses, the pounds melted away from his huge frame. His ruddy, heavy-jowled face grew thinner and whiter, and the shadow of his black beard stood out against his pallor. His big, slightly bulging eyes popped more than ever from his sunken cheeks. He was bald now, except for a fringe of black hair curving downward from above his ears around the back of his skull and a few black strands brushed straight back from his high narrow forehead. The skin on his forehead and knobby skull was slack and dull. He had weighed two hundred and forty pounds when he had the first heart attack. Within six months he weighed only a hundred and seventy.

During those months when, alternately frightened and disbelieving, he struggled to regain his health, he sat long hours in the platform rocker by the dining room fire. What else could he do? He was not allowed to drive a car or work. He did not care to read. Once or twice a day in fine weather he walked slowly along the three blocks to the hotel coffee shop to sit at the counter, sipping a glass of milk and chatting with the men who came in for the morning paper and a few minutes' gossip over a cup of coffee. But no one had much time for him. People were too busy. Sometimes he sat for an hour, sipping his milk, smoking one of his two cigars a day, chatting perhaps five minutes to one old friend after another who folded and refolded his newspaper restlessly, and sometimes, bored and outraged in the presence of imminent death, left him in the middle of a sentence. "Yes, Charlie. You tell em, boy. See you tomorrow, fella."

He began to go to the barbershop every day to be shaved. "I haven't the energy to shave myself," he said to Sarah D. who hadn't the money to pay for his shaves.

"Maybe I could learn to shave you," she said.

But he wouldn't let her try. The ritual of the steaming towel, the massage, the foaming lather, the carefully stropped razor filled a part of his empty day. A visit with the barber, who was always willing to talk, or to listen, was something to look forward to. And the barber could not be in a hurry to get away, for he was not going anywhere.

After the coffee shop and the barbershop, there were still hours to be filled. And so he sat in the platform rocker in the dining room with his head bent attentively toward the radio. He did not seem to care what the program was, but listened indiscriminately to recipes, sermons, news, fashion features, soap operas, and race music.

At three o'clock he would begin to listen expectantly for his son to come in from school. On bad days, when he got home, Billy would sit down with his father for a game of checkers or a chat. But often Charlie waited in vain, for the boy would stay out until suppertime at baseball or football practice, or playing with his friends. At five Charlie would begin to wait for his wife and daughter who never failed when they came in to give him a lively account of their day, to consult him about their problems, and to try to ease his loneliness.

During the months of Charlie's convalescence from his first heart attack, Charlotte McGovern was in and out of Homochitto, visiting her mother and sisters for a day or a weekend, as she had for years. She and Sis went over and over the difficulties and possibilities of the family situation. As had always been the case with them all, they found their greatest pleasure, or in this instance, solace, in long conversations about their circumstances. Many things went unsaid in these conversations, for they were always too private to speak much of themselves; but each one held up to the other her personal mirror; and then they exhaustively compared the reflections they found there. It was almost never necessary for one of them to act alone, because it was always possible to correct one's private decision by comparing it to the common fund of family reflections. Charlotte and Sis knew quite well that they could not talk freely to Sarah D. about Charlie's illness; their mother had reached an age where they had begun consistently to spare her; but they could say to each other what they could not say to either Sarah D. or Kate; and then they could devise the means to put their concern to work. With their mother and Charlie almost always at home, it was difficult for the two sisters to find a place to be alone together. They fell into the habit, in the early evening, of crossing the street to the little Confederate Memorial Park in the shadow of the Cathedral. Here on a green slat bench under the dense shade of the live-oak trees, they sat by the round pool where the goldfish lived. Old men in shirt sleeves reading their evening papers, nursemaids, in stiff uniforms, sat on the benches nearby; children fed crumbs to the fish and climbed over the ancient cannon; the fountain murmured cool evening music and the two sisters examined their problems.

They had been sitting together silently for some time one evening when Charlotte began tentatively, "How are *you* feeling?" she asked. "You look as if the strain is beginning to tell. You haven't a pound of meat on your bones, Sis."

Sis shook her head. Then, "I can hardly bear to look at him," she said. "When I come in at noon and at night, I can hardly bear to look at him. I can't tell you how pitiful he is. So thin and pale. My God, if I didn't know it, I would never believe he was Charlie Dupré. And his eyes, Charlotte. His eyes are so terrible. He looks at you with those scared, pleading eyes, and it's like he's already dead — dead and buried and waiting to be told whether he's going to heaven or hell. 'I saw a fellow yesterday,' he'll say, 'a tugboat captain I knew in Greenville. Ran into him in the coffee shop. He's on his way upriver to Cairo. He's got a scheme,' he'll say, 'a real money-maker, and he's going to let me in on it.' And all the time his eyes, as if they didn't have anything to do with the rest of him, are saying, 'Please pretend you believe me.' What can you say? 'Yes,' I'll say, 'that's wonderful, Charlie,' wanting to run out of the room. 'I might as well face it,' he'll say, 'it's possible, just possible (mind you, I don't mean I think it's going to happen) that I'll have another one of these attacks. I've got to think about providing for Sarah D. and the children.' 'Now, Charlie,' I'll say, 'we don't want you to have to think about *anything* for a while but getting well.' Do you know what he told me? He said this tugboat captain had told him you could invest fifty thousand dollars in a barge and make twenty per cent profit on it. You could clear your investment in five years. Like he had fifty cents, much less fifty thousand dollars! 'It sounds like a good thing, Charlie,' I said. I try to be serious with him. 'Bankers,' he said. 'Bankers.' You know how he is about bankers. But in the end the eyes always win. 'I've got to be patient,' he said. 'I know I'm not a good risk. I've got to take care of myself a while.' "

Sis shrugged uneasily and bending over to the grass at her feet picked out a four-leafed clover. "Look," she said. "We need a bushel of these." Then she sighed. "I know I oughtn't to talk like that about Charlie," she said, "not even to you. But it's hard, hard. And there's no one else to talk to. I wouldn't dare mention him to Mama. She simply has no time for him at all. She's perfectly awful to him, Charlotte. She acts as if she thinks he's *pretending* to be sick. You know I hate to face it, Charlotte, but Mama's getting senile. There are some things she is absolutely unreasonable about. Like the platform rocker. You know how we've all always stumbled over that devilish chair and barked our shins on it? Well, last week she stumbled over it and had a nasty fall. We thought at first her wrist was broken. And do you know what she said? She insisted (fortunately not in his hearing) that Charlie had stuck his foot out and tripped her." Sis laughed helplessly. "Can't you just hear her?" she said. "Muttering around the house for days, 'Damn his big feet. They reach halfway across the dining room.' And that's not all. She has this fixation about food, or rather about Charlie and food. When she hears him puttering around in the kitchen, she'll drop everything and go back there to pick at him about eating too much. I've seen her stand in front of the icebox to keep him from getting to it. Isn't that absurd? And the poor fellow never loses his temper. 'Now, Mrs. A.,' he'll say, 'come on, Mrs. A. I just want to get a little slice of roast.' Do you wonder Sarah D. has an ulcer? I don't see how she stands up to it as well as she does. It breaks my heart to have her see Charlie like that. Whatever else was the matter, he was always so strong and healthy and handsome." She twisted the cloverleaf around and around between her fingers and let it fall at her feet. "Charlotte," she said, "she has to wait on him hand and foot. It throws me into a rage the way he orders her around. (You see, there I go. In a way, I'm as bad as Mama is about him.) He never seems to realize that she works hard all day and comes home worn out. He'll send her to the kitchen for a glass of water. But in the morning he can walk three blocks to the coffee shop. I have to bite my tongue. And she never says a word. She's always patient and cheerful with him."

"If Mama won't let him open the icebox, maybe he has to send Sarah D.," Charlotte said.

Sis did not smile. "I know in a way it's funny," she said, "and I know we have to make the best of it, but it's hard, hard. Just think, my dear — Sarah D.'s been working all her life, ever since she was eighteen years old. And now this! She may have Charlie to support until it kills her."

Charlotte's eyes filled with tears. "I'd give anything in the world to be able to take some of this off your shoulders," she said.

"There," Sis said, "I knew I shouldn't have talked to you about it. It just distresses you needlessly."

"You ought to know better than to pay any attention to my tears. I've always cried if anyone looked too hard at me."

"Look," Sis said, "here's another four-leafed clover. And here's another. We're sitting in a patch of them."

"Besides, whether you talk to me about it or not, I'm distressed. After all, I'm here often enough to see very well what's going on. Just to sit through a meal with you all and feel the friction between Mama and Charlie makes me wonder why you don't all have ulcers. And I've had to listen to Charlie's grand schemes, too."

"Well, don't exaggerate our troubles," Sis said. "There are alleviating factors, after all. Charlotte and Billy keep us lively. Young folks in the house. It makes all the difference. And Charlotte is a saint. She's the only person who can do anything with Mama any more. You know Mama worships the ground she walks on. Charlotte's never too tired or too busy or too preoccupied to be sweet to her. She doesn't even seem to realize that she's doing anything out of the ordinary. She pours oil on the troubled waters without a thought for what's the matter. She's the one who keeps relations between Charlie and Mama from breaking into an open quarrel."

"That's plain enough," Charlotte said. "And she seems absolutely unconscious of the conflict, doesn't she?"

"Conscious or not," Sis said, "she . . ."

"She's always been an odd child," Charlotte said.

"Odd! She's not odd. She's marvelous. God knows what we've done to deserve her."

"Oh, Sis, I didn't mean odd in a bad way," Charlotte said. "You know what I mean. Slow and dreamy. Sometimes I think she hasn't grown up at all. Why at her age *my* girls . . ." She paused uncertainly and blushed at her own frankness. "I mean grown up physically," she said. "She's, she's . . . I mean, do you think she's ever been — awakened?"

Sis stared at Charlotte incredulously.

"I mean felt any sort of desire for a man. Do you think she has, *really*? I've never seen a girl who was so indifferent to men, to going out. And I've certainly never heard that she had so much as a 'crush.' Haven't you ever thought about that? After all, she's twenty-one years old. Just think back about Sarah D. at her age, or four or five years younger for that matter, and you'll see what I mean."

"Well!" Sis said. "She has beaus enough, if you ask me. I don't see why a girl should have to have her mind on men twenty-four hours a day. Besides, she has a heavy burden on her young shoulders. And I for one would be drawn and quartered if I could relieve her of it, and give her the time and heart for . . . *men*. If that's what she needs."

"Don't be huffy, Sis," Charlotte said. "I'm not criticizing Charlotte. I'm thinking and talking about her in the same way I do about my own. I know how much it means to you all to have Charlotte at home, and I wouldn't upset you about her or *anything*, for the world." She sighed and laid her hand on Sis's for a moment. "The Lord knows my heart aches for you all," she said.

Indeed, they all knew quite well, regardless of their varying opinions of young Charlotte, that she and Billy kept their lives from sinking into apathy and despair. The weight of the dying man was almost too much for three frail and tired women to sustain. Charlotte's personality fitted her peculiarly well for her task. She had always been a slow dreamer; now she dreamed her way cheerfully along, a buffer between so many tense and ailing people. As Sis had said, nothing bothered her. She did not seem to mind their obsessive, single-minded interest in her affairs. When she came into the house, they fixed their attention on her instead of on the conviction that

each one of them kept buried beneath the day's trivia: *It's
too late for things to get better. They can only get worse.* It
was as if a soft wind had blown the house full of warm sleeping life. She sat quietly on the parlor love seat or at the dining room table, and filled the room with her mysterious presence.

Charlotte was big, like her father, long-limbed and heavy.
Heavy, short, dark lashes fringed her speckled green and
hazel eyes; her golden skin and tawny, thick, brown-gold
hair shone under the evening lamps. She had not one feature
or mannerism of her mother and aunts. The small-boned,
dark-haired, pale-skinned Creole had vanished. Perhaps it
was her very appearance, so different from their own, that
made her baffling to them. Every evening they watched her
and thought how beautiful she was. Indeed, Sarah D. and Sis
thought her the most beautiful woman in the world, when in
truth, except for the lovely tawny coloring, she was not particularly beautiful. Her head and face were a trifle too small,
and her figure left a good deal to be desired. She had that body
peculiar to some big women who seem made not so much for
love as for bearing and raising children — small breasts, heavy
hips, and big, sturdy legs.

In the morning at breakfast the family sat and watched her
eat her way methodically and slowly through a plateful of grits
and bacon and scrambled eggs, and a mound of hot biscuits
dripping with molasses, and worried about her figure.

"You ought to cut down on the hot biscuits, Charlotte,"
Charlie would say. "You're gaining weight."

"You're a fine one to talk," Kate would mutter.

"What's that, Mrs. A?"

"Now, Gran," Charlotte would say, smiling at Kate, "Daddy
and I *like* to eat."

"But seriously, darling. . ."

"I'm going on a diet," she would say to her father. "Next
week I'm going on a diet." And sometimes, to please them, she

did. But not for long. She was too fond of biscuits and molasses.

In the park, Sis turned to Charlotte, her face drawn with emotion. "There's nothing I wouldn't do to make her happy," she said. "*Nothing.*"

"I still think what I said is true," Charlotte said. "After all, you want her to marry, don't you? She needs somebody to come along and stir her up a bit. Don't you agree?"

Sis did not answer. She bent again to the grass at her feet, and sorted absorbedly through the clovers growing there.

"Never mind, never mind," Charlotte said. "I'm sure all I really mean is, she's a Dupré. You know the unconscious way of doing things all the Dupré women have. I guess I'm just not used to it. While Billy's all Anderson. He reminds me more of Father every day."

"No, indeed," Sis said. "I see the resemblance to Sarah D., but *Father?* No, I don't see that. None of Father's grandchildren is like him."

"Why, Sis, he's the living, breathing image of Father," Charlotte said. "All he needs is a little mustache. And he's going to be small, too. You can tell it from his wrists and ankles."

"Yes, that's his cross right now," Sis said. "He's convinced he's going to be no bigger than Will, and it's about to drive him crazy. Too bad he can't get some of Charlie's height."

"He'll survive, I reckon," Charlotte said. "Will manages to make as much commotion as most men twice his size."

"Mama thinks he looks like Father, too," Sis said, "so I suppose he must, but I can't see it."

"To get back to Mama," Charlotte said, "I've been trying to think how I might get her to Eureka for a few weeks. I know you all need a rest."

Sis laughed. "If we could just get her out of her room long enough to clean it up, it would be a help," she said. "You know what a pack rat she's always been, and lately she's gotten so she won't allow Sally to touch anything in the room except to make the bed. It's a disgrace."

"I've asked her twice this spring already, and she's refused."

"Well, she thinks the roof will cave in if she's not here to hold it up," Sis said, "but we really do need to get her out of town for a few days, long enough to give us a little breather."

The two woman sat quietly watching the fountain and the children. At last Charlotte began again. "I really didn't mean to upset you about Charlotte," she said. "All right?"

Sis nodded. "I had something on my mind I wanted to say to you about Charlotte anyway," she said. "I'm glad you brought her up. The queerest situation has developed since Charlie came home from the hospital. He's begun to play the heavy father. Not only with Billy, but with Charlotte, too. Billy doesn't seem to mind, and besides, a little heavy fathering at his age, even if he's never had it before, isn't going to hurt him. But with Charlotte it's another matter. He wants a pedigree on every man she goes out with, he stays awake until she comes in from a date, he tells her what time she has to be home, he cross-questions her about her affairs, he's even begun to advise her about managing her money."

"*Charlie?*"

"I know it sounds ridiculous," Sis said, "but it's the truth."

"Too bad he didn't think of taking on some of his responsibilities fifteen years ago — when Charlotte and Billy needed a father. Do you remember the winter Billy was born — when Charlotte was six? Sarah D. worked up until two weeks before she had Billy."

"I don't know what anybody can do about it," Sis said. "I suppose the truth is, he just hasn't got anything else to do. But I'm afraid Charlotte is going to get tired of humoring him one of these days. Fortunately, she doesn't seem to notice it. Isn't that fantastic?"

"Sarah D. ought to be able to put the quietus on him,"

Charlotte said. "After all, Charlotte's a grown woman, earning her own living."

"*Ought!*" Sis said. "*Ought* and *can* are two different matters."

"I tell you what I really think," Charlotte went on. "Why Sarah D. waits on him hand and foot, why she lets him impose on the children and on her. She knows as well as anyone that it's partly her fault he's like he is, and she . . ."

Sis interrupted. "You ought to understand," she said, "that it's not all bad. Billy *needs* his father. Charlie has taken a lot of time with him this spring. Of course, he can't get out with him. But he's given him a lot of attention."

"Yes, but it's Sarah D. I'm talking about," Charlotte said. "Sarah D. knows if she'd gone with Charlie twenty years ago, fifteen, even ten years ago, one of those times when he had a fair job, if she'd been willing to gamble on him and leave Homochitto, if she'd thrown all the responsibility for their lives on him, it might have been the making of him. She didn't do it, she could never have done it, but she's bound to say to herself sometimes, If I *had* . . ."

Sis looked at Charlotte with an ironic smile. "*You* can say that," she said.

"But it's true. And now here she is saddled with him — an invalid, an old man at fifty. I have to close my mind to it when I go to bed at night, or I'd never go to sleep."

"Don't be too sure, my dear, that there aren't other reasons. For my part, I think she worships the ground he walks on."

Charlotte was silent for a moment, as if checking this strange notion against the data in her mind. "But *why* . . . why would she never . . ." She shook her head wonderingly and shivered as if a cold wind had struck her. "I don't see how you can keep on loving a man you can't respect," she said.

"There are lots of ways to love people," Sis said.

"If she does, that certainly doesn't make it any easier for her, does it?"

"Do you remember how beautifully they used to dance together?" Sis asked abruptly. "I've seen them in the pavilion at the Elysian Club waltzing, summer nights when we used to have dances there, remember? They were so light and lovely and happy, I could have wept for joy. When I want to remember everything lovely about young folks, I think of them."

"And the Charleston," Charlotte said. "Do you remember when Bud Scott's band used to come up from Natchez for the Charleston contests? Charlie and Sarah D. could out-Charleston the Castles." She laughed aloud. "Wasn't Sarah D. practicing the Charleston upstairs when little Jean Dupré fell off the parlor wall?"

"And Mama fainted and I poured a pitcher of lemonade on her," Sis said. "How could I ever forget that? But you know I never did think she really fainted. She just felt she had to do something adequate to the occasion."

"That was all a long, long time ago," Charlotte said. "There never was a young girl gayer or more charming than Sarah D. She was in love with love."

"She's stood by him a long time."

"Anyhow," Charlotte said, "whether she loves him or is taking care of him because she has to (she certainly couldn't turn him out, could she?) is her business. Our business is to do what we can to help her, and you're the one to decide what I can do."

"Go ahead," Sis said, "get Mama to go home with you, if you can, and keep her as long as she'll stay. Put it to her that she neglects you and it hurts your feelings. That ought to do the trick. After that, I have another idea. I've been mulling it over for weeks, and I've hesitated to mention it to you because in a way it seems high-handed. It's a round-about way of getting Charlie to take a little pressure off Charlotte and Sarah D. What would Anna think of spending the winter over here? There are plenty of jobs at Camp Mc-Clure; she could transfer, I'm sure. If she were here, she'd undoubtedly go out with Charlotte a lot. Charlie might ease off worrying so much about her. He'd be bound to respect *Anna's* right to live her own life, and that might give him a start on letting Charlotte alone. And since Anna's three years older, he might consider her a bit of a chaperon. She could pay board, and that would help with the finances. Do you think Anna might do it? Or do you think it's a foolish idea?"

"I could talk to her about it," Charlotte said. "There's certainly nothing to keep her in Eureka."

"I suppose the truth is I'm just clutching at straws," Sis said.

After this conversation Charlotte persuaded her mother to go to Eureka. Kate did not want to go, but she went, because Charlotte made her feel that otherwise she would be offended. It was the only way to get Kate out of Homochitto. As Sis had said, Kate felt, indeed desperately needed to feel, that she was indispensable to her daughters' household. In her heart she must have been afraid that if she stayed away, it would become apparent even to her that everyone could get along without her. In Eureka, to occupy her mother, Charlotte got out everything in the house that needed to be mended or altered. Although Kate's eyes were failing her, she never admitted to anyone that she could no longer sew so beautifully as she once had; and now she got out her sewing basket, and seemed to gather all her strength to be gay and busy.

"You've been saving everything in the house for me to alter," she said with her old mock ferocity. "I don't believe there is such a thing in Eureka as a sewing lady."

"No one as good as you, Mama," Charlotte said. "You ought to know that," and she quietly put away the unevenly hemmed dresses and botched darns to be done again after Kate left.

Kate stayed two weeks, not a day longer, and then demanded to be taken home. "I've got to get back," she said. "Here it is

June and I've never done the spring housecleaning or put away the woolen clothes. Everything will be eaten up with moths."

Anna drove her back to Homochitto and stayed on there.

❧

Homochitto
June 28, 1944

Dearest Mama,

I wish you could have seen Gran when we got here and she discovered that the girls had cleaned up her room while she was gone. She was furious. She's spent the last week pottering around in there getting it good and messy again. Says she couldn't find a thing when she got home. She's lost all great-grandmother's old wigs and that big box of letters from the cousins in California and half her quilting scraps and that enormous sack of wool she is always talking about carding and getting made into comforts. I don't know about the rest of the stuff, but I'd be willing to bet the girls threw away those horrible old wigs, although they won't admit a thing.

I am comfortably settled, Mama, staying with Charlotte in the bedroom in Charlie and Sarah D.'s old apartment upstairs. Sis has moved into their old living room. We keep the icebox hooked up in the kitchenette and it's very convenient, almost like having an apartment to ourselves. Gran wanted me to take the upstairs bedroom in the wing, over hers, but it hasn't been used for so long, it would have had to be painted. Besides I like staying with Charlotte, and it's more convenient to be in the house. I don't know why Gran insists on staying out in the wing, especially in the winter when she has to go outdoors to get to her room. I should think the girls would worry about her being way back there where they couldn't hear her if she called. But of course you couldn't budge her with a crowbar.

Everything is fine here (as far as I am concerned, that is). The hours are pretty strenuous, as we have to be at work at eight and don't get off until five. We have a car pool and it takes a good forty minutes to pick everyone up and make the drive, there's so much traffic going out. That means I have to be on my way by seven-twenty and don't get home until nearly six. Charlie gets up in the morning and fixes breakfast for Charlotte, himself, and me, as everyone else eats at eight. Did you know he has a little job? Isn't that *grand?* I don't know what he does, but it's something at the police station, sitting down, and only for half a day. At least he's making his own pocket money and paying for his share of the groceries. Anyway, he has to get up, too, so he cooks. He's really a good cook, Mama. You know he's always said he was, but I never believed him. At any rate, he can certainly make biscuits, and he fries a mean egg. I know it isn't right for him to cook for us every day but he wants to. It would be simple enough for us to fix ourselves a cup of coffee and a piece of toast in the morning, but honestly, he seems to like to do it. You might as well not try to help him. He wants to do it himself. He's so proud of his biscuits!

Mama, the craziest thing happened the other night. Charlotte and I had dates with two boys from the 112th (mine was Jim Coleman who used to be stationed in Eureka, remember him? And he brought a friend for Ch.). We were planning to go out to the Blue Slipper and meet a crowd of others, and when the boys came to get us, they'd had a couple of drinks. I don't mean they were drunk, or even tight, but they were feeling pretty good, and you could certainly smell it. I didn't think anything about it one way or the other; we stopped in the parlor to chat a minute with Sarah D. and Charlie, and then left. But apparently (from what Sis told me afterwards) as soon as we left, Charlie began raising cain. No daughter of his was going out with a drunken soldier, what did Sarah D. have in her mind, letting us leave with the boys in the condition they were in, etc., etc. S.D. didn't argue with him. His blood pressure is so high, she never crosses him about anything, and Sis said he really did look like he was going to have a stroke, all red in the face and short-winded and excited. The two of them tried to reason with him a little bit, said they didn't think the boys were tight, they'd just had a drink, or at the most maybe two, that I was along, etc. But he swore he'd seen Charlotte's date stumble going down the steps, that she'd had to grab him to keep him from falling. (By the way, Charlotte's date was a darling boy from New Orleans, Gerry (Gerard) Griswold. I'm sure you know the name. Isn't he a distant cousin of Father's? I know we're related to all those

Griswolds someway. Not my type by any manner of means — you know what an odd-ball I am — but just as nice as he could be, and would be a grand person to squire Charlotte around. He seemed quite taken with her, too, has called a couple of times since for dates, but she won't go out with him again for reasons I am about to explain to you.) To go on with the tale, Charlie said he would have stopped us before we got away, but we had driven off before he could get to the door. Finally, to pacify him, Sarah D. said she'd call the Slipper and see if we'd gotten there safely. Which of course we had. But that didn't settle him down. He kept on about it, and was worrying so about whether we'd get home safely and what people would think, what would happen to our reputations. (How about that! Did you know reputations were so fragile in Homochitto? I wish I had a nickel for every drunk cousin I've run into at the Blue Slipper.) He said we must both come home immediately and must get one of the other boys in the party to bring us, not those two drunks. Fortunately, Sarah D. put the quietus on his plans for me. She told him after all, as far as they were concerned, I was simply a boarder in their house. It was none of their business who I went out with. I don't know what I would have done if she hadn't. I would really have been over a barrel. But poor Charlotte! Nothing would do but Sarah D. must call out there again and tell Charlotte her father said she must come home. Charlotte really handled it very well. She came back to the table and called me aside and told me what was going on, and we decided that she should say her father had gotten sick suddenly and she had to go home, and that when she got there she should just say to Gerry not to come in, or even see her to the door; and that way Charlie wouldn't know who had brought her home. That's what she did, and jumped out of the car real quick and said, "Don't bother to see me in, I'd better hurry," and ran.

Now, Mama, Charlotte's twenty-one years old and has been earning her own living for three years. Most of the time for the first twenty years of her life Charlie wasn't even within yelling distance, much less there to tell her what to do and what not to do. Isn't it incredible that in his old age when she's grown, he should suddenly assume his obligations? Of course he's sick now, and everybody has to humor him and do what he says, or his blood pressure will go up, or he'll have another heart attack. That's some racket, isn't it? You know, people are always talking about tyranny and the evils of force, but it seems to me that half the time the shoe's on the other foot. It's not the strong ones who tyrannize, but the weak and sickly ones. The strong ones can afford to be magnanimous, and so, before they know what's happened to them, some invalid is in charge of their lives.

To go on with the tale, Sis told me the next day (she was seething with Charlie, not only for doing Charlotte that way, but for putting Sarah D. on the spot) that Charlotte came in the dining room where they were all sitting (Billy was in bed, of course), and she looked so pretty — she did look lovely that night. She had on the shade of golden brown that's just the color of her hair, and a green scarf, and her eyes were green, green. Also that brown dress makes her look not so thick through the middle . . . Well, Charlotte came in the dining room and stood there. Gran was listening to the radio and pretending she didn't know anything about what was happening, had her head right up in it practically, and her eyes shut. Sis said she was trying to read, and Sarah D. and Charlie were sitting one on each side of the fireplace, like Gog and Magog, Charlie with his arms folded, very grim, and Sarah D. looking like she could die. Charlotte stood there a minute and looked from one to another of them, and Sarah D. said, kind of timid, "Hello, darling." Charlotte didn't say anything for what seemed ages, and neither did Charlie. It was like, Sis said, like he didn't feel any explanations were necessary. To him it was perfectly obvious that he had done the only thing any self-respecting father could do. He was waiting for *Charlotte* to explain. At last when Sis said she didn't think she could stand one more tick of the clock, Charlotte spread her skirt out like she might curtsy, and turned all the way around once, and then she said, "Well, here I am. Now you've got me, what are you going to do with me?" I didn't know she had an ironic bone in her body. Did you? But you can see from that she understands what's happening as well as anyone.

I agreed to try to lend a hand with this, Mama, but I don't know that my being here is doing any good. Charlie hardly sees anyone but himself and Charlotte. Don't worry, though, I'm going to stay. And besides, aside from family complications, I'm having a grand time.

Tell Father I went out to see Grandmother and Teen night before last, and they are fine.

Love to all,
A.

P.S. Charlotte hasn't mentioned the incident — not once! She goes her way as if nothing happened — wasn't mad with anyone. And she won't give Gerry another date.

Again, love, A.

Eureka
July 5th, 1944

Dearest Anna,

I am glad to hear you are all settled and have the arrangements worked out to get to and from work. You didn't say a word about the job, but I reckon it is more or less the same as it was over here. Your father and I are saving gas coupons and plan to come over for a couple of days, probably Friday week, if K. is home and settled by then. Tell Sarah D. she won't have to put us up. We're going to stay out at your grandmother's.

I never heard such an absurd rigamarole as Charlie's performance with Charlotte. I feel so sorry for the girls in their present situation that I simply cannot bear to think of it. I often ask myself what I have done in my life to have deserved so much good fortune — fine, healthy children, a husband like your father, and now, even with the war, having little Ralph in the Navy and in a fairly safe station (I even think sometimes they invented hearing aids just in time for my deafness) while *they*, who've always worked so hard, go from one trouble to another.

I know what your father would say: "How unsearchable are His judgments, and His ways past finding out." You know, I say it for a joke, but I believe it too — your father is such a *good* man, I think maybe the Lord keeps a special eye on him, and under the circumstances, naturally I benefit, too.

This year, my dear, you are in a position that I have longed to be able to fill. You can be a big help to Sarah D. and Sis, not only with the board, but with your cheerful young presence, and I know you will do your best to keep the household lively. As for Charlie, of course we must take into consideration that he is a sick man. Poor old fellow, he's never been overburdened with brains, goodness knows, but in his behalf, I have always felt, as I told Sis the other day, that if Sarah D. had been willing to leave Homochitto during those early years and "cleave only unto him," he might have been a different person. But you know how the girls and Mama have always been about Homochitto. You'd think there was no other decent place in the world to live. Oh, I know too well how furious he can make you when he talks about buying and selling the world, while all the time you know Sarah D. is buying the groceries and paying the taxes on her salary and Sis's. But you must take it in your stride and keep your mouth closed. It's out of character for me to say this. I can hear you now: "Mama's a fine one to talk. She's always had less time for him than anyone, and never hesitated to tell him so." And that's true; I'll never stop grieving for what he has made of Sarah D.'s life. But I would never tell him *now*, no matter how much he might provoke me, and besides, I am thinking mainly of what you can do to help out, not what's past and done with.

I am delighted to hear you have already gotten acquainted with some of the boys at McClure. I know you are going to have a happy time. Be on the lookout for an attractive man for Charlotte. Wouldn't it be grand if she could marry a rich Yankee! (Or even better, a rich Southerner, although they're harder to find.)

I am enclosing a letter from Ralph. I had another that I wanted to send you, saying he had gone up into Scotland on leave, but can't find it. Said he had a grand time. Letter from Katherine yesterday, but it was just a note. She is packing to come home. I am sure Mac must be out of the country by now, although she has not heard anything from him one way or another. I don't suppose I am any different from millions of other people, but I often feel as if I were reliving my own early married life with Katherine. The war — the upheaval of everyone's lives — and now being pregnant, as I was, so far from home. But even in that I was luckier than most people. Your father never went overseas at all, though he broke his neck trying to get there.

By the way, I read in the paper a few days ago that Taylor Kelly had been killed off the coast of France. This terrible war! He was flying an attack bomber off an aircraft carrier, as I think you know.

I don't know what the circumstances were, but I understand the Kellys have heard from his commanding officer that he will be posthumously awarded the Navy Cross. His poor little wife. And she has a young baby, too, hasn't she?

Must stop now and get to work on Jeremiah. We are doing the prophets in our auxiliary, and next week is my week to talk.

A heartful of love
M.

P.S. Be sure to take Ralph's letter out to Gm. and Teen to read.

Anna was sitting on the front gallery after work reading her mother's letter, and she read the next-to-last paragraph over three times.

By the way, she said to herself, and then, *She puts it at the tail end like it's nothing to me any more.* But she had not thought of Taylor, herself, in months. *She puts it at the tail end,* she said to herself again. The comfortable noises of the dusky street, the cries of children playing in the park, the steady patter of the fountain, the twitter of desultory conversation between Gran and Sis and Charlotte broke through her concentration, strange and almost unidentifiable, like the noises in a night club in the sickening moment between pleasantly tight and drunkly dizzy, when the floor feels underfoot as it does when your foot is asleep, and everything in the room stands out separately.

Billy Dupré lay on the long green bench at the end of the front porch and with one knee cocked up on the other, idly scraped his foot back and forth across the screen. The light through the slatted blind at the west end of the porch lay across his pale face and black hair in wavery bars.

"Don't scrape your foot on the screen, Billy," Sis said. "It gives me goose flesh."

"Come over here and tickle my foot, Billy," Sarah D. said. "I'll give you a nickel."

"Oh, boy, oh, boy," Bill said. "Gee whiz. Great." He looked across the porch at his father as much as to say disgustedly,

"Women!" Then he got up and went out in the front yard where he stood swinging the gate to and fro. The iron gate screamed rhythmically as he swung it, and Anna shivered. *I think I'm going to vomit*, she thought.

Sarah D.'s voice reached her. "Anna, you're a million miles away. I said, 'What does your mother have to say?' "

Anna folded the letter and put it back in the envelope and put the envelope in her pocket.

"Taylor Kelly's dead," she said.

"Dead? Dead?"

"Who's that?" Charlie said. "A friend of yours?"

"I used to go with him," she said. "He was shot down over France."

"Poor little boy," Gran said. "Poor little fellow."

"I've got to go dress," Anna said. "I've got a date."

Upstairs she lay down on her bed and looked a long time at the ceiling. Then she got up and took the letter from the envelope and read the next to last paragraph again.

"I always intended to marry him," she said aloud. "I knew we would marry some day. He would never have stayed married to that girl. Never."

She saw him again, as she had seen him a thousand times. He came hurrying toward her along the sidewalk, with his long, bouncy stride, grinning and swinging his arms, looking eagerly to see if she was sitting on the front steps waiting for him. "Wait'll I tell you . . ." And then again, as she had last seen him, for he had come to see her in the summer of 1942 when he was on leave, after he got his wings and before he married. They had gone out together several times for the first time since the end of their love affair, stiff at first, but then friendly and at ease. He had been painfully thin, and his big head made his slight body seem even frailer than it was. He had been in his Navy dress whites, high-collared, stiff white tunic and crackling pants, and she had never seen anyone who looked so ridiculous in a uniform. "I'm learning Spanish in my spare time," he had told her, "and reading law. I've fooled around too long. War or no war, I haven't any more time to waste."

Anna began to cry quietly, sitting on the side of the bed with her head in her hands, and then she lay down and buried her face in the pillow and pounded noiselessly on the mattress with her fist.

After a little while she sat up again and pressed her hands against the sides of her head as if to crush the shell of skull. "He's alive in my head," she whispered, "but he's not alive anywhere in the world."

The heart-shattering loss of all the lovely young men, all the slender lads in their shining uniforms, the boys who wanted so passionately to live; all the babies unconceived, the love wasted, the fame unsought, the houses unbuilt, the joy and eagerness smeared across a thousand desolate islands and ruined cities, rocked her so bitterly that nausea swept over her and she went into the bathroom and vomited. Afterward she turned on the bath water and undressed. When she was naked she went to the basin and splashed cold water on her face. Then she opened the bathroom door and yelled downstairs, "Say, Charlotte, fix me a drink, will you?" She sat on the lid of the toilet, naked, with a cold washcloth on her eyes until she heard Charlotte on the stairs. Then she went to the door, opened it a crack, and took the drink.

"Are you all right?" Charlotte asked anxiously.

"Sure."

Sitting on the toilet again, she drank the drink and smoked three cigarettes. She heard Charlotte moving about in the bedroom dressing for the evening and then the sound of her feet on the stairs. The front-door bell rang and she heard Charlotte's voice in the parlor, and then the gruff answering voices of their dates for the evening. Hers was a young captain from Camp McClure, green-eyed and curly-haired, a gentle, virginal boy who thought Thomas Wolfe was the greatest novelist of the twentieth century, and whose outfit was scheduled to ship out any day. He wanted to marry her, and she had not the heart to tell him she would make his life miserable. She got into the tub, bathed hurriedly, dressed, made herself up more heavily and more carefully than usual, and went downstairs.

Charlie had wandered into the parlor, presumably to inspect the young men, and all three men rose as she came in. Charlotte, who had been sitting on the love seat beside her father, got up too, and crossed the room to stand beside her, her eyes shadowed with an expression Anna had never seen in them before, a look of conscious sorrow and compassion that made the tears start in Anna's eyes again.

Charlie cleared his throat and ran his hand nervously over his bald head. "Now, you boys take good care of these girls and bring them home early, y'understand? Eh?" He spoke in his deepest, most pontifical voice and then laughed self-consciously, as if to say, "Between us men," or "We all know women must be protected from themselves."

Anna looked at him blankly, her heart still pounding and all the muscles of her body tight. She said nothing; but, *Why couldn't it have been you?* she thought ruthlessly. *Why couldn't you be dead, useless old man, instead of poor lovely, clumsy Taylor?* One thought flashed briefly into her mind: *He never could even drive a car worth a damn. How could he fly an airplane?*

As they left, Charlotte turned back. "Matter of fact, Daddy," she said, "we'll probably be late. It's a party at the officers' club, you know, and we may go on from there. Just leave the front door open and don't worry about us. We're big girls now."

❧

It is true that death stirs passions other than sorrow. Only a death can make one feel alive in a particular horror-stricken way, can make dread whisper in the veins, *You, too. You, too.*

Someday you're going to die. And when one hears that whisper, then, if it is ever to happen, the world bursts upon the senses and all the passions of life shake loose from their old moorings and demand to be used.

It seemed to Anna that the death of Taylor Kelly had just such an effect upon Charlotte Dupré, who had never even known him. At any rate, when they came in that night, Charlotte demanded that Anna tell her everything about Taylor, the story of their courtship, and how it had ended in frustration and exhaustion. *How did you feel? How did he feel?* she seemed to be saying, as if she had no data on her own feelings and must use Anna's to find out what to do with them, as if after sleeping twenty years behind the thorny hedge of her taboos, a dark prince had awakened her.

To Anna, who had expected nothing but silence and reserve from her family, it was a welcome release, and at the end of the sad little story she wept again.

Still maneuvering cautiously on the surface of her dangerous emotions, Charlotte listened and questioned, and said nothing of herself. There were many things about her own life that she could not yet afford to know. But one vital depth had been touched. The surface had been pierced, and her life burst through, clear and fresh, as if an underground river had been tapped.

The next time Gerry Griswold called her, she went out with him, and within a month they were involved in a headlong courtship.

Charlie looked on amazed at the spectacle of his placid, docile daughter become unmanageable. But he had not forgotten how to keep his fancies working. He had had more than his share of practice at pretending that failure was success.

He made one or two feeble attempts to keep Charlotte from seeing Gerry. "His family may be fine, sugar; but I know these New Orleans men. I've lived there. And let me tell you that the city of New Orleans is nothing but a cesspool of vice and corruption. Why, if I thought that a daughter of mine . . ."

But Charlotte kissed him lightly on top of the head. "Now behave, Daddy," she said. "New Orleans may be a cesspool of vice and corruption, but Gerry isn't. And besides, you wouldn't talk like that if you heard the nice things he says about you."

For a while he continued to stay up until she came in at night, and to call her to task if it was late; but she only listened, and then turned away to climb the stairs to her room, looking as if she'd just seen a vision of paradise.

Without a word to each other or to Charlotte, Sarah D. and Sis lent a hand. "Charlotte tells me Gerry's father was an old beau of your cousin Augustine's," Sis would say to Charlie, or "Will writes he ran into Mr. Griswold the other day at the International Club, and he said he really appreciates our being nice to Gerry." And Sarah D., adroitly putting the correct face-saving words in his mouth, "You were so right to be cautious, darling — that first night, I mean. But I can tell he's redeemed himself with you. Still, I think maybe we should warn Charlotte not to rush into anything hasty. After all, she's never really cared seriously about a boy before."

"No, no," he would say. "Charlotte's got a good head on her shoulders. Let the child alone, Sarah D. She has to make up her own mind."

Within a few weeks Charlie was telling his friends at the coffee shop that Gerry Griswold was madly in love with Charlotte. "One of the New Orleans Griswolds, you know. I met the old man when I was with Delta Lines down there. He's on the Board. But Charlotte's no fool," he would add. "He's a nice boy, but she's not going to be rushed into anything. 'Marry in haste and repent in leisure,' I tell her. She'll take her time."

As for Anna, no one except Charlotte mentioned Taylor's death to her after the evening she heard of it. They were all too deeply absorbed in Charlotte's beau. She grieved bitterly for Taylor, but she felt that she had no right to her grief, and that her family was right to ignore it. Perhaps it did not even occur to them that his death was a blow to her. They knew that the love affair had been over for years, and that she had seriously considered marrying at least one other man in the interval. But at the same time, Anna felt robbed of the right to be grief-stricken. She had been struck by the most piercing of sorrows — the loss of a life unused — and there was no comfort for her.

She knew that she might be kidding herself when she thought again and again: *I always meant to marry him some day.* But none of the facts she knew affected the physical fact of her grief. Alone, when the thought of him came uninvited to her mind, she would double up, as if someone had driven a fist into her belly. And sometimes, typing at a form in her office, she would find herself whispering some phrase that meant what his death meant to her: "The young men are dying," she would whisper, or "Waste and desolation, waste and desolation, waste and desolation."

To even the closest observer, however, her feelings were not apparent. She went out a great deal in the evenings. If she had no date, she served as a hostess at the local U.S.O., and danced night after night with strange young men from Milwaukee or Brooklyn or Albuquerque; scrubbed, crew-cut soldiers in heavy G.I. shoes; men she would never see again, who drifted, bewildered and bewildering, through a succession of alien scenes where fortuitous circumstance might be expected to bring at any moment what normal times took years to evolve: passion, marriage, separation, pain, the disgrace of cowardice, the accolades of heroism, and finally, abruptly, senselessly, a violent death.

She felt herself to be at a pause in her life, to be waiting for things to begin again, on a different plane, in a different way, for different purposes. She could be a young girl no longer. She did not see that there was anything she could do while she waited except to go on night after night dancing with the soldiers in their G.I. shoes, but she knew what she was waiting for. *I am ready to get married,* she told herself, in almost the same words her mother had used in 1916. *I'm going to find a man who is as strong and as intelligent as I am, a man I can trust, and . . .*

※

The warm, brown autumn days of the South drew in toward the late November rains and the brief, sodden chill of winter. On the hills around Homochitto dogwood trees flamed in the dusty jungles of green live-oak and cedar and magnolia; in the Negro cabin yards golden berries hung heavy among the bare lyres of chinaberry fronds; and coxcomb dropped gold and orange feathers in the broom-marked dust. There were fewer and fewer men at Camp McClure, as one outfit after another shipped out for ports of embarkation. Most of Anna's beaus were gone, and Charlotte was seeing only Gerry Griswold. On Sunday afternoons the two girls were often alone, and if the weather was fair, they went to the country with Sis. Sometimes they fished the pasture ponds for bream, but they were not serious fishermen, and sometimes they spent whole afternoons sitting on a creek bank in desultory conversation. Charlotte, too, was waiting, even more specifically than Anna; and they had a tacit understanding that they could not bear to wait in the Anderson dining room where Charlie sat, waiting, too, with his head bent toward the radio; where Gran waited, alert, for the moment when Charlie would get up and go to the kitchen to fix himself a sandwich.

On a creek bank, at the end of one of these sunny afternoons of wandering, Charlotte told Anna and Sis that she and Gerry were to be married. The three women had been a long time silent together and had quite suddenly burst into a flurry of conversation, as if to bring themselves out of their absorption before they started for town.

"Do you remember how much fun we used to have on picnics out here when we were little?" Anna said. She was sitting on a fallen tree trunk washed by the spring floods to the high edge of a sandy beach that stretched to the creek channel where now, in the cold autumn light, a trickle of clean, icy water twinkled over the gravelly stream bed.

Charlotte, sitting in the sand with her back against the log, picked up a smooth egg-shaped rock, and began to knock it against a piece of pudding stone. "This looks like Indian paint rock," she said. "Remember how Gran used to paint us?"

"Remember the time Gran got caught in the quicksand," Anna said, "and Katherine got so scared?"

"I don't remember that."

"She wasn't really caught," Sis said. "She was just making a production to amuse you kids, and she was a little too convincing for Katherine."

"*Was* she? I always thought we saved her life," Anna said.

"Look," Charlotte said. "It is." The shell of the sun-baked lump of clay had broken, and she held the two halves in her hand like a broken egg, dripping its yolk of pure liquid ocher pigment over her fingers. "Look at the color. Wouldn't we have loved that for war paint?"

Anna sighed. "It all seems so long ago," she said. "So many things have happened."

Sis looked sidewise at her tenderly. "You've had rather a stormy youth, my dear," she said. "You've always taken things hard — like me."

Charlotte put down the dripping bowls of yellow and began to sort the rocks at her feet, looking down at them intently as she spoke. "You all ought to relax," she said. "*Come what may*, that's what I always say."

"I can't help it," Anna said. "I can't help it. And now . . . Now I think about poor Taylor and it breaks my heart. I think about him all the time."

"Poor little boy," Sis said. "Poor little boy."

"I can't help it."

"But my dear," Sis said, "think how fortunate you are you got through that affair without marrying him. You can see now — I don't mean on account of his death, of course — but you can see what a mistake it would have been."

Anna looked at her in astonishment. *That from you,* she thought. But she dared not say it. She shook her head. Then, "Yes," she said. "But if it had been possible, if we'd been a little older . . ."

"It would never have worked," Sis said positively. "I know you can see that now. Marry your own kind."

So that's what you think. She thought of what Charlie had told her that night in New Orleans, of the diamonds pawned, the nights of agony. *After all that, it's "Marry your own kind." There must be more to it than that it was a mistake, a social blunder.* Aloud, Anna said, "We could have managed. Taylor had his faults, but — who hasn't?"

"Here's another," Charlotte said. She put a second broken clay ball, this one full of bright sienna liquid, at their feet. "We stopped at a good spot."

"I remember how happy Gran was when your mother married your father," Sis said. "That's the kind of match that works."

"After all there's not just one kind of anything."

"A marriage needs a lot of *weight* behind it," Sis said.

"If people love each other . . ." Charlotte said, and then broke off shyly and bent her face over the pile of rocks at her feet.

They were silent for a few minutes. Then, "Sis, did you see by last night's paper that old Mr. James Anderson died in Baton Rouge?" Anna asked idly. "Wasn't he related to us?"

"My Lord, I thought he'd been dead for years," Sis said. "Let's see, his grandfather and your great-grandfather Anderson (you know, Thomas, the one in the silhouette with his hands under his coattails) were first cousins. That makes him your — first, second — heavens, Anna, that's down to about seventh or eighth. I can't keep track after fifth."

"But Gran said . . ."

"Well, it was complicated," Sis said. "Aunt Alice, Gran's aunt, raised him. He was her husband's first cousin on the other side, his mother's side. And both his parents died in the yellow fever, you know. So Gran feels closer . . ."

"*Whoa.* Stop," Anna said. "I never heard anything so involved."

Sis bent over and picking up a handful of sand, sifted it slowly through her fingers. "Some day you'll be interested in all that, children," she said, "believe it or not."

"I'm already interested," Anna said. "I've been interested in all those old dead people ever since Gran first told me the story about Henry Dupré drinking the barrel of whiskey in the cellar." But she had responded automatically, saying what she knew would please Sis, while all her attention was concentrated on a queer turning over and re-arrangement of data at the bottom of her mind. Listening to Sis's remarks on the bases of successful marriages, she had felt something begin to move, to rise irresistibly toward the light. It had begun when Sis had said, "Marry your own kind," and she had seen as if on a lighted screen Charlie's picture of Alderan furious, dripping with sweat, sitting in the bus station café, saying, "I gave you all the room I could, but you've got to back me into a corner"; and Charlie, "Me? *Me?*" and Alderan, "Yes, all of you. You're all alike."

She almost spoke aloud: *But he wasn't afraid. He was never afraid of Father. He thought Father was afraid of him. That's why he didn't show up for the fight. He knew Father didn't have a gun; yes, the man in the café must have told him. And so he thought Father was afraid of him. And after that he just didn't bother. That hasn't occurred to a single one of them. To them he's nothing but a cardboard villain, not a man at all. They'll never see that they could have been villains to him*

— baffling, unmanageable, hard-headed villains — that they were so foreign to him, he never really understood a single thing about any of them, any more than they did about him. He was miserable, miserable and humiliated by what his own misery had got him into. To think Father was a coward — that would have given him one shred of dignity to begin over again with. I'll bet this very day he can say to himself, "He wouldn't fight me. The bastard wouldn't fight me."

She smiled at her own passionate interest in all those buried passions. *Reckon the reason I'm so excited,* she thought, *is, if I can see that, then I'm getting somewhere at last, I may even have something useful to tell my children.*

"Anna, where are you?" Charlotte said. "Did you hear what I was saying?"

"Huh?"

"I said, if you all can get your mind off past generations for a few minutes, I've got something to tell you about future ones."

"Huh?"

"I've been trying to get up the nerve to tell you all afternoon. Gerry and I are going to get married."

Anna brought herself back to the creek bank with an effort.

"Wonderful," she said. "Charlotte, that's wonderful."

Sis sat up straight and dusted the sand off her hands. "Does your father . . . ?" she began.

"Gerry's talking to him this afternoon," Charlotte said. "Asking him for my hand. Isn't that absurd? I told Daddy and Mama right after church this morning, and told them not to say anything. I wanted to tell you all, myself."

"And your mother? Are she and your father pleased?" Sis asked. "You're not rushing into this too quickly, are you, Charlotte?"

"Of *course* they're pleased. They're tickled to death. You know they've both been crazy about Gerry from the beginning."

"We're *all* crazy about him," Sis said. "He's a darling fellow. Now, you see," she turned to Anna. "This is exactly what I was talking about. This is a marriage that will work."

•§§•

Charlie Dupré had a slight heart attack the day after Gerry called to ask for Charlotte's hand. He was sitting in the dining room with Sarah D. and Billy and Anna when it happened. Charlotte was out with Gerry, and Sis and Gran had unobtrusively left the dining room a few minutes earlier when Charlie began to relate for the third or fourth time his conversation with Gerry the day before.

"I told him," he was saying, "I made it absolutely clear to him that Charlotte has led a sheltered life. She's never lived away from home, and she's always had us to fall back on. After all, the boy should understand that. Am I right, eh? Sarah D.?"

"Of course, darling."

Billy was sitting on the day bed under the huge, heavy gold-framed mirror. He had his face close to the glass and his chin stuck out like a man shaving. "Do you think I could grow a mustache in time for the wedding?" he asked, thoughtfully rubbing the downy black beginnings of a beard on his pale cheek.

His father looked at him seriously. "I doubt it, old man," he said. "You'd be surprised how long it takes to grow a beard. It seems to go fast for a couple of days, and then it slows down to nothing."

Billy leaned back against the pillows and stared grimly at his parents. "Nobody has seen fit to ask *me*," he said, "but I think Charlotte is entirely too young to marry."

But Charlie was intent again on his story. "I also told him," he said, "that we didn't have any two-headed uncles hidden in the attic. All the freaks in this family are allowed to sit in the parlor. Ha." He paused and frowned as he felt the faint beginning of pain in his left arm. "He's a fine, straightforward, manly

fellow. None of this New Orleans fancy-business about him."
And then, "I told him we felt we were not losing a daughter,
but gaining a son. He appreciated that. And after all, we need
another man in the family, eh, Bill? We've always been outnumbered."

"And Lord, Lord, isn't he good-looking?" Anna said. "I'll
take him if Charlotte changes her mind."

Charlie leaned back in the big platform rocker. "I feel
queer, Sarah D.," he said. "I better take some of the heart medicine." He began to fumble at his jacket pocket.

Sarah D. got up quickly, got the bottle of digitalis tablets
out of his pocket and gave him one, at the same time telling
Anna to call the doctor.

Billy picked up the telephone on the table at the end of the
day bed. "I'll do it," he said.

"Not necessary," Charlie said. "I'll be all right in a minute."

"Be quiet and stay still, darling," Sarah D. said. "It's no use
to take any unnecessary chances."

Billy completed the call and then sat white-faced and wide-
eyed watching his father.

"It's all right, son," Charlie said. "I'm not very sick."

Gran was still in her room in the wing and did not hear the
doctor's arrival, or any of the comings and goings to get Charlie into bed, but Sis had come back into the dining room just as
the doctor arrived. It was apparent from Charlie's breathing
that he had a return of the edema that had almost killed him
after the first attack, but the doctor said that it was slight, and
prescribed the medicine that was used to dry up the fluid in his
lungs. The heart action was good, he told them, but of course
Charlie must stay quiet until they could decide how serious the
attack was.

After he left, the three women held a conference in the dining room. Sarah D. sat down on the day bed beside Billy and
put her arm around him. She seemed as much to be leaning on
him as drawing him to her for comfort, and he sat up straight

and stiff, his face made even more childish by his pitiful attempt at self-control and manliness. Now and then he timidly
patted his mother's hand. Sarah D., who in the weeks of Charlotte's courtship had begun to be her old lighthearted, joking
self, was once more tense and sad-eyed; the tiny vertical lines
around her mouth were noticeably deeper, almost as if she
had just had her teeth pulled. She began the conversation
matter-of-factly.

"You mustn't be upset, Billy," she said. "Cousin Jimmy says
that a return of the edema was to be expected. And Daddy is
feeling much better now. He's going to be all right." She
seemed to be talking to herself as much as to the boy, and now
she drew herself up and took her arm from around Billy's
shoulders. "We've got to decide right away before Charlotte
comes home what to say to her. We don't want to make her
unhappy now if we can help it."

"How long does Jimmy think it will take Charlie to get over
this?" Sis asked.

Sarah D. shook her head. "Over it?" she said. "He's just
going to *have* it off and on, that's all." And then, "He wants
him to stay quiet for a few days, but he said there was a good
chance he might get up for the wedding."

"Then perhaps we shouldn't say anything at all to Charlotte," Sis said. She turned to the boy and with one sentence
put on him the responsibility he was so anxious to assume.
"What do you think, Billy?"

"Don't tell her," Billy said. His voice was low and hoarse,
and he did not trust himself to say more without weeping.

"For one thing," Sarah D. said, "it's not a bit of use for us
to try to make Charlie do anything he doesn't want to do. He's
going to do as he pleases. And if he wants to go on with the
wedding, and get up and give Charlotte away, he's going to
do it."

"If he's going to have these attacks from time to time, we
may as well go on with our plans and trust in the Lord to get

him well enough for the wedding," Sis said. "No matter when we plan it, he might be sick."

"I think we should do whatever Daddy wants us to do," Billy said, still in a low, hoarse voice. "Ask him."

"He wants to go on with the plans for the wedding, darling," Sarah D. said, "and he has already told me not to tell Charlotte about this attack. But I want to be sure we are doing the right thing."

Anna had been sitting quietly at the dining room table taking no part in the conversation, but now she spoke. "Two things," she said. "One, how are you going to keep Charlotte from knowing he's sick, when he's in bed; and two, what about Gran?"

They were all silent, looking to Sarah D. for a decision, and she answered immediately. "I think we should tell Charlotte and Mama that Charlie is having a little difficulty with his breathing, that the doctor thinks it is a bad cold, and that he advised Charlie to stay in bed for a few days and to take it easy until time for the wedding," she said. "You know, if we don't deceive Mama, too, she'll be bound to give it away to Charlotte one way or another, and if we are going to try to get through the wedding without getting Charlotte upset, then we ought to do a good job of it."

They carried out the deception successfully. Charlie obeyed the doctor's orders to the letter and took fanatically good care of himself. "I'm going to give her away, if it kills me," he told Sarah D. "After all, she's mine. Who else could do it?"

The edema subsided after two or three days, and as for the frightening pains in his arm, if he felt any more, he quietly took his digitalis and said nothing. But he lost even more weight, and when, a few days before the wedding, he got up and began to sit quietly in the dining room watching the comings and goings and preparations, his suits, although they had been altered for him after the first attack, hung loosely on him again.

Going in and out of the house on the dozens of errands that had to be run to the florist, the caterer, the gift shop, the jewelry store, the bootlegger, and the grocery, Anna, passing him sitting patiently by the radio in the dining room, could scarcely bear to look at him.

"It's his eyes," she told her mother, when Charlotte and Ralph and Katherine arrived from Eureka for the wedding. "I can't bear to look into his eyes. Sometimes he looks like he's pleading with you for something, and sometimes like he's saying (I know it's terrible and melodramatic to say this, but it's true), like he's saying, *I know horrors. God keep you from the horrors I know.* And no matter what anyone says to him, or what he answers, his eyes are saying, *What's the use? Why talk to me about foolishness?* Except Charlotte and Billy. I think he manages to hide it from them."

"I know," Charlotte said. "I've seen it. And Sis said the same thing last summer. Only now it's worse."

Charlotte and Gerry were married a few days later. Patriotism as well as poverty forbade the entertaining and expense of a peacetime wedding, but the two young people did not care. Charlotte had the same indifference to appearances, the same arrogant acceptance of idiosyncracy that was characteristic of all her family. Like most of them, she had not yet given much thought to the maintenance of status because she had been taught quite subtly and almost without words that hers was unassailable. It would be some years yet before any of the Andersons or McGoverns would begin to realize with baffled frustration that no one any longer knew or cared what their status was, and even then, lifelong training and habit would prevent their trying to do anything about it.

As for Gerry, like most men he was interested chiefly in getting the ordeal over with as quickly as possible.

"Just one thing," Charlotte had said when she and the family were discussing the plans, "I want it to be gay, a real party. I don't mean the ceremony, of course. But afterwards. I want to invite everybody I like to the reception, and I want plenty of champagne and everybody to have a grand time."

"Champagne!" Sis said. "Mercy, aren't we fancy!"

"If Charlotte wants champagne, we'll have champagne," Charlie said.

Both Sarah D. and Sis had some small savings which they spent for the trousseau; and Ralph and Charlotte and Will and Eunice gave the rehearsal party and the reception. Ralph got his mother's permission to use her house for the reception. For the first time since old Mr. McGovern's death in 1922 the McGovern house was thrown open to wind, flowers, music, dancing, and young people.

The two old ladies, Miss Celestine and Miss Julia, who still lived there alone together, were nervously delighted with the preparations and went from room to room watching everything and occasionally intervening with a warning about the state of the chair legs, or the venerable age of a potted plant. Julius, decrepit, but still as formal as a queen's chamberlain in his worn and purplish uniform, stood on a ladder and strung garlands of white japonicas around the capitals of the half columns in the drawing rooms, while Miss Celestine, peering anxiously up at him through her pince-nez, stood by to catch him if he fell. "Be careful, Julius," she would say tensely from time to time. "Now don't go up another step. Mercy."

Ralph bustled happily to and fro with cases of champagne to be chilled, while Charlotte McGovern gave orders to the two Negro men who were moving the horsehair-covered parlor furniture to make room for the orchestra and dancing. Miss Julia in a pastel house dress and pompon-trimmed, black leather house slippers followed behind Charlotte, watching the moving of every chair and table.

"My dear, this is delightful," she would say to Ralph if he paused beside her for a moment. "Delightful. I wonder we haven't done it before. So much excitement and so many handsome young people." Or to one of Anna's beaus who had offered to lend a hand, "Ash tray? No, I don't believe we have an ash tray, Captain Hope. We don't smoke, you know. Sister, what shall this young man put his ashes in? Ah, here's a nice shell right here on the étagère. Will this do?"

The weather that January was unseasonably springlike, and Anna and her beaus brought armfuls and basketfuls of paper-white narcissus, early jonquils, and burning bush to the pantry, where Katherine, already heavy and clumsy in the seventh month of her pregnancy, sat at the pantry table and arranged them for every table and pier stand in the house.

Will and Eunice arrived too late for the preparations, but Eunice had had the wedding cake made in New Orleans, and they had brought it on the back seat of the car. In the trunk Will had a case of whiskey for those who did not care for champagne. He was relatively sober. "Afraid to take a drink," he told Charlotte, "on account of that damned cake. Did you ever hear of a cake keeping a man sober? Eunice would have skinned me if I'd let anything happen to it. And here's the whiskey. My God, it's heavy. Get one of those men out here to help me. How's Charlie?"

"The preacher," Charlotte said, kissing him absent-mindedly on the cheek. "Will, I just realized I forgot the preacher. What's he going to drink?"

"My God, woman, why can't he drink what everybody else drinks? Is he a Baptist? A Mormon?"

"Will, you take the name of the Lord in vain every other breath," Charlotte said. "He doesn't drink and neither does his wife."

"Don't worry about it, Charlotte," Eunice said. "I'll fix a fruit punch for the preacher and the old ladies. Give me the car keys, Will."

"You won't need much, honey," Will called after her as she left. "Very few old ladies in Homochitto drink fruit punch."

Anna stood up with Charlotte for her marriage and one of

the young officers from Camp McClure stood up with Gerry. At the ceremony itself no one was present except close relatives, the Andersons and Duprés and their families, Mr. and Mrs. Griswold from New Orleans, Gerry's younger sister, two aunts and uncles and two great-aunts. Gerry came of a large family, but all three of his brothers were in the service and overseas. The wedding guests were ranged around the parlor walls as they had been for Sis's wedding thirteen years earlier, but here the resemblance to the earlier ceremony ended. The tension in the air for Charlotte's wedding was a tension of joy. The parlor was glowing with candlelight, and the improvised altar in front of the fireplace was a mass of white japonicas. For once nobody was in mourning. All the perennial mourners had either died or gone into pastels.

Charlie Dupré had bought a new navy blue suit for the wedding; and a suit that fitted made a considerable improvement in his appearance. Whatever the expression that had haunted Sis and Anna, he seemed to will it away for the day. Tall and haggard, but marked by a distinction and confidence that were also a product of his illness, he escorted Charlotte into the parlor and down to the altar with all his old grace and poise. Quietly serious, he played his brief ritual part, and then stepped to Sarah D.'s side. There he stood listening intently and seriously to the service and looking at his daughter's tawny hair and golden cheek, half hidden beneath her short veil. Midway in the service, he took Sarah D.'s hand, put it on his arm, and covered it with his other hand. She looked at him, dry-eyed and smiling, and then looked back at Charlotte. None of the Andersons believed in crying in public if one could avoid it.

Afterwards in the double drawing rooms at the McGovern house he stood beside Sarah D. in the receiving line for half an hour, greeting friends and cousins, introducing the Griswolds, easy, charming, and obviously happy. Then, when the orchestra began to play, he swept his daughter into his arms and danced. The crystal chandeliers and the candles in their tall hurricane shades gleamed and were reflected back and forth in the two huge pier mirrors at either end of the drawing rooms. The wide, worn oak floor boards shone with wax. The air was sweet with the perfume of narcissus. Charlotte caught up her train and followed her father, whirling once around the room and back, where he spun her into Gerry's arms and stopped once more beside Sarah D.

"May I have this dance, sweetheart?" he said, bowing over her hand with mock ceremony.

The wedding had been at five. At seven Gerry and Charlotte drove away in a shower of rice. After they had gone, the party settled into a comfortably joyous mood. The crowd gradually thinned out until only the two families and a few of Charlotte's close friends and their beaus were left. The erect and dashing young men in uniform whirled the girls about the floor, and among them uncles and cousins danced sedately and a little drunkenly with their wives and old sweethearts. At the sidelines, sitting around the parlor and drawing room walls on the Victorian sofas and parlor chairs that had been shoved out of the way for the dancers, were the old folks — more cousins and great-aunts and uncles — all but Kate, who as always preferred the young folks to her own contemporaries, and had gone outside with several of the young men, where, from the shouts of laughter that could be heard in the parlor, she was keeping them entertained with wild tales of the old days. Sarah D. sat in the front drawing room and talked with the Griswolds, but she could not help watching Charlie anxiously all the time she talked. The young girls had discovered that Charlie could dance better than most of their beaus, and he was greatly in demand. He had drunk only two glasses of champagne, and he sat down frequently between dances to rest; but after five minutes he would be up and dancing again, looking down from his great height at his partner, never seeming to have to stoop to her, no matter how small she was, as he guided her about the room. Charlotte and Sis, sitting across the drawing room from Sarah D., also watched him anxiously.

"I wish he'd stop," Charlotte said in a low voice. "He's wearing himself out."

"But he's having such a grand time," Sis said. "Maybe, after all, it's good for him."

"Sarah D. never takes her eyes off of him," Charlotte said. "See her over there?"

Just then Charlie danced by them and the music stopped. He and his partner sat down, breathless, and Charlie, smoothing the top of his bald head as if his hair were out of place, turned to his sisters-in-law with an ironic smile. "No fool like an old fool, is there?"

"Don't wear yourself out, Charlie," Sis said.

"After all, your only daughter doesn't get married every day," he said. "You have to give her a send-off, don't you?"

Anna came into the room from the front gallery where she had been listening to her grandmother entertaining the young men, came over and sat down beside her mother. Leaning forward and talking across the two women, she said, "Charlie, it's my turn now. I've been waiting in line. Don't you know I'm supposed to be the maid of honor?" And then, to his partner, "You don't mind, do you, Jenny? He's only danced with me once all evening."

The orchestra was playing again, "Tales from the Vienna Woods."

Charlie rose obediently. "Where have you been?" he said. "I was looking for you a little while ago." He took her hand and swung it gently, as if she were a child.

Anna smiled back at him. She thought that if she could not say to him how heroic she thought he was, her heart would burst. But she knew, too, that he would recoil from a word, from even a look of sympathy, that he could not allow anyone to recognize the control that kept him standing with them, erect and lighthearted, full of all his strength and love.

"Well, two things," she said. "One, a bunch of us have been outside with Gran. She's trying to teach the boys to whistle through their fingers. Did you know she could? It's deafening." She paused as a piercing whistle sounded from outside. "Listen. Did you ever hear such a noise? And two, Eunice had me in a corner of the pantry for half an hour, telling me what a wonderful, brilliant, handsome, charming fellow Will is, and before that *I* had Will in another corner of the pantry for half an hour delivering a monologue on the state of the world."

"Come on," Charlie said. "This one'll be over, and I know you love to waltz."

He stepped out on the floor and looked across the room at Sarah D. For an instant a puzzled, questioning expression crossed his face, as if he were listening to some faint, imperfectly heard admonition from his heart. Sarah D. half rose from her chair, but he smiled at her and drew Anna into his arms.

"Now, my dear," he said. "I've gotten Charlotte married off. I'm going to see what I can arrange for you." He held his broad shoulders back, and looked around the room, smiling like a king on his subjects. "Wasn't it a beautiful wedding?" he said. "Wasn't she lovely? Did you ever see a lovelier bride?" And they danced lightly away.

"Come on," Sis said to Charlotte. "I'm going over to chat with the Griswolds. You find Ralph and tell him to ask Sarah D. to dance and get her mind off Charlie, and then tell Eunice to go visit with the Griswold aunts." And, as Charlotte started away, "Wait. Tell Will to ask Mrs. Griswold to dance, will you? They look a little sticky over there. They're probably feeling the strain."

∗

Three months later Charlie Dupré was dead. Young Charlotte did not know until the very end how sick he was. His severe attacks of edema — hours of agonized choking and gasping for breath until the medicine began to dry up the fluid in his lungs — usually came late at night or in the early hours of the morning, and neither he nor Sarah D. told Charlotte about them. They wanted to give her a few months to settle into her marriage before she had to be burdened again with her father's illness. Besides, Gerry expected every day that his outfit would ship out for overseas, and the family felt that Charlotte had enough to worry about. When she came to see them, usually in the afternoon after work, Charlie got up, if he possibly could, and dressed and sat in the dining room for her visit. He talked seriously and intensely to Gerry of his schemes, of buying into the tow-boat business, of renting a farm, of contracting to cut timber for the paper mill in nearby Natchez. Of himself and his illness he never talked.

The day after his death, waiting in the upstairs bedroom before the funeral began, Charlotte said matter-of-factly to Anna, "Daddy never thought about himself, did he? All this last year he's been thinking only about how he could make Mama secure. He knew he was going to die, and he was thinking only about Mama and Billy and me. He never could succeed, everything's an awful mess, worse than if he hadn't tried to do anything, but that's what he was thinking about."

Anna, who had been in the room when Charlie lapsed into the final coma, could not answer. She could only keep patting Charlotte on the shoulder and saying over and over again, "I know, I know." But in her heart she said, *He did succeed. He never flagged this time, or failed in his resolution, not to the very end. At the last, when he could hardly speak for choking, he found breath to say, "Don't call the children, sweetheart. I'm going to be all right." He used on dying all the courage and intelligence and self-denial that he could never find to use in his life. This one time, he was a success.*

Death and Homecoming

～§ WILL CAME HOME the day after his mother's third accident. He was sober when he arrived and he stayed sober until the day he left. In someone else this might not have seemed extraordinary, but no one in the family could remember an occasion in ten years when he had come home *completely* sober. He might *get* sober in the course of a visit, but he arrived "well organized," as Charlotte put it.

Will knew perfectly well that his drinking distressed "the girls"; it distressed them not half so much as it sometimes did him. They would have been astonished and incredulous if they had known that he worked hard to keep it under control, that he had for years thought of himself as a juggler desperately keeping aloft the whirling spheres of his appetites and his necessities. They would have said that he cared not at all for appearances or for his responsibilities, where he would have considered that he spent an agonizing amount of his energy on maintaining both. It never ceased to surprise him that Charlotte could show so plainly how much she disapproved of his being tight when he had been timing his drinks carefully all day to keep from getting dead drunk. Besides, he considered his sisters, particularly Charlotte, who was always the most disapproving of the three, too innocent and ignorant to set themselves up as judges of his habits. Charlotte gave herself away with *Oh, Will, not in the morning!* As if a man who needed a drink gave a damn whether it was 10 A.M. or 10 P.M.

But Charlotte and Sis and Sarah D. had never *needed* a drink in their lives, as far as Will knew, so he might as well have been whistling when he said he *could not* stay dry all the way from New Orleans to Homochitto. It never occurred to him to try to explain what he meant to them, but he sometimes wondered to himself how they could have dealt all their lives with their own appetites, their own passions, and still have so little understanding of his. He would shake his head, and say to himself, *Women!* — aware when he said it that it explained nothing. For he knew that no matter what he said or thought about them, they could make him feel guilty with no more than a shrug, or a raised eyebrow. *We're all a little bit crazy,* he would say to himself. *I'm just more tolerant of their craziness than they are of mine.* And then: *What's the point, after all? It'll ruin my visit. And if I let myself go, we'll all have a grand time.*

At least half the time he was right. His visits would turn out to be occasions, spectacular or absurd, as it struck him; and his mother and sisters, in spite of their initial disapproval, would talk about them for weeks afterward, and laugh at the ridiculous scrapes into which he got himself and them.

The weekend usually began in La Place, a few miles outside New Orleans on the airline highway to Baton Rouge. Will and Eunice would stop there at a restaurant and bar to settle their nerves after the ordeal of battling the wild New Orleans traffic (drivers who, Will said, were *completely prodigal* of life and limb, their own or the other fellow's). The juke box blared and bubbled in a corner while over a drink they decided which of Will's nieces and cousins they would stop to see in Baton Rouge.

Such a beginning might lead to anything, including not going to Homochitto at all. Will always intended to go home, if he had telephoned his mother that he was coming. He did not want to worry and disappoint her. But going home was hard for him. When he had been young, he had been too busy; and

now he had other reasons for staying away. Old, hopelessly
unpayable debts reproached him, when he allowed himself to
think of them. Seeing his mother and sisters alone together,
struggling to deal cheerfully with poverty and illness, made him
vaguely aware that there might, *must* have been something he
could have done so that their lives would be different. He
pushed these unpleasant thoughts to the bottom of his mind
and poured a highball on top of them, and in a little while the
unpleasantness misted over and was replaced by the more
bearable conviction that either he or Homochitto, one or the
other, was not real. After a few more drinks even the faint
unpleasantness that accompanied this idea vanished. His un-
realities merged, joined forces, and lent strength to each other.
He decided either that he and the world were both figments of
his imagination, or that his character had gained a force capable of shielding his threatened home . . . that he was a Ulys-
ses returning to draw the unbendable bow. In the first case
he was a god and in the second a hero. As a god, he could sit
back and gently shake the ice in his highball, contemplating the
world he had created, a faint mysterious smile, an infinite,
tender sympathy for all the poor human creatures who had to
struggle to live, lighting his face. *Never mind, you poor bastards,* he seemed to say, *I see it all, I understand, but I'm beyond it.* If he went the other way, and the hero took over,
then, as Eunice said, it was *Katy, bar the door.* Then it was
death before dishonor, by God, suh, and bring out the dueling
pistols. Will alone still stood for the broadsword virtues, and
woe to the man who thought it was funny. All his gerunds got
strong *g*'s on the ends. He paid old debts with next month's
salary, found widows and orphans to befriend, and picked a
fight with the two-hundred-pound truck driver in the next
booth who looked twice at his wife. He might end up in a
blood bank, giving his life's blood for the men overseas, or he
might buy each of his sisters a $25 bottle of Christmas Night
perfume.

The women, too, had their masks, put on for his visits. Sarah D. shook off the cares that were destroying her and became again the belle of the twenties who had once danced the Charleston better than any one in Homochitto. Charlotte played the role of fall guy for Will's extravagant stories: the naïve overprotected wife who failed to get the point of a faintly off-color story, thereby making it infinitely funnier to everyone else. Sis had for the few days of Will's visits a proper object for her passionate devotion to love and duty, and Will bloomed in the warmth of her quiet attention.

In Baton Rouge, whatever direction Will's drunk had taken, he was welcomed as if his relatives could not think of an excuse, other than his visits, for a party. Will did not believe they had been waiting for him; he knew their party habits as well as his own. But by the same token he recognized their enthusiasm as genuine. Everybody delightedly kissed everybody else, the bottles were brought out, and they all began to talk at once. Other exiles from Homochitto gathered, as the news spread that Will and Eunice were in town. If it was summer, the party adjourned to the back yard, the host dragged hoses and sprinklers away, and nurses were gotten to take the children to the park. By the time dusk cooled the parched summer grass, plans for the evening were being concocted in various corners of the yard. Sometimes momentum would whirl all the celebrants in exile into their cars and away into the night — parents, children, lovers, and neighbors, home to Homochitto, perpetually refusing to be discouraged by the prospect of bleak Mondays.

Before crossing the Mississippi state line the caravan came to a halt, to stock up on liquor before they had to pay bootleg prices. Then the party broke up and each family went its own way, toward the dark houses where long-suffering relatives would bed them down. By the time Will and Eunice pulled up before the shabby old house sleeping behind its wrought-iron fence in the shadow of the Cathedral, to the soft rain of the fountain in the park, they were fit for nothing but bed. Sis and Sarah D. would extract them from the car; the inevitable argument always followed whether Will could carry the luggage, and then he would stumble up the front steps, cursing and banging the suitcases against his shins, and putting them down against the screen door, so that he could not get it open without backing up and starting over. Sis and Sarah D. would be standing behind him at the foot of the steps, arms outstretched to grab him if he fell backward, while Eunice leaned on the creaking iron gate, shaking her head and muttering lectures to herself as she prepared to act at least half sober when she greeted Kate.

Whether deliberately, or because she had always been one who was busy in the back room at something absorbing, Kate, even in the years before she was a cripple, usually missed all this. The banging of doors and suitcases would finally bring her into the parlor, her glasses hooked behind her ears and pushed up on top of her head, peering through the darkness of the porch toward the vague figures of her children, who had by now surmounted the difficulty of opening the screen door and were coming in.

"Mama, here they are at last."

"Will?" She always embraced him, clinging to his slight figure as passionately as she had the night he had run away from home, and she had thought he was drowned.

"Well, here we are Mama. Here we are."

"Don't knock my specs off, darling. Where on *earth* have you been so long?"

Twice in the two years preceding Kate's last fall in 1950 she had broken her arm. She was eighty-three the first time, and in a woman of her age a broken arm was no slight accident. But the wonder of it to her daughters was that it hadn't happened ten years earlier. She stubbornly refused to recognize the toll that time had taken of her agility and cataracts of her vision, and persisted in attempting what a woman of sixty might have hesitated to undertake. The strength and vitality that had been her family's bulwark in the years after Mr. Anderson's death, when they were still children, was their burden in her old age, when she was no longer able to put it to any practical use. She wanted to do everything for herself and most things for other people. Opposition was a challenge to which she had never failed to rise, and as she grew older, her unreasonableness took the exasperating forms that senility thrust upon it.

The first accident happened on the way home from the grocery store. She *would* go, although Lizzie, the cook, implored her to stay at home, and even dared to tell her that Miss Sis had done bought everything they needed the day before, muttering to herself — when she saw that the old lady had no intention of listening to her — that Miss Kate was just going out of sheer devilish contrariness.

Lizzie ordinarily kept up the same pretense that Sis and Sarah D. struggled to maintain — that their mother's pottering about the house and kitchen was indispensable to the smooth ordering of their lives; that the continuous rearrangement of their clothes, furniture, and belongings with which Kate occupied her days, the cleaning out of the icebox, the cancellation of orders to grocer, yardman, and dry-cleaner, the re-arranged dinner menus, the total dislocation of routine which her feeble yet inexorable interference brought into their lives was the same efficient service of love she had always given them.

But that day Lizzie tried to keep her at home. They stood first on the front porch and then on the sidewalk in front of the house, arguing; Kate, still erect and slender, wearing a black straw sailor hat cocked sideways on her head (she could no longer see more than a blurred image of herself in the mirror); and Lizzie, even more eccentric looking than her mistress, in men's shoes cut out at the toes to favor her corns and flowered house dress that hung loosely about her tall skinny black body.

"Now Lizzie," Kate said, "go on in the house and let me alone. You hear me!"

Lizzie shook her head. "You suppose to stay home," she said. "Or else I'm suppose to go with you."

They stared at each other stubbornly and then Kate shrugged and set out at a rapid walk with Lizzie following and taking her arm to steady her at every crossing.

"You *know* I can walk to the grocery store by myself," Kate said, impatiently shaking off Lizzie's hand.

"Miss Sis say I got to keep you company. You *knows* you can't see so good no more, Miss Kate. What Miss Sis going to say if she find out I let you go off without me?"

"We don't have to tell her, do we?"

"She don't miss nothing. She can find out anyway, us tell her or not."

"I am perfectly capable of looking out for myself," Kate said.

"You spry, all right," Lizzie said. "You about the spryest old lady in Homochitto. I ain't disputing that."

"You could go on back to the house and finish your work and get off early."

"I *likes* to get a little airing, Miss Kate. And you know I can't get off, nohow, till Miss Sarah D. gets home from work."

"You're supposed to be working for *me*. I'm head of the house."

"Yas'm."

"Well, I say for you to go on back home."

"We's practically there, now, Miss Kate. I'll just wait out here whiles you do your shopping, if I worries you so much. And then I can keep you company on the way home. Ain't that all right?"

"No! It's not all right. I'm sick of the sight of you. If I find you waiting out here for me when I come out, you're fired. *Fired!* You understand?"

"Now, Miss Kate, you fires me one way, Miss Sis skins me the other. What I'm going to do?"

She was still there when Kate came out with her bag of groceries. "Why don't you let me take the sack, Miss Kate?"

"Oh, *God*," Kate said, and she grinned at Lizzie. "I believe Sis *hired* you to *torment* me." She handed the sack to Lizzie, more to free her hands for a dramatic gesture than to save herself the effort of carrying it, and pressed her temples with the heels of her hands as if trying to crack her own skull. "If I could give one order, one *reasonable* order, and expect it to be carried out!"

"Now, Miss Kate, les you and me let bygones be bygones," Lizzie said.

"Why is it, just tell me why it is that I never tell you to have black-eyed peas for lunch but you have butterbeans?"

"I cooks what I sees in the icebox," Lizzie said. "I can't cook no black-eyed peas if they ain't none."

"Well today we'll have black-eyed peas," Kate said. "I'm sick of butter beans."

She stopped, as if a thought had just struck her, and got her coin purse out of her pocket. "Lizzie, we forgot to get any salt meat. There's not a piece in the house. Here. Go back and get a pound of salt meat."

"I can't go back and leave you by yourself," Lizzie said.

"Go on and get it," Kate said. "We can't cook black-eyed peas without salt meat. And I'll walk along slow, so you can catch up with me. I'll even let you carry the sack."

"Miss Sis'll be mad at me."

"Go on, you devil. What do you think I'm going to do, jump on a broomstick and fly off?"

So Lizzie went. At the next corner, stepping down from the curbing into the street, Kate fell and broke her right wrist.

For a day or two she was in severe shock, but she quickly began to recover. Young Dr. Shields, the grandson of one of Kate's girlhood beaus, set the bone and told the girls that it was entirely possible it would not knit, Kate was so old. But it did knit, as quickly as a child's.

Will was busy the week Kate broke her arm. Sarah D. telephoned him the day it happened, but he explained that the company was in the midst of important negotiations with the union and he could not possibly get away. He had not been home in more than a year, as he and Eunice had been in New York the preceding December and had missed their usual hasty Christmas visit. Sarah D. had seen him in the summer when she had visited Gerry and Charlotte in New Orleans. "Mama would love to have a little glimpse of you," she had told him then, and he had promised to come in the fall. But it was November when she broke her arm and he had still not been able to get away. When he began to tell Sarah D. on the telephone that he could not come until the negotiations with the union were completed, she interrupted him.

"You *have* to, Will," she said. "Next week at the latest. *Please.*"

"All right," he said. "I'll try."

He came and paid his duty call. But his mind was elsewhere, and it did not seem to occur to him that he might better adopt another role than that of the prodigal son.

Kate was already home from the hospital when he arrived, lying in a rented hospital bed in her room, plotting new ways to outwit her children and attendants and get her own way. The old French sleigh bed on which she had slept all her life, on top of all the mattresses and feather beds she could squeeze into it, was made up for the colored practical nurse who slept in the room with her. The girls had had the hospital bed fitted with wooden sides to keep Kate from trying to get up alone the instant the nurse's back was turned. The hospital bed was the first necessity the girls had thought of after the accident. It would have been impossible to nurse an invalid in the sleigh bed. Making it up was like making up a rowboat full of mattresses. The solid curving head and foot and the swelling sides contained with difficulty their cargo of feathers and wool, and all the mattresses and feather beds had to be turned frequently or they got lumpy and uncomfortable. To make room for the hospital bed, Charlotte, who had supervised the rearranging of her mother's room, had had the old bed shoved against the inside wall, blocking the door to the parlor. She had taken the stack of cardboard boxes from under the front window to make room for an extra chair, and had stored them in an empty armoire upstairs. Kate missed her boxes as soon as she was brought home from the hospital, even though there was another stack by the armoire and still another shoved under the sleigh bed, and Charlotte promised to return them to her as soon as she was well enough to get rid of the hospital bed.

With the removal of the three boxes under the window, Kate's room began to suffer the slow, imperceptible loss of its properties that was to continue until it was stripped after the third accident of everything over which anyone might stumble, everything that would collect dust, or get in the way of a broom, or have to be moved about unnecessarily. But there was a great deal to be moved out of the crowded room, and the process was so gradual that only one who was not there every day would have noticed it. In the beginning, when she first came home, everything except the three boxes was where Kate was accustomed to seeing it. Two huge walnut armoires stood at right angles to each other against the walls in one corner, towering almost to the high ceiling. A washstand with its bowl and pitcher, unused since the advent of bathrooms, but never discarded, was across the room from them. Her chest of drawers was jammed up against the foot of the sleigh bed, leaving just room enough to get the door into the dining room open. Two cane-bottomed rocking chairs were drawn up to the gas space heater in front of the old coal grate. On one side of the space heater was a low prayer stool with Anderson carved roughly into its surface. Kate had brought it home when the interior of the church had been remodeled in 1910. On the other side was a round, spool-legged sewing table under which three bricks were neatly stacked. "You never know when you'll need a hot brick for a long winter trip," Kate would say to explain them, but in reality she had uprooted them from the courtyard at Bois Sauvage when the family had moved to town after Mr. Anderson's death. The mantel, the sewing table, the chest of drawers, and the wall over the fireplace were crowded with pictures of her children, grandchildren, and great-grandchildren, as well as of nieces, nephews, and cousins, silhouettes of great-uncles and grandfathers, and photographs of portraits belonging to other members of the family. One wall, her "gallery of heroes," was plastered with pictures of men in uniform. Occupying the place of honor were a photograph of Will in his World War I private's uniform and a framed newspaper picture of General MacArthur, for whom she had conceived a passionate admiration during World War II. Surrounding them were the faces of all the handsome and vulnerable young men of the family, sons, and sons- and grandsons-in-law, who had gone off to all the wars since 1861. Her eldest brother, James, killed at Shiloh when he was sixteen, was half visible in a fading daguerreotype, his mouth stern, his eyes ready to fill with childhood's easy tears; Brother Charlie was there, a veteran of the Spanish-American War, although he had gotten no farther than Florida where he had been poisoned on improperly canned meat, and sent home. A full-length photograph of Gerry Griswold in battle jacket and paratrooper boots hung next to Brother Charlie. Ralph, his face above the high collar of his major's tunic already marked for duty by the cleft chin and straight lips, looked firmly out upon an unmanageable universe where circumstance begged the compromise that honor forbade. Below him in a row his two sons-in-law, and young Ralph, cocky as a rooster in his rakish seaman's cap, divided his gentle immovability by three, and it was still enough for them all. All the men in Kate's gallery were heroes, touched by the call to service, happier, nobler, and more predictable when they wore their country's uniform. She poked fun at herself for hanging their pictures on her wall, but she never took them down.

The removal of Kate's boxes was a bone of contention all through that first illness. There was no place to keep them in the crowded room, but no one could tell her that. She was furious. None of her children had been allowed to touch anything in her room without permission since she had begun her collection, the first tangible herald of her old age.

Charlotte, to whom necessity was a more demanding reality than the past, did not recognize her action as anything but practical. She moved the boxes, but she intended to return them when she could. They contained nothing of any value, but she knew her mother valued them, and she would not have taken advantage of Kate's helplessness if she had not had to. She had often thought of her mother's life in the past few years as tedious, alone day after long day in the empty house. She did not know that the days had passed for Kate as swiftly as the drawing of a deep and painful breath, passed in musing over her life and the lives of her intimates, dead so long that no one else remembered them, but imprisoned for her in all her talismans, ready to be released when she picked up a pair of wool cards, an old deed, an unmended shawl, a box of stereopticon prints, or a letter she was too blind to read.

Twenty years had gone by since Kate had dragged a dust-covered trunk full of quilt scraps out of the storeroom in the wing and begun to rummage through it, the twenty years between sixty-three and eighty-three. The years that saw Kate's eldest grandchildren reach maturity, marry, bear their first children, fight a war, and then painfully take up the broken

threads of their lives, the years that saw their first loves burn
and die and new loves spring from the ashes, the years of the
fullness of their lives, when so much happens that forty years
are not enough to contain it all — for Kate these years spun by
so fast they seemed no more than the interval between pulling
a piece of lace from the first trunk and deciphering an old letter in the last. She had gathered her life into her room, and
put it in trunks and boxes and drawers, and daydreamed over
it, until she saw or at least sensed in her age and semi-blind-
ness that it was being cruelly stripped away to make room for
her death.

Kate had dresses in her boxes, ranging in style from a high-
necked, bustle-backed gray faille sewn with cut-steel bead designs that had been in her own trousseau, to Sarah D.'s flat-
bosomed, knee-length white chiffon wedding dress. Sometimes
she had spent a whole morning trying dresses on one of her
granddaughters and telling them of the occasions when they
had been worn. She read the letters and diaries over to herself until she could no longer see them, and by then they were
so familiar she could recognize them by touch. Sometimes even
if she could decipher the signature she could not remember
who had written them. (*Darling*, one began, and was signed
Charlie; was it from her Uncle Charlie to his first wife, or was
it from Brother Charlie to Clara? The date was undecipher-
able.) She had planned new dresses with collars of heavy
ivory-colored lace; pieced bits of velvet and shotsilk together
for a quilt one morning and in the afternoon swept them back
into the trunk, her design forgotten. She would fall into a
reverie over a photograph of herself at twenty, corseted and
high-bosomed, gazing out from beneath seductively drooping
eyelids. In those days her lids had drooped just enough to
give her an *air*; now she could not raise them to see the dust
on top of the icebox. The picture had been taken on a visit
to Brother Charlie in California, the time she had fallen so

desperately in love with . . . With whom? Ah, Mr. Carr, of course. And he had been quite wealthy, but that was years later, long after she married Mr. Anderson. Yes, she had met him again in St. Louis during the yellow fever, when she was there with all the children, all *four* of them, and Mr. Carr had been a bachelor still, but rich, and bald as Uncle Ned. Will had been so bad, so *terrible* they had almost gotten put out of the hotel. And Mr. Carr had been so nice, so gallant; in spite of the years and the children, he had sent her a dozen beautiful red roses and taken her out to dinner.

"Here," she would say to Anna McGovern or Charlotte Dupré, "here's what I looked like when Mr. Carr fell in love with me. Just think, if I'd married him, we'd all be rich as sin."

"But we'd be somebody else, Gran."

Kate would grin fiercely at them, her automatic signal that she did not mean to be taken seriously. "Never mind. What difference would that make, if we were rich?"

The grandchildren had seldom needed to ask questions about the pictures and letters Kate brought out, for as the years passed she made them as familiar with her talismans as she was. To Anna particularly Kate's stories made her family's past almost as real as her own. She never tired of them, and drew Kate on to repeat them and to sing again and again in her cracked, quavering voice the songs her mother had sung to her.

But now Kate's granddaughters were all grown and married and far away. There were great-grandchildren, babies and toddlers whom she would never be able to see properly, never have time to know. To Anna and Katherine and Charlotte it was a bitter thought that Gran could not be to their children what she had been to them, but to Kate it was a matter of indifference. She could not keep track of their names and ages, much less cherish them and spend herself on them in as she had on her own. She drew inward. Even her grandchildren sometimes disappeared into the haze outside or were confused with their parents or cousins, all but Charlotte Dupré who had always been her favorite.

≈§≈

"Roll me up, please, Charlotte. I'm tired of lying down."

Kate drew up her knees and squirmed restlessly, twisting the sheet and pulling it loose from the foot of the bed. She had been waiting too long for Will and was beginning to be cross. Charlotte had rolled her mother up and down half-a-dozen times in the course of an hour, but she got up without comment, turned the crank at the foot of the bed, and tucked in the sheet. Then she sat down again in the rocker beside the bed and took up the hooked rug she was working on.

"I forgot to tell you, Mama, I had a letter from Anna this morning. If she can find someone to keep the children, she's planning to come down to see you next week."

The screened door of the front porch banged, and Will shouted, "Hey, anybody home?" There was a noise of greetings in the parlor. Kate sat up.

"Give me my teeth quick, Charlotte," she said. "No use worrying Will by looking any worse than I have to." With her left hand she put them awkwardly in, and then brushed back the fine hair straggling loose from the three big tortoise-shell hairpins that held it twisted up on top of her head.

Will came into the room, anything but a hero in his rumpled gray suit, his tie loosened at the neck and his collar unbuttoned. The fresh, dark, masculine beauty that gave his photograph its charm, the fine-boned, precisely articulated strength were blurred and distorted by years of hard work and dissipation, but there was still a hint in his straight, determined mouth and the bony structure of his face that the framework of beauty was there, to be put to use in his old age, if he didn't kill himself drinking. Now he was simply middle-aged and beginning to be tireder than he had ever thought he could be. His balding head was corrugated with the imprint of the gray felt hat he had taken off as he came into the house. The wings of his small, straight nose were marked with tiny branches of red, and the deep sockets of his eyes were as bruised and puckered as if someone had driven both fists into them. His firm mouth and chin announced to the world what his eyes denied, that despite all evidence to the contrary he was still in control of his destiny.

"Will! Ah, here's my darling." Kate held out her arms to him, waggling the cast that encased the right one from fingertips to above the elbow at the makeshift side rails on her bed. "Look what they've done to me. They've got me penned up like a hog in the slaughter pen."

He put his arms gently around her, and then stood back and rapped the side rail. "What kind of damn-foolishness have you been up to, Mama? Rolling out of bed?"

Charlotte kissed him on the cheek. "She won't pay any attention to the doctor," she said. "He told her not to get up without someone to help her into her chair. But yesterday, the minute we turned our backs, she got out of bed and started for the kitchen. Of course she fell again. Thank God she didn't break anything else."

"Where was the nurse?"

"Ha!" Kate said. "She was asleep. Lazy, no-count thing. I don't know why they keep her. Her feet are so big they stretch halfway across the room. She's exhausted all the time from dragging them around. And I fell over them. I would have been fine if I hadn't fallen over her feet."

"Now, Mama."

"Yes, I'm lying," Kate said. "I admit it."

"She won't listen to reason," Charlotte said. "Will you, Mama?"

"What were you up to, anyhow?" Will asked. "After the sherry bottle?"

Kate patted the mattress of her bed. "I keep my sherry

right under here where I can lay my hands on it without getting up," she said. "I was after the butcher knife."

"The butcher knife! What for, for God's sake?"

"I'm going to cut this cast off," Kate said. "It's driving me crazy." She pushed her finger under the edge of the cast and scratched at her wrist. "I would have gotten it off yesterday, if I hadn't fallen."

"You see," Charlotte said, patting her mother's thin hand and rubbing her fingers gently over the swollen veins, "She's incorrigible."

"And they all talk about me as if I weren't here," Kate said. "It makes me feel like the corpse at the funeral."

"There's more to all this than meets the eye, Mama," Will said. "You've been doing some mighty fancy staggering around lately."

Kate laughed. Nothing pleased her more than the fiction that she was a heavy drinker. "Ralph brings it to me," she said. "I have to drink it up."

"Whose feet were in the way the day you broke your arm?"

"I was sober as a judge. It never would have happened if it hadn't been for that old fool, Ben McCrory."

"What did he have to do with it?" Charlotte asked. She had not heard this version of her mother's accident.

"I stopped to talk to him," Kate said. "You know, Will, I don't see as well as I used to, but I couldn't miss Ben. Ever since he had his seventieth birthday last year, he's taken to plopping himself down on the curb to rest, whenever he feels like it. He says it's the privilege of old age to be conspicuous and ridiculous. If you ask me, it's nothing but affectation. Anyhow, there he sat, right in front of me on the corner of Lee and Pine. I almost fell over him, and then I stopped to help him. You can't help thinking he's sick when you see him like that, all dressed up in his black coat and string tie, so proper and dignified, sitting on the curb with his coattails trailing in the gutter. And his face is so red he looks like he might have a stroke any day. I was trying to help him up, and he was trying to make me let him alone, when I fell."

"You'd better concentrate on helping yourself and quit trying to be a good Samaritan," Will said, winking at Charlotte.

"Oh, Mama, you know that's not true," Charlotte said.

"Let me draw a long bow, Charlotte," Kate said. "It's more entertaining than the truth. The truth is that I misjudged the distance from the corner of the Super-drug building (isn't that what they call that plastic monstrosity that's gone up on the site of the old Aldridge house?) between the building and the curb. I thought I had one more step of sidewalk, and I stepped on air. It could happen to anybody — any half-blind, simple-minded old body like me."

Kate lay back, quiet for a moment and frowning, as if she were seeking a way to tell him exactly what it had been like. Then she sat up again. "Will, I just lay there in the street," she said. "I just lay there. I couldn't speak a word. For the longest time I felt my brain still bumping against the sides of my head. At least ten people must have seen me fall. It gave me the strangest feeling when they gathered round and started talking about what to do with me — as if I weren't there. And, Will," she said, leaning forward and shaking her cast at him again, "the strangest thing of all. *Not a one of them knew who I was. Not a single one.* Even old Ben McCrory would have been a comfort. At least he could have told them where to take me."

"Imagine that!" Charlotte said. "Imagine *Mama* falling down on the main street of Homochitto and nobody knowing who she was!"

"That's one advantage of New Orleans," Will said. "You don't expect folks to know you, and so you're not disappointed when they don't."

"Oh, I wasn't *disappointed*," Kate said. "It didn't make any *difference*. I simply couldn't *conceive* of such a thing."

She fell back against the rolled-up head of her bed, and closed her eyes. "Lizzie finally came," she said. "I suppose they would have put me in the charity ward if she hadn't. She had gotten the salt meat I sent her for, and was poking along, slow as molasses in January, but at least she had sense enough to say she knew me, and to get someone to call Jimmie Shields and the girls." She opened her eyes, as if new dramatic possibilities of the situation had occurred to her. "I might have *disappeared*," she said. "Suppose Lizzie hadn't come, and I had gone into a coma and died. No one would ever have known what happened to me. Why, I'd be buried in potter's field right this minute in a ten-dollar pine coffin."

Will and Charlotte laughed. "I expect we would have looked for you, Mama," Charlotte said.

"Where's Eunice?" Kate said to Will. "You brought her, didn't you?"

Will nodded. "She'll be along in a minute, Mama," he said. "She stopped in the parlor with Sarah D. Where's Sis?"

"She'll be down in a minute, I reckon," Charlotte said. She went upstairs right after supper."

When Eunice came into the room the faint smell of whiskey that Will had brought in became more noticeable. Charlotte sniffed, but said nothing.

"Give Will and Eunice a glass of sherry, Charlotte," Kate said, "and call the girls. Let's all have a little glass of sherry." She rooted with her good hand under the edge of her mattress and brought out the bottle. "My wine cellar."

"You, too, Mama?" Charlotte asked, taking the bottle.

"Of course. This is an occasion. Will hasn't been home since . . . How long has it been, Will?"

"It's been over a year," Sarah D. said in the doorway. "They haven't been here since he got the vice-presidency last May a year ago. Remember? The time we had the party out at the Blue Slipper, when Will got carried away making toasts and fell over backwards in his chair. You remember how mad you got because we all laughed at him, Eunice?"

"Just the same he might have hurt himself," Eunice said.

"The Lord looks after fools and drunkards," Sarah D. said. She crossed the room and put her arm around Will's waist. "We knew you weren't hurt, darlin'," she said, "and you *were* funny."

"Now, pour us some sherry, Charlotte," Kate said, "and Will, tell us what you've been doing with yourself."

"Not I, Charlotte," Will said. "I have some bourbon in the car. I'll fix a highball for Eunice and me. Anybody else want a drink? This deserves a party — we can call it a knitting party. But nobody has to knit except Mama."

"Sherry for me," Kate said. "Whiskey makes me too woozy."

The tone of the weekend was set. Kate took part in its beginning, but her fall the day before had set back her recovery more than any of them realized to begin with and she did not get up again until the following week. It astonished the girls that her weakness and lassitude escaped Will's notice, but he took whatever his mother said at face value and resolutely refused to probe any deeper.

As for Kate, she excused her weakness with the same sort of courage she had ridiculed and understood so well in old Ben McCrory, by saying she was bored with them all, and wished they would go away.

"Go on, all of you," she commanded abruptly that first evening, after they had sat with her perhaps half an hour. "Sis, send Lizzie in here. She's better company than the lot of you. You too, Will. I'm sick of looking at you."

The three sisters looked at each other, all of them feeling the same twist of pain and pity. Kate had been waiting for him, had thought of nothing but his visit for a week.

Charlotte bent over the pillow and kissed her forehead. "You'll feel better in the morning, Mama," she said. "Maybe you'll be up to taking a nice long ride with Will and Eunice."

Will and Eunice spent a night and a day in Homochitto, and then went back to New Orleans, leaving the four women to their long ordeal. The following week, when Kate was up and about the house again, Charlotte went back to Eureka. Sarah D. and Sis settled into the routine of work and nursing, waiting patiently for Kate to regain her strength, to put to use again the wry humor that illumined their pleasures and gave the lie to their frustrations. But they waited, finally, without hope. Bewildered and exhausted, they saw her summon her strength and concentrate her force for the duration of a short visit from a friend or cousin who would go away amused and astonished, while with them, her daughters, she sank day after day into a morass of pain and boredom.

Kate had been for years a master of the art of growing old. She had never tried to look younger than she was, letting the agility of her mind and body make its own statement, without apologizing for her face. She had suffered hardship and tragedy, but she had always found the world fascinating and had been able to communicate her fascination. She had always known how to use the pleasant shock to a solicitous young person of a faintly risqué remark, or an incongruously youthful ambition.

And she could still do it, still *had* to do it. But she could not sustain the effort long.

Her callers always went away saying to the girls, as they saw them to the door, "I don't see how she does it. She's as bright and full of life as she was fifteen years ago."

Their sense of privacy and family loyalty gave Sis and Sarah D. no choice but to agree, knowing all the time they nodded and smiled that as soon as they had walked out of the door of her room, Kate had probably put her head down on her hands and begun to moan.

They did not openly question Kate's right to punish them for her suffering, but neither did they at first recognize the important fact that might have given them the strength and the means to deal with her. They kept making the same advances and the same responses to her that they had made all their adult lives. They could not see that she was not the same person. She was different, not simply in health and in age, but in her soul.

When Charlotte came for her next visit, she spent one day and night in her mother's house, and then she said to Ralph, "Things are *bad* at home."

"What's the matter?" he asked.

"Mama's wearing Sis and Sarah D. out," Charlotte said. "Sarah D. looks like she's been pulled through a keyhole."

Ralph shook his head sympathetically. "Sarah D.'s thin," he said. "I've never seen her so thin."

"Mama shouldn't be so unreasonable."

"She's old, Charlotte," Ralph said. "And besides that, she's sick. There's no use in your saying she ought to be different."

"But she's not senile," Charlotte said. "She has perfectly good sense, and she owes it to the girls to try to be cheerful and to make life a little easier for them."

To Sis and Sarah D.'s blindness, Charlotte added her own notion of how things should be, and in spite of Ralph's warning, she called her mother to task.

"Mama, you've got to think about the girls," she said. "You've got to make an effort for them. Sis looks like something the cat dragged in, and even Sarah D. is getting skinny. You've got to be more cheerful for them."

Kate was sitting in the low cane-bottomed rocker in her room. She had drawn her chair close to the fire and had a pile of old wool from a worn-out comfort and a pair of wool cards in a basket at her feet, but she was not working. When Charlotte had sat down on the opposite side of the battered gas space heater and begun to talk, Kate had begun to rub the knot on her right wrist. Now she compressed her lips and appeared to be listening to some deep sound within herself.

"Mama," Charlotte said again, "try to be a little more cheerful."

"I do, I do," Kate said. "Nobody knows the effort I make."

"I see you making an effort for Jimmie Shields and Aunt Annie Hunt, and Alice and Mary, but as soon as all the visitors go home, you stop trying. I see what you *can* do when you want to. If I didn't I wouldn't fuss at you, Mama. But the girls need you to make an effort for *them*, and the company, as far as that's concerned, makes no difference at all."

"They don't need me any more," Kate said. She stopped rubbing the knot on her healed wrist, and began to moan. "Oh, oh," she said, "it never stops hurting, never, never."

"There," Charlotte said. "That's what I mean. Don't you see what it does to them to hear you moan so, night after night? Even if it hurts, can't you hold back a little when Sarah D. and Sis are home, and treat *them* like company? They're so *tired*. Moan to Lizzie and me. We know it hurts and we'll moan with you. They need you to be cheerful."

"Everything I do is wrong," Kate said. "I see it. I can't even use the telephone. Don't think I don't see it. I'm useless. Useless."

Charlotte drew her chair closer to her mother's and laid her hand on her arm. "Mama," she said, "you know that's not true. We've always needed you, and we still need you. That's what I'm trying to tell you."

"Not Sis and Sarah D.," Kate said. "They're never . . . never . . ." She broke off and pulled away from Charlotte. "They sowed the wind," she said furiously. "Now they're reaping the whirlwind."

"What in the *world* are you talking about?"

"They wouldn't listen to me when they were young. If they had, they wouldn't *have* to listen to me now."

Charlotte half rose from her chair, and then sat down again, shaking her head in bewilderment.

"You needn't try to walk away from it or shrug it off," Kate said. "*You* know what I mean."

"I don't, Mama. I haven't the faintest idea what you're talking about."

Kate leaned forward in her chair and spoke in a passionate whisper. "I'll tell you then, if you forget so easily. If either one of them had married a decent man, they'd have enough money to put me in an old ladies' home and *nobody* would have to listen to me."

The tears started in Charlotte's eyes. "Don't be ridiculous," she said. "How can you, how *can* you say such a thing?"

"Sis," Kate said, paying no attention to Charlotte's distress. "I *begged* her. Didn't I? You were here. I went on my *knees* to her, and she wouldn't listen."

"Mama, that's all over and done with years ago. And God knows she's suffered enough for it without your punishing her any more."

"I'll never forgive her," Kate said. "Never."

Charlotte leaned back wearily in her chair and closed her eyes. The fire hissed quietly and Kate's rocker creaked as she rocked herself to and fro, saying no more, but smiling to herself and nodding every now and then, as if to say, There. I've said it and I'm glad. In a few minutes Charlotte sat forward again and took her mother's good hand in her own. "Darling," she said, "we all have to forgive each other every day. We *have* to. Maybe if you ask him, God will take all that old bitterness out of your heart."

"I don't want Him to," Kate said.

Charlotte looked at Kate as if she had never seen her before. "I know you don't mean that," she said. "There's nothing Sis wouldn't do and hasn't done for you."

"Humpph," Kate said, but her senseless anger had subsided and she glanced at Charlotte sheepishly as she said it.

"Mama," Charlotte said, "you've given your whole life to us. You've worked and grieved and rejoiced for us for sixty years. And of course you've been furious with us, sometimes, all of us. We understand that. But what you've got to see is that you must do something different for us now, something different from any of the things you've ever done for us. You have to accept *our* gifts to you. Let us be useful now, and you be ornamental and enjoy it."

"Ah, my dear," Kate said, "I see all that. You're wonderful daughters to me. But I don't *want* to give up. I can't let go. I can't."

"I'm going to teach you how to use the dial phone before I leave this trip," Charlotte said. "I'm sure you can learn to dial by touch."

Kate nodded. "Of course I can, if someone will just show me how," she said. She leaned down to the basket at her feet, and pulled out a pile of wool and the cards and began to work. "See here," she said, "when I get all this wool carded, I'm going to make a new comfort for Sarah D.'s bed."

Without thinking, Charlotte sighed.

Kate dropped the cards and leaned forward in her chair. "I know I'll never finish it," she said. "I know it. Just let me alone. For God's sake let me alone."

Charlotte's heart was cold and heavy as a stone.

"I'm tired," Kate said. "I'm tired. I wish I were dead."

∗⸙∗

The second time Kate broke her arm, Charlotte came as promptly as usual. Her children were all grown and gone, and it was easy for her to leave home and settle down in Homochitto for an indefinite stay, as long as she thought her mother needed her. She knew the long days were lonely for Kate, alone except for servants in the empty house, and she submerged herself in her mother's life, spending hour after hour every day sitting beside her, talking, talking, and listening. Both women had inexhaustible stores of reminiscences and family stories and were content to spend days analyzing the intricacies of family relationships. Prevented by her increasing deafness from taking pleasure in the radio or the movies or television, Charlotte had always put conversation to use as an unfailing source of amusement; she liked to visit and she seemed unaware of her own patience and forbearance. That winter, simply by an indefinitely prolonged marathon of conversation, she kept Kate tied to the real world with countless frail threads of participation in the lives of her children and her children's children. Most particularly she kept her sane because she demanded nothing of her, no understanding of their problems, no feeling for their joys or tragedies, but simply the effortless entertainment of hearing about their recipes, their vacations, their new draperies, their children's antics and ailments, their quarrels with their neighbors, their husbands' promotions, in short the simple furniture of their lives. Any demand would have been too much for Kate, whose difficulties, no matter how heavy the cast on her arm, were almost all in her mind and heart. Charlotte acted instinctively on this assumption, although for a long time she could not bring herself to admit it. She must have known in her heart that one push, one reasonable demand would have been enough to make Kate turn her face to the wall. The wall was there, blank and quiet and inviting. Charlotte must have felt, too, as everyone has at some time in his life, the temptation to huddle against it, to pull up the covers and leave the world to its weariness. But what she did instead was to charm Kate out, day after day, with loving, patient tenderness.

Away from the sickroom with her own children and with Ralph, she protested every step of the way. She could not give up the notion that Kate could do better, if she would just *try*.

Perhaps it was the vitality of Kate's body that made the disintegration of her personality so mysterious to Charlotte. The tired old heart beat steadily, calmly on; the broken bone again manufactured the necessary calcium and knit, as if her body had no knowledge that it had now served its exhausted tenant eighty-four long years. She got up; she talked again of hanging curtains and clearing out closets. But inexorably, far down in the deepest convolutions of her brain, the tiny blood vessels hardened. The mist drew in, like the fog over the river on a cold winter morning, opening for a moment to a gust of wind, closing again over all the landscape of her life. The projects she planned, the tests to which she drove herself, were even more short-lived than those spurts of energy that had pulled her together long enough after the first accident to send visitors away saying, "Kate is remarkable; I don't see how she does it."

Chasms of depression yawned at her feet and she had not the strength to draw back. She told Sis and Sarah D. over and over again how much she hated to be a burden to them. "Old people ought to be disposed of, like sick mules," she would say.

She insisted upon being brought to the table in her wheel chair during the weeks before she could walk alone, and would allow no one to feed her. She could not see her food and pushed it round and round her plate in an effort to get a bite onto her fork. Eventually her daughters became accustomed to this struggle to eat, but for weeks they sat at every meal, unable not to stare at her plate, half paralyzed with the effort not to reach across the table and help her. She would *not* be helped, and as a result, she ate almost nothing. Before the winter was out Sis had an ulcer, undoubtedly from enduring the tension of those dreary meals.

Day after slow day the evidence piled up, and Charlotte and Sis and Sarah D. admitted to themselves at last that there was nothing they could do to make their mother happy. They could not stop trying, they could enjoy their brief successes when for a moment, with all the last strength of her life, Kate helped them sustain their make-believe; but that was all. There was no way for them not to see that her personality had suffered a total reverse. Self-pity had replaced humor and malice charity. She declared a final war, not on the whole human race, but on those who loved and served her — her family and her servants.

She had been served all her life by Negroes. Her relations with them had been like those with her grandchildren, whom she threatened in accents of mock ferocity to "snatch bald-headed," but who were not expected to pay the least attention. She had quarreled with them, made unreasonable demands upon them, and in response to their tolerance, had made unreasonable demands upon herself in their behalf. But now she hated them all. She would scarcely let her Negro practical nurse touch her, and was so rude that one nurse followed another in rapid succession until she was well enough to need only Lizzie, who refused to be insulted, and treated her like a wayward child.

"Miss Kate's wo' out," she said to Charlotte one day in the kitchen where she was clashing pans together to relieve her feelings after the ordeal of getting Kate dressed.

"What do you mean, Lizzie?" Charlotte had followed her out of her mother's room to make a lame apology for her mother's behavior.

"All they lives folks keep waiting for better times," Lizzie said, "and Miss Kate done more waiting and had things worse in her time than she would have expected. But she always made the best of things and hoped for better times. Now it ain't no use for her to hope no more. Times won't never get better for *her*. More than likely they'll get worse. What's the use in her being good to old Lizzie?" She put down the saucepan which she had been furiously rubbing with a scouring pad and turned around to Charlotte with her hands raised and the water running down her arms and dripping off her elbows. "Miss Kate knows I forgive her," she said, "but she ain't got time to forgive herself."

Charlotte shook her head. She was not sure she understood what Lizzie was talking about, or, as she put it to herself, she didn't think Lizzie was sure what she was talking about. She could never have allowed herself to think that there might be a day when she too would not have time to forgive herself, and when Lizzie's forgiveness might weigh heavily on her.

"I hope I can give up when I'm old, Lizzie," she said. "I hope

I have sense enough left to give up, and let my family take care of me, and stop trying to thread needles when I can't see the eyes."

"No, ma'am," Lizzie said. "I don't see you giving up. I see you making it by yourself, holding your breath to the end. You ain't like Miss Kate. You ain't going to try to make it for everybody. But mind you don't shut your heart and think you can bear your own misery. It makes your folks feel just as bad when they can't help you bear your misery as it makes you feel when you can't bear your own. Your folks' hearts is going to ache for you, all by yourself, just like yours aches for your mama. You got to give a little. That's the way it is with you. Remember, you told me one time how when you was little and trying to make a dress for your doll, your mama would come to show you how, and she could do it so good, she'd always end up making it for you? Well, now you got it fixed in your head you just *got* to do it yourself, or there ain't no satisfaction in it. But you can't do it all yourself, no more than Miss Kate can do it all for you."

"When the time comes, I'm going to say to myself, I've tried to serve the Lord and my family, and now I'm through. I can't do any more."

Lizzie shook her head. "The time don't *never* come, Miss Charlotte, not so as you'd notice it, not from one day to the next. But I know you. Your straight back got to bend, and you got to say *Help me* before you die, if you mean to go easy. Everybody has got their own way of suffering, and nobody's way is strange to them.

"Look at Miss Kate. Many a day I hear her, when Miss Sis and Miss Sarah D. go off to work in the morning, holler after them, 'Wear your rubbers. Take your umbrella.' Now anybody that'll holler *wear your rubbers* after a grown person has got some strange notions about how folks manage to get along. And so when they gets old and the rubbers all wore out, and the umbrellas got holes in them, they gets mad. They feels like they not only got to remind you to wear them, they also got to figure out some way to patch them up. And they too blind and tired to do it.

"It's the same way with everything," she said. "You watch her with Miss Sis and Miss Sarah D. She can't forgive them because they got to work, and it ain't right for ladies to work. She always telling them, same as she tells me how no-good I am, how they daddy worked so hard to leave them fixed so they could live like ladies, and how she can't understand what happened. Now, Miss Charlotte, you know that ain't the way it was, and that ain't the way it is. She's just mad with them because she sees they ain't a thing she can do to help them out, and they ain't never going to be. Why she don't treat you thataway, she see you fixed up; Mr. Ralph, he come in, fat and rich, and bring her a bottle of wine, and she don't have to be mad at you, cause you don't make her feel bad."

"But she *has* changed," Charlotte said. "The hardest thing to understand is how she's changed. She never used to be bad to you. And not only that, all these years, and all the things that have happened to her and to us, she's never been mean. Unreasonable, sometimes, and always wanting things done her way — but never mean. And she's not childish, like old Miss Ella Watkins. You can't blame it on that. She understands everything that's going on, but she gets more selfish and unreasonable every day."

"That ain't it, Miss Charlotte," Lizzie said. "I nursed plenty old folks, and what you got to see about them is, even if they don't make you put hair ribbons in they hair and play doll babies with them, like Miss Ella, they still like children. You might think they as smart as they ever been, but it ain't so. Children ain't got at what makes grown folks do like they do, and old folks is beginning to forget it. You don't tell no children how things is. You *could* tell them, and later on they asks you why you didn't and feels like you cheated them. But it ain't no way to tell them. They ain't got there yet. They brains and they hearts ain't growed big enough to take it in. When they gits here they is shut up like tight little buds, and then they begins to open and open, and when they gits bloomed out, they goes to seed. And what I thinks about old folks is this: like children ain't got at things yet, well, old folks is forgot them. Death done blowed his cold wind on them, done blowed they bones bare, done blowed out of they heads all it took so long to git. They waiting and shivering, and can't nobody rightly expect them to be good-natured."

Will was in Washington on business at the time of the second accident. He sent Kate a postcard with the Washington Monument on it, and then the family heard no more from him for six weeks. By the time he got to Homochitto, Kate was up, and as active as she was ever to be. When he came, she made an effort that was quite evident to her daughters to be her old alert and unsinkable self. She seemed to concentrate her force and review her difficulties and make her plans to overcome them with a forethought and consistency that astonished the girls. She told them before he came that she was not feeling well enough to come to the table, and would eat in her room for a few days. All of them recognized and forbore to comment upon the subterfuge. The ritual of a visit from Will demanded the same behavior from them, but they had not thought their mother capable of making the effort.

Fortunately for Kate's masquerade, Will arrived late at night, and by the time she was up the next morning and ready for him, he had already begun to drink. She had breakfast in her room. Lizzie helped her dress and combed her thin, fine white hair into a softer style than the usual knot twisted up on top of her head and precariously held by two or three big tortoise-shell hairpins. Then she powdered the old skin, soft and clear and wrinkled as worn linen fresh from a wind-blown line, carefully brushing the powder out of the deep wrinkles.

Will and Eunice were standing in the parlor, debating the advisability of making a trip to the bootlegger's before the day began, when Kate came into the room. She had bullied Lizzie into letting her come alone, and she walked carefully, avoiding the vague shapes of furniture that looked in her way. Will started forward to guide her to a chair.

"Never mind, Will," she said. "You're as shaky as I am. Why, I'm trotting in and out, and up and down the steps a dozen times a day." She steadied herself with her good hand on the back of the love seat. "Why," she said, "I'm feeling so frisky I believe I could slide down the banisters, if our stairs had banisters."

"No wonder you break an arm every year," he said. "You ought to start acting your age. Why, you're old enough to be my mother."

"Come on, Mother," Eunice said. She called Kate Mother with the formal and unnatural inflection that daughters-in-law give the word, a pause before and after, and a formal roll to the "r" that said, *See how generous I am. We're friends, even though I stole your son.* "Will, give Mother a hand and stop clowning."

"Mama's the one who's clowning," he said.

"Would you like to drive to the bootlegger's with us, Mother?" Eunice said. "It's a lovely morning for a spin."

Kate nodded and smiled. She was very fond of her daughter-in-law, although she had been astonished when Will had married her, and had not been quite sure what to do with this big, talkative woman when he had brought her home as a bride. Convinced of Will's irresistible charm, she had thought he could marry anyone who was fortunate enough to be chosen by him, and had said to herself that if she were a man, she would not have chosen Eunice.

"Why," she had said to her daughters, "she's two inches taller than he is."

And they had held their tongues regarding their own private conviction: that it was equally mysterious what Eunice had seen in Will.

As the years passed, Eunice's virtues had become more apparent to Kate. The most important of these was that she adored her husband. She clucked and fussed over him like a large distracted hen, waited on him hand and foot one day, and the next batted her eyes at him with the awkward coyness that some big women use to convince men of their femininity. Then, too, Eunice was a steady worker and a hardheaded business-woman. She always had a good job and was ready to throw her resources into the breach when Will had been on a gambling spree or wrecked himself with a week-long drunk. She had bought their home, and she made sure that Will did not throw it away or get his hands on the back log of savings which she had laid by for *real* emergencies.

There was only one flaw in the marriage as far as Kate was concerned — there had been no children. She longed for a grandson who bore her husband's name — William Augustin Anderson; and she was sure that Will would "settle down" if only he had children. But neither Will nor Eunice, as far as the family could see, felt the lack. Eunice had had one mis-carriage, but they had never talked of adoption, and Eunice seemed content to mother Will, Will to be mothered.

"What on *earth* would he do without her?" That was the consensus of family opinion, and they all had a healthy respect for her, although Charlotte might still say privately to Ralph, "Charm or no charm, I don't see how she puts up with him."

Kate went with Will and Eunice to the bootlegger's and after-wards to a drive-in for a drink, and then for a drive. She in-sisted that the outing had done her good. But despite her pro-tests she was exhausted. She had made her effort to hold the center of the stage, and even with a willing audience it had been too strenuous for her. She took to her hospital bed after lunch and Will, semi-comatose with whiskey and food, followed her into her room to sit beside her and visit.

"They're so good to me, Will," she said. "The girls. You're all so good to me. When I think how some children treat their parents . . ."

Will's face settled into the mask of bantering tenderness that was his shield whenever conversation threatened to get too serious. "It's a pleasure to be good to you, Mama," he said, bowing with mock gallantry. "You're the queen bee around here."

"Ah, my darling," she said, "I don't know what I'd do without you." *Poor fellow,* she thought, *he's tired. He needs to take a nap.* "Sit a little closer to me, Will, so I can see you." She peered anxiously into his face. *Aren't those dark shadows under his eyes? Yes, he's tired.* "If only you were here, Will," she said, "we'd take better care of you than you take of yourself."

"Eunice takes better care of me than I deserve," Will said. "And besides, I don't think you could support me in the style to which I am accustomed."

Kate laughed. "I know you can't even come home very often, much less stay," she said. "But you work too hard, my dear. And I was just thinking, besides, thinking what a joy it would be to have you here."

"I'm going to fly to England on business sometime next month," he said. "It'll be a nice vacation. Eunice may go, too, if she can get off at the same time."

"Grand," Kate said. "Grand." She began to rub the knot on her wrist with her good hand, realized what she was doing, and quickly put her bad arm under the cover. "How long will you be gone?" she said.

"Three weeks, at least," he said. "Probably longer."

Wouldn't it be fine if one of the girls could go? I wish . . .

Of course he'd suggest it if he thought they could. But, work-ing . . . And maybe he couldn't afford to take them. "Will," she said, "while I have you to myself there's something I want to talk to you about. It's about the girls. I'm distressed about Sarah D. and Sis. They work too hard. Too hard. I know it's all right for you. You're a man, and it's different. Your work is important. But they're so frail, and they're getting too old to work all day long every day. I think they should stop working. Don't you, Will? Every day, rain or shine, getting up so early and besides that, *walking.* All that, and then on top of it coming home to take care of me. It's too much for them." She hesitated. "Charlotte doesn't think they look well, either one of them," she said.

Will laughed ruefully. "Mama, you aren't thinking about what you're saying," he said. "Sarah D. and Sis have been working for twenty-five years. They'd be lost at home with nothing to do. And besides, there's the little matter of eating and paying the rent. They can't afford to stop work. In time, of course, when they're older . . . But then they'll have their Social Security to fall back on."

"But there ought to be some way . . . I can't understand why we can't figure out some way . . . Even if they had a little rest — six months or so."

Will twisted uneasily in his chair, then reached into his pocket for a cigarette and began to smoke.

I can't help seeing him, as plainly as if he were a child again, Kate thought. *Blind. But I see* him. *I don't want to, don't want to see him turn away.* "Have you moved, Will? It's dark in here with the shades drawn."

"No, Mama, I'm still here, but getting sleepy."

Kate held doggedly to her unreasonable concern for Sarah D. and Sis. It shut out for a moment the thoughts of Will that struck so heavily at her heart.

"You and Ralph between you . . ." she said.

"Mama, Sarah D. and Sis are grown women. Grown! Old

enough to be grandmothers. They want to lead their own lives. They'd be miserable if they were sitting idle, taking money from Ralph . . . even if he had that kind of money."

But, you? You leave yourself out of it.

"I'm a silly old woman," Kate said. "I know the girls have to work. I know they enjoy it. Sometimes I get a fool notion in my head and it sticks like a cocklebur."

She put her good hand under the cover and began again to rub the knot above the old break. For a moment all her own motives and Will's were painfully clear to her. She said to herself what she had not allowed herself to say for many years: *I want him to help us. Just once in all the years of his life, I want him to see how much I need him. I am tired. I've waited and waited, and now I'm tired. It's too late to wait any longer. Tomorrow, next week, next year, yes, as soon as that, I'll be dead. Please, my son, my darling boy, please come home to me. My strength is gone and only you can sustain me. Only your strength can make me ready to die.*

"Will," she said. "Will, are you asleep?"

"Almost," he said.

If I say it, he might not understand. No one seems to understand what I am talking about these days. Am I so unreasonable? Crazy old woman? But how can they know? No one ever told me what it would be like. And if I do say it, and he does understand, what then? He still might not . . . All the tears in the sea couldn't wash that out of my heart, nor all the wine in the world out of his. Wait. Still wait. Some day . . . But hurry, she thought. *Hurry, hurry.*

"Alice was here to see me a few days ago," she said. "She asked about you and Eunice."

"Ummmm," Will said.

"She brought Liza and the baby with her. Wasn't that nice? Liza was only here a couple of days."

"Liza? The baby?"

"I don't mean Liza. The other one. Mary's child. And her

baby. His baby." Kate closed her eyes and her lips moved as she frowned and tried to find the faulty connection where her brain had betrayed her. A tear slid down and she put up her hand as if to cover her eyes for thought and carefully smeared it away. "Fenton," she said. "Fenton's wife."

"I thought they were in California," Will said.

"Home," she said. "Home for a visit."

"Ummmm."

What day is this? Kate said soundlessly to the ceiling. *Did they come?*

"Did you say something, Mama?"

"A young man was here from Baton Rouge the other day," Kate said. "A friend of Fenton's. Do you know he wanted to buy the furniture out of my room? Right out from under me!"

"Better sell it," Will said, "if you can get anything for it."

"But it's yours, darling. I told him I had given it all to you."

Will looked around. This was an old story.

"I'll never have a place big enough for it, Mama," he said. "That old wardrobe is as big as an efficiency apartment." He laughed. "I might move into it," he said, "but it would be close quarters for Eunice."

"Fabulous price," Kate said. "He offered me a fabulous price for that old sleigh bed. He was carried away with it."

Will rose and stretched. "I'm sleepy, Mama," he said. "May I lie down on your fabulous bed for a catnap?"

"Go on, darling. I'll nap, too. Wake me up in time for dinner."

"Ummmm," Will said. "Supper."

Wednesday? Kate said. *Fenton was here on Wednesday. Will on Friday. Too late to talk. Saturday morning took a ride. Yes, Saturday afternoon. Now it's —* Then she spoke aloud very softly. "Saturday. Mr. Anderson died on a Saturday. Forty years, gone. Long, forty long years. I have four children," she said. "Charlotte, Anna, Sarah D. and Will. I have five grandchildren, six great-grandchildren, and another coming. I am in my room. Charlotte has taken away my boxes, but it *is* my room." She began to moan.

From the bed Will softly snored.

❧

Sunday afternoon when they left, Will and Eunice stopped at the front gate to talk to Sarah D. and Sis. Charlotte was not there. Ralph had come over from Eureka the night before, and they had gone out to spend the day with his mother and aunt.

Will swung the gate nervously, ready to be on his way. "Mama's remarkable," he said. "It's wonderful how she's stood up. And she seems so happy. I don't see how she does it."

"She was making an effort for you, Will," Sis said. "She was happy to see you."

"You can't keep up an effort for two days if it's too much for you," he said. "I wish I had half her strength."

"Mama's been known to keep up an effort for years," Sarah D. said.

"She's not so cheerful all the time," Sis said. "Sometimes she's miserable — more so now that she's getting stronger and is beginning to feel hemmed in again."

The gate screamed on its rusty hinges, and Sarah D. put her hand on it to stop the swinging. "I don't know what we're going to do with her, Will," she said. "She's so *unreasonable*."

"She seems reasonable enough to me," Will said. "Of course her mind wanders sometimes; she gets a little bit mixed up; but, my God, she's eighty-four years old."

"Lizzie can't do anything with her now that she's able to walk," Sarah D. said, "and Mama fires any other nurse we get. Of course she fires Lizzie too, every day, but Lizzie just doesn't pay any attention."

"One of these days she's going to slip off from Lizzie and fall again," Sis said. "It's just a matter of time. Lizzie may be faithful, but she's not overburdened with brains."

"It's the nights that get us down," Sarah D. said. "We can't keep a practical nurse to sleep in the room with her any more, and she keeps Sis and me up so much, it wears us out. Even when Charlotte's here, it doesn't help much. She's too deaf to sleep in the room with mother."

"Hire competent nurses, if you need them," Will said, "registered nurses. Although from what I've seen this weekend, she can get along all right without them. You all are borrowing trouble. Reason with her."

"Reasoning with her is about like reasoning with you," Sarah D. said. "We might as well talk to the wind."

"Who would pay for a registered nurse at twelve dollars a day?" Sis said. "Sarah D. and I can't, and God knows Charlotte shouldn't be asked. Ralph is already in debt up to his ears on account of Mama. And if Ralph doesn't keep his head above water, God *knows* what will happen to us all."

Will laughed. "I have boundless confidence in Ralph's ability to keep his head above water," he said.

"But, *Will* — " Sis said.

"Draw on me if you need to," Will said. "Do whatever's necessary."

Sis gripped the top round of the wrought-iron fence and yawned the gaping, gasping yawn of unbearable tension. "Go on, Will," she said. "Eunice. It's getting late. You all can get back to New Orleans before dark if you start now. I hate to think of you driving after dark." She let go the fence and gave Eunice a dry, light kiss on the cheek. "Take care of yourself, Eunice. Don't work too hard."

Sarah D. put her arm around Will's waist. "Bye-bye, honey," she said. "Hurry back."

After they had gone the two women sat down together on the front steps, and Sis leaned over and began to pull grass from the chinks in the brick walk at her feet. The old house behind them sat wide and low under the ancient laurel trees. It was now the only residence in the block. The red brick mansion on one side with its round Rapunzel's tower had been torn down and replaced by a new dime store. On the other, the clapboard house where distant cousins had once lived was a mass of dust and rubble. It had been bought and razed to make way for a new supermarket.

Sarah D. looked down the block at the hideously empty lot. "If we sold the house . . ." she said.

Sis shook her head without looking up from the grass. "Not as long as Mama lives," she said. "You know it would kill her."

Their nearest neighbor, who lived in the next block, came toward them along the deserted sidewalk, her heels clicking in the Sunday afternoon quiet. "How's your mother today?"

"She's fine, Mrs. Callahan. She'll be out again in a few days."

"I told Mr. Callahan, 'They can't keep Mrs. Anderson down. She'll be out again, bright as a chipmunk, before you know it.' "

Sis forced a courteous smile, and the heels clicked gaily away.

"What would have been the use of saying anything?" Sarah D. said. "He knows."

Neither of them said any of the things their hearts were full of: that Will's last check had been turned down at the bank; that they were old and tired; that they could scarcely sustain the thought of going into the house to their mother, who by now would be in the depths of a reaction from Will's visit; that the heavy burden lay on them, no matter how much money Ralph and Charlotte poured into the house; that, in spite of knowing this, they were burdened also, and galled with the obligation of taking Ralph's money and driving him deeper and deeper into debt; that Will would not assume his share of the responsibility or give the measure of loving concern that would have eased the vise in which they felt themselves slowly squeezed to death. They did not even think this last to themselves, for they were past missing what had never been given. Sarah D. stood up and turned toward the house. A bright square of early afternoon sunlight shone on the wide worn boards of the gallery floor and lighted the open door to the parlor. Beyond the door, the light dimmed to twilight in the shuttered parlor. The house was quiet.

"Maybe Mama is napping," Sis said.

From the bedroom where Kate lay resting in her narrow, barred bed, with Lizzie sitting vigilant beside the hissing fire, the two sisters heard voices, one inquiring, querulous, the other gentle and slurred.

Sis rose, too. "Come on, my dear," she said. "It's getting chilly." She smiled at Sarah D. "You can get used to hanging, if you hang long enough," she said.

❦

The third time Kate fell, the time Will came home sober and stayed sober, was different from the beginning, not only because of his sobriety, but because he didn't bring Eunice. Until Charlotte told them the reason, Sarah D. and Sis were glad she had not come. They were always a little bit uneasy in the presence of her heavy-handed proprietary devotion to Will, and now there was so much to do, so much to think about that they were glad not to have her there.

Sarah D. had telephoned Charlotte immediately after the accident, and she had come the same day, but she had not been able to reach Will, who was not in his office or at home. His secretary had said that she thought he was at the races, and that Mrs. Anderson was out of town, so they had put off trying to reach him again until night. Then Charlotte left the others at the hospital and went home to call. By this time Kate was under sedation, and what examination was possible had been completed.

Young Dr. Shields, his high, round brow wrinkled by a combination of professional gravity and familial concern, his long, sorrowful mouth held carefully, as if he reminded himself not to be exasperated with Kate because she persisted in abusing her poor body, told them that the pelvis seemed to be broken, probably hopelessly shattered, although of course X-rays could not be made for some time.

"What?" Will had shouted into the telephone at Charlotte. "What?"

Charlotte tallked on calmly. "She's resting now. Jimmie gave her a sedative this afternoon and we hope she'll sleep all night. I'm going to stay over here until she's able to come home from the hospital, and help the girls get some sort of workable arrangement set up at home."

"But how is she?" Will said. "My God, a broken pelvis! She'll never walk again."

"There's no way to tell about that, yet," Charlotte said. "You know how quickly her arm knit, both times. Nobody thought she could get over those. Jimmie says her heart is sound. We'll have to wait and see."

"What was she doing? How did she fall? Why wasn't somebody looking out for her?"

The wires fairly throbbed with Charlotte's silence. "I bit my tongue," she told Sarah D. later. (She wouldn't have dared criticize Will to Sis.) "Why wasn't somebody looking out for her, indeed!"

"Are you there?" Will said. "Operator, operator!"

"Never mind," she said. "I'm here. I don't know, Will. Sis and Sarah D. were at work, of course. It happened in the early afternoon. And you know how Mama bullies Lizzie. Lizzie said she tried to persuade her not to do it. She thought she *had* persuaded her. But even Lizzie has to go to the bathroom sometimes, and as soon as she turned her back . . . You know what Mama was doing? She put a ladder in the bathtub, in the *bathtub*, the back bathroom, with the tub against the window, you know, and tried to hang the curtains. Sarah D. had gotten them down, and Lizzie had washed and ironed them, and was planning to help Sarah D. hang them when she came home from work. As soon as the girls got out of the house after lunch, Mama began to nag Lizzie about hanging those curtains. She wanted to surprise Sarah D. and save her the trouble of doing it when she got home. Well, she finally let Lizzie talk her out of it, and even lay down for a nap, but the instant Lizzie went out to the wing to her bathroom, Mama sneaked back to the storeroom, got the ladder, *by herself,* and put it in the tub. By the time Lizzie got into the house, she had gotten the curtains strung on the rod and was climbing up. Lizzie grabbed the ladder to keep it from slipping, and began to beg her to come down. Then, Lizzie said, Mama got terribly excited and kept shouting, 'Get out of here, you black devil,' waving the curtain rod at her and tangling them both in yards of white organdy ruffles. Lizzie began to cry and beg and threaten to tell Sarah D. on her, but she couldn't let go of the ladder to go and get help. Mama made one swipe too many at her, hollering, 'I was hanging curtains before you were born,' and hit her on the head with the rod. Lizzie dodged and down they all came. Lizzie said she tried to catch Mama, but the ladder knocked her down as it fell, and Mama came down across the side of the tub. It's a blessing Lizzie didn't get her skull fractured."

"I'm coming up," Will said. "I'll catch the first plane."

Charlotte was surprised at the urgency in his voice. "Wait until Friday afternoon, if you don't want to leave work," she said. "Mama is not dying. We'll call you if anything goes wrong. There's not a thing you can do here."

("All we need is Will," she told Sarah D. afterward. "Raising cain and tearing up the pea patch. Excited as he sounded, he's sure to get on a bender, and then we'll have two invalids to nurse instead of one.")

"I'll be there tomorrow," Will said.

When he came the next afternoon, Kate had gone into a coma. She had never regained consciousness after the first sedative had taken effect.

"Shock," Charlotte told him as they drove in from the airport. "Don't be surprised at the way she looks. She was almost this bad for a day or two when she fell last time."

"All right," he said.

"Where's Eunice?" Charlotte asked. "Your secretary told us she was not at home."

"Out of town."

"Where has she gone? Vacationing?"

He shrugged. "I don't know."

Charlotte quickly glanced at him sitting beside her, and then looked back at the narrow, winding road.

"What do you mean, you don't know? You're bound to know where she is."

"Oh, I suppose she's in Dallas visiting Frances and Deck," he said.

They drove on in silence a mile or more through the tunnel made by high shale bluffs and overhanging trees on each side of the road.

"I may as well tell you," he said. "Eunice has left me. Three months ago."

"Oh, *Will*," Charlotte said.

"I tried to get hold of her when you called," he said, "but she *is* out of town. She would have come up here with me, anyway, if she'd known Mama had hurt herself again."

Tears filled Charlotte's eyes.

"Now don't start crying," he said. "You'll make me cry."

"I can't help it," she said. "You know how I am."

"I didn't see any point in worrying you all with it," Will said. "I didn't want to tell Mama. There was no point in her knowing. She could live the rest of her life without knowing, and Eunice would help us keep it from her."

"Will, what on earth will you do without her?"

"I'm getting along fine," he said. "I have a nice little apartment on St. Ann. She helped me get it set up, as a matter of fact. We haven't quarreled, Charlotte. It was all perfectly pleasant and amicable."

Charlotte shook her head impatiently. "How can you leave somebody you've been living with for twenty years *pleasantly?*" she said. "That's beyond me."

"*You* couldn't," he said, "but we can. The world changes and I change. You and Ralph are the only people left in the world who think it doesn't change."

Charlotte looked at him again. "That's not true," she said. "We stay the same *because* everything else changes. That's just one way of getting along. Somebody has to always be in the same place, to keep track of where everybody else is."

He laughed. "A singlehanded battle against the theory of relativity," he said.

"Oh, Will, you know what I mean. And never mind joking. I'm so distressed for you and Eunice, I could stop the car and boo-hoo right here in the middle of the road. I'm . . . I'm overcome. What on earth . . . ?"

"There's no use going into it," he said. "You've always known what a no-account bastard I am. Well, after all these years Eunice has finally realized that you're right."

"But . . ."

"It's better this way," he said. "I was never meant to be a married man. I love my freedom too much." He stroked the top of his head gently and absently in a characteristic gesture, as if he was still wondering where all his hair had gone to. "Charlotte," he said, "I'll tell Sis and Sarah D. about it eventually. I hate to distress them now, but I know it's just a matter of time until somebody comes home from New Orleans and tells them that I've moved. But there's not a bit of use telling Mama."

"You couldn't tell her now, anyway," Charlotte said. She turned the car off the highway into the street that led to the hospital. "She's still sleeping — unconscious."

"Well, anyhow, I will tell them," he said, "or you can, when things have settled down a little bit."

"Will, I'm so *sorry,*" Charlotte said.

He shrugged. "Can't be helped."

In the bare white hospital room he stood and looked down at his mother. Her thin wispy snow-white hair was drawn back from her face and twisted into a knot on top of her head. Without its false teeth, her mouth was drawn, the bloodless lips caved in over the gums, the cheeks sunken. Her lower jaw had dropped slackly open and she breathed noisily through her mouth. Her crumpled skin was still soft and white, and she looked like an ancient, unbelievably clean white monkey, a dying monkey, whose brain no longer knew that the body it had once controlled still drew its living breath of air.

"She looks so old," he said. "As old as God."

"I told you," Charlotte said.

"She looks *terrible*," he said. "Isn't there anything else we can do?"

"Jimmie says not. This afternoon he said he didn't think the bone could ever be set. If it were, there's only a chance the break would knit, and the cast would have to extend from above her waist to below her knees. Just the business of keeping her in a cast, immobile like that, might kill her. He said judging from the other two breaks, he thinks it will probably be best just to keep her quiet, that there is a possibility it may knit without a cast. You know how miserable even those little ones on her arm made her. At least this way she'll be more comfortable."

"That sounds crazy to me," he said. "Impossible. Jimmie must be out of his mind. How could she be moved at all? How could she even go to the bathroom?"

"God knows how we are going to manage," Charlotte said. "But Jimmie will show us how to handle her. After all, it must be possible, or he wouldn't want to try it."

"What about pneumonia?" he said. "Isn't he afraid she'll get pneumonia?"

"There's always the chance she will," Charlotte said. "But what's the use of borrowing trouble?"

"Call in another doctor."

"Will, we have to wait. Another doctor couldn't do anything. And there's something else to consider. Jimmie treats Mama for nothing, just like old Dr. Shields did. It's not a bit necessary, of course; they're only third cousins. But he insists, and I think it's wonderful. No telling how long we'll have to have nurses, and we've got to try to keep expenses down as much as we can."

"Expenses be damned," he said.

"Jimmie would call in someone else if he thought it was necessary."

Charlotte looked down at her mother's face, peaceful and withdrawn, her head resting quietly on the pillow. She reached down and tenderly brushed a strand of hair back from Kate's forehead. Her heart was full of love and sorrow and an intimate knowledge of the future — years of nursing a miserable, rebellious invalid, years of suffering for her mother, and for Sarah D., Sis, and herself.

Die, she said silently. *Go on and die.* Her eyes filled with the tears that she always felt came too easily, but that now at least were justified.

Will, too, leaned over the bed and stared at Kate tensely, as if willing her back to consciousness.

"Oh, Will," Charlotte said. "I wish God would take her. I wish she would never wake up."

He stared at her unbelievingly, contempt and anger in his face. Then he looked down at his mother again. "I want her to speak to me," he said. "If only she knew that *I* was here."

"There have been lots of times when she's wanted you here and you weren't," Charlotte said. "But this time it doesn't make any difference."

Will opened the front gate and held it for Sarah D. and Charlotte to pass in ahead of him. The house had been painted five years earlier. The first thing Will thought was that he had not realized it. On other visits he had not missed the patterns of cracked and peeling paint that were familiar to him from childhood. Nor had he seen that the wicker porch furniture had been replaced with light metal and canvas chairs, glaringly out of place in the old-fashioned gallery. Only the green bench at the west end of the gallery in the shade of the queen's wreath vine was the same. The fountain in the park across the street murmured its cool distant music. The house breathed on him its familiar odor, compounded of dust and wax, mossy fountain, sweet olive tree, and thousands of days of cooking — bacon, coffee, hot biscuits, greens — with a new fraction added: sickness and old age. The huge brass knocker on the front door shone, newly polished but green in the curves and creases. Something: the smooth white paint? the new smell? the sound of the gate, so intimately bound up with all his arrivals and departures? Something caught and concentrated his attention, released the suppressed anxious excitement that comes with sudden disaster, the ambiguous feeling almost like joy that an enormous effort is required of one; and turned it outward toward the house. Or perhaps his consciousness of the place, the time, was waiting for some trigger to release it, where always before he had wanted *not* to see.

I haven't looked in twenty years. More? Yes, Eunice and I were married in twenty-nine. I must have looked then. Must have wondered how she saw it, what she thought. Goddamned arrogant, I probably didn't care. Funny though, I always thought it was funny, her wanting to get married here, when we were all strangers to her. No family of her own, she said. And it suited me — I didn't give a damn. Just something to get through with I said then; they mumble a few words over you, and that makes it legal, makes everybody happy. Go right on

to bed, children. Blessings on you. Oh, wasn't I the bohemian
— half-assed bohemian! Foolishness. Obviously, if there were
children — I saw that. I wasn't a half-wit. And then, too, in-
heritance laws. Makes everything simple. But they have com-
mon-law marriage in Louisiana, Mississippi, too. Doubt if I was
thinking about dying. I simply didn't mean any of it, did I? I
would never have . . . A bragging, posturing young jackass.
How did she manage to put up with me? Good thing for the
race, that foolishness. If people didn't marry young, before
they knew what they were doing, they'd never . . . But it
didn't work with us, did it? One miscarriage, and then . . .
And finally, all thrown away, twenty years down the drain.

He stopped inside the dining room door, still looking, put
his hat on the tall, lyre-shaped hat and umbrella stand against
the wall to his left, and examined the curving arms and
clouded oval mirror.

"Charlotte!" he shouted, "where did this monstrosity
come from? I never saw it before."

Charlotte, who had already hung up her coat and started
with Sarah D. toward the kitchen, turned back. "Mary left it
to the girls," she said. "Along with great-grandfather. You've
seen it, Will. It's been here a couple of years."

"Gave me a turn. I thought for a minute it was a skeleton —
dinosaur or something. Ribs — " He indicated the arms.
"Backbone, neckbone, and — " He pointed to the large vase-
like attachment in the center of the base. "Unusual beast.
What would this be, its belly?"

"That's for umbrellas, nut," Charlotte said. She laid her
hand fondly on one of the branches. "Somebody had to take
it. And besides, the portrait, that darling one of him as an
old man, went with it. It's hanging in the parlor. Mary told
the girls they had to promise to give the hatrack a home if she
left them the portrait."

"And has it been happy here?" Will asked gravely.

"It's happy wherever great-grandfather is," Charlotte said.

"And Mama adores it. Are you hungry, Will? Sarah D. and I are going to see what we can scare up for supper."

"Not very. Don't fix anything for me." As she crossed the room toward the kitchen, he moved on and stood staring with his hands in his pockets at two small pictures hanging side by side to the right of the hatrack — one an enlarged snapshot of himself and Eunice taken immediately after their wedding, standing arm in arm by the front gate, the other a formal one of Sarah D. in her wedding dress.

"I'll fix you a sandwich," Charlotte said from the door. "You ought to eat something. There's a cold roast back here, and some of Sis's good pepper relish."

Hands in his pockets, head tilted slightly back, Will stared at the picture of himself, small and natty in a double-breasted summer suit, with a straw boater cocked at a jaunty angle on his head, holding Eunice's elbow and grinning proudly into the camera, as much as to say, look what I've got. Eunice, tall and fair in the graceless, almost ankle-length fashion of the early thirties, looked shyly at Will from beneath the brim of a deep-crowned cloche.

He thought of the passion of those first years of his marriage; and unbidden, the memory of one thing Eunice had said to him then came into his mind. "I want to know everything about you, Will. *Everything.*" *Maybe she loved me too much,* he said to himself, and then, *Gone. Like two other people.* He shook his head slightly, and with hands still in his pockets moved back to peer at himself questioningly in the cloudy mirror. Then he turned and examined the room.

Sometime in the preceeding ten years it had been repapered above the wainscot with a cheap, nondescript ivory paper patterned with stylized tendrils of beige-colored vine.

I wonder when. Not during the war. They wouldn't have spent money on wallpaper during the war. Must have been since '45. But everything else stays the same, that's why you don't look at it.

He moved to the center of the room and ran his hand over the surface of the square oak dining table: *Father pulled it out of the river. After the wreck of the old* River Queen. And crossing the room, stared at himself again, this time full length in the huge mirror above the scroll-backed day bed. "Well, here I am," he said softly.

"Did you say something, Will?" Sarah D. called from the kitchen.

He raised his voice. "You've had the sideboard done over, haven't you?" he said.

"Charlotte did that just before she was married," Sarah D. said. "My Charlotte. She got interested in fixing up the house. She did one post of my bed, too, but she never did finish. Do you want tomatoes on your sandwich?"

"Um hum." He continued to look around him after she went back to the kitchen, and at last crossed the room again and stood with his back to the space heater that stood in front of the old coal grate.

Not a decent-looking piece of furniture in the room except the day bed. Mirror of course, if you like mirrors. Oh, the sideboard's not bad, after all, now it's got all that black varnish off and you can see the wood. Bit heavy, but I've always liked that Empire stuff. But the table! Did Eunice think it was awful that first visit? Nobody had any money then. It was no shabbier than any place else. And — face it — it all meant something to her. The mirror, the silver service, even the table, with attached legend of having been fished out of the river after the wreck of a stern wheeler. Passports. Yes, and I knew it. I knew it. I've used them when I needed to. Kind of pitiful to need such battered passports. He sighed and rubbed his fingers up and down the middle of his forehead.

Too many things to take into account. Too many different reasons why we're all what we are. She ought to see that. How can anybody expect . . . ? But, women! He shrugged and his lips moved like an old man's talking to himself, acting out some private quarrel as he sits sunning himself in the park. *Women!* *Always in the middle of things. They can't make a detached observation, any of them, if their lives depend on it. They never — what is it? Never size things up, make an objective evaluation, and then act on it.* But he corrected himself scrupulously. *Foolishness,* he said to himself. *You see, I am just as bad as she is, as they all are. Because what I was saying before was, yes, that she couldn't see everyone was like that, couldn't see there was too much for anyone to take into account, to act on reasonably, that a man's impulses are mysterious even to himself and most of the time he knows he is dreaming.*

Who was it in War and Peace *knew all that? Bagration? Yes. He was the only one who saw that everything was so complex, that a battle had to sort of fight itself. No one man, no general, could plan and carry out an action. All a good general could do was to listen, to observe, to push a little here when things were going the way he wanted, and hold back a little when they were going wrong. And that's what I have to do while I'm here — push a little here, hold back a little there, get this household operating so it will be tolerable for everybody. Get right down to it, isn't that what a woman does? Hmmm? Passivity. Female trait. Androgynous, he was— Bagration. And, let's face it, I'm not. If there's anything I'm not, anything I've fought against, it's being like, being trapped by — females. Yes, the time comes when someone has to take things in hand, act. There's got to be someone doing something for Bagration to encourage — or hold back.*

And Mama will see what I'm doing, that's the main thing. Trying to make her comfortable, to cut through all the passivity, the defeatism. It's enough to drive a man to drink, *the way they all sit back — waiting, waiting. But Mama knows how I . . . And it doesn't take much. A little time, a little money, intelligence, force. I can make it up to her for all the times when I couldn't—so many pressures, and so forth and so forth. She always understood that. Hell. Who could have*

*done anything but leave and stay gone? Always too much ex-
pected, too many demands, and that dead weight of how things
were and ever would be. They. Going down, going down. And
pulling.* He shivered. *And then, I had to keep my own head
above water. I never wanted, never — never abandoned. But
God, it's all so painful. And what can you do most of the time?
Have to be a millionaire.* He looked once more around the
drab, shabby room; he thought of his own small house in the
Garden District, clean and sunny, his father's books in the
shelves against the study wall, his father's sturdy pine plantation desk, shining with wax, newly refinished, the comfortable,
tailored sofa in its immaculate, soft blue slip cover. *All that
costs money. Yes. I need to be a millionaire, that's all. No
moral issue involoved. Money. And empty, now. Eunice,
where?*

The quiet voices of the women in the kitchen penetrated his
reverie, and he sighed and crossed the dining room to join
them. In the big, drafty kitchen he sat down and absent-
mindedly watched Sarah D. put a plate in front of him with
a sandwich on it. He rubbed his finger across the bleached
and scoured surface of the pine kitchen table, staring down
at it.

"This is a nice little table, Sarah D.," he said. "Too bad to
keep it back here and let it get ruined."

"I know," she said. "One of these days when we catch our
breath, we're going to get it fixed. But Mama never has liked
it; that's why it's back here. She thinks pine is a little bit dé-
classé."

*Furniture! For God's sake why am I talking about furni-
ture?*

He began abruptly: "The first thing we need to do before we
bring Mama home," he said, "is to make the house more comfortable, more workable. Look at your bathroom, for example. It's a damn nuisance to have to go all the way to the back
of the house from Mama's room and cross that cold back hall

to get to the bathroom. Now, my idea would be to cut off a corner of Mama's room and build her a small bath."

Sarah D., who had been puttering with her own sandwich at the counter, drew up a chair to the table and sat down opposite him. "You want a drink, Will?" she asked. "There's a little whiskey in the safe."

He shook his head impatiently.

Charlotte, who was already sitting at the table, erect and corseted as always, but with heavy, downward lines of pain and weariness etching the soft roundness of her face, had not been listening to the other two, but smoking and staring fixedly through the wall opposite her. Now she roused herself with an effort. "You must be exhausted, Will," she said.

Will raised his voice slightly. "Charlotte, I was saying I think we should make some plans right now, while we have a little peace and quiet," he said, "and tomorrow I can begin to get things underway."

"Underway?" she said in a puzzled voice. "Underway?" She got up. "I believe I'll have a glass of sherry, Sarah D.," she said. "It might help me sleep. How about you?"

Sarah D. nodded, and Charlotte went to the old-fashioned screened kitchen safe in the corner of the room and got out a decanter.

"Wineglasses in the dining room," Sarah D. said.

"I know." She got them, came back to the table, and poured out the wine for herself and Sarah D. "Are you sure you won't join us, Will?"

He shook his head.

Sarah D. grinned at him. "Never thought I'd see the day when Charlotte and I would be drinking and you'd be dry," she said.

"After all," Will said, "I won't be able to stay here all the time. I'll have to be going back and forth to New Orleans, and I want to get as much done here as I can before I leave."

Charlotte sipped her sherry and seemed to be searching her mind for something to say.

"Of course, we know you can't stay long," Sarah D. said. "And there isn't much anyone can do now, is there?"

"That's what I'm *talking* about, sweetheart," Will said. "There are several things I think I could do to help you all out."

"Oh," Sarah D. said. "Well . . ."

"Here's what I think: As I said, you need to cut off a corner of the bedroom and put in a bath for Mama. Like this." He picked up a knife and drew a square on the table, and then a small square inside it. "See," he said. "On the outside corner there, next to the driveway. It could easily be done, and you can see how much more convenient it would be. And then . . ."

"We can't do that, honey," Sarah D. said. "You know we have to have two beds in the room. Someone has to sleep in there with Mama. And that huge armoire takes up so much space. And you know how much company Mama always has. It would be so crowded we'd be falling over each other's feet."

"Well, as far as that's concerned," Will said, "we could add it to the outside of the house, here, and cut a door through. That's no problem."

"Will, Mama's still in a coma," Charlotte said. "Don't you think we should wait and see how she gets along before we do anything?"

"Nonsense," Will said. "You know she's going to want to come home as soon as she comes to. She hates hospitals."

"Yes, I suppose she will," Charlotte said. She glanced at Sarah D. who raised her eyebrows and shrugged slightly, as much as to say, *I don't know what to make of it.*

Will's sandwich lay untouched on his plate and he smoked nervously and steadily. "Here's another thing," he said. "I know you all think the world of Jimmie Shields, and of course he's a nice boy. I like him, myself. But, let's face it, he's nothing but a general practitioner, and a young, inexperienced one at that. He couldn't possibly know anything about complicated fractures, much less geriatrics."

"Geriatrics?" Sarah D. said. "What's that?"

Charlotte leaned forward and thumped her hearing aid to make sure it was working. "What did you say?"

"Geriatrics. The medical specialty that deals with the diseases of old age."

Sarah D. laughed. "Well if he doesn't know anything about old age, it's not because he hasn't had the experience," she said. "Mama's an advanced course, all by herself."

Will smiled impatiently. "But what I mean is, of *course* we'll have to call in specialists. A good bone man, and a geriatrician. I can call Arthur McCain in New Orleans in the morning, or tonight, as far as that goes. He's a good friend of ours, an ENT man, but he knows all the doctors, and can tell us who to get."

"But . . ."

"We can fly them up here in no time. Tomorrow, if necessary."

Charlotte took another sip of sherry. "Settle down, Will," she said. "You're going a little too fast for us."

"Now, as for the bathroom," Will said.

"We're only ten feet from the line on that side of the house," Sarah D. said. "I don't believe we could get a permit to add a bath over there. Besides, you know, it would block up the driveway."

"That kind of difficulty can be dealt with," Will said. "All I need to do is to talk to the right people and explain that this is an emergency."

"Oh!" Sarah D. said.

"Will, Sarah D. said it would block the driveway," Charlotte said.

"That's no problem," Will said. "We could open the driveway into the alley on the back — tear down a section of the wall back there."

"Tear down the wall!" Sarah D. said. "Why, you'd have Mama to bury if you touched a brick of that wall."

Will put out his cigarette, leaned forward, and began to speak slowly and gently in the patient tone of a man dealing with children or mental defectives. "Now, don't *worry* about it," he said. "I don't want you girls to have to bother your heads with *any* of it. I want to take all the burden of the arrangements off your hands. I want you to be free to rest, and to take care of yourselves and Mama. You won't have to think about any of it for a minute. Okay?"

And, indeed, Sarah D. and Charlotte looked as bewildered and baffled as children. He looked at them intently for a moment and then sat back in his chair. "Now, the first thing in the morning I'll talk to Jimmie," he said. "I know he'll be delighted to get some expert advice. And you can see for yourselves that it is absolutely essential for him to get some. The *idea* of his saying the break probably shouldn't be set. Ridiculous. Why, Mama'll be a cripple for life if we don't get that pelvis set."

"For *life*," Charlotte muttered in a low, ironic voice.

"You see? You don't want that, do you?"

Sarah D. reached across the table and patted Will's hand. He was trembling now with the suppressed excitement of getting his schemes under way. "My dear," she said, "I know you're upset. We all are. Charlotte and I have had very little sleep, and you probably didn't sleep last night either. We are all too tired to try to make sensible decisions about anything. Let's hold off a day or two. The fracture can't be set until the swelling is reduced, and by then we'll also know how strong Mama is and what she can take. Frankly, Sis and I couldn't possibly cope with anything like putting in a bathroom right now. Later, maybe, when the dust settles. And it is too soon yet, I think, to call in a specialist. Besides, there is a good bone man right here in Homochitto whom I'm sure Jimmie will consult. A young fellow who has just been here three or four years. You could ask your friend in New Orleans about him when you call. But let's not do anything right now except try to get a good night's sleep."

"Don't you see, Sarah D.," Will said exasperatedly, "we need to get in touch with somebody who knows his business, *immediately. Immediately.*"

"All right, Will," Charlotte said. "We'll do something about it in the morning. But you know, after you talk to your doctor friend, we'll still have to act through Jimmie. None of us would hurt his feelings for the world. He's been so grand to Mama — she worships the ground he walks on." She laughed. "You know how she is about soldiers and doctors," she said. "She says Jimmie could put his shoes under her bed any night."

Sarah D. tiredly changed the subject. "How is Eunice, darling? In all the confusion I haven't even asked you."

Will got up abruptly. "Charlotte will tell you," he said. "I'm going to bed."

"You haven't touched your sandwich," Sarah D. said. "You ought to try to eat something."

He shook his head and turned away, but paused in the doorway. "Another thing," he said, "you have a wheel chair, don't you? From last time? But we'll need one of those walkers. I've heard they're a big help."

"Um-humm," Charlotte said. "That's a good idea."

"At least drink a glass of milk," Sarah D. said. "You're going to make yourself sick."

But he shook his head again.

"The upstairs bedroom is ready for you," she said. "If you need anything, holler. Breakfast at eight in the morning, but sleep later, if you can. I have to get on to work, and Charlotte will be going to the hospital early to let Sis come home."

The two women were silent after he left until Sarah D. heard the water running in the upstairs bathroom. Then she leaned close to the hearing aid which she knew was clipped to Charlotte's brassière strap. "What in the world do you suppose has gotten into him?" she said. "He's certainly got ants in his pants."

Charlotte nodded. "Sounds like he's gonna reorganize us, doesn't it? But maybe he'll slow down tomorrow."

"I hate to say it, but I believe he's easier to manage tight than sober," Sarah D. said. "And what did he mean, you'd tell me about Eunice? Is something wrong with Eunice?"

Charlotte sighed. "She's left him," she said.

"Oh, Lord. Oh my Lord." Tears welled in Sarah D.'s eyes.

"Yes," Charlotte said. "I could break right down and cry. Did cry when he told me."

"Poor fellow. No wonder he's so keyed up."

"Apparently she's been gone a good while — a couple of months," Charlotte said. She shook her head. "What in the *world* is he going to do? Who's going to take care of him? Not that you can blame Eunice. If he were my husband, I'd have left him years ago."

"Oh, Lord," Sarah D. said again. She wiped the tears from her eyes and ate the last bite of her sandwich. "What happened?" she asked.

"I don't know," Charlotte said. "He told me on the way in from the airport, but he was pretty vague about why. I suppose she got sick of his drinking so much. Or maybe he's been involved with another woman. More likely that. She wouldn't be so apt to leave him on account of the drinking, do you think?"

Sarah D. shook her head. "She ought to be used to that, goodness knows, and besides, he seems much better than usual to me."

"That might have happened since she left," Charlotte said. "Although I can't believe Will would quit drinking to get her to come back. That wouldn't be like him at all."

"Eunice likes a little nip herself," Sarah D. said.

"You don't suppose he's sober on account of *us?*" Charlotte said. "I mean, the accident and everything. Trying to help. He seems so different, somehow. Maybe that's part of it."

"I don't know what to make of him," Sarah D. said. "I've never seen him act so queer." She laughed. "I'll say one thing for us," she said. "You've got to hand it to us. We managed to get through that whole conversation without once mentioning money. I never thought you could be so self-contained."

"I bit my tongue," Charlotte said. "Bathroom, indeed! Or rather, I was so overcome, I couldn't even think about money. But you know who'd end up paying for it — if it weren't a pipe dream, I mean." Then the indignation faded from her face and voice. "Poor fellow," she said thoughtfully. "The truth is, he seemed so upset I couldn't bear to say a word."

"Maybe he'll have something else on his mind tomorrow," Sarah D. said. "Maybe we can just rock along and not let it come to a head until he wears the notion out."

⋙§⋘

But Will was unmanageable. The next day before he went to the hospital he ordered a walker for his mother and called his doctor friend in New Orleans. The doctor recommended several orthopedists, adding, after naming the ones whose work he knew in New Orleans, that there was a young fellow practicing in Homochitto who was considered pretty good. Will did not mention this to his sisters; he could not believe that a doctor who chose to practice in Homochitto could be competent. Nor did he say that his friend had been annoyingly vague on the subject of geriatricians. "Better take care of the break first," was all he had said. "I'll look into the other for you when the time comes."

"But what is this jerry-whatchamacallit going to *do?*" Charlotte asked her sisters privately after another abortive conversation with Will. "What does Will *want* with him?"

"Maybe he thinks he can make Mama young again," Sarah D. said.

"Don't you all be so hard on Will," Sis said. "He's only trying to help, poor fellow."

The skirmish continued for two days, while Kate lay collapsed and quiet beneath the white covers in the white hospital room. A nurse, and usually one of the children, sat beside her. There was not much to do except to keep her clean and watch the slow draining of the glucose bottle hooked to the iron stand beside her bed and attached by a long tube to her withered arm. In her weakness and deathlike trance, Kate's old, toothless mouth hung open, and they greased her lips and moistened her tongue from time to time to keep the skin from cracking. She had become an object to them, like a broken chair, glued together and set in a vise, maddeningly occupying the very spot where one was most likely to stumble over it. They could scarcely believe that she might still be *there*, somewhere inside the frail, broken body, as intensely alive as she had ever been, acting out in sleep some familiar, private dream. They spoke of her in her presence as if she were not there, or as if she were a baby, murmuring endearing encouragement to her as they wet her lips with bits of soft, wet cotton.

All but Will, who scarcely ever spoke when he was in the room, but sat or stood staring at her face, at the drooping lids as if willing them to open, at the slack, lifeless mouth, waiting for the old, brave, mocking smile. Sometimes his attention was so concentrated, he watched with such fascination every slight change in her expression, every random movement of her body that it seemed as if he were trying to enter her dream, to join her if she would not come out to him.

She moaned softly now and then and stirred as if to wake, and sometimes her eyelids fluttered. Occasionally she muttered something unintelligible or even spoke a few words quite clearly without opening her eyes. "Mr. Anderson? Mr. Anderson?" she would say. "Dinner's ready." Or, "I *told*

Will . . ." What? To hurry? Not to be late? The rest blurred into a wordless murmur. Once, in the querulous, distressed voice of a sick child, she called out for her own mother, dead forty years. Will was alone in the room with her. He patted her hand and brushed the hair back from her forehead as tenderly as a woman. "Yes?" he said. "Yes? What is it, darling?" But she said no more. He sat down on the hard, straight-backed chair by her bed. He hunched his shoulders and bent his head forward until the chin touched his breast, as if he were shrinking into himself against the cold, and sat warming his cold hands between his thighs. When Charlotte came into the room a little while later, he began to talk immediately about his plans for taking Kate home. Charlotte listened without comment, but her face, always too open for discretion, had on it an expression of barely tolerant impatience.

After supper the third night Will was in Homochitto, the four children went back to the hospital together, and having looked in on their mother and seen her lying inert in exactly the position they had left her in two hours earlier, went to the little sun parlor at the end of the corridor and sat down together — waiting, although they scarcely knew what for. In a low, insistent voice Will began again his compulsive planning for the future. Sarah D. and Charlotte half listened, gazing absently down the dim, hushed corridor, turning the pages of old magazines, smoking abstractedly. Then with increasing anxiety they watched Sis as she tapped her foot and clenched and unclenched her fists.

One very old man, in a gray flannel bathrobe, emaciated and toothless, sat in a wheel chair at the other end of the room and coughed a dry, persistent cough. Someone — his son? — was visiting him, and sat beside him in silence for half an hour. All this time Will was talking, talking, and Charlotte and Sarah D. were watching Sis and occasionally trying to deflect the conversation into other channels. At the end of half an hour, as if a bell had run, the younger man got up without a word and wheeled the old man away. The dry cough and squeaking wheels receded down the corridor.

As soon as a distant door had closed on the sound, Sis burst out in a kind of stage whisper, never forgetting that they were supposed to be quiet. "Will, you've *got* to stop this," she said. "You've got to let us alone. You're driving us all crazy."

Will stared at her in amazement.

"All this foolishness about walkers and bathrooms and physiotherapists. We simply can't listen to it any more."

Will stood up. "You!" he said. "*I'm* driving *you* crazy! You damn, stubborn, stupid, hide-bound — *women!* I'm *trying* to *help* you. What the hell is the matter with you, anyway? You damn — damn — hardheaded — women!" He was almost shouting.

"Be quiet, Will," Sarah D. said. "Don't make a scene."

"What the hell do I care whether I make a scene or not? What I want to know is, what's the *matter* with you all? You sit around and sit around like you're at a wake, or a tea party, I can't tell which. You talk about anything in the world except Mama. You won't do a damn thing, and you won't let anybody else do a damn thing."

"Mama may not get well at *all*, Will," Charlotte said. "No matter what anybody does. Can't you get it through your head that the doctors don't even know whether she's going to live?"

"What *can* we do?" Sarah D. said. "What do you *expect* us to talk about?"

Sis continued in her stage whisper as if the others had not spoken. "There is *nothing to do*, Will, nothing. Nothing. No use to order any equipment, no use to hire a physiotherapist. Nothing to do but wait. You're like a child thinking he can make Christmas hurry up and get here. You say you're trying to help, but you're not thinking about us, or about Mama. What are you thinking about? What do you want? What do you think Mama's got to give you — now?" She was shivering uncontrollably. "Grow up, Will," she said. "You're supposed to be an intelligent man. Grow up."

"Hellfire! Hellfire! Yes, I'm intelligent. I'm the only one of us who is. You all are the ones who are wrong. You're behaving like, like *sheep*, like . . . You're absolutely wrong. There are plenty of things to do, plenty of things, if you wouldn't just sit there thinking over and over to yourselves that it's hopeless. And I'm going to do them, do whatever seems like a good idea, no matter what any of you says. I'm the man of the family, the head of the house, and it's my responsibility, and I'm willing to assume it."

Sarah D. was saying over and over, "Shh, shh; no use to quarrel about it; we all love Mama; we all want to do what's best for her. Shh, shh." Neither Will nor Sis heard her. Charlotte sat looking from Will to Sis as if she had never seen either of them before, and said nothing.

Still whispering, Sis leaned forward. "All right, you're asking for it, Will. Listen to me. We'd be perfectly agreeable to your playing to your heart's content with your gadgets and your specialists. Perfectly. But who's going to pay for it? Answer me that. No, don't. We already know. We'll end up paying for it, after you go back to New Orleans to the races and Pat O'Brien's, and all your — *commitments*. Hasn't it always been that way?"

Without a word Will took out his wallet, pulled a checkbook from it, sat down, wrote out a check for a thousand dollars, tore it out, and handed it to Sis. She took it by one corner, held it between her thumb and forefinger, and after a glance at it, shook her head stubbornly. "Anybody can write a check," she said. "Give me your checkbook. I can write a check for a million dollars." She dropped the check onto the table beside her. "Do you forget so easily that you have done that to us before?"

"It's good," he said. "Go cash it in the morning. Now. I'm going to get Mama well in spite of all of you. So you may as well get used to the idea." He looked from one to another of the three women, who all stayed silent under his gaze. "Do you keep everything I've ever said or done in your books and balance them every month?" he asked. Still they said nothing, already, even Sis, appalled at the way the quarrel was growing. "Do you know what I've always thought about you all?" he said. "I've thought that Charlotte was the most righteous and unbending, and that Sarah D. was the gayest and most courageous, and that *you*," he looked at Sis, "were the most loving and forgiving. Loving and forgiving!"

Charlotte got up and left the room.

Sarah D. stared coldly at Will. "How *could* you say such a thing to Charlotte?" she said. "You must be out of your mind. Or does it gall you so terribly that *Ralph* has always done what you wouldn't do?"

Will was still standing over them looking furiously from one to the other. Now he turned away, crossed the room, and stood with his back to them, hands in his pockets, staring out into the darkness. No one said anything.

The silence lengthened, broken only by the clocklike hum and whirr of the hospital all around them. Then Sis spoke. "Will . . ." she said tentatively.

"Never mind," he said without turning around. "Don't go on with it. We've said too much already, all of us."

"I'm sorry, Will," Sis said quickly. "I'm sorry. We're all so tired we don't know what we're saying half the time. Please . . ."

They heard light footsteps approaching down the hall, and Kate's nurse came into the room, smiling and expectant. "Mrs. Anderson is awake," she said. "She's waked up. Mrs. McGovern says for you all to come."

Will nodded at Sis and crossing the room touched her lightly on the shoulder. Then they followed the nurse down the hall toward their mother's room. All three of them were shaken and astonished by the violence of their quarrel; and the two women were both sorry for what they had said, each one saying to herself, *and at a time like this, too, with Mama . . . But it's true; there's no getting around it; it's true just the same.* For they both knew that they had been on the verge of quarreling with Will half a dozen times in the three days since his arrival, held back only by the sense of something different and desperate in him, a frantic, self-absorbed grief that had filled them with unease. *Charlotte would have spoken out eventually, if Sis hadn't,* Sarah D. said to herself. *She can never resist the temptation to say what she thinks to Will.*

They said nothing to each other, and did not even look at each other as they filed down the hall.

At the door of their mother's room they found the Presbyterian minister standing, waiting for them, and in their confusion and excitement over the quarrel and over Kate's rousing from her coma, they allowed him to follow them into the room. They gathered around the bed. Charlotte already stood beside Kate on the far side, next to the stand with the glucose bottle on it, holding Kate's hand and smiling encouragingly at her.

Kate's mouth was firmly closed and her eyes were open, although the drooping lids gave the impression that she could scarcely keep them so. Her thin snow-white hair was twisted up on top of her head, and her sunken cheeks above the toothless gums made her look like a victim of slow starvation. Everything — face, hair, thin, clawlike hands, covers, walls — everything was white; as if the whole room with her in it had been washed and bleached and left a long time in the sun. Kate's thin body, barely fleshed sticks of crumbling calcium, lay as still under the seersucker bedspread as if she were dead; but her face had on it an expression of perfect consciousness.

"Where my teef?" she was saying to Charlotte as they came in. "I want to talk."

She turned her head carefully toward the door when she heard them enter, and looked slowly from one to another.

The nurse had gone around the bed, and looking over Charlotte's shoulder, was checking the position of the needle taped to Kate's arm. The minister stood unobtrusively in the background.

". . . a short prayer," he muttered to Will. "Don't want . . . Didn't mean to intrude."

Will did not even hear, but stood looking at his mother, the tears welling in his eyes.

Kate saw the minister, and an expression of anguished terror crossed her face. She reached her trembling left hand along the sheet toward Sis. "I'm dying," she whispered. "Troof. Tell me troof."

Sis shook her head. "No, no, Mama. You're not dying. You're going to be *all right*." She took the thin hand in hers and stroked it gently. "You're pretty sick," she said. "You've got to take care of yourself, but you're getting better. Much better."

"What's — the matter?"

"Remember, Mama," Sarah D. said, "you fell off the ladder. Aren't you ashamed of yourself?"

"Hanging curtains," Kate said. "I . . . wanted . . . get those . . . curtains up . . . before . . . you . . . got . . . home."

"That's right, and you hit the tub on the way down, but you're going to be all right."

"If . . . Lizzie . . . had . . . let . . . me . . . alone . . ." Kate said, "I . . . could have . . . done it. Damn nig."

"You've got to stay quiet and be very, very good for a while," Sarah D. said.

Kate looked all around the room once more, and when she spoke again, her voice was stronger. "What's he doing here?" She waved her hand vaguely in the direction of the minister. "Planning my funeral, isn't he? That's what he's here for."

Sarah D. giggled nervously. "Mama, he just stopped in to ask about you, that's all. Everybody's been so worried about you. Nobody's planning your funeral."

Kate's eyes shifted to Charlotte. "And you came over, Charlotte. That's grand. Grand. Children . . . all well?"

Charlotte nodded and gestured toward Will. "We're all here, Mama," she said. "But we don't want to tire you out. We want you to rest and sleep and get your strength back."

"Sleep," Kate murmured. "Have I been 'sleep long? Dreaming. About Will. Time he ran away. Remember? And we found him . . . He came out. Remember?" She smiled and added in a stronger voice, "The children always loved that story, didn't they?"

"I'd better go now," the minister was saying to Will in a low voice. "I'm afraid I've upset your mother. If you'll call on me for anything you need . . ."

But Will stood as if in a trance, staring at Kate, quietly wiping away the tears that continued to come into his eyes.

The three sisters all seemed to realize at once that they were being rude.

"We *would* like you to pray with us, Mr. Stewart," Sis said. "Wouldn't we, Mama? The Lord knows we need all the prayers we can get."

"Yes. Please." Charlotte nodded encouragingly at him.

"It's just that we were a little bit excited," Sarah D. explained. "You see, you came in just as Mama woke up for the first time, and we . . ."

The minister raised his hand in benediction and closed his eyes. While he prayed, Kate continued to look vaguely around the room. She tried to move her right arm, and when she could not, examined it with interest — the needle, the tube, the board to which her arm was strapped, and the bottle suspended from its metal hook.

In the middle of the prayer she spoke. "What's all this?" she asked Sis. "What are they doing with my arm?"

Sis leaned over and whispered in her ear. "It's glucose, darling. Help you get your strength back."

The minister ended his prayer abruptly and discreetly. Sarah D. saw him to the door. It was only after he was gone that Kate focused her attention on him again. "Not yet," she called after him. "Old Nick's not going to get me yet." Then she looked at Will and frowned. "Or is he?" she said. "Is he already here?"

"Mama." Charlotte leaned over the bed. "Will's been so concerned about you. He's been here all week."

"Will?"

He moved forward and stood beside Sis.

Kate looked at Sis. "Who is this young man?" she asked, "and what is he doing in my room?"

"It's me, Mama," Will said. He leaned over her to kiss her, but she feebly put her hand against his chest.

"Charlotte?" she said. "Sis?"

"Don't you know your own son, old dear?" Charlotte said lightly. "He's lost some weight, hasn't he? And I believe he looks ten years younger since you waked up."

Kate tried to move away from Will who was still bending over her, and cried out sharply.

"Here, Mrs. Anderson," the nurse said. "You've got to lie still if you want that leg to get well." She shook her head sternly at Will and motioned him away. "Too much excitement," she said. "I believe you'd all better go out for a little while and let her rest."

"I'll just sit here quietly until she falls asleep," Sis said. "It's my night to sleep here. The rest of you may as well go home."

The other three filed docilely out as the nurse settled Kate more comfortably on her pillow and prepared a hypodermic syringe to give her a sedative. As they closed the door softly behind them, they heard her querulous voice speaking to Sis.

"Where is Will, anyhow?" she was saying. "It seems as if when a person is lying at death's door, a person's only son

could take one day off and come to see her. It seems that way
to me. Doesn't it to you?"

❦

Quarrels can be and usually are forgotten, even when the
antagonists say to themselves and to each other, "I'll *never* forgive, never forget." But their effects, like the effects of all
events past and sinking to the dark at the bottom of the mind,
continue to be visible — rings on the surface of the pool long
after the stone is buried in the mud. That was what Will had
meant when he had said to himself at the beginning of his visit,
Too many things to take into account . . .

The sisters could not have taken Will at face value then because a thousand forgotten memories already made up their
conception of what his behavior meant. It would not have
made any difference if they had cashed the check and found
that it was good. No, that's not quite true. The good check
would also have taken its place in the complex structure of
their conception and changed the relation of every part to
every other part. But not one part, remembered or forgotten, could be taken away. The structure would have collapsed. So with the quarrel. It added itself to their relationship, regardless of their desire to forget it.

But in their common concern for their mother and for
each other, and particularly in their vaguely understood but
acutely felt confrontation with Will's distress, they pushed
the quarrel down. By tacit common consent, no one mentioned it. The wounds were left to heal as best they could,
ignored, and the three women outdid themselves in courtesy
and consideration. An abyss had briefly opened among them,
like a crack in the heaving of an earthquake, a yawning abyss
that all their background, their training, the habit and central
meaning of their lives, made intolerable to them. They had
never been willing to cut themselves off from one another, to

act in the arrogance of their individuality, not even Sis, who in her deepest trouble had come home, had crawled into the den like a wounded beast, unable to conceive of doing anything else. In joy and sorrow they had lived in and for the common life of the family. They had stubbornly loved and supported one another whether they understood one another or not; yes, they had loved one another, had clung together, even when it seemed to them that their hearts were full of hatred. Toward the outer world of strangers, of incomprehensible mystery, they might turn their suspicions, their cruelties. *Here,* at home, they brought to bear everything that was best, that was most human in them: patience, courage, hope, loyalty, tenderness. They had, all, in their time, even in the darkest nights of their lives, acted so. They did not know how to act in any other way. But if it is true that not one of them would have wished to face a life alone, it is also true that on a cold winter morning, pregnant, with the children sick and no money in the bank, they would not have known how to turn their faces to the wall and refuse to get up.

And this was true to a degree even of Will, who had tried hardest to break away. What the sisters resented so bitterly in him, after all, was not his failure to help them, not even the suffering he had caused Kate, not those in themselves, but what they signified — that he *would* go it alone, that he did not need his family, or would not admit that he needed them, that he would not store up credit in the family fund against his own future. Their moral code, the reasons they adduced to themselves for censuring him, the strict sense of individual responsibility for the common good, were after all only the ethical expression of a feeling that went far deeper than morals or ethics would ever have gone with them. As Anna had said that night in New Orleans after she and Charlotte had bound up Will's wound and thrown away his torn and bloody clothes, there were loyalties they could call up, loyalties overriding conscience, caution, habit, distaste, inexperience, and fear; and

Will, *Will* of all people, had been able to put them to his service.

And now in this last crisis of their mother's life, in spite of their refusal to take Will's efforts for Kate at face value, they all obscurely knew what was moving in him. Clearly he had been wrong from the beginning. After all he had had to come home. His time had come, and he heaved and turned like a dumb, suffering animal while they bestirred themselves stiffly to make room for him.

Kate continued not to know him. Charlotte and Sis and Sarah D. could scarcely believe it; hourly they expected her to give a glad cry of recognition when he came into her room. Of course, there were other delusions in her poor, wandering mind, and the girls repeated them faithfully to Will, as if it might comfort him to know that she was lost in a wild landscape of her own invention, that he was not the only part of her life she had forgotten. Sometimes she did not know one or another of her daughters; once she mistook the doctor for her husband; she conceived a violent, persistent dislike for one of her nurses and told Charlotte that "that woman" *deliberately* tickled her every time she changed the bed or bathed her or put her on the bedpan. But the fact remained that she *never* knew Will, and would become so upset when "that strange young man" came into her room that at last he had to stay out altogether. She seemed from the moment she first mistook him for the devil to have him entwined in her mind with some notion about death, as if she half thought he was coming to get her. To make Will's suffering more acute, she asked for him constantly, and was so restless and unhappy because he did not come that the girls, having given up their efforts to convince her that he was *here*, told her he had been on a business trip to Europe when she fell and was now on his way home as quickly as the boat could bring him. They trusted to luck she would have forgotten the existence of airplanes; and she seemed content, at least for a time, with their explanations.

Will subsided to a silent misery. He abandoned his many projects and after three days of vain waiting to greet his mother returned to New Orleans. Once there, he neither wrote nor telephoned. The girls did not know where he was or what he was doing, and in the intervals of their concern for Kate were afraid that he might have "gone on a bender" without Eunice to care for him and nurse him back to sobriety. They tried to reach him at his office and at his apartment, but no one answered the telephone at his apartment, and his secretary did not know where he was. Finally, after weighing the matter among themselves (they considered calling Eunice to come home and help him, but decided against it), they delegated Sis to call George Ransome, an old and intimate friend of Will's in New Orleans, to find him and report to them. Then they decided to call Eunice and tell her of Kate's accident without saying anything specific about Will's strange behavior.

"After all," Charlotte said, "we *should*. Regardless of what's happened between her and Will, she's been a member of the family for nearly twenty-five years, and she's very fond of Mama."

They located her at a home of a friend in Dallas and told her of Kate's fall. They told her also that Will had been in Homochitto, had told them of the separation, and was now back in New Orleans, "very upset and not like himself."

"Now, that's all we can do," Sis said after she had hung up. "She said she was going home first, and that she wanted to come up and help us."

That was Monday, ten days after the accident. Kate had begun to improve, and with returning strength was more and more unhappy at having to stay in the hospital.

"I *need* to be at home," she told Charlotte. "It's so hard for the girls to keep things running smoothly when they both have to work."

For his own reasons Dr. Shields agreed with Kate. The bone specialist had confirmed his decision that the pelvis would be better left unset. Very little could be done for Kate in the hospital; and he knew the hospital staff would be as delighted to say goodbye to her as she to them. Charlotte arranged for nurses, Sis and Sarah D. got her room ready, and she was taken home.

Eunice came up in the middle of the week, and Charlotte went to Eureka for a few days to see about her husband and her house. While she was gone, Eunice organized the sickroom and took over the nursing with the efficiency of a born supervisor. She cared for Kate with a matter-of-fact breezy ease that her sisters-in-law called "midwestern"; but they needed her desperately, and in the two months that she helped them care for Kate her devotion was so real and so endearing, they none of them ever again allowed themselves to think critically of her. Two days after Eunice arrived, they dismissed the registered nurses, and old Sally, the practical nurse who had helped them when Kate had broken her arm, came back. During the next month Charlotte and Eunice alternated weeks in Homochitto, so that Kate would not be left all day without a member of the family in the house with her.

Physically, Kate improved slowly, but her fancies and moods were still unpredictable. She moved backward and forward in time; sometimes she knew them and sometimes she did not. They watched her hopefully, not hoping anything for *her*, but thinking that perhaps her mind would clear, that they could tell Will to come home and be sure she would know him, unwilling to subject him to the pain of another visit like his first one.

They tried to explain to Eunice what had happened and how distressed Will had been, but they were not quite sure what *had* happened and they were correspondingly vague. Charlotte at last put it as clearly as she could. "He was missing *you*, Eunice," she said. "That's the long and short of it. I believe he was missing you, and he wanted Mama to comfort him."

The two women were sitting together in Kate's room one morning, and Kate was dozing.

"You think so?" Eunice said without inflection, as if she were only mildly curious. She sighed and then began to talk slowly and thoughtfully, weighing her words, as if to be sure she was saying what she meant.

"You know, Charlotte," she said, "I've never had much family — just Mama and Daddy, and they've been dead so long. You all are all the family I have and I've always been — I've appreciated your taking me in so generously." She hesitated. "It might have been different," she said. And then, "I still feel that way. Being separated from Will hasn't changed my feeling about you."

There was an embarrassed silence as Charlotte cast about in her mind for something to say.

"Oh, now, Eunice," she began, "you know we . . ."

But Eunice interrupted her. "Sometimes I think I have been more concerned, fonder of you all, than Will has been," she said. "Will has his troubles. And then, too, he's a man. But that's neither here nor there. I reckon what is to the point is, I've always seen how much Mother loves him. It's a burden to him. Is that an awful thing to say? No. Hear me out. The reason I see it so well is — I've always loved him too much, too. That may be one reason I've been so fond of her. We're in the same boat, not rivals for his undivided attention, but both admiring hangers-on. We've been married more than twenty years, and at a party I still think he's the most attractive man in the room. Isn't that a hell of a note?

"But a while back I just gave out. I can't explain to you how or why, but I gave out. I suppose there are times in your life when everything seems to heave and turn over inside you and when it all settles down again, nothing is the same, all your motives and intentions are changed. That was the way it was with me. I didn't care any more. I had given out of caring. And

now, all this you tell me about your mama not knowing him —
maybe she gave out, too." She laughed ruefully. "She had a lot
more staying power than I had, didn't she? But poor Will.
Where does it leave him?"

Charlotte glanced toward the bed. Kate was still sleeping.

"I don't want to say anything, Eunice," she said, "to interfere
in your business, or anything like that. I know I shouldn't, and
besides, I'm not smart enough to advise you. But . . ." She
paused, and then went on more firmly. "But I will say this one
thing. Please think about it again. *Please.* Don't give him up.
If there is any sense in anything he has done, it's that he needs
you, whether he has the gumption to know it or not."

Eunice shrugged. "I can't do anything," she said. "I simply
can't make a move in his direction."

The two women were quiet for a long time. Then Charlotte
spoke again. "Do you mind if I pray for you all?" she
said timidly. "I know the Lord will help you, if we just ask
Him."

"I've been doing some praying myself," Eunice said. "But
I'm not very good at it." She smiled. "Maybe you'd better get
Ralph to put in a word," she said. "Will always says he's got a
private line to God."

❦

The fourth week Kate had a relapse.

After he had examined her, Dr. Shields, sitting in a straight-
backed chair at the dining room table, his medical bag in front
of him, told them that she had pneumonia. Sarah D. was
sitting beside him and Sis across the table. Eunice was in the
room with Kate.

Sarah D. nodded. "We were pretty sure she did when her
fever went up so high in the night," she said.

Restlessly the young doctor rubbed his hand back and forth
across the top of his medical bag, opened it, and stared in as if

he expected to see something surprising there. His long body
was jackknifed awkwardly into the small chair and his thin
young face was serious. "You know your mama is an old, old
lady," he said. "She's had a long life."

Sis smiled kindly at him. "Yes," she said helpfully. "Mama
has had a full life. She's had hard times, but she's always . . ."
She broke off. "She's had a way of living," she said. "I don't
suppose she's ever been bored in her life — or boring."

"Ten years ago there would have been no treatment for
pneumonia worth mentioning," Dr. Shields said. "No anti-
biotics. And with the complication of the broken pelvis . . ."
He hesitated. Then, "Sarah D.," he said, "Sis. I have to speak
plainly to you. You know I love Cousin Kate. She . . . I *love*
her. And I *know* . . ." He stopped again, then went on. "I
have two alternatives," he said. "I could take her back to the
hospital. If we started her on penicillin and glucose and oxygen
right away, we'd have maybe a fifty-fifty chance to pull her
through this attack. But the bone is not knitting. She's going
to have to be bedridden. That means in a month, two months,
she'd probably have another attack. And then, if she came
through that one, another. I could give her six months, maybe
even a year of — pain. That's what I could do for her. The
other alternative is to keep her at home. To do nothing, or
nothing except make her as comfortable as we can." He shook
his head angrily, snapped the bag shut, opened it again. "I've
been thinking about all this, about what might happen, since
the day she fell," he said. "That's one reason I wanted to get
her out of the hospital — to give myself and you a choice in
the matter. Because once she's in the hospital there isn't much
choice. Everything that can be done to keep her alive has to be
done. And I can't do it. I can't put her through all that suffering, can't keep her hanging on just so that she can suffer again
and more. If you want to try to get her well, I'll call in another
doctor for you."

"We've *all* thought about it, Jimmie," Sis said. "It's not your responsibility. We know that." She could not say anything more for a moment and leaning forward touched him once lightly on the shoulder — the habitual family gesture of sympathy and understanding.

"Yes, it *is* my responsibility," he said. "But yours, too."

"We'll call Will and Charlotte," Sarah D. said. "We can't do anything without them."

He pulled at his tie as if it were too tight and then snapped his bag shut and stood up. "I don't see any reason for you to get a registered nurse," he said. "Sally knows how to take care of her better than anyone. Keep her warm and dry, and try to get as much liquid down her as you can. That's very important. We don't want the kidneys to get blocked. Keep a pitcher of fruit juice for her and see that she drinks a little every hour or so. Give her clear soups and Jello if she can swallow it. Aspirin for the fever. I don't believe she can swallow a tablet. Give her ten grains dissolved in a teaspoonful of water every three or four hours. Try to get her to drink a little water as often as you can. And don't forget to keep her lips greased and her tongue wet. That's all, I reckon, except to get Will and Charlotte here. I want you all to decide what you are going to do, today if possible."

Sarah D. and Sis walked with him in silence through the house. At the front door he paused. "I'll look in again late this afternoon," he said. "Call me if you need me." He looked around the dim parlor and still hesitated, as if there were some one thing he could say.

"It's all right, Jimmie," Sarah D. said. "We understand."

"I remember one time when I was a kid — eleven or twelve," he said abruptly, "coming with Grandfather to see Cousin Kate. My shirttail was out, I reckon, and my face was probably dirty. She told me that all little boys ought to be kept in a bureau drawer from the time they were six until they were eighteen. 'Boys!' she said. 'Boys!' " He imitated her tone of mock revulsion. "She taught me to whistle on my fingers that afternoon. My own father couldn't do that." He smiled. "I reckon I thought she was a boy herself, I liked her so much. And when we left the house, Grandfather told me he'd been engaged to her once. Did you know that?"

Sarah D. laughed. "Yes, Mama's always said she was engaged to your grandfather and our father at the same time."

Dr. Shields went on slowly. "And then — you know, Grandfather was always a great quoter — then he recited all that wonderful short thing that Enobarbus says about Cleopatra. I've never read it or heard it since without thinking of Cousin Kate."

He recited slowly in a low voice: "Age cannot wither her, nor custom stale/ Her infinite variety; other women cloy/ The appetites they feed, but she makes hungry/ Where most she satisfies; for vilest things/ Become themselves in her, that the holy priests/ Bless her when she is riggish."

He grinned suddenly. "Do you suppose he quoted it to her when they were courting?" he said. "Wouldn't she have gotten a kick out of being compared to Cleopatra? Do you reckon she kept a straight face?"

❦

Charlotte and Will arrived late that afternoon, one by plane and the other by car, and the four children held a council in the dining room while Kate lay feverish and half conscious in the front bedroom. The in-laws were there, too, Ralph and Eunice; and one grandchild, young Charlotte, who had come up on the plane with Will; but they took no part in the decision, sitting quietly by and listening to the matter-of-fact conversation among the others. Sis explained briefly what the doctor had said. "He wants us to decide tonight," she finished. "If we are going to take her back to the hospital, we should do so right away."

"So we have to decide," Charlotte said, speaking to them all, but her words meant for Will, "whether we're going to drag it on and on — put her through maybe months of suffering — or let God take her when He's ready."

If Will felt even a twinge of revulsion at Charlotte's way of putting it, at what he might once have called her sanctimoniousness, his face did not show it. The room was silent for a few moments except for the steady hissing of the gas space heater. Then Will spoke. He was sitting with his fists on his cheeks, his elbows on the table, watching them, and he did not move.

"All right," he said. "All right."

"Do you mean . . . ?"

"Let her go," he said.

Charlotte nodded.

"Sis and I . . ." Sarah D. said. "We can't see any point to . . . We can't . . . either."

"Let her go," Will said again. He got up and left the room and the house. Eunice followed him and they did not come back until late that night.

They went to the hotel coffee shop and sat at a corner table half hidden by a straggly potted palm. They each drank two cans of beer, talking desultorily. Will gave Eunice the news of New Orleans, and she spoke briefly of Kate's symptoms, of her own weariness, and of how his sisters were bearing up. Then, still restless, unwilling to go home, Will drove her a long way into the country, through deep shale tunnels overhung by live-oak trees, lighted in the occasional open spaces by the cool brilliance of the October moon. They did not speak of reconciliation, but, at home, when they paused in the dining room to turn out the light and the fire before going to their separate rooms, they both knew that the separation was over, that they were ready to take up again the burdens of their life together, to try once more to love and support each other.

They parted, and for a little while the old house creaked with their quiet footsteps as they prepared for bed; and the cooling walls popped and settled. Sarah D. and Sis, sleeping lightly and restlessly, heard them come in, and even Charlotte was roused by the vibration of the house when Will slammed the front door. For a long time they were all restless in their beds, hearing Sally when she got up to care for Kate, hearing the Cathedral clock strike one and then two. They dozed and wakened and dozed again, and in the dark night the old house was filled with their waking and sleeping dreams, with scraps of their childhood that drifted from room to room, with the fullness of their responsibilities, breaking on them when the Cathedral bell boomed out in the still night, with the bitter sorrow of having to let their mother die; as if they all, and even Kate, dreamed a common dream, and waking to the same sick anxiety, were comforted by one another's presence.

No more was said about the decision taken that night, except to tell Dr. Shields that they would keep Kate at home. For three weeks they nursed her constantly and tenderly. The house was full of people all that time. Grandchildren and cousins and nieces came and went, traveling from New Orleans, and Memphis, and Baton Rouge to spend a day, to go in and speak, to talk quietly with whoever was sitting beside Kate's bed — going away and then, restless and helpless under the weight of the ordeal that continued in Homochitto, returning, as if their presence might lend strength to the women who watched dry-eyed in the bedroom there.

Some days Kate would rouse from her coma for a moment, smile, speak, hold out her hand to one of them, or dredge up a random recollection from the past that seemed to blow like a light, shifting breeze through her dreaming mind. Again, she might be conscious all day, or all night, restless, filled with a delirious anxiety.

Eunice and Charlotte stayed in Homochitto, Charlotte going home occasionally for a day or two to see that Ralph was being fed properly and that her house was in order. Will returned to New Orleans. Toward the end of the third week, when Dr. Shields thought Kate could not live more than a day or two longer, the sisters sent for Will and he came back. Eunice met him at the airport and they drove to the house where Charlotte and the practical nurse were with Kate. Sis and Sarah D. were both at work. Eunice went upstairs to the bedroom where she stayed with Sis, and Will put his hat on the hatrack and his suitcase beside it, and went in to his mother. It was the first time he had seen her conscious since she had left the hospital.

When he entered the room, Charlotte was trying to feed her a little orange juice from a teaspooon. Sally, on the other side of the bed, had a strong brown arm supporting her head and shoulders. Kate's eyes were open and she had an expression of impatient distaste on her face.

"Now, dearest, now sweetheart," Charlotte was saying, "drink just a little for me, just one more spoonful."

"No," Kate said. "Ugh."

The floor vibrated under Will's step, and Charlotte looked up. He came over to her where she stood by the head of the bed, kissed her lightly on the cheek, and looked down without expression at his mother's face. Clearly he had ceased to expect from her whatever it was he had needed so desperately at the beginning of her illness, and like his sisters now he stood and looked at her, unable to understand what was happening either to her or to them all. Unlike the women, he could not mask his bewilderment, his anguish, his occasional guilty frivolity, the drive of his own life toward its own goals behind the constant, exhausting activity of service. Except to fulfill his role, to do what was expected of him, he was not needed.

Why am I here, after all? he said to himself. *What's the use in any of it?*

Charlotte whispered to him, "She roused a little this morning and she's been sort of half conscious ever since. And now, see? She doesn't want any more orange juice."

As Charlotte put the spoon to her lips, Kate made the unmistakable face of a child forced to take medicine, and feebly pushed it away. Charlotte put the spoon and glass on the table and Sally settled Kate against her pillows.

"It's so hard to get any liquids down her," Charlotte said. Then, as Kate closed her eyes and turned her head away from them, "Sit down, Will. Let's sit down a minute. Have you a cigarette?"

He silently gave her one, took one himself, and lighted both.

Kate turned her head from side to side, eyes closed. "Sally?" she whispered hoarsely. "Sally? Sally? Sally?"

"She calls for Sally like that all the time," Charlotte said. "But we can't ever figure out what she wants with her."

"Yes'm. Here I'm is," Sally said. "I'm right here, Miss Kate. What you want, honey?"

"Sally? Sally? Sally?"

"Yes ma'am. Yes ma'am."

"Sally? Sally?" Kate turned her head from side to side, her ravaged face, every ounce of flesh melted away from beneath the dry, wrinkled parchment skin, seeming no longer human, but the very embodiment of death. "You — find — glasses," she said. "All water . . . under . . . and find . . . glasses."

"You want a drink of water, honey?"

Kate shook her head. "Glasses," she said. "All water . . . under . . . slipping . . . slipping. Long, long, long. Find . . . glasses. I'll . . . see . . . see . . . all went . . . went . . . too . . . gone."

"I believe she want her glasses, Miss Charlotte."

Charlotte shrugged. But she got up and went over to the bed. "Mama, you wouldn't be comfortable with your glasses on," she said.

Kate turned her head from side to side. "Sally?" she said. "Sally?"

Charlotte sat down again. "She's been talking like that all morning," she said, "but she recognized me a little while ago. She said my name."

"Sally? Sally?"

"Jimmie says not much longer," Charlotte said. "Her veins are collapsing."

"My God, Charlotte," Will said in a fierce whisper, "she'll hear you."

"She's been asking for you again, yesterday and today," Charlotte said. "Maybe . . ." She did not add that sometimes Kate repeated his name over and over as she was now repeating Sally's.

"It doesn't matter," Will said. "That's all right, Charlotte."

Kate turned her head toward them and half opened her eyes, sunk deep in the white, crumpled face. She raised her heavy lids, those lids once so seductively, so provocatively veiling her sharp, merry green eyes. "I hear you, Charlotte," she said faintly but clearly. "Who are you talking to?"

Charlotte got up and, motioning Will to follow her, went quickly to her mother's bed. She bent over and took Kate's hand, but Kate had closed her eyes and turned away again.

"Sally?" she said.

"Mama," Charlotte said, "It's *Will*, darling. Here's Will come to see you."

Kate roused and opened her eyes again. She looked at her two children. "Orange . . . juice," she said. "You . . . know . . . I *hate* . . . orange juice."

"Here's Will, Mama," Charlotte said again.

Kate's hand moved along the white bedspread. "Will?" she said. "Will?"

"Hello, sweetheart," Will said. "Got a kiss for your wandering son?" He bent toward her and his lips touched her dry cheek.

She looked at him and, raising her hand, touched the rough surface of his coat sleeve. "Will!" she said. "Visiting? So nice . . . so lovely . . . to have . . . you with me."

He put his arms around her and, lifting her gently, held her against him for a moment.

"Charlotte, Will is here," she said clearly. "Isn't that grand? Get . . . my . . . sherry . . . will you? Celebration." She closed her eyes as he laid her down again. "Grand!" she whispered. "Ah, grand!"

She did not speak again. That same night, shortly after the Cathedral clock struck three, she died at last.

◆§◆

At nine o'clock on the morning of Kate Anderson's funeral the Presbyterian Church in Homochitto was quiet and almost empty. The minister sat reading in his study; upstairs in the choir loft the organist sorted through his music; outside the janitor was sweeping the three steps that led up from the sidewalk to the small banked yard in front of the church.

The church stood back from the street on a low, terraced hill, surrounded by a waist-high brick retaining wall; austere and massive in its solid simplicity, the warm beige of its plaster walls crumbled away here and there by wind and rain to the rosy brick beneath. Its great oak doors were open to the soft air of an Indian summer day; sunlight streamed through the clear, chaste glass of the long windows and gleamed on the rows of white box pews.

Eighty-five years had passed since Kate had been held up squalling to the font beside the pulpit and received her name — Kate McCrory Dupré — bearing witness from the beginning to the mixture of bloods, Creole and Scottish, Catholic and Protestant, that she and her children had all perforce to accommodate. Thirty-four years had passed since the Sunday morning when Charlotte had watched Ralph's strong young profile as he stood in the Henshaw pew beside his mother and sang:

> Bles't be the tie that binds
> Our hearts in Christian love;
> The fellowship of kindred minds
> Is like to that above.

A hundred and fifty years had passed since the church had been built in a new, raw land by settlers long rooted in an austere faith. A hundred and fifty years — not the full span of two lives as long as Kate's. But already the land, and the symbols so lovingly and solidly constructed by the sojourners there, were old, an anachronism in a bewildering world, clung to tenaciously by men and women who could find nothing else so solid in the whirlwind of their lives.

There are places, buildings, everywhere, that are so strongly associated with the lives of certain people that they seem to those who love or hate them to possess a brooding, immobile life of their own; and this was true of the Presbyterian Church in Homochitto. Every one of all Kate's family gathering for her funeral had felt, clearly or obscurely, at one time or another, that that square, spare, sturdy, beautiful building *lived*, that somehow the molecules crystallized in its walls of brick and plaster were the same molecules that flowed in their own frail, impermanent veins. It didn't matter that the notion was a silly and unreasonable one. They had all felt it, had cherished the feeling, and had longed on occasion to express it.

This inexpressibly strong feeling welled up in Anna McGovern Glover's heart the morning of the funeral when she and her husband drove past the church on the way to her grandmother's house.

They had driven south the day before from the small Delta town of Philippi, and had spent the night, along with Katherine and Mac, at the old McGovern house where Julia and Celestine, a bit feebler than they had been five years earlier, still lived, still attended by a stooped and graying but punctilious Julius. Anna, like her sister and brother and the other scattered members of the family, had been waiting all month for her grandmother to die. She had come south to Homochitto for a day and night twice during that long month, leaving her two children at home with a nurse and her husband. There had been nothing to do in Homochitto, nothing to do but wait, and she had returned, restless and sorrowful, to her own family. When the telephone had rung the preceding morning, she had known the instant she heard her mother's voice that it was over. Gran was dead. Charlotte had told her that they would like her husband to be a pallbearer. Kate was to be carried to her grave by her two grandsons and three grandsons-in-law, and three great-nephews. The funeral was to be the following morning at ten o'clock.

And so she had returned, bringing with her her young, skeptical husband, son of a Northern father and a Southern Jewish mother, an alien to his wife's rigidly idiosyncratic background, who would nonetheless bear his share of Kate's weightless body in its plain steel-gray coffin.

As they drove past the church, Anna glanced at him and then away. His tall, slender body was slumped over the wheel, for if he sat up straight, his head almost touched the roof of the car. His profile with its straight, jutting nose, small, delicately cut mouth, and broad forehead was perfectly expressionless, but she knew he was miserable. He considered funerals barbaric. *He really doesn't want anything said about any strong emotion except in books,* she thought. *He's so afraid it may turn out to be false.* There was no way, she knew, to tell him what she was thinking. *You can't tell anyone anything he doesn't know already,* she said to herself. *Except once in a while by a miracle. Isn't that a queer way for people to be? How could you explain that a person might go on being a Presbyterian, even if he weren't a Christian any more — even if he thought it was a grim idea at best? Was it Will said that? That night in New Orleans when he was so drunk? Or maybe it's so obvious it's not worth mentioning,* she thought. *And besides,* reacting against herself in the light of her husband's clear-headed rootless intellectuality, *maybe it's nothing but sentimentality. But it's true,* she added stubbornly. *Obvious and sentimental or not, I have to take it into account. It's a fact.*

"Isn't it a beautiful church?" she said aloud, making a half-hearted effort in spite of herself.

By that time they were drawing up to the curb in front of Kate's house, and he looked up at the Cathedral towering above them across the street. "As churches go," he said.

"No, I meant the Presbyterian Church," she said.

"They're both beautiful buildings," he said. "I never have been able to understand how those people could build such fine houses and buildings, and then stuff them with all that horrible Victorian furniture. Like having a neoclassical ego and a rococo id."

As Anna opened the car door to get out, another car stopped behind theirs and young Billy Dupré got out. He had driven down that morning from Vicksburg, where he was working. Sarah D., who was sitting on the front gallery with half a dozen callers had gotten up to greet Anna and Richard, but when she saw Billy, she turned toward him instead. She held out her arms to him, and, stooping toward her, he gathered her to him and began to weep.

"Don't cry, darling," she said. "You mustn't cry."

But he was laughing, too. "I know it," he said. "I don't know what came over me." And then anxiously, "How are you, Mother? Are you all right?"

Anna and Richard joined them, and the two men shook hands reservedly, Billy intent on controlling himself, and Richard on ignoring Billy's tears. The two men were as different as if they had come from opposite sides of the world. Billy, small and dark like his Uncle Will, had his father's heavy, placid manner. Tears were alien to him and he could not have accounted for the sudden impulse of sorrow that had made him weep. He moved through the world like his sister Charlotte, unselfconscious, hardly aware of his own life as an entity separate from his surroundings. Richard, alert, charged with energy, cynical with the cynicism that fears its own sentimentality, shy yet master of himself, was the epitome of the self-

conscious intellectual. He knew quite well why he did everything he did — too well for comfort, perhaps. But if he had
few illusions about himself, it was also true that he sometimes
failed to give himself credit for his best impulses.

Anna kissed Billy on the cheek and put her arm around Sarah
D. "Hi, sweety," she said to Billy. She had seen Sarah D. the
night before.

"I'm all right," Sarah D. said to Billy. "Tired but all right.
Charlotte and Gerry are inside."

"Where's Mama?" Anna said as they started up the steps.

"She and Ralph are in the dining room," Sarah D. said.
"Go on back, children. Margaret and Norman Stone have been
waiting to speak to you and Richard. They're with your
mama."

"Where's Gran?" Billy said.

"In the parlor," Sarah D. said. "The coffin is closed,
darling. We thought . . ."

"I didn't want to see her," Billy said. "I just wanted to know
where she was."

"We never let them take her away," Sarah D. said. "She's
been right here ever since she died."

There was an air of ritual celebration, of unmistakable quiet
gaiety, almost of a party, in the Anderson house as Anna and
Richard walked through. People were coming and going,
cousins and intimate friends who felt enough at home with the
family to know they were welcome even an hour before the
funeral. A great many of them were young people — friends of
the five grandchildren who had grown up under Kate's feet,
familiars of her sharp tongue and merry laugh. There would
have been no way for any of them to mourn her death. They
had loved her — not so passionately as the grandchildren to
whom she had been a bountiful source of joy and courage, but
with the love that all good men give to gallantry and high spirits.
Now they were together because of her life, not her death.
They all knew this, and knew that the others knew it, as clearly

as if they had said it to each other. Greeting friends, one after another, some of whom she had not seen in years, Anna recognized and suppressed in herself, a vague guilty excitement. Like an actor walking onstage to say his one line, she could scarcely resist the egocentric thrill of being the center of everyone's attention. *I'm awful*, she told herself. *Don't you suppose I'll ever get over being self-important?*

She and Richard joined Ralph and Charlotte in the dining room, and the next hour was confusedly taken up with greetings and reminiscences, and with arranging and rearranging the funeral procession. Who was to go in what car and what order were the cars to be in? Everyone had a suggestion, and the harried funeral director listened mournfully to them all and changed the order of the cars in front of the house half a dozen times. It gave them all something to think about. Then, gradually, the house emptied of company. At five minutes to ten the pallbearers took up the coffin from the trestles in the parlor, carried it out the front door, across the gallery where the queen's wreath vine rustled in the light morning wind, down the steps and through the creaking iron gate. The family followed. Anna got into the car with Ralph and Charlotte, first behind the pallbearers' car; Katherine had been assigned to look after Aunt Annie Hunt, and she helped her into her car; young Charlotte and Sarah D. got into the back seat; Sis rode with Will and Eunice. Two of Kate's nieces who had driven down from Port Gibson followed them; and last came Julius, the McGovern chauffeur, who had been borrowed to bring Lizzie and Sally.

The procession started up. The Cathedral clock across the street struck ten, and in the cool depths of the church the choir began to chant: "Gaudeamus omnes in domino, Diem festum celebrantes sub honore sanctorum omnium."

"It's All Saints' Day," Charlotte said. "I had forgotten yesterday was Halloween. They're having a High Mass."

As if they had been before her eyes again, Anna saw the summer mornings of her childhood, the orphans marching past the park to Mass, led by the sisters in their winged white hats and wide-swinging dark blue habits. Her heart contracted with pain as she seemed to hear Kate's voice saying contentedly in her ear, *Listen to the music, Anna. Isn't it lovely?* Kate had lived in the shadow of the Cathedral, had counted the hours of her life by its bell, and now its choir sang for her one last time the sweet morning music she had loved. It was as if they, too, were joining in the celebration of a long life drawn to its close.

Grandmother McCrory would turn over in her grave if she knew how fond I've gotten of those Catholics, Kate said in Anna's ear.

The little procession turned the corner by the Cathedral and drove past the side of the park toward the Presbyterian Church. The soft rain of the fountain murmured below the swelling music of the Mass, and the shouts of two small children feeding bread crumbs to the goldfish broke into Anna's dream.

Suddenly Charlotte spoke. "Nobody touched her," she said. "Nobody touched her but us."

Anna patted her mother on the shoulder. "I know," she said. "Sarah D. told me."

"Eunice and Sally laid her out," Charlotte said.

"I know."

In front of the church they all got out of their cars and Julius escorted Sally and Lizzie around to the side entrance of the church near which a pew had been set aside for them. At the church door the family paused in confusion, each of Kate's four children deferring to the other three.

"Ralph, you and Charlotte go first," Sarah D. said. "Charlotte is eldest."

Ralph obediently took his wife's arm, but she shook her head and held back, motioning Sis and Sarah D. to go in before her. They had borne the heavy load of their mother's old age, and she did not intend to precede them. But neither Sis nor Sarah D. would go in first.

"Go on, Will," Sis said. "You're head of the family, now."

But Will, being youngest, held back, too.

Always practical, Eunice took Will's arm. "Come on, honey," she whispered. "Somebody's got to go first, and this is the way the girls want it."

So they went in, two and two, the heavy footsteps of the pall-bearers swinging in unison ahead of them, sounding dull but loud above the soft chords of the organ: Will and Eunice, Sis, supported by Anna, Sarah D. with young Charlotte, Ralph and Charlotte, Katherine and Aunt Annie Hunt, and last the two nieces from Port Gibson.

All old Homochitto is here, Anna thought, glancing down the aisle into the half-filled church. *Only a funeral like Gran's would get some of these folks out.*

Quiet and expressionless, they passed the empty Anderson pew at the back of the church as the minister began to read aloud from the pulpit: " 'I am the resurrection, and the life, saith the Lord: he that believeth in me, though he were dead, yet shall he live: and whosoever liveth and believeth in me, shall never die.' "

They passed the McGee pew where Kate's indestructible beau, Mr. James McGee, sat, bent and solitary, cured of drink by having outlived it. *"Pickled,"* Kate said in Anna's ear. *"You couldn't kill him if you tried."*

"God is our refuge and our strength," the minister read, "a very present help in trouble. Therefore will not we fear."

They passed Julia McGovern and Celestine Henshaw in the Henshaw pew at the front of the church and turned in at the two empty pews directly in front of them.

"Our Father which art in heaven, hallowed be Thy name.

"Thy Kingdom come, Thy will be done, on earth as it is in heaven . . .

"Lord thou has been our dwelling place in all generations.

"Before the mountains were brought forth, or ever thou hadst formed the earth and the world, even from everlasting to everlasting, thou art God."

Anna's heart began to pound. She knew perfectly well that she must conduct herself with dry-eyed, emotionless dignity. But it seemed to her, there in the high, square, airy church, with Gran's body resting at the foot of the pulpit, that everything she had ever seen or heard of in the life of her family and in her own life was taking its place in an ordered whole.

"For a thousand years in thy sight are but as yesterday when it is past, and as a watch in the night.

"Thou carriest them away as with a flood . . ."

She looked up at the paneled ceiling of the church and saw again the Sundays of her childhood when with Marjorie at her side she had searched the labyrinthine church walls for the treasure hidden there; felt again for a piercing instant the sexual thrill of their imagined trials and torments, and nodded her head as if in greeting and goodbye to her old mirror self, as other scenes flashed on her memory in a blinding radiance of sorrow, understanding, and affirmation. She saw Gran on a summer Saturday, skirts hiked up, wading the creek and screaming with feigned terror at the quicksand sucking around her ankles; heard her father's voice out of the still winter night: "Charlotte, Sis has had another miscarriage"; and her mother's reply, "Oh, Ralph, not again"; saw Gran with her head bowed on the gate at Sis's wedding; heard Alderan saying in the parlor, "My daddy named me for a star"; and, dressed in his dirty khakis, looking at her and saying, "I'll bet you've never seen your father dressed like this"; and Charlie, standing in the kitchen door at Christmas time saying, "But I was just trying to help. I was just trying to cheer us up"; and on his deathbed, "Don't call the children, sweetheart. I'm going to be all right"; Will drunk in Galatoire's saying, "All men are brothers. See?" and leaning against the wall of Katherine's apartment on St.

Ann Street saying, "You — got — key, Charlie? Anybody — got — key?" And most important of all, that flash of insight on the creek bank with Sis and Charlotte the afternoon Charlotte had told them she and Gerry were engaged — the sunlight on the cold, sparkling water, the sand grating against her shoes, Sis sitting on the log, gentle, graying, and inflexible, saying, "The day will come, children, when you'll be interested in things like that"; when like a clap she'd seen that Alderan was a *man*, a real human being, that he too had been able to suffer, to feel desire and shame; when she had known beyond doubt that he had run away because he thought Ralph was afraid, that he had scorned to confront a man who refused to carry a gun.

Whatever you say about them, she thought, *however far you may go away, your reasons for going would never include the one that they were ignoble. They live by their own lights, and they blame their failures on themselves. And what could they have given me — what could anyone give a child — more precious than the habit of moral consciousness, the conviction that one must be a man, must look after his own, must undertake, must dare, and always every man in the shadow of death? That's what makes the inflexibility bearable. Because you've got to see, too, that the very rigidity that galls so bitterly, the hanging on with locked jaws like Rikki-Tikki, even if the life is battered out of you, is what makes their life together possible, makes it possible to survive in the middle of the whirlwind. Yes, a man's strength is his weakness, and if you deny one half, you have to throw away the other. And then, at last,* she thought, *you have to think about love, about the terrible burden of love, about being created every day in the image of every human being who loves you, about the impossibility of ever seeing yourself, the fate of always being caught, even in your life's most secret moments, in the rays of someone else's light. Every one of them sees in every other, in me, his own heart's desire, his own creation, sees the whole world through*

*his own band of the spectrum. As if he might be looking
through green glasses and said to you, "But your face is green,
green." And lighted up so strangely, you look in the mirror and
say, "But that's not my face."*

*But there! There's the answer. If there are enough of us.
Yes!* She looked around her at them all, each in his separate
self mourning as she mourned, each one his own loss. *Yes, and
there are enough. So that they must look through all the bands
of the spectrum and the light is mingled, and the color vanishes
in radiance, and one sees oneself whole. Everything is realized
at once, and one gains oneself.*

While she had been absorbed in her reverie they had risen
and sung "Rock of Ages, Cleft for me," and now they had sat
down again, and the minister was reading: "I will lift up mine
eyes to the hills from whence cometh my help.

"My help cometh from the Lord, which made heaven and
earth."

She knew that her mother and Sis and Sarah D. had told the
minister what to read for the service, and now she tried to put
her attention on what he was reading, but another memory
intervened.

Strangely, she heard once more that strange preacher's voice
in the church in Eureka preaching to her in the summer of her
grief and confusion. What had he said then that had seemed
so senseless? "No man buys life or love but with the willingness
to die." And, "Beloved, let us give all things to each other and
to God — our loneliness and absence and defeat; our doubt,
that other name for death; and pain and joy. And all these gifts
accept from Him and from each other. For all that a man can
know of God is that love and trust are His human voice. Trust
Him to give thee a voice with which to pray, for He *is* thy
prayer. Trust Him, though His face be hidden from thee;
for trust is the mirror of His love, and the opening lock that
lets through the torrent of His life. In God's name who made
us quick, and made us know we die." She realized with a shiver

that she remembered what he had said word for word, as if she had said it herself, had written it down and said it over and over to herself, remembered it in the same way she remembered the turning points in her own and her family's life, printed on her brain like the illustrations in a familiar book.

"Let us listen to the reading of God's word from the New Testament, the Book of Romans," the minister said.

"And we know that all things work together for good to them that love God, to them who are called according to his purpose.

"For whom he did foreknow, he also did predestinate to be conformed to the image of his Son, that he might be the firstborn among many brethren.

"Moreover whom he did predestinate, them he also called: and whom he called, them he also justified: and whom he justified, them he also glorified.

"What shall we then say to these things? If God be for us, who can be against us?"

Anna compressed her lips to keep from speaking aloud. *No!* she said to herself. *No! That's not the way it is. There's a key, yes, like Will said. But that's not it. The key is not just for us.* But then she corrected herself, looking around again at her family. *Not just for you,* she thought. *I know, you open your doors, you make room for each other, for me, even for Richard since he's mine, and Sally and Lizzie, since they're yours. But suppose we weren't yours? What about all the poor bastards who are only human beings, predestined — yes, to joy and death; and justified only in their own humanity. Isn't God, can't you be for us all?*

And naming Richard to herself, considering what a dose he was for them to swallow, an unbeliever, a grief like her own apostasy that her mother and father would bear to their graves, she knew that to her his very differentness was one of the most important things about him. He was *outside,* a living symbol of her refusal to be enclosed, to exorcise with primeval magic the grisly specter of death, to say, *We alone are the Men, the Chosen, the Elect.*

"For I am persuaded that neither death, nor life, nor angels, nor principalities, nor powers, nor things present, nor things to come,

"Nor height, nor depth, nor any other creature, shall be able to separate us from the love of God, which is in Christ Jesus our Lord.

"Grace be with you, mercy, and peace, from God the Father, and from the Lord Jesus Christ, the Son of the Father, in truth and love. Amen."

They followed Kate's body out of the church and into the high, clear day; only now, on the way out, Julius and Sally and Lizzie walked behind the family. Sally and Lizzie were weeping, and outside the church Sis let go of Anna's arm and dropped back to comfort them.

Then they all got into their cars and watched the pallbearers load the coffin into the hearse.

Anna sat quiet beside her mother.

"This funeral is real, *old* Homochitto," Charlotte said, watching the people come out of the church. "You don't see all these folks together very often any more."

"I was just thinking the same thing," Anna said.

"Gran and your grandmother McGovern and Teen are just about the last of their kind," Charlotte said.

"Aunt Annie Hunt," Anna said. "And I saw Mr. Jimmie McGee in church. There are a few left."

"Yes, a few," Charlotte said.

We'll be starting up in a minute, Anna said to herself. *We'll be driving past the old yellow fever hospital and into the cemetery under the blue-green cedar trees where a place is saved for Gran next to Grandfather, by the azalea that Great-grandmother Dupré planted.*

The words of the minister sounded again. *Grace be with you, Mercy and peace, in truth and love.*

But let none of us be outside at last. Let not one man be outside another's pale. Let the inside be opened instead. Let me take in humility all they give, and give in return all that I have. Let me accept even exclusion, and say Yes to all the human world. That's what the preacher meant. Oh let me now and all my days bless every life that quickens under the hand of God.